Warlord

The Sanctuary Series
Volume 6

Robert J. Crane

Warlord
The Sanctuary Series, Volume 6

Copyright © 2015 Midian Press
All Rights Reserved.

1st Edition

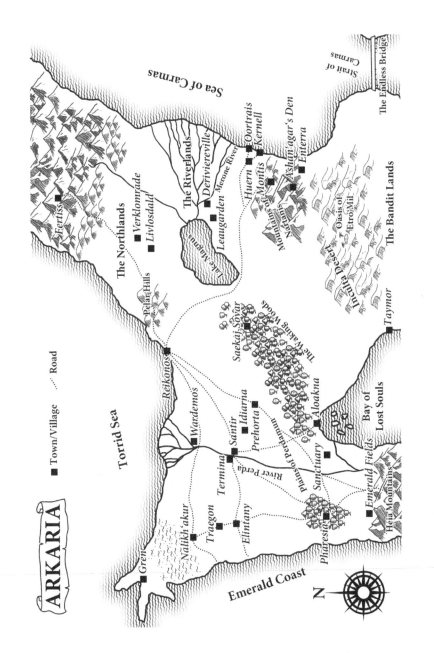

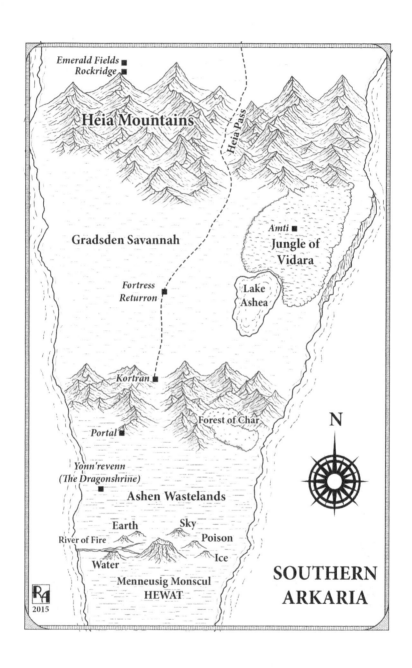

Emerald Fields
Rockridge

Heia Mountains

Heia Pass

Gradsden Savannah

Amti

Jungle of
Vidara

Fortress
Returron

Lake
Ashea

Kortran

Forest of Char

N

Portal

Yonn'revenn
(The Dragonshrine)

Ashen Wastelands

Earth   Sky

River of Fire   Poison

                                    Ice

Water

Menneusig Monscul
HEWAT

SOUTHERN
ARKARIA

RA
2015

NOW

Prologue

I have become death, Cyrus Davidon thought as he looked out across the endless waves of brown grass that covered the Plains of Perdamun. Scorched earth reached up to the edges of the cracked and damaged curtain wall that stretched around Sanctuary, stones fallen out, an enormous V-shaped gap carved into it only a hundred feet from where Cyrus stood next to the granite memorial stone. It even smelled like death, as though a pile of rotting corpses lingered somewhere over the horizon, the smell blown on the wind and forcing its way into Cyrus's mouth, crawling down his throat.

The tingle of the air's chill ran over his flesh beneath his black armor, and he shivered in the dusk air. *In the absence of Mortus, I am the closest thing to death that walks this world. I have become death … and it has cost me everything.* His eyes swept the horizon for signs of life, but save for the grass that stubbornly clung to it, he found nothing.

"I am death," Cyrus whispered, his voice lost under the breeze. Or so he thought.

"Well, at least you know who you are," Vaste's calm amusement cut across the gap between them. He turned and saw the troll standing under the grand gates, watching him.

Cyrus bit back an angry retort. "Didn't know you were there," he said instead.

"Would it have mattered if you did, Mr. Death?"

Cyrus took a breath of the air and then a step toward the troll. His foot sank into the sodden ground, drenched by rain but still lifeless. "Perhaps not," Cyrus said. "But you don't need to call me that."

"I didn't start it, you did," Vaste said, giving him a raised eyebrow. "I mean, calling yourself death? That's grim, even for this place." He swept a hand around to encompass the whole of Sanctuary, looming

3

large in the falling darkness beyond the wall. "Come on," he said, a little more gently, "let's go back inside."

Cyrus cast another eye across the Plains of Perdamun before nodding his head. *It is grim, even for this place.*

But that makes it no less true, Cyrus thought as he took the troll's invitation and followed him back into the halls of Sanctuary ... into halls empty of all but the whispering voices of the dead ...

... Into the only place where I still belong.

THREE YEARS EARLIER

1.

Who are you?

The question echoed in Cyrus Davidon's ears as he stared at the ashen ground beneath his plate-mailed boots. His sense of balance was askew; he felt as though he stood on a slanted hill even though the ground appeared flat all around him, clear to the horizon. It was a dark sky; not night, but as if clouds had rolled in on a clear day. The dim light was forbidding, reminding him of twilight in the north in the wintertime.

Cyrus tested his footing, and the world moved as he did so, shifting around him as though his strength was enough to topple it with one hard step. He brought his hands up to steady himself, but futilely; the world shifted again and seemed to straighten out. Despite the dark sky, the air was hot, like the breath of summer coming down the back of his neck, his armor taking up the heat and baking him like his own personal oven.

He clinked his fingers reassuringly on the hilt of Praelior, his sword. The world around him may have been unpredictable, unfamiliar, and mad, but at least there were some things he could count on. He didn't draw his blade, not yet, but he let his fingers dance across it, sinking into the soft layer of padding that separated him from the hard metal that protected him during battle and war.

There's no battle or war at present, though, Cyrus thought, viewing his surroundings through a hazy eye and a clouded mind. *There's nothing to be afraid of but—*

Who are you? the voice came again, rattling the earth beneath him and shifting the dark ash beneath his feet. It moved like it had been stirred by the wind, but it hadn't; there was no wind to speak of. This was a simple movement of the earth, like shifting sands, and suddenly his legs felt unsteady again, as though the ground beneath them might give way.

"My name is Cyrus Davidon," he called it into the dark sky. He clenched Praelior's hilt in his fingers, forgoing the gentle, reassuring stroke and progressing to taking a firm grip, waiting for the power in the blade to wash over him—

Except it didn't.

Cyrus took a sharp breath and tasted the air. It was thick with the smoky smell of ash, as though the movement of the ground had dislodged it and dispersed it into the air, a thick cloud that was part of the haze around him. He coughed, choking on it as he tried to clear his lungs. It passed after a moment of hacking, though the rough traces of it felt like they left a mark on his throat, dry dust stretching from the back of his mouth on down, leaving him with a scratchy sense beneath the gorget that protected his neck.

Who are you? The voice was deep and hollow, rushing over the world around him with a rising fury. The ashen sand blew with the arrival of the question, and Cyrus turned his face away from its unseen origin as a cloud blew past. Reflexively, he squinted his eyes shut against it, but still some particle lodged painfully in the corner of his right eye. He resisted the urge to move his hand off his sword and dig at it, instead moving his left, pressing mailed fingers through the gap of his helm to do so. The rush of wind subsided and tears sprang out from beneath his heavy lids. He opened his one good eye and picked at the other in an ungainly fashion, the thick fingers of his gauntlet preventing him from doing much other than pushing gently at it.

"What the hells?" Cyrus muttered to himself as he realized his failure and merely tried to blink the eye clear with tears. It worked after a moment, and he was able to reopen it without the sense that someone had lodged a boulder beneath the lid. "I already told you who I am," he said, now looking around for the source of the voice.

WHO ARE YOU? This time the voice was a bellow that shook the earth, not a mere twist of perspective and balance the way it had moved with his feet earlier, but a full-on rocking of the ground beneath his feet as though some army of titans the size of buildings had marched past him at a run, their enormous feet causing the earth itself to protest at their weight.

Well, that's about enough of this shit, Cyrus thought, as the dust began to settle. This time he'd closed his eyes in time and raised a gauntlet to protect them. "My name is Cyrus Davidon. I am the Guildmaster of Sanctuary, Lord of Perdamun and Warden of the Southern Plains!" he called in challenge. He stared into the dark skies.

WHO ARE YOU? The world rocked on its foundation again, even harsher if it was possible, as though a god had grabbed hold of the flat earth of Arkaria and given it a hard tug. Cyrus barely kept his feet this time, and the gusting of wind was like the force of a cyclone in the low country. If there had been trees anywhere in sight, he would have feared they'd have been torn up and thrown wildly at him, but when the angry question subsided and he blinked his eyes open and looked around, he saw nothing but dark skies and ashen earth in every direction.

"I keep bloody well telling you," Cyrus said, borrowing one of Vara's favorite words as he pushed back to his feet, "but apparently you don't like my answer." He looked once more, trying to find a face to direct his query to. "So ... who the hell are you?"

WHO ... ARE ... YOU? This time the question came with a mighty crack as the earth beneath Cyrus broke in two. It came like the rushing of a loosed river, tearing across the land at him as though it were a bolt of lightning streaking from the heavens to a tall tree. Even with his hand on Praelior, he felt nothing—no speed, no ability to react. It came as quickly as anything he'd ever seen and it split the earth between his legs and yanked them hard apart as though it meant to tear him asunder.

Cyrus fell, hand leaving his sword. He lost the ground beneath him, a flailing reaction to the fall that he had not seen coming. The earth yawned wide beneath his legs and he fell, catching himself with one of his thrown hands. The clink of his gauntlet against hard stone was preceded by the yanking force of his sharp descent suddenly coming to an abrupt halt. He felt the pain of it down his joints, rattling in his helm, the padding of his armor not doing nearly enough to defray the force that came with the harsh stop.

He dangled on the side of a newly made cliff, eyes drifting down into the impenetrable darkness below. It was as though a new shade of black had been invented purely for the purpose of this rift. He stared into it, almost fearing he could see eyes staring back at him out of it, compound eyes that glistened without a hint of light, attached to a mouth that would swallow him up, but only after grinding him to loose meat upon flat, unrelenting teeth.

Cyrus swung his other arm up once he'd gotten the sense of himself and his surroundings and managed to land it on the ledge next to the first with a clack of gauntlet upon stone. It came just in time, too, as the ash from above poured down upon him like water into a gutter. He turned his head in time to miss the worst of it, but he still received a full nose of the dark, silky cinders. It billowed around him in a cloud even as it rushed over his armor, sneaking into the cracks and tickling his flesh beneath his chainmail and clothes.

It stopped after another moment and all was silent for a bit. Cyrus hung there, waiting to see if more would come. When none immediately followed, he began to pull, his muscles forcing themselves against the armor as he began to strain. With Praelior as his aid, lifting his own bulk was an easy matter. Without it ... well ...

"Ungh," Cyrus muttered, lifting with all his strength. His armor groaned, a curious sound that he could not recall hearing before. He pulled up far enough to place an elbow on the rocky outcropping above, just as the voice thundered out once more ...

... but this time from below him.

WHO ARE YOU? it asked again, louder than ever, as though it had ripped his helm from his head and shouted it directly into his open ear. It rattled his head, drove all his thoughts out and left him without the concentration to formulate an answer. His grip betrayed him and his arm slipped, and Cyrus was left clutching the ledge above with but one hand, and then only his fingers as his palm wrenched free with a cracking of stone and a rain of small pebbles upon him from above.

"I just can't seem to find an answer that will satisfy you," Cyrus said, hanging by his fingertips. He looked down into the blackness below, his shoulder muscles straining, on fire with the exertion. "What do you want? I'm a warrior. I'm a general. I'm a—"

WHO ARE YOU? This time it wasn't just the darkness that asked. Red eyes gleamed in the ebony chasm, like someone had lit twin fires beneath him, burning bright in the midst of an endless sea of blackness. *WHO ARE YOU?* The voice rattled across the rock and through his armor, into his very bones. The force of it drove the ash

10

into fine clouds, blotting out the already dark sky and surrounding Cyrus in artificial night.

He hung there for another moment, sweating, sticky, his face covered in the fine ash that had started to drip in beads of sweat down into his eyes, where it burned. "I don't know what you want from me," Cyrus said to the eyes in the dark, "but—"

With one last bellowing question—*WHO ARE YOU?*—the rock beneath Cyrus's hand cracked and turned him loose from his perch. He thrashed his feet around but found no purchase, and he dropped into the darkness below and the ruby light of the twin eyes swelled with his fall, until they swallowed him whole—

2.

"Cyrus," came the soft whisper in his ear as long, gentle fingers brushed against his shoulder, shaking him awake as lightly as if he were being touched by a morning breeze, "you're dreaming. Wake up."

Despite the nightmarish vision he'd been caught up in only a moment earlier, he was still slow to open his eyes. When he finally pried them apart, they quickly captured the setting around him: wood supports lining the ceiling, the circular construction of the cap of a vast tower, and a smooth, pale face hovering just above him, her blond hair flowing over each shoulder unrestrained by her usual ponytail.

"That was not a dream," Cyrus rasped, levering himself up. Vara's hand was upon his bare chest, lightly, her delicate fingers touching his skin with little more pressure than he might have found from having a small bird perched upon him. He ran his fingers, thick and rough, over a day's worth of beard growth on his jaw as he exhaled. There was a foul taste in his mouth, not unlike the ash he'd dreamed of.

"No, I expect it wasn't, given the noises you were making." Vara brushed hair back to reveal the delicate points of her elven ears. A few light freckles showed on her nose, summer's kiss upon his lady's skin. He blinked the afterimage of his nightmare away as he stared into her beautiful, concerned face. Her hair was a little mussed from where it had been pressed against the pillow that now rested beneath her elbow. She lowered her voice, but the concern so evident on her face seeped into it nonetheless. "Cyrus, the war has been over for months."

"Huh?" He stared at her, perplexed, until he realized what she was talking about. "No, it wasn't—I wasn't at Leaugarden." *Not this time, anyway.* That battle had figured in more than a few of his nightmares of late, and the elf's assumption was reasonable—though wrong, in this instance. His eyes trailed around the room until they fell upon the wooden dummy that held his armor, stationed at the end of the bed. A matching figure holding silver-gleaming armor designed for the slim woman in bed next to him stood next to his own, so close that they could have held gauntlets with one another. *Still not quite used to that— but I do like seeing this particular sign of the changing times. Unlike ... others.*

"Oh, good," Vara said, and the exhalation of relief that followed stirred the hair upon his chest. She laid her head upon his shoulder, and he found his eyes drawn to the part of her hair, to the faint, pale skin peeking out between the flowing golden locks. "What was it this time, then?"

"I don't know," Cyrus said, clearing his throat, which felt as scratchy as if he'd swallowed a thistle—or a face full of ash. "Some loud voice asking, 'Who are you?' as the world fell apart around me."

"I hope you answered them appropriately."

"I did." Cyrus rubbed at his bare throat, fingers finding the ridged scar above it, bare of the rough stubble that sprang up on the rest of his neck. "Apparently, whoever it was did not find my answer satisfactory."

She ran her fingers down his chest, her breath stirring against the hair. "Did you tell them your full titles?"

"Of course," he answered before really thinking about it. He paused afterward, realizing he'd been tricked. "Oh, you—"

"I always get a bit irritable when you recite all of them as well," she said, pulling away enough for him to see the twinkle of amusement in her striking blue eyes. "Not only does it take all day, Guildmaster of Sanctuary, but it makes you sound a bit windy."

"Oh, does it?" He snaked an arm around her bare back and pulled her close, drawing a laugh. She did not resist as he pressed her naked chest to his own and drew her face to his and kissed her. He felt her tongue work its way through his lips and did not resist; she did not taste like ashes, that was certain.

When she was done, she pulled her lips from his and opened her eyes slowly. She gave him a canny look, like she could read his intention, but she asked anyway. "What do you have in mind here,

Warden of the Southern Plains?"

"Well ..."

She let out a slight groan and shifted in his arms. "I should have known."

"What?" He ran fingers over her back, finding the scar and letting his touch run over it. She no longer stiffened at his touching of it; in fact, she did not seem to notice at all anymore. *Almost like the one on my back, though I don't care if I ever see Aisling again. If I were to run across Archenous Derregnault, though ... well, I shouldn't mind if I got a chance to cross blades with that bastard.*

"I would swear you have but two interests," she said, leaning her forehead against his chest, tucking it into the curve under his chin so that he could smell her hair. It wafted a clean scent, like fresh soap. "War and sex, with perhaps an occasional allowance to be made for the intake of enough food to continue both."

"Well," he said, his fingers on her shoulders now, "war and sex are both hungry businesses."

"Yes, and your appetites for both are certainly vast." She pulled her head up so that she could look at him with those eyes. "Almost as large as your—" she halted, and Cyrus felt his eyebrows spike upwards, "—land holdings, Lord of Perdamun." Her eyes gleamed again, this time with amusement that caused her lips to curl in a smile. "What did you think I was going to say?"

"Something a great deal more complimentary," Cyrus said, looking directly into her eyes and letting her look back into his, "and more pertinent to the matter at hand."

"Ohhh," she let out a sigh. "It is the middle of the night, and you've woken me from a sound sleep. I do not know if you noticed upon my kiss, but a poor taste lingers in my mouth—"

"Sorry about that."

She raised an eyebrow in amusement. "It was not your doing, on this occasion, though I might suggest drinking fruit juices more regularly in the future." She pursed her lips and looked vaguely ... pouty, for once, he decided. "I can promise you that on the morrow, I will be fully happy to engage in almost whatever you wish to partake in—within reason—when I am fully awake. But for tonight ..." Her voice entered the territory of a plea. "Can we not just go back to sleep?"

"I suppo—"

He was cut off mid-thought by the sound of a trumpeting from somewhere in the night. It echoed and resonated through the stone walls around them, stripped of the volume he knew it would have contained only a floor below in the officer's quarters. It was followed by another blast, and then the ringing of persistent bells, and the sound of shouting—faint, but growing in intensity with every passing second—filled the night.

"ALARUM! ALARUM!"

Cyrus's eyes met Vara's, and he saw hers widen in surprise as they both hurried to leave the warm, comforting sheets behind for the cold suits of armor that sat on the mannequins at the end of the bed, waiting for their wearers.

3.

"I'm amazed at how fast you changed from 'Let's just go back to sleep' to being ready for action," Cyrus grumbled as they descended the stairs. Vara loped along ahead of him, taking them three at a time, her hand on her sword.

She shot him a serious look. "If you'd lived through the year of the siege, you might be a bit more circumspect about this and a little less grumpy." He could see the tension in her shoulders even through the armor, in the way she held herself, in the tight lines around her eyes, and the way the humor she'd displayed in bed had vanished the moment the shouts, bells and trumpets had reached them.

"If you'd acceded to my desires about five minutes ago, maybe then I'd be less grumpy, but otherwise—"

"What the hell is going on?" J'anda Aimant's thin voice sounded surprisingly strong as he rushed down the steps behind Cyrus. He wore full-length blue robes with runes stitched into the luxurious material, and vestments hung over his neck like a scarf with ancient lettering that marked him as an enchanter. He carried with him a long staff of metal that came to a glassy orb at the tip. It glowed purple from deep within, some magic that looked as though it might leak out at any moment. In spite of wrinkled blue skin and an aged look that had drained some of the vibrancy from his step, the enchanter easily caught up with both Cyrus and Vara, his quickness belying his appearance.

He's been different since he returned from Saekaj Sovar, Cyrus thought, watching the dark elf's speedy approach. *Faster, more energetic. Enough to put to lie the appearance of age he picked up in Luukessia.* He glanced at the orb atop the staff and wondered, not for the first time, exactly where

16

J'anda had gotten it. Answers, however, had not been forthcoming. "No idea," Cyrus said. "Other than a bellowing of 'ALARUM' from what sounds like the foyer."

"Could it be danger at the walls?" Vara asked, and a thin streak of worry laced through her voice, almost causing it to crack a bit. "Some siege force, perhaps?"

"I looked out the balcony windows while you were putting on your greaves," Cyrus said, eyeing her. "There's nothing on the plains and a full moon shines down."

"The portal in the foyer, then," J'anda said as they came to a great clot of people upon the stairs. The staircase was jammed full, and Cyrus stopped before running full-on into a familiar, black-robed, green-skinned figure.

"Hihi," Vaste said, turning to look up at the three of them. He looked past Cyrus and Vara to J'anda. "What, did you go to bed with these two tonight?"

"No," J'anda said, voice strangely husky. "It takes me a little longer to dress these days."

"You certainly weren't slow coming down those stairs," Cyrus noted, and his eyes fell to the staff again.

J'anda reached forward and swiftly tapped Cyrus on the head with one of the metal fingers that clutched the globe at the tip of his staff. It made a tinging noise that echoed in Cyrus's ear, and it actually hurt a little from the impact, causing Cyrus to step down onto the stair beside Vaste. Cyrus shook off the ringing from his ears and looked up to see the enchanter smiling at him. "Why do you ask questions you already know the answer to?" J'anda asked.

Cyrus opened his mouth, trying to clear the ringing in his ears. "What's it called?"

"Rasnareke," J'anda said, flourishing the staff, purple orb glowing, "the Ward of Justice."

"Who gave it to—"

Something else clanged on the top of Cyrus's helm, and he cringed, looking back to see Vaste staring at him with black pupils buried in a yellow iris, his white wooden staff still held guiltily high. "Oh, I'm sorry. I saw him do it and thought maybe it was 'Bop Cyrus on the Head Day.' Which, I might add, would easily be my favorite holiday save for 'Beat the Stuffing Out of Ryin Day.'"

"Did someone say my name?" Ryin Ayend's high voice shouted from across the open space of the staircase's spiral. Cyrus looked down to see him half a circle away, looking around for the speaker.

Cyrus adjusted his helm again, slightly, less out of need than in hope for the ringing in his ears to stop, and his gaze fell to Vara. "Usually in the past," he said as her eyes met his, "you would take several people knocking me about the skull as an opportunity to land a hit of your own."

She raised an eyebrow at him. "Things are not as they were in the past, though, are they?" She smiled, just a trace. "However much I might occasionally wish it in the middle of the night, you randy little—"

"Okay," Vaste said and turned abruptly with a twirl of his robes, "This is just so adorable I think I'm going to be nauseous." He paused. "Yes. Yes, that's nausea. Clearly a reaction to your oh-so-cutesy natures, and it's manifesting in—" He brought up a hand and placed it over his lips. "Going to vomit. Yes. It's happening." He looked over the side of the staircase and down. "Ryin! Come here! I have need of your robes to catch my regurgitation."

Cyrus looked across the gap and saw Ryin looking around again, once more apparently searching for whoever called his name. "You're going to give that poor man an ache in his neck."

"The nausea's passed," Vaste announced, straightening up.

"Are you certain?" Vara asked, looking at him innocently.

"Mostly," the troll said, regarding her with a healthy dose of suspicion. "Why?"

Vara grasped Cyrus by his newly shortened hair and dragged his head down for a kiss, long and passionate, and interrupted by a heaving noise from Vaste. "I'm just going to jump off here," the troll said, leaning over the edge of the staircase. "Make sure no one resurrects me at the bottom."

Vara laughed in a somewhat evil way at his discomfort. "After years of you tormenting me, troll, I see nothing but advantage in this."

Vaste's lips pursed and faded to an almost yellow color. "This is what you get for wishing people well. From now on I'm wishing you nothing but ill." The faint sound of someone shouting "Alarum!" below wafted its way up to them as the clot on the stairs began to work its way loose and movement resumed. "On second thought," he said, "perhaps I'll wait on that until we see how this works out."

"A prudent gesture," came the voice of Curatio as he slid into place next to J'anda. The healer looked more than a little disheveled, his face almost as pale as his white robes. For as long as Cyrus had known him, Curatio had looked nearly ageless, for he indeed was. *But now*, Cyrus thought as he looked the elder elf up and down, *he looks like he was dragged from deepest sleep and set upon a by a pack of angry rock giants.*

"Are you quite all right, Curatio?" Vara asked with more than a touch of concern. "You don't look—"

"I'm fine, thank you," the healer said brusquely. He ran a hand through his hair, smoothing it. "I apparently did not wake immediately upon the sounding of the alarm." *He's another one that hasn't been right for a while*, Cyrus thought. "Do we have any idea what has prompted this middle of the night awakening?"

"No army at the walls," Cyrus said, nodding to the empty space that stretched stories below to the foyer. "Maybe a battle down there at the portal?"

Vara listened carefully, and Curatio did the same, tipping an ear toward the shaft running through the middle of the tower. "No sound of swords clanging," she said, shaking her head. "Just shouting. A great lot of bloody, indiscernible shouting."

"It bodes ill," Curatio pronounced, and Cyrus could not find it in himself to disagree. Cyrus looked with concern over the edge of the great drop. "Alarms called in the night, no sign of an army or battle …" His voice trailed off, and Cyrus felt his thoughts swirl as he considered possibilities, none of them making any sense.

No battle, no invaders. No threats—the dark elves declared peace and Terian is at the head of their government … could he have changed his mind about burying the old grudge? Cyrus looked down again as the slow shuffle of the spiral continued, and he did all within his power to keep from trying to strong-arm his way past Vaste and down the stairs.

He looked over at Vara and smiled in what he tried to make a reassuring way. "It'll be all right," he said, easily as much for himself as anyone else present.

"I know," she said, returning his smile, but lightly, as she did everything. She leaned forward and gave him another soft kiss on the lips.

"Well," Curatio said, "that was … very nearly sickening."

"Thank you!" Vaste bellowed, drawing every eye in the spiral for two whole floors. He lowered his voice. "I tried to tell them exactly that earlier, and I don't think they believed me."

"Or perhaps we simply were hoping you would eventually jump, thus sparing us all your rancid troll wit, which is nearly as sour as your breath," Vara said.

"You should talk." Vaste waved a hand in front of his nose as he looked up at her. "You kiss him with that mouth? Did you swallow a—"

Vara flushed red as a ripple of reaction ran through the spiral below them. Cyrus noticed it in the form of a hush that fell, whispers straining to reach across the gap as his eyes found Ryin, who was listening intently to someone ahead of him in the line. When the druid heard what was said, his head rocked back and he blinked three times in rapid succession. "Ryin!" Cyrus called, drawing the man's gaze toward him as the rumor raced up the spiral. "What is it?"

"I could have told you," Vara said, voice a quiet whisper behind him. He turned to look her in the eyes, again, but found the mirth that had been present only moments before had fled as surely as the desert dwellers of the Inculta disappeared at sunrise. There was a tentativeness behind her eyes, a hesitance that caused him to quiver as her ears reddened at the tips, with her blond hair now drawn back in its severe ponytail, as it always was when she was ready for battle.

"What is it?" Cyrus asked, swallowing heavily. A sense of nervous anticipation flowed through him freely, and he placed his hand upon Praelior as much for the feeling it provided as for a place to rest it.

"The Emerald Fields," Vara said, her voice with a quiver of its own. Cyrus's stomach dropped as though someone had shoved it over the edge of the stairwell. "The titans of Kortran have come through the Heia Pass … and they're attacking the town as we speak."

4.

The flash of a teleportation spell faded into dark night, and the smell of flames and smoke reached Cyrus's nose before his eyes regained their sight. The orange glow on the horizon was the first sign of the trouble ahead, and Cyrus found himself giving orders before his mind had caught up with his balance. It was a hot night in the middle of summer, the moisture thick in the air as if a hard rain were imminent. "Keep a tight formation! We don't know how many we're dealing with, or what we'll find when we get there." He didn't wait for acknowledgment before beginning his run, pushing out in front of his army of some three hundred. Flashes behind him told him that more were on their way in, and he trusted them to follow close behind him.

"This is like a waking nightmare," Vara said at his side as they headed toward the town in the distance. The clank of her silver armor was subtle compared to the shouts and screams that came from ahead, the cries in the night of battle and terror. "How many people did we have stationed here?"

"Maybe five hundred at the portal," Thad said, causing Cyrus to turn his head to look at the warrior in blood-red armor. He already had his sword drawn, a plain-looking weapon of mystical steel that had been procured from one of their endless trips to the Realm of Purgatory. *It'll be enough to cut a crease in titan skin, that's certain.* "We pulled half the garrison last year at Administrator Tiernan's request."

"And they'd have been in poor position to deal with anything out of the south," Cyrus said, his long legs making less stride than they could have. He held himself under control to keep from outpacing his army. "They were meant to defend the portal against invaders, not the town against an army out of the south." He pursed his lips into a tight line, his fearful anticipation growing with each step closer to the flames of war that beat in the near distance. His jog was not enough for him, not nearly. He longed to run, to lope along the worn and dusty road from the portal to the town, to use every bit of the speed that Praelior granted him to charge headlong into battle.

"I know your mind," Vara whispered at his ear. "But even you, with that sword, would find difficulty against an army of titans."

Cyrus nodded his acknowledgment, unable to find sufficient words to express the muddled rage seething under the surface. *Titans are twenty feet tall and with all the proportionate strength that entails; a stray hand could cripple me with one good blow, and they're not slow creatures, either.* "I'll maintain discipline," Cyrus said at last.

"I did not worry about it," she said, "I merely wished to reassure you at following your better instincts. I know it is difficult. I, too, long to run ahead in order to inflict my singular rage upon these creatures, but without magical support, even we would be at a great disadvantage."

Cyrus breathed a hard breath, and it seemed to stick in his lungs like he'd taken in a bone that had lodged in his chest. The night sky was dark overhead but light in front of them, flames dancing into the night and giving the smoky clouds hanging ominously over the town a subtle glow. It brought to mind another battle he'd fought. "Does this remind you of—"

"Santir, yes," Vara said quietly. She was breathing a little louder now, not panting by any means, but he could hear her exertions. "On the night of the Termina battle."

The mere memory caused Cyrus to swallow heavily. "I hope we're not walking into anything as bad as that ... massacre."

They crested a small rise and the town came into view. At least a quarter of it was burning, flames billowing into the air in the northwest side of the main street. Houses farther off the avenue were catching as well, a stiff wind coming out of the east and carrying the fire between the wooden structures that made up the town. Large, shadowed figures loomed over the buildings and smaller ones ran to and fro in great numbers, their screams all blending together as the survivors attempted to flee.

"Son of a bitch," Martaina Proelius breathed, and Cyrus started slightly to find the elven ranger at his shoulder. She had her bow in hand and looked prepared to draw and fire it, even from here.

"Hold," Cyrus said and put up a hand that caught the glow of the fires and turned his skin a sickly shade of yellow. He spun and looked over the army behind him, straining to raise himself up slightly. They filled the ground behind him all the way to the portal, already numbering several thousand. A flash near the portal forced him to avert his eyes for a few seconds, and when he turned back he saw a few hundred on horseback, plainly teleported directly from the stables. "Thad, keep the cavalry out of the fight in town. The last thing we need is to have them riding down our own people in tight confines. Send them around on the northern reaches through the fields, see if they can rally survivors. Have them gather anyone they find and escort them back to the portal for evacuation to Sanctuary."

"Aye, sir," Thad said, saluting sharply with the hand he did not carry his sword in. "Anything else?"

"Where's Odellan?" Cyrus called, and his eyes alighted on the familiar winged helm of the elf somewhere in the second formation that had teleported in. "Never mind. I'm sure he's got his own group under control—just repeat my orders to him as he passes."

"Aye."

"Army of Sanctuary, on me!" Cyrus called and started forward again at a slightly faster pace. He came down the small hill toward the town, looking hard at the first of the titans ahead of him. He could judge the height by the size of the buildings it moved near. The beast was easily taller than a two-story building and tore through a thatched-roof hut with a fearsome roar. This one had gotten away from his comrades that were filling the streets of the town, dark, shadowed towers in the streets of this small city.

Cyrus waited for the sound of the army's motion to betray him to the titan he stalked, but the creature was far too busy tearing the roof off the building ahead of it. It rummaged about in the house like a man through small chest, a stray hand destroying the wooden side of the structure. It made a low, horrible chortling noise and drew a massive fist out with something that looked like a small doll clutched inside it. With a sickening sense of disgust, Cyrus realized it was a person, a human being, though a hard squeeze by the beast ended that life without so much as an audible squeal. The titan threw the body over its shoulder without a care, and then turned back to the house as a cry from within the building echoed in the night.

Cyrus held back no longer, letting his blade carry him forward on legs now stronger and faster than any stallion's. He reached the squatting titan and leapt into the air, landing with a hard clank upon a shoulder, causing the creature to look up in utter bewilderment. Its face was rough and ugly, like a rotted fruit, the eyes under its dome-shaped helm, tangerine with the reflection of the fires burning beyond. A smell wafted from it, sweat and body odor of an intensity Cyrus could remember only from a Society of Arms barracks after a long week of military exercises. The smell almost made him gag, but he sublimated his disgust and threw it into a thrust of his sword instead, driving Praelior into a gaping eye and following behind it with all his force.

The titan screamed as the blade pierced him. Cyrus pushed into the socket with fury, driving his hand into the orb as gelatinous blood came rushing out. He buried his hand up to the wrist, not considering that he was attaching his fate to the creature's, but as the first shocks of movement surged through the titan's massive frame, Cyrus realized his error.

Should have gone for the neck, he thought as the beast jerked to its feet. A hand came up to swat at him, and it hit his armor with harsh force, striking him as if he were a bothersome fly. The rattle of rough flesh against his metal armor echoed through Cyrus's bones like the quaking of the earth in his dream and drove him slightly deeper into the eyeball, burying him almost to the shoulder. *Shit.*

As the striking hand withdrew, Cyrus pulled hard against the entrapping eyeball, ripping free of it only with great effort and all his Praelior-enhanced strength. The soft tissue resisted and tugged at the edges of his gauntlets and vambraces, and the shrieking of the giant beast raged around him like a thunderstorm. He maintained his footing as he withdrew thanks only to the balance granted him by his sword. It was a precarious place to stand; Cyrus knew it and meant to remove himself from the perch as quickly as possible.

The titan stood up on wobbly legs, raising a hand to deliver another smack. It was hardly likely to injure someone who had only months earlier been knocked about by a god, but Cyrus had certainly felt the first blow, even if it had caused him no harm. He watched the titan turn its face away from him, exposing a neck that had no gorget upon it. Cyrus struck swiftly, opening the vein that flowed in exactly the same place as it would have on a human. His reward was a geyser of dark-tinted liquid that looked almost black in the firelight. Cyrus did not bother to dodge away from his portion, receiving the spray upon his black armor.

The titan's steps became unsteady, and one of its hands rose in panic. Cyrus leapt from atop the shoulder and felt the shock run from his feet up through his knees and legs as he landed. It hurt, and he counted himself fortunate indeed to feel the breath of a healing spell only a moment later, though nothing had been obviously broken in his sudden descent.

He cleared out of the shadow of the titan as a fire spell struck the beast's already scarred-looking face in the side that still contained an eyeball. The creature fell, probably more from the wound Cyrus had inflicted rather than the spell. It landed on its knees and then folded at the midsection, crashing into the house that it had been rifling through upon his approach. Cyrus cringed, looking away, letting the anger rage over him at his failure to protect the occupants within. The wooden planks that made up the walls were broken and scattered, all support lost when the titan had landed upon it, knocking it entirely flat.

"You bastards," Cyrus whispered but allowed himself only a moment before his mind moved on, seeking his next target. He found it shortly but hesitated as he stared at the towering creature that stood only a hundred feet down the street.

It was a titan, obviously, clad in the same steel armored breastplate that the rest of them wore. They had helms, they had breast and backplates, but little else, as though they simply ran out of metal before being able to cover themselves in any further protection. This one wore the same dome-like helm as the one he'd just killed, but instead of bearing a weapon in its hands, it seemed to be …

It seemed to be playing with fire.

Flames sprouted from its very skin and shot out to the thatched roof of a building on the south side of the road. A crackling sound of glee came out of the beast as its small effort was rewarded with a burgeoning flame that lit the house ablaze. It moved to the next uninhibited, and Cyrus watched for a sign of a torch, a hint of something other than—

"It's casting a bloody fire spell," Vara breathed as the titan's hands sprung aflame again. "It's—"

"Yes, I saw," Cyrus cut her off, a flame of his own growing within, rage mingling with stunned disbelief.

"Titans cannot use magic," J'anda breathed from next to them. "They cannot—"

"And yet they are," came Curatio's quiet voice from out of the night. "Plainly."

That was the great equalizer, Cyrus realized as the titan squealed in perverse joy as it lit another home aflame. They may have been the largest creatures in Arkaria other than the dragons, the fiercest warriors, the most frightening—

But they couldn't use magic. That was the only thing holding them back from coming north, from crushing their way through the pass at will, from stomping through the northern lands and—he looked around at the carnage, the fire streaking its way into the darkened sky. Hints of despair came through, settling on him like they were finding the cracks in his armor and piercing him with a truth that was as thick as the smoke in the air.

Now they know magic.

Now there's nothing holding them back.

5.

"Strike him down!" Cyrus shouted as the horror passed back to rage, the implications of what they'd seen falling by the wayside as muffled shouts came from out of the house that the titan was lighting ablaze. "Spell casters! Bombard!"

Cyrus charged forward as bursts of ice, fire and lightning heralded his arrival. They struck the titan spell caster, drawing his ire and surprise. The titan whipped his massive frame around as Cyrus charged at the creature's knees, right at head level for him. The titan's right sleeve was on fire, and another bolt of lightning drew a scream as it crackled across the metal helm. Cyrus ran past the creature's leg and buried Praelior into the tendon at the back of the foot as a howl of agony split the night above him.

Vara slid into place behind the other foot only moments after him and struck a mirrored blow. The titan stumbled and fell, and Cyrus blanched as he saw a ranger and a warrior crushed beneath the falling body. Others of Sanctuary's army swept in upon the head as the creature landed, and Cyrus found himself moving on to the next target, the next battle.

"This is not a fight we have fought before," Vara cautioned him as they swept down the street at the head of a shouting, clamoring army. Cyrus saw rage on the faces that followed him, and not just from the ones wearing the livery of Luukessia's three kingdoms. "This is different. These things can harm us more certainly than—"

"I know," Cyrus said, softening his voice more than he would have for anyone else. "I just watched our own people killed by the fall of that thing." *In a way, my nightmare was less frightening than this battle that I've awoken to …*

He was back under control, pacing himself to keep his army with him. The next titan was already waiting for them, having heard the fall of its comrade. It bore an evil smirk beneath hair that hung down under its helm's steel lip, and a short beard grew out of its potato-skin-like jawline. It swept at them, trying to stomp on Cyrus at the lead. He dodged the massive foot and buried his blade in the calf, drawing a sharp gasp of pain from his foe as he jumped on the leather shoe and struck swiftly again, this time into the gaps in the bones of the ankle.

The titan staggered at the attack, and Cyrus leapt for the knee, driving Praelior into its underside and prompting the titan to howl as it came down, the joint twisting and buckling under the pressure. Cyrus moved well clear, shoving two rangers out of the way, their green cloaks billowing as he elbowed them back to give the titan room to fall.

The beast landed on its haunches, its arse ending up in one of the flaming buildings. It moaned almost pitifully then tried to stand in panic as the fire rose around it. Cyrus drove his blade through its heavy trousers, a coarse cotton that his weapon ripped with ease. He cut a hard X into the gnarled flesh then parted it with a gauntlet as he tore at the edges. It peeled back enough for him to see a red tube running through, and he thrust Praelior home and opened the artery, stepping clear as the titan screamed out in the night.

The titan struck blindly at where Cyrus had been, but Cyrus was already gone, backing away from the doomed creature. He pushed his army back, hectoring them away from the battle that he'd already finished. "Leave it be," he said, striding around the leg and back to his course down the street. The titan struggled to remove itself from the burning building, but failed, and the smell of burning flesh combined with its shrieks to pierce the night and add to Cyrus's sickened stomach.

"We need to find the leader of this war party," Cyrus mumbled, knowing she'd hear him.

"Toward the square!" Vara called from behind him.

He did not ask her if she were sure; he knew that she was. He merely made for the next titan down the street, but before he could reach it, it jerked as though an unseen something had climbed onto its back. Its eyes alighted on Cyrus for only a moment before they went blank, and the creature stood at its full height, almost at attention.

"Hold," J'anda said, coming alongside Cyrus brandishing that marvelous staff of his. "This one is mine."

Cyrus stared up into the vacant eyes of the beast. "You sure you can hold it?"

"What an insulting question," J'anda said. "I'm going to ignore that and pretend you asked something else instead, such as how I am faring in this warm and sweaty night."

Cyrus dipped his head in acknowledgment as a bead of sweat rolled down his forehead. He started down the street but J'anda's titan broke into a run ahead of him. J'anda's pet made a break for the next foe, a titan who was leaning over a wagon to pick it up, and slammed a fist into that gawking titan's jaw upon approach. The sound of large bones breaking echoed in the fire-lit night as Cyrus did his best to keep up with the new warrior in his army.

"Give me a moment," J'anda said from beside him, almost maintaining Cyrus's pace. He paused and his arms went akimbo, purple light dancing from the spell spitting forth out of his hands. The spell light flickered and shot into the night, disappearing as a new titan, sprinting toward J'anda's pet with fearsome rage in his eyes, halted mid-stride and stood, back stiff, eyes dull.

"Now you've got two," Cyrus said, and he started to huff as he tried to navigate around J'anda's first enchanted titan before it broke into a run again down the street. "Save some for the rest of us, will you?"

"Perhaps," the enchanter said quietly, breaking into a jog again as Cyrus paused to wait for the rest of his leading element to catch up. *This is new; J'anda is usually at the back of the fight, and now he's at the fore with me. I would say nothing good can come of this change, especially given his frailty, but damned if he isn't holding more than his own.* The two pet titans sprang upon one of their own down the street, catching him by surprise and killing him with a flurry of well-placed blows that culminated in a punch to the temple that sprayed a fountain of dark liquid into the night.

The square was ahead, and the sounds of battle rang out in the night. It was only a few hundred feet in front of Cyrus, but the street between him and the open area was utter chaos. The survivors he'd seen from the hill had thinned, and corpses lay dead in the dust. Cyrus tried not to look down as he nearly tripped over a small body and felt his heart sink when he realized it was a child. "Curatio!" Cyrus called, looking back at the fire-lit faces behind him. "Can we revive these people?"

"I am working on it," Curatio said, hands glowing red as his spell drained his infinite life. "As best I can, in any case, as we go." The red persisted, reflected in his eyes. Lines and wrinkles on the healer's face caught shadows from the dancing fires around them. If he had looked worn before, now he had pallor about him that even the fiery night's glow could not make warm. The town of Emerald Fields was burning on either side of them. "We need more healers."

"Like I've never heard that one before," Cyrus muttered, stalking back toward the square. He listened carefully, catching sight of Vara picking her way around bodies as J'anda's titans brawled with two others just ahead, blocking their view. "It sounds like fighting up there. Actual fighting, not slaughter." He cast a tense look back at his army, still hurrying to keep up with him, ranks filling in, people breaking off to enter buildings on either side, dashing back out with ash-blackened faces. *Trying to save whoever they can*, Cyrus thought. *Admirable. I didn't have to order it.*

He caught a glimpse of Andren a row behind him and Vaste off to the side a little, the troll's usual smirk replaced by an expression of drawn horror. His lower teeth bulged out as always, but his mouth lay slightly open, the shock of what he was seeing uncontrolled in his expression. His white-crystal-tipped staff rested lightly in his hands, and it was at that moment that Cyrus realized the true graveness of the spectacle about them. *If Vaste is stunned into horrified silence ...*

... then this is an atrocity like nothing we've seen before.

This place ... it's home to so many of our number. His jaw tightened as the rage ran through him again. *Someone will pay for this transgression.*

"Sanctuary Army!" Cyrus called, pooling his rage and letting it spill from his lips. "On me! Let us strike down these enormous bastards and make them pray for swift death and mercy they will not find from us!"

A hoarse cry broke through the ashy, smoke-filled air, and Cyrus turned to charge. One of J'anda's pets was dead in the street, the broken body of its foe atop it. They blocked Cyrus's view of anything but the tops of titan heads beyond; of J'anda's surviving pet throttling the life out of another titan, thick fingers wrapped around a neck and squeezing as it bowed the back of its adversary in fury, pressing forward to the death. The dying titan's mouth was open, and a gagging noise was all that came out, loud as a horse's whinny. A snapping filled the night as bones broke and sinews ripped, and the hard slaps of the titan's hands against the bare forearms of its assailant ceased as the corpse fell to the ground with a thud that caused Vara to lose her footing for a moment.

Cyrus, however, followed the surviving titan through the smoke, toward the square … and stopped at the edge, stunned at the sight his eyes beheld there.

6.

It was clear to Cyrus that the titans counted on hardened hands to beat their foes to death with slaps and strikes that could shatter bone and rend asunder the flesh of their smaller prey. Here, in the square, however, they had finally met a foe their equal, and four of the massive creatures were having at it, matched against their lone opponent whose gravelly voice did not hold back any of his obvious fury.

"GRAAAAAAAAAAGH!" The bellow of the rock giant was sharp in Cyrus's ears. Stony hands struck at the groin of a titan and brought him to his knees, retching, as the rock giant grabbed at an ear and ripped it off. It was hardly an equal battle by size; the rock giant was roughly half the height of the titans, but he seemed to have more than enough fire to take the creatures on. He threw the ear into the face of a titan coming at him from the side as a third grasped hold of his smaller arm in the way an adult might manhandle a misbehaving child in the Reikonos markets. The titan dragged the rock giant for three paces before the rocky creature dug in, dropping low and ripping his arm free, leaving bloody wounds on the titan's hand where the jutted, stony skin tore great rents in its palm. The titan who had lost his ear came back to his stumbling feet, one hand clutching his grievous wound, and the rock giant found himself encircled once more. Any other, less courageous creature might have fled under the assault of so many obviously superior enemies.

But Fortin the Rapacious is no coward, Cyrus thought.

Before the titans could spring against him, Fortin bellowed again, giving his opponents pause, and leapt high to land an enraged punch upon the jaw of the titan who had just laid hands upon him. The sound of bone breaking was as loud as the crunch he'd heard earlier when J'anda's pets had struck down their own with furious punches. The titan's eyes fluttered and he went limp, toppling over backward into a general store that collapsed under the fall of the beast. Makeshift carpentry went asunder in an instant and the rest of the structure fell in on top of the downed enemy.

"AHHHHH!" Fortin's yell crackled in the night once again, and he came at the next of his enemies as J'anda's pet charged forth in front of Cyrus, intercepting one that went to attack the rock giant while his back was turned. J'anda's titan grabbed his opposite number by the wrist at the apogee of his attack on Fortin; pulling him off balance, J'anda's pet dragged him to the ground and stomped his throat without mercy as Fortin tackled the knees of his own opponent, breaking bones and pulling his foe to the ground in a screaming, pummeling brawl that saw a rocky hand raised and lowered in fury again and again until it came up glinting with dark blood in the square's light, the shouts of the titan silenced.

Cyrus did not issue an order, sprinting instead toward the last of the unoccupied titans. It was moving to drag Fortin off its fellow, grasping him around the waist and lifting him under an arm. The rock giant threw back his elbows ineffectually, clanging against the titan's soot-covered breastplate. He writhed and squirmed and shouted as Cyrus came in and drilled Praelior into the back of a dirtied, crusted leather boot, ripping his blade into the sensitive spot behind the ankle and drawing a surprised scream out of the titan.

Fortin dropped immediately, wriggling out of his imprisonment and punching squarely into his enemy's knee. This caused the titan to topple faster, and as soon as his head dipped low enough, Fortin grabbed hold of it, bringing his hands together and pulling hard. With no chinstrap to keep it in place, the helm came off with ease. Fortin let it fall and planted his massive hands, so small next to the titan's giant skull, on the beast's temples. He squeezed them together, and the titan's screams ceased in seconds, before Cyrus could do much more than start to open an artery.

The titan died, and Fortin moved swiftly to kill the other, hefting the helm that he'd tossed aside and bringing it down on his prone enemy over and over, using a hard corner as a cudgel and finishing the titan in seconds. Cyrus snaked out from behind one of the fallen and called to the rock giant. "Fortin!"

When the rock giant turned, there was no mistaking the killing instinct present in his hard features. His face, usually inscrutable, was jagged lines of pure rage, covered with scarlet blood along every crag and crevice of his skin. He breathed into the hot night and Cyrus could nearly imagine the steam pouring out of his nostrils. His fury did not soften even as the trace of recognition flickered across his stony face. "Lord Davidon," he said, rough and gravelly.

"How many are there, Fortin?" Cyrus asked, approaching the rock giant slowly. While he did not doubt Fortin's ability to tell friend from foe, he had been in the rage of battle like this before. *Anger overwhelms him; best not get in his way.*

"Too many," Fortin said, and his voice cracked. "Half a hundred, I think. Spell casters in with them. They have them now—"

"We know," Cyrus said. He could feel the heat of the flames. "Did anyone make it out of town?"

"Administrator Tiernan led the retreat toward the woods," Fortin gestured toward a copse of trees in the distance. "But … not enough." His head swung around as a shout echoed in the night from behind him. "We have to stop them, have to kill them—"

"Yes," Cyrus said, "we'll—" But he was cut off by a new entrant on the far side of the square.

The loud footsteps should have given the approach away, but at that very moment one of the burning buildings collapsed just off the square, and a cloud of dust whipped over Cyrus. When it cleared, he looked up toward the shadow he'd seen coming a moment earlier. *J'anda's pet?* he wondered. *No, it was over—*

Cyrus saw Fortin again as the dust cleared, his frightening features still clouded by the haze of ash and smoke. But he only saw them for a moment before a massive hand descended and drove the rock giant into the earth. The sound of rock cracking was as loud as any building collapse. Fortin did not even have a chance to cry out before his body bent unnaturally, and Cyrus knew that he was dead.

The attacker swept out of the cloud of dust, black sleeves catching white ash in their fine thread. He was a titan, and wore shining silver armor that gleamed with crimson, dozens of spots of blood smeared across it like a butcher's apron. His helm matched the look of his breastplate but carried rather more dust, and hid a face even rougher than the other titans; more scarred, somehow, and with a furious twinkle in his eyes he stared down at Cyrus.

"Lord Cyrus Davidon," Talikartin the Guardian said in a deep voice as rough as his complexion. "At last, we meet again."

7.

Cyrus was well past the point where fear could hold him in sway, even at the sight of so frightening a visage as Talikartin the Guardian's. "At last indeed," Cyrus said, low and rough, his voice almost unrecognizable to his ears. "How long has it been?"

"Some five years gone now," Talikartin said, tilting his massive head to regard Cyrus, the light of the fires flickering across his rough cheeks. "I have waited for you to return as you promised, but I grew tired after a time and have come north to find you."

"I'm surprised you know my name," Cyrus said, holding Praelior tight in hand. "It was so very long ago, after all."

"Your legend reaches even our ears in the southern lands." Talikartin brandished a mailed fist, and his gauntlet, so different than the bare hands of his confederates, glinted with blood. It ran in down the furrows in his armor, dripping onto the dusty street in great splashes. "Do you know how many people have invaded my city under my watch, become known to us, and survived in the way you and your guild did?" He took a step closer, and the ground shook beneath Cyrus's feet. "You came to claim bounties upon the heads of my fellows issued by those accursed, scheming, cowardly, hidden elves of Amti." His eyes glinted. "Do you know how many bounties have been paid in the days since your attack?" He smiled, and his teeth showed hints of blood in the saliva that covered them in a liquid shine. "Not one. I have killed … so many of you northerners since that day, simply hoping that one day I would see your taunting, black-armored form creep into my city once more, so that I could show you my gratitude at our reunion."

"Here I am," Cyrus said, arms spread wide. Talikartin was almost forty feet away from him, not an easy distance to close when his foe's reach was such an advantage. Cyrus kept an eye fixed on the creature, waiting for him to make a move other than to threaten. "You came all this way; I presume you won't leave without paying your regards."

"I will give you the full regard of the titans of Kortran, yes," Talikartin said, stepping closer to him. *Thirty paces.* "Though I have heard it was not you who stole Ferocis from us."

"Don't need it," Cyrus said, brandishing Praelior. "Got my own sword. I could give you the name of the guy who did take it, if you'd like—though I doubt very much you're going to survive the next few minutes to do anything with that information—"

Talikartin swept forward with alarming speed and Cyrus was forced to dodge to the side, throwing himself to the dirt as the titan struck at him. Cyrus rolled and came back to his feet in a crouch, clutching his weapon. *Without Praelior, I would have taken that hit squarely. I bet that would have hurt.*

The titan moved sideways, not closing the gap between them at all and thwarting Cyrus as he started to head in Talikartin's direction. Cyrus spun to follow the evasion and ducked just in time to avoid a hard smash of the sort that he'd just watched kill Fortin.

"Too slow!" Cyrus taunted, dodging in closer to Talikartin's feet. But the titan was certainly fast enough, and his limbs were long enough that he could sweep them in a grand arc that made it difficult for Cyrus to dodge him. Cyrus drove closer, forcing Talikartin to stoop as Cyrus moved in to strike a blow of his own. The titan took a step back and swept another attack at Cyrus, this one forcing him to make a small retreat.

"What's the matter?" Cyrus called up at his much taller foe. The silver helm caught the light of a building burning just behind him. "Afraid to face me?"

"Stand toe to toe with me," Talikartin said, "then we will talk of courage, mite."

"I'm trying to get to your toe just now," Cyrus said, dodging a thrown hand, "you're not making it easy, chickenshit."

"Hah!" Talikartin's laugh was a harsh bark. "I know of your sword, your speed, your armor—the Death of Gods, they call you and yours. If you think I am fool enough to merely wait for you to come at me, you know nothing of battle or war."

"I know a lot about both," Cyrus said, coming in low and charging at Talikartin's steel boot. He made a leap of the sort he'd seen Vara employ on dozens of occasions, landing ten feet from his target, just as the titan stepped backward again. "And I'm about to teach you everything I—"

The backhand hit Cyrus unexpectedly, a hard snap that knocked him over on his back. His armor rang like a temple bell. His backplate hit the dirt and a cloud of it puffed up around him. He caught a lungful and choked, the taste of blood heavy on his tongue. He started to get up, pushing to his feet, and then a hard pressure closed on his leg as his feet were yanked from beneath him.

Cyrus found himself dangling upside-down, like a plucked thread hanging from massive fingers. His blood rushed to the dome of his skull as he stared into mighty eyes and a cruel smile. "Not so much as you should know," Talikartin said. "Not enough to keep to the ranks of your little army." He spun Cyrus, hanging by his knee, and a cracking in the joint told the warrior everything he needed to about the strength of the beast that held him. As he came around he caught sight of the Army of Sanctuary facing a half dozen titans, Vara in the midst of them, looking across the square at him, the fire behind her casting her distinctive form in silhouette and reminding him for a brief flash of the first time they'd met.

"A man of true strength becomes a warlord," Talikartin said, staring at him with those massive eyes. "What are you called? Warden? What is that, but a glorified shield for the kingdoms of men and elves and other insects? Instead of taking what you want, you protect what others hold dear." The titan scoffed, a deep noise in his throat. "How pathetic."

"Aren't you called Talikartin the *Guardian?*" Cyrus asked, dangling by his leg, preparing his next move, a swipe at the fingers that held him.

"Do you know what I protect?" Talikartin asked and pulled him slightly closer to the eye. *Or maybe I just poke him good, see what that gets me*—"The plunder of a warlord so great that serving him is nothing but glory of itself. He is not a man, not a mite, and to do his bidding nets me everything I desire." The titan grunted. "What has your service as shield given you, fool?"

Cyrus's breath caught in his throat as he started to respond, but he knew the delay was too great even before the first word left his mouth. "It's given me—" Before he could even finish, Cyrus felt himself lifted high with shocking speed, as though the very force which held him to the earth had been reversed, and just as he reached a height and could see the whole of the Emerald Fields, of the battle—Sanctuary looked to be winning—Talikartin ripped him down, and Cyrus felt a great tearing in his groin as he was brought to the dirt again with a great and terrible smashing, like the time he'd ridden the Dragonlord into the earth—

8.

Cyrus awoke to blood spouting out of his mouth, pain in his every limb, and a feeling like someone had ground up his innards under a stone press. It reminded him of drowning, but this time the pungent stink of his own blood was upon his tongue, in his eyes, red everywhere—

"Hold on," came Vara's voice, as tight as a cursed belt, the life squeezed from it. He couldn't see her, couldn't feel her touch, couldn't see any light but the orange of blazing flames tinted as sharply red as if someone had painted his eyes.

"I don't know if I can do this!" Andren's voice came, strained. "I mean—he's—he's just—"

"Just keep him alive for a moment, you great bloody idiot!"

Cyrus tried to move and felt bones grind against one another, fresh pain surging through him. He could barely draw thoughts one to the other; it was all agony and paralysis, helplessness coupled with a feeling as though he couldn't even move significant swaths of his body—

"What the holy horned hell have you done?" Vaste cried, his voice so loud, so filled with fear that it was almost unrecognizeable.

"Heal him!" Vara shouted, and something ran across Cyrus's flesh, a tickle that did little to assuage his pain. "Just do—"

"Are you jesting?" Vaste asked, and the panic was obvious in his tone. "I mean, me having to ask you this should—for the sake of the gods—do you have any idea what you're *doing*—"

"I am trying to save his life," Vara said, low and harsh, most of it escaping like a hiss. "Why don't you aid me, since you're such a damned expert—"

"He's—"

"Oh my—"

"We need Curatio for this," Vaste said, firm, serious. He waited a breath, and then shouted, "*CURATIO!*"

"For—I mean—holy—what the—"

Other voices were joining in now, frightening, frightened, and awestruck. The thump of feet against the street was a constant sound, but there was none of the thudding of titans running about, not now. A strange peace settled over Cyrus as the pain started to fade …

"Aw, shits, he's dying—"

The light drifted out of his view like a candle snuffed in a light wind, a puff and gone—

—then consciousness returned with the pain, harsh and unrelenting, and all the way up his arm this time, present now in a way it hadn't been before. Before it had simply been numb, or gone, but now it screamed at him.

"Yes," Curatio's soft voice said, straining. "And then—" He muttered something under his breath, and the pain receded from his arm's joints, feeling instead like it was originating on the surface. "Then—yes, like that—" The healer murmured again, and this time his left leg screamed in pain for a brief second before it started to fade. "Almost—"

A moment passed in which Cyrus felt as though he'd fallen into a sleep, then snapped back to a wakeful state with the sky dark orange above him. He could feel his own breath coming now, and when he raised a hand, it responded. His whole body was now at his command, and all of it hurt with that strange, phantom pain of wounds now healed. Cyrus grunted, the noise deep and full of discomfort.

"Oh, thank Vidara," Vara said, drifting into his vision, her cheeks red.

"What the—hell …" Cyrus moaned, sitting up, his head woozy with the aftereffects of a resurrection spell.

"Talikartin the Guardian smashed you into the ground about twelve good times before J'anda's titan combined with one of Mendicant's spells drove him off," Andren said, blurring into focus. "We had a merry time trying to put you back together again."

Cyrus sat there, taking stock of the world around him. The air was still thick with the smell of smoke, and he could feel blood or sweat or both dripping down his skin inside his armor. It was hot, miserably so, and the sky was still dark with night, fires blazing all around him. Cyrus could not tell if it was the harsh heat of summer baking the Emerald Fields long after the sun had fled for the day, or simply all the fires still burning around him that was doing it, but it was as uncomfortable as sitting too close to a hearth.

The taste of blood still tainted his saliva, dripping off his tongue when he went to speak. "Did ..." He blinked and looked around the square. Fortin sat on his knees a short distance away, a strange noise coming from the rock giant, something that almost sounded akin to ... sobbing?

"Where ... did they go?" Cyrus asked, the weight of all that had happened settling down on him. "Talikartin, I mean?"

"Cast the return spell and disappeared," Vara said. "Some of the other survivors went as well, flashing into the night ..."

Cyrus pushed himself up on unsteady legs. Vara tried to grasp him under the arm, but he waved her off and she relented, though he saw the tension in the way she held herself. He got to his feet and Andren stood up next to him. "Shouldn't you be off ... healing people?"

"I ..." Andren's mouth flapped open and shut, and he swiveled his head to look down the street. Without another word, he broke into a run off toward one of the main thoroughfares that led west, robes flapping behind him. Cyrus could see other Sanctuary members in that direction, shouting as they ducked into and out of buildings, carrying bundles—bodies—both large and small.

"Gods," Vara whispered, and she sidled up to him, her armor clinking lightly against his. This time he did not brush her away, he let her lean against him as he did the same against her.

Fires raged, crackling all around them, punctuated by the rough, heaving sobs of the weeping rock giant as they stood there under the fiery night sky and watched the town of Emerald Fields burn.

9.

"How many did we lose?" Cyrus asked as dawn broke over the eastern horizon. The ruined streets were teeming with life, with the refugees of Emerald Fields, with the Army of Sanctuary still pulling the living and the dead out of the wreckage, with a steady flow of arrivals from the homesteads further out coming to render aid or simply see the smoky remnants of their city. He stood in a rough circle of the Sanctuary officers, all downcast eyes and long faces. Joining them was Administrator Cattrine Tiernan, who had reappeared shortly after the end of the battle in the company of several hundred children and women whom she had helped hide in the woods.

"Two dozen warriors and rangers," Odellan said, his winged helmet under his arm, his long, blond hair matted down with sweat and the night's efforts. His golden skin was darkened with soot, and his normally pristine breastplate carried hints of black ash in the ornate art fashioned into the metal. "Crushed beyond any hope of resurrection or simply missing until the hour of resurrection passed."

His words hung in the silence, and Cyrus turned his gaze to Administrator Tiernan, her brown hair in only a slightly better state than Odellan's. She was wearing naught but a nightgown, a very simple cloth dressing that was stained with dirt from her flight out of the town. "Do you have ... any idea?" Cyrus asked.

"About our losses?" She blinked, her eyes surprisingly clear, her face absent any emotion at all. He suspected she was beyond exhaustion; they all were, really, but no one had poured more of their efforts into Emerald Fields over this last year and more than she. "I know it would have been considerably more if you hadn't driven them

43

off when you did, but … no. No idea. No counting as yet, not even of the corpses."

Cyrus swallowed, words feeling like they lodged in his throat. *It would have been much less if I hadn't pissed off the titans about five years ago, apparently …*

"You had a population in excess of one hundred thousand, yes?" This came from Curatio, whose complexion looked even more washed out in the pale dawn light. The sky held a purple tinge, and it reflected on his white skin, making him look like some sort of dark elven hybrid. "How many lived here in the town?"

"Not as many as you'd think," Cattrine said, stirred back to life by the query. "Perhaps less than a quarter, and it looks as though the titans simply came over Rockridge, ignoring the mines, and came down into town. All the farms are north of here, and thus should be safe."

"This entire area should have been safe," Vara said, and on her scarlet cheeks there was the first brewing of anger. "The pass over the Heia Mountains—"

"Has always been ridiculously porous," Cyrus said, catching a flash of anger in her eyes. "Don't you remember? We went through a few years ago on a three-day march and ended up finding a few titans up there even then. That was before the war, when the King of the Elves had less to worry about."

"The war is over," Vara said sharply.

"And the losses were great, as well you know," Curatio said, rather limply. "Garrisoning the pass—"

"Is now a priority," came a sharp voice as Nyad edged her way into the circle. Her crimson robes looked fresh, and she carried a staff high, her face flushed with some emotion Cyrus couldn't quite pin down at first blush. "I just got back from Pharesia."

Cyrus glanced at Vara, expecting her to say something, but she held her tongue, much to his surprise. "I take it you have something to tell us?" *I didn't even realize she'd gone; but then again, you could just about move an army in here right now and I wouldn't have any idea about it unless they were titan-sized …*

"My father wants to hire Sanctuary to garrison the Heia Pass until such time as he can maneuver troops from the northern expanse near Nalikh'akur to here," Nyad said, more straight-backed than Cyrus could recall seeing her. She looked at Vara. "The King wishes to know if the Lady of Nalikh'akur has any objection to moving troops out of her holdfast?"

"None," Vara said swiftly, and Cyrus caught something ... strange ... pass between her and Cattrine Tiernan without a word spoken. "Bring them down here. Sanctuary will even provide the wizards if it'll spare them the march."

Cyrus paused. "That was ... fast."

"And not voted on," Ryin said with a hint of ire. His face was just as soot-blackened as the rest of theirs.

"All in favor?" Cyrus asked with a certain weariness.

"Aye," came the chorus, just as weary.

"Aye as well," Ryin said, looking a little put out. "But we could have voted first, that's all I'm trying to say."

"We could also string you up by that high beam there," Vaste said, pointing his staff toward a piece of wood that extended out of a broken structure, "by your feet, so you were just a few feet above the ground, and then we could take turns thumping you with this," he brandished the white staff, "or something suitably blunt, until you stopped being so gods-damned contentious all the time. It could take a while, I'll be the first to admit, but I think we'll all agree it's worth it once it's done—and perhaps during every single satisfying whack of the wood against your thick gourd—"

"That's about enough of that," Cyrus said, waving a hand to cut him off. "We'll garrison the pass, help King Danay move his soldiers down to reinforce us, and—" He paused as a dark elven man in a white robe approached, his hands pushed inside his heavy sleeves. Cyrus squinted, trying to recognize the fellow, but he was utterly unfamiliar. "Yes? I'm sorry, we're in the middle of an officer meeting at present—"

"I don't mean to interrupt," he said, and his face was long as he pushed back his hood. Cyrus heard a squeal of surprise and turned to see Erith smiling broadly at the dark elf. "I only came to speak to Administrator Tiernan."

"Dahveed Thalless," Cattrine said with subtle bow. "What brings you to Emerald Fields on ..." Her gaze ran over the smoking wreckage around them; the fires had mostly burned out or been put out by this point. "Well, now?"

"I come with the condolences of the Sovereign," the healer said, bowing deeply. His accent was unusual. "As one of your chief trading partners—" Cyrus stiffened at that, "—he directs me to offer you skilled carpenters as well as whatever other aid you might need from the Sovereignty."

"Terian—wait—what?" Cyrus shook his head. He rubbed at his forehead with a bare hand and it came back smudged with dried blood and ash. "You trade with—" Cyrus stared at Cattrine, who looked back at him flatly. "You hate him." He spun to look at Curatio, who was standing, quite still, just across the circle. "I'm not—am I losing my mind? She hated him, didn't she?"

"Many things have changed since our days in Luukessia, Guildmaster," Cattrine said, still without a hint of emotion. "The Sovereign of Saekaj and Sovar bought a considerable amount of our first harvest of the season only a few months back."

Cyrus turned to say something to Vara, but her ears were red enough at the tips that he stopped himself before he did. *She knows something of this.* His eyes narrowed and flitted to Curatio. *So does he.* He turned to look at Vaste and found the troll already shrugging with a plainly feigned innocence. "We'll discuss this later," Cyrus said and quickly dropped the subject.

"Is there anything we can do for you immediately?" the healer, Dahveed Thalless asked. He spoke with a slow cadence, and his eyes found Erith mid-sentence and offered a smile of his own, something reassuring and laced with a kindness that Cyrus did not immediately associate with dark elves, save perhaps J'anda.

"We have need of strong hands," Cattrine said. "To help clear the rubble and build anew, to help harvest more lumber in the east, and …" Her voice drifted off, and for a moment Cyrus was certain she would fall over on her feet, she looked so dazed and tired.

"We will send help immediately," Dahveed said with a bow. "We have many eager to work from Sovar, and with our first seed planted above Saekaj and Sovar for the season, plenty of hands to send in aid. The first will begin to arrive in hours." With that, he bowed once more, met Cyrus's eyes for only a second, offering an enigmatic smile, and then moved away from the circle. Cyrus watched him walking back to a curious-looking man who seemed like some sort of druid, perhaps. His long hair was pulled back in a queue that hung to his belt, and he sat on air, a Falcon's Essence spell keeping him aloft. Dahveed spoke to him in low tones for a moment, and the man nodded, then disappeared in the light of a return spell.

"You look like you wish to say something, Lord Davidon." Cattrine's voice nudged him out of his observation of the dark elven healer.

"I have nothing to add of note," Cyrus said, shaking his head. "You'll need help, as much as you can get, and our army is hardly of great use in rebuilding. At destroying, perhaps, but not rebuilding." He let his gaze drift to Erith, who broke away from the circle of officers and moved toward Dahveed, leaving them behind without so much as a word. She, too, looked tired from the night's exertions, from their efforts at bringing back the dead and healing the wounded. She fell into conversation with the dark elven man so easily that Cyrus knew there was some long association there. "All I have left are only questions I'm too tired to ask at present, and that you're not obligated to answer in any case," Cyrus finished.

"Yes," Cattrine said. Her voice expressed weariness and choked desperation, but she was strong enough and skilled enough at hiding it that she smothered it before even another breath of it came out. "We will need help. Again."

As for Cyrus, he looked over the town all around, the smoking wreckage, at the hell he had once more indirectly inflicted on these people, and as he caught Vara's eye he knew she saw the truth in his.

When will these days of war finally end?

10.

Days passed under sunny and cloudless skies. Cyrus spent the majority of them in the central tower of Sanctuary, in and out of Council meetings, and few enough actually out in the world, either at the Heia Pass or in the Emerald Fields aiding the reconstruction. He had been at the site twice in the last week, enough to satisfy himself that he had no skill to contribute, and once to the garrison in the pass to inspect the preparations. That was dull work, and when Martaina made her report to tell him that nothing had come through since the titans almost a fortnight ago, it was enough for him to gladly make his retreat back to the Tower of the Guildmaster.

Now he stood in the middle of the breezy space, all four balconies open to the gusts from the Plains of Perdamun, and looked out onto the grasslands below. There were still tents within the curtain wall, the last of the Emerald Fields refugees who had been evacuated after the attack seemingly content to shelter on the Sanctuary grounds. There were children, there were the aged and infirm, those who would not or could not fight. Whole divisions of the Luukessian cavalrymen were sweeping the southern end of the Elven Kingdom even now, making certain that not so much as a single titan remained north of the mountainous divide between the southern lands of their residence and the north, which desired them not.

"You sulk, still," Vara said as the door to the tower opened. The elf ascended up through the narrow slit that held the stairs. He did not turn to greet her, merely cocked his head in response to her observation, letting the wind stir his hair as he stood with gauntlets clenched behind him.

"There's little else to do," Cyrus said, looking north and catching

48

movement at the portal in the distance. A single figure, ahorse, rode south toward the Sanctuary gates, a traveling cloak billowing grandly behind them. It was blue, the color of the Torrid Sea off the shores before the tideturn where the currents grew rough, and it caught his eye as it moved against the dark green grasses of the plain.

"There is much to do, Guildmaster," she said, coming to stand just behind his shoulder. "Always so much to do, as well you know."

"There's little I want to do, then," Cyrus said, turning his head to regard her with his careful stare. *Surely she knows what I want to do, truly.*

"Oh, you're not back to that again, are you?" She eyed him. "Because we can, but I'd rather either wait until the fall of night and douse the lamps, or else close these doors and draw the curtains, because last time Vaste made the rudest comment after apparently overhearing us—"

"Not that," Cyrus said, waving her off in frustration. He paused. "Well … maybe later," he conceded. "But I meant …" He lowered his voice, ashamed, "… revenge."

"Ah, the prickly path," Vara said, eyebrows arching even as her face fell a notch. "I had assumed you would bring it up before now."

"I assumed you'd assume it before now," Cyrus said, turning to look back over the plains. The figure on the horse was gone, in the shadow of the tower by this time. "In the past, you've never hesitated to think me certain to snap straight to vengeance."

"In the past, I was not sharing your bed," Vara said with enough crispness to remind him of a fall day, "and I had not seen you pass on nearly so many opportunities as you have in the past few years." Her voice softened. "Besides, I assumed you would consult the Council and perhaps myself before launching a full-scale invasion of Kortran."

"You knew I'd want to, though, didn't you?" He bowed his head slightly.

"You wouldn't be Cyrus Davidon if you didn't want to strike back at those who did harm to your own," she said quietly. She looked around, as though she were afraid someone were watching. "You wouldn't be the man I've come to care for if you didn't possess that finely honed protective instinct, as though all Arkaria were under your wing."

"It's not all Arkaria," he said. "But it is a people I feel a great obligation to." He strained as hot anger bubbled up. "They'd just become independent, just gotten their feet underneath them, and now—" He pulled his hand out of his gauntlet and wiped a sweaty palm over his upper lip, freshly shaven. "Gods, the timing. Why now?"

"Because this was the moment the titans chose to be enormous jackasses, presumably."

"Who taught them magic?" Cyrus asked, turning to face her. "Something is amiss here. The titans are not a civilized people, they don't have Leagues, and they've never had magic instruction until now—"

"Something is amiss, I agree," Vara said, nodding. "But to assume some nefarious evil at the heart of this is ... well, it's a bit much, as such things go." She cracked the faintest smile. "I know it won't stop you from blaming yourself, but long before you came into the picture, the titans were more than happy to strike through the pass. In fact, if you recall—"

"Alaric lost his wife to Talikartin," Cyrus said, memory jarred loose by Vara's mere suggestion.

"Yes," Vara said, her voice suddenly ghostly in its reduction to near-whisper. "He did."

Cyrus stared down at her, their difference in height somehow all the more striking in this moment. "I fear it, you know."

"You don't have a wife," she said, playfully, an impish smile returning to her features, but still somehow less cheerful than it might have been a few moments before.

"Yet," he said, and smiled back at her. "I—" A knock sounded at the door, causing him to frown. "Yes?" he called.

The door at the base of the stairs clicked open a crack to reveal a ranger, a human, thin and wiry with dark hair. "There's an envoy to see you, sir," she said, breathless from the ascent.

"From where?" Cyrus asked, frowning. He glanced at Vara, but she maintained her distance.

"Amti, sir."

"I'll be down in a few minutes," Cyrus said, pondering that one, "assemble the—"

"Orders already went out, sir," the ranger said. "The envoy asked to meet with all of you."

Cyrus felt his eyebrow rise. "Did they? How ... presumptuous of them." *Giving orders already? I can't imagine what sort of arrogant prig this elf must be*—

"The order to assemble came from Lord Curatio, sir," the ranger said. "He and Larana are speaking to the envoy even now." The ranger lowered her voice, like she was passing on some form of forbidden knowledge. "They seem to know this lady envoy quite well, if I may say so."

"What?" Cyrus blinked and looked at Vara, who held a look of undisguised curiosity of her own. "And yes, you may say so, along with anything else you know that might shed light on this mysterious envoy before I meet them face to face. What's your name, young lady?"

The lady ranger paused for a moment, slipping just a little further inside the door. "Carisse Sevoux, m'lord. Of the Riverlands."

Cyrus watched her, could see the bubbling excitement beneath her youthful facade. It was not well hidden. "Spill it, Carisse Sevoux. Who am I dealing with?"

"Only caught her name, sir," Sevoux said with a hint of pride. "Said it was Cora."

It took Cyrus a moment more to get there than it did Vara, who stiffened immediately. He started to reach out for her, but the elven paladin was already in motion, sprinting toward the stairs. Carisse Sevoux scarcely had time to dodge out of the way, flattening against the wall of the stairway trench before Vara shot past, her armored boots clanging hard with every step.

"It would appear Lady Vara knows this envoy as well," Sevoux said as she pulled herself off the wall, lithe figure balancing on the tips of her toes, silent.

"She should," Cyrus said, taking a breath as he moved toward the stairs himself. "I feel like I know her as well, though we've never met."

Sevoux looked up at him, tanned face perplexed. "Sir?"

"Cora is the last surviving founder of Sanctuary," Cyrus said, making his way down the stairs and opening the door for Carisse Sevoux, whose mouth opened just a hint in surprise. *Can't say I'm not surprised either*, Cyrus thought as he let the ranger walk through the door first before stepping through and pulling it shut behind him. "And as far as I know, this is the first time she's set foot in this place in … years."

11.

Cyrus decided he liked Cora immediately, though it would have been hard not to. She was an elf, of course, but with hair that was a lustrous auburn, an unusual shade for elves in Cyrus's experience. It reminded him of autumn foliage in the north for some reason, and her handshake was firm, her eyes clear and hazel when he looked into them. There was also a hint of familiarity about her in that regal bearing, the august presence he'd come to expect from elves. The dark blue cloak that she wore drawn about her shoulders hid spell caster vestments from his sight, hinting only that they were there by the small bit that stuck out of the collar.

"It is good to be back in this place," Cora said in a light voice, less serious than many of the elves he'd met. They stood in the Council Chamber, around the table, with an extra chair pulled up to accommodate their guest. "Though it has changed considerably since last I was here." She looked around the room with an appraising eye. "The table was smaller then, I think."

"Same table," Cyrus said, settling back in his enormously high-backed chair. Suddenly he felt the pressure of the Guildmaster medallion strung round his neck, and felt self-conscious about the chair he was inhabiting. *When she was an officer of this guild, I was not even a member. Now I am the Master of Sanctuary and she is not even a member. Sometimes I forget the history of this place predates me by some considerable margin.* "We haven't replaced it."

"Indeed?" Cora looked it over again. "Memory is a most malleable thing, I suppose, making days that were a struggle seem like halcyon stuff after a sufficient distance of years. Merely shrinking a Council Chamber seems an easy task compared to that." She forced a smile. "I am sad to say that I recognize few enough of the faces around me."

"But a few of us recognize yours," J'anda said with a smile of his own, warm, sincere and genuine.

"Oh, J'anda," Cora said with a tinge of regret. "It does my heart ill to see you this way."

"You would have outlived me in any case," J'anda said, but now his smile was tinged with sadness. "Such is the fate of you elder elves."

Curatio cleared his throat. "Who are you calling elder, exactly?"

Cora glanced over at him. "Did that finally come out, then, oh, ageless healer?"

Curatio looked chastened for a moment. "Indeed. It was quite dramatic in the way it did."

Cyrus watched the interplay between the two of them and felt a faint aura of suspicion. *She knew he was one of the Old Ones? That was a closely guarded secret until just three years ago.* Cora's eyes met his, cool, composed, and he wondered not for the first time what exactly he faced in this elven woman. *How many secrets did the founding members of this guild know that even I am not aware of?*

And how many did—does—Alaric keep still, wherever he may be?

"I apologize for coming to you in this manner, and at this hour," Cora said. She dropped her gaze to the table and ran her fingers over the smooth grains of the wood.

"The dinner hour is always a poor time for a meeting," Vaste agreed. "Second only to the breakfast hour and just behind the lunching one, or on the afternoon occasions when Larana decides to bake fresh fruit pies—"

"Vaste," Cyrus said, taking up the Guildmaster's sworn duty to rope the troll back on topic.

"The smell of tart apples, sugar and pastry crust fill the air in the foyer, like magic wafting off the fingers of an expert caster—"

"Vaste," Curatio said, somewhat more sternly.

"I'm hungry," the troll said, more than a little plaintively. He sulked for a few seconds then looked to Cora. "Oh, fine, then, proceed. I'll just sit here, starving. Ignore my stomach's rumblings."

"Just as easily as I ignore the rumblings of the rest of you," Cora said a bit playfully, poking at the troll. "As I was saying ... the timing is poor for my approach, and yet necessary. Word of what happened in your protectorate of Emerald Fields has reached our ears in Amti—"

"I'm sorry," Samwen Longwell said, and Cyrus detected a hint of danger lurking behind the dragoon's eyes, "but I can't recall hearing of this 'Amti' place that you represent. It's not on the maps of Arkaria that I've studied."

"Amti is a colony of elves in the southern lands, beyond the Heia Pass," Odellan said, leaning forward, his winged helm gleaming upon the table and his blond hair in perfect order this day. "They were founded roughly a century ago to exploit some of the resources discovered in the Jungle of Vidara—"

"What sort of resources?" Longwell asked.

"I'd be curious to know that, myself," Ryin added, casting a look around the table. "Especially as they're not terribly far from Kortran, and I'd imagine the titans give them some considerable amount of trouble."

"Considerable is understating it," Cora said, leaning back in her seat, her cloak spilling open to reveal robes of the deepest blue, more cerulean than her dark cloak. "What resources we harvest are sent back to the Heia Pass in convoys that only made it roughly one out of five times, until recently."

"Good gods," J'anda murmured.

"Why keep sending them, then?" Vaste asked.

"Because they have to pay their taxes," Nyad said, drawing every eye in the room. "They're a protectorate of the Elven Kingdom. It is required."

"They don't sound terribly protected," Vaste said.

"We're not," Cora agreed, looking quite comfortable where she sat. "We live under constant threat. The only reason the titans have not destroyed us utterly is that the town of Amti remains safely hidden." She drew a sharp breath then let it out in a hiss. "But I do not believe it will remain so for much longer."

"You have traitors," Cyrus said, and she snapped around to look at him.

Cora watched him carefully, as though she could read his thoughts. "Know that, do you?"

"The last time I was in Kortran," Cyrus said, "we caught an elf named Erart there. He claimed to be a prisoner."

"Good memory, remembering his name like that," Vaste said. "I confess I'm surprised; as many times as you've died and been resurrected, I'm surprised you didn't lose that trivial bit of knowledge."

Cyrus felt a sudden tightness in his chest. "It doesn't seem to be the trivial bits of knowledge that are lost in resurrection." He shifted his gaze back to Cora. "Have there been others?"

"Probably," she said. "Captives from the caravans we send that are ambushed, desperately seeking to survive in any way they can. Frustrated outcasts searching out favor they will never find from the titans."

"How have they not betrayed you yet?" Cyrus asked. "Being in Kortran, as prisoners or traitors—it would seem they'd have to give away your secret."

"No," she said, looking just a bit proud, though it was mixed with a coyness that Cyrus found strangely compelling. "They can't."

"Why's that?" Longwell asked, sounding thoroughly irritated.

"Because they don't know exactly where Amti is," Cora said, matching Longwell's fire with her own ice. Cyrus watched as the dragoon sat back, seemingly halted in his advance.

"Why have you come to us now?" Cyrus asked. A pop in the fire to his side punctuated his question.

Cora let a poignant silence linger a moment longer than necessary before speaking. "When I left this guild, it was scarcely more than a hundred people on a good day." She swept her gaze around the Council Chambers once more. "Now I hear you have over twenty thousand at your command." The number prickled at Cyrus. *It would have been more if not for Leaugarden.* "Before, Sanctuary was hardly a bulwark against anything, let alone an army capable of rendering the sort of aid that Alaric promised in our purpose when we founded this guild." She pursed her lips carefully, and glanced at Vara, who remained silent but flushed just slightly enough that Cyrus detected the quiet something that passed between them. "Now you've become the fulfillment of that promise, and Alaric is no longer here to see it. A great regret, I am sure."

"You seek our aid in your cause," Cyrus said, and she met his eyes with her own, and her meaning was made plain.

"I would seek any aid I could find at this point," Cora said, unsmiling, "but the rest of Arkaria is painfully thin on help. The King of the Elves would draw a line at the Heia Mountains, the River Perda, and the swamps of the north, and desire to pay attention to none of what goes on beyond those boundaries, even though he supposedly rules us in Amti. She looked pointedly at Nyad, who flushed and turned away from her gaze. "Here I come to a place I left, most reluctantly, with my … pride in hand, as it were." Her tanned skin showed no embarrassment, but her expression spoke of that reluctance in the tilt of her chin, her inability to look up as she spoke, and the slow way in which her words made their way out. "If you defend the Emerald Fields, then we have a common enemy, you and I." Now she looked up. "The titans are a relentless foe, and a threat to all who have opposed them. Vengeance is more than a simple word with them; it is a way of life that they embrace with a fervor that Vaste reserves for pie."

"You just had to poke a spear into that open wound," Vaste grunted.

"They are consummate warriors and they only grow more deadly and dangerous now that they know magic," she said.

"How did they learn that?" Curatio asked, placing his elbows upon the table.

"We do not know," Cora said, and now she looked more serious than ever. "We only know that now our ability to send caravans across the Gradsden Savanna is almost completely compromised. It is a recent development, I can tell you that much."

"Why don't we just blame Goliath now and get it over with," Vaste said. "All in favor?"

"Goliath is not responsible for all the problems in Arkaria," Vara said with a frown. "Though it certainly feels like it, sometimes."

"They were trying to consort with the titans a few years ago," Erith said, speaking up for the first time.

"Yeah," Cyrus said, frowning, "I remember that. They were killing dragonkin down in the Ashen Wastelands in hopes of earning titan favor."

"I'm just going to go ahead and pick Goliath in the pool right now," Vaste said. "I'm putting a hundred gold on them, all right? Who else wants in? I'll give you odds on weird suggestions."

"I'll take forty gold on the dragons," Mendicant said softly, as though he were trying to both make his bet and respect the meeting at the same time.

"That's a sucker's bet," Andren said, still clean-shaven and with his hair cut short. Cyrus had still not quite adjusted to seeing the elf without his long, mussed hair and bushy, unkempt beard. The healer made no attempt to keep his voice low. "Give me two hundred on heretics from the bandit lands."

"Eighty gold says Pretnam Urides is involved somehow," Erith offered.

"Now we're talking," Vaste said, nodding. "I'll give you two-to-one on that."

"My money's on the dark elves," Odellan said.

"Put some coins where your mouth is, then, nobleman," Andren sniped.

"Fifty gold, then," Odellan said with a nod. "What odds can I get on that?"

"What the hells?" Cyrus asked, frown creasing his brow. "Is this a Council meeting or a betting pool?"

"Can't it be both?" Andren asked innocently.

"You are all idiots," Vara said with utter annoyance. She then lowered her voice slightly. "Also, I'll place fifty gold on the gnomes being responsible in some fashion."

"Dammit, Vara," Cyrus said, slapping his head with a gauntleted hand. "Curatio?" He looked to the healer for some sort of support.

"Yes," Curatio said, nodding sagely. "Perhaps a different time might be more opportune for these sort of activities—though I would like to register my bet of three hundred gold on dwarven mercenaries right now, before it's gone—"

"Clearly, this meeting needs to be adjourned so that all of you can get out of my sight," Cyrus said, avoiding the gaze of Cora, whose amusement it was impossible to mistake even out of the corner of his eye. "And make your wagers. But before we do that, I would suggest," he let that word have all the emphasis, "that perhaps it might be wise, given Cora's history with our guild, to send a small, exploratory expedition to the southern lands in order to assess the situation in Amti." He glanced at her for only a moment. "If that would be acceptable?"

"Our leaders would love to plead their case to you directly," Cora said. "And we would welcome the opportunity to show you the state of things. I can guarantee safe passage to an even half-dozen of you. Any more than that and it becomes rather … complicated."

Cyrus narrowed his eyes, trying to suss out the meaning of that one. "All in favor?" he asked.

"Aye," came the chorus.

Cyrus paused, frowning, and looked to Ryin. "No 'nay'?"

Ryin looked weary. "I've just spent a week teleporting materials to Emerald Fields and trying to apply my very modest skills at carpentry to reconstructing one of their dining halls. I'm afraid I don't have it in me to make a contrarian argument to your request to send a mere expedition of six people into the south." He pursed his lips. "While I don't doubt your ability to make trouble with even so modest a number … I was there the night you were killed by Talikartin, and I heard every word he said, voice booming across the square." Ryin leaned forward. "In case it is not apparent to all, there is no need to worry about you starting some war in the south; the titans have made plain, in my opinion, that they are at war with us … and now we need only fear what form their next reprisal will take, for it seems certain that fall it eventually will." The druid's voice went hollow and quiet as his reply drew to a surprisingly dire close. "And better to know more about them for when that day comes … than less."

12.

Cyrus had forgotten the heat of the Gradsden Savanna in the intervening years since last he had been here. As soon as they appeared at the portal, he began to sweat in earnest. Within five minutes, his underclothes were drenched in sweat, beads running down his head even as tall grass brushed his armor and helm as they walked, a distracting noise that had him perpetually alert for threats.

"I don't remember the grass being this tall when I last I passed this way," Vara said, at his side. She was quite right; the savanna grasses now reached a foot above Cyrus's head, a strange spectacle to him.

"Time was," Cora said, leading the way through the thick grass, "we would simply use the druid spell Falcon's Essence and make our way to the cover of the Jungle of Vidara, secure in the knowledge that the titans would not be able to catch us under its influence. Now," she said ruefully, "we cannot go high enough to avoid their spellcraft, nor outrun them once their cessation spells strip the enchantment before they fall upon us."

"A dramatic change," Curatio said, his white cowl covering the top of his head. Sweat marks were already showing where his hair was transferring its moisture onto the cloth. "I imagine it came as something of a rude surprise."

"We have no wizards," Cora said, "and only two druids, which makes teleporting convoys impossible unless we were able to find some brave soul mercenary enough to undertake the trip and bind themselves within our town." She pursed her lips and looked back to the course ahead, sparing only a glance at Mendicant, who trailed slightly behind her on his short legs, almost walking on all fours, his wizard's robe cut to avoid dragging his hem.

Cyrus looked at the last two members of their small party. Martaina Proelius was one of them, her green cloak drifting behind her in a very similar manner to the way Cora's did, though Martaina's seemed even quieter as it trailed in her wake. Martaina's eyes darted about, as though they could pierce the thick curtain of green grasses that fenced them in on all sides.

Their last party member kept his quiet, as per usual. Scuddar In'shara was a man of the Inculta desert folk who had been passing through the foyer as Cyrus assembled his team. Scuddar had been with Sanctuary for some five years now. He was a warrior without armor, a scimitar as his weapon, but his strange style of fighting was indisputably effective. Able to keep his cool in situations where Cyrus had seen others falter, Scuddar had proven himself more than capable in any number of actions, including holding the line of retreat across the Endless Bridge from Luukessia.

Scuddar was also a man of terribly few words, which Cyrus found much to his liking, especially at the moment. It was the same reason he'd chosen Mendicant over Nyad when the time had come to pick a wizard to accompany them.

"Everything seems so bloody dire," Vara mused aloud. "The timing is peculiar as well, just as the north seems to have gotten its shite together."

"Outside of the sudden magical concerns, this threat of the titans has been a long time coming," Cora said, fingers brushing their way through fat blades of grass that looked like they would not have been out of place in a swamp, though these were considerably larger. "They have hounded us since first our colonial forces came in contact with their patrols here on the savanna. Were it not for the dragons as a constant threat to the titans' south, I imagine they would have made destroying us their greatest priority by now."

"Probably why they haven't come north in great numbers, either," Cyrus said, grunting as he stepped over a rut that Vara leapt with a loping grace that he felt certain he lacked without having a hand on Praelior. "Pull enough of their army off their southern borders and they're vulnerable to that threat." He ran his tongue over his teeth and found the taste of his breakfast still lingering there—eggs and bread fresh from Sanctuary's ovens. "The dragons are not to be dismissed out of hand, I've heard."

"Indeed they are not," Cora said, curiously muted about the subject. "We don't see them north of Kortran very much, unfortunately. The titans have bows the length of their entire bodies, taken from the trees of the jungle and the mountains, strung with a twine so powerful it could hold up a hundred elves, and nocked with arrows the size of our northern trees." She grew hushed as she spoke. "I have seen them issue a hail of them into the air, once, when I was spying within Kortran. They brought down a lesser dragon, piercing its scales as though they were hunting a simple bird."

"You've been in Kortran?" Cyrus asked, drawing a smile out of Cora.

"Many times," she said. "It used to be easy for the magically endowed to slip beneath the noses of the titans. Now I would not risk it, given their capacity for seeing through invisibility spells and all manner of illusions. Truly, this boon of magic for them has been nothing less than a curse for the rest of us."

"Hmm," Cyrus grunted.

"Have you thought of trying to strike up an alliance with the dragons?" Mendicant asked. Cyrus glanced down at the goblin, who looked at Cora earnestly while he waited for an answer. Cyrus suspected he knew what was coming, having a vague recollection of asking the question himself once upon a time.

"Dragons do not treat with us lesser beings," Cora said, "let alone consider us as worthy enough to be allies. Theirs is a strange mind, a slithering sort of reason that makes conversation difficult, even among those of their kind that speak our languages."

"I've spoken with one before," Cyrus said, trudging along. The ground was growing stickier, a hint of wet dew sliding down to slick the dirt.

"I heard about your experience with Ashan'agar," Cora said. "We all did. I confess, I am surprised that you were able to bring him down."

Cyrus shrugged. "I took one of his eyes at our first meeting, and the second one when next we encountered one another. As I was on his back at the time, it was fairly easy to steer him into a collision with the ground that he could not survive." He looked to his side and noticed Vara holding her breath almost imperceptibly.

"Easy to steer a dragon?" Cora asked, seemingly amused by his humble tale. "I don't believe I've ever heard anyone claim that before."

"He was frightened, blind and flailing," Cyrus said calmly. "Fear can tame any beast it takes hold of."

Curatio let out a small chuckle. "You'll have to excuse our new Guildmaster, Cora. He suffers from an unfailing lack of self-aggrandizement, even over as worthy a deed as defeating Ashan'agar's attempts to control his mind."

Cora raised little more than an eyebrow. "We should expect nothing less from one of so distinguished a lineage as his."

Cyrus felt a curious chill run up his back, a tickle unrelated to the rivers of sweat dripping their way down his back. "My lineage?"

Cora paused, thinking it over. "I have to apologize. Human speech is not my first language, naturally, and that word was ill chosen. I meant to say something similar, the line not being one of family but one of your current office." She smiled faintly. "As in, the last Master of Sanctuary—he, too, possessed some small gift for understating his abilities and successes."

Cyrus felt a small cloud of darkness drift over his emotions at the mere mention of Alaric. "Indeed, the Ghost is—I mean, *was*—a rare sort of man in almost every regard." He caught a most curious look from Curatio at his slip, a probing glance if ever he'd seen one.

"Indeed," Curatio said, surveying Cyrus further before turning his head and fluffing his cowl to block the direct line of sight between the two of them. "Indeed he was."

13.

By a few hours after nightfall, they had reached the edge of the Jungle of Vidara. It had loomed in the twilight for the last several hours, visible even over the tall grasses, a shadowed start of a tree line that hinted at greater cover than the slow path they were currently carving across the savanna.

"Why don't the titans simply station a guard patrol at the portal like anyone else?" Vara asked as they drew closer to the jungle's edge. "It would seem the easiest way of interdicting anyone traveling to these lands, if they were of a mind to control everything."

"A very good question," Cora said, speaking with a calm stillness. "Which I do not know the answer to. I am only grateful that they have not done so as yet, for they presumably know the locations of the portals and certainly do not lack for patrols across the savanna these days. They reach their hand out further and further with each month, it seems."

"I am so ill of seemingly unstoppable, unfathomably powerful armies," Vara said, and Cyrus nodded silent agreement as they reached the shade of the first large trees of the jungle.

Here, as they took a break to rest, Cyrus could not help but be awed by what he saw. From a distance, the trees of the jungle had looked impressive. Up close, they were, quite simply, a seemingly perfect fit for everything else he'd seen in these lands—enormous, far larger than their northern counterparts, even greater in size than the Iliarad'ouran woods that surrounded Pharesia, though the atmosphere was strikingly similar.

"Looks familiar, does it not?" Vara asked as they rested under the boughs of a tree that stretched so high above them that Cyrus knew a titan would easily find shade beneath it.

"Yes," he said.

"Feels a little like home," Martaina breathed, her cloak softly rustling as she placed a bare hand on the rough bark of the massive tree. "Like the woods I grew up in, so tall."

"Curatio?" Cora asked, nudging the elder elf slightly with a finger.

"Hm?" Curatio stirred, sitting on a root, his white robes revealing the dirt of the bark as he moved. "Oh, yes. Seeds of southern trees were brought north long ago, in the days of old, and planted around the lands where Pharesia now sits. They were few at first, but as they took root, they squeezed out many of the smaller, native trees with their prodigious shade, and the Iliarad'ouran woods sprung up over the course of many thousands of years, forcing the native trees to either die or seek their home elsewhere."

Cyrus listened, then stiffened. "'Seek their home elsewhere'? Curatio, trees can't move. They're rooted to the ground. It's where the word comes from, in fact."

Curatio smiled thinly. "I think if you search your memory, you will recall a time in the last year where that statement was put to lie."

"You're talking about in the Realm of Life?" Vara asked, springing to it before Cyrus could so much as form the thought. "Curatio, that's Vidara's realm. Of course the trees there have special dispensation to do odd things. They're under the auspices of the goddess."

"Oh, I'm sorry," Curatio said, not remotely contrite and smiling with more than a little self-assured sarcasm, "I didn't realize that you already knew everything at a mere thirty-three years of age, my dear. I apologize. Please, tell me more of this apocryphal tale, then." He waited, knowing full well that the burning scarlet on Vara's cheeks insured that she would not. "Shall I continue?"

"I could stand to hear a little more about it," Mendicant asked, and Cyrus heard a hunger in the goblin's words. Martaina, for her part, watched the scene unfold with a hand in front of her mouth, tentative, as though she knew what was about to be said and was preparing herself, cautiously. Scuddar, meanwhile, had his white robes wrapped in the manner of a scarf around his mouth as usual, hiding his expression.

"Niamh once told me she used to speak to the trees and the trees would talk back," Cyrus said as Curatio turned slightly to look at him as he spoke. "Were these the trees she was talking about?"

"Probably," Curatio said. "Though the trees she was speaking of—I wouldn't even be able to hazard a guess where they went beyond a general direction perhaps."

"What direction is that?" Mendicant asked.

"South," Curatio answered without reservation. "For there are no other directions they could have gone—north would see them freezing in the mountains beyond Fertiss, east and west we are hemmed in by the Sea of Carmas and the Torrid, but south—they could have gone beyond the Dragonlands, if they were very fortunate or had the blessing of those beasts, or through the bandit lands to whatever lies beyond."

"What lies beyond?" Cyrus asked.

"I don't know," Curatio said with a shrug.

"I feel like there's more that you're not telling us," Cyrus said.

"That should be a feeling you are long accustomed to by now," Curatio said with a smile as he stood. "We should continue before darkness grows too deep, yes?" This question was directed at Cora, who nodded subtly, and they proceeded.

Their walk was quiet and subdued after that, the sounds of the jungle growing louder around them as they went deeper and deeper into it. They threaded along a path that was hardly defined, with plenty of undergrowth springing up around them to make the journey more difficult. "This is one of our greatest defenses," Cora said, plucking a plant the size of a small bush, thick and leafy. "The titans cannot see our footsteps because with them already being so small, these aid in hiding them further."

"Useful," Martaina opined, walking so lightly that Cyrus doubted she even left footprints. "It doesn't make it too easy for me to track here, either, save for the bigger beasts that plainly inhabit this place."

"Bigger ... beasts?" Mendicant asked, halting in his walk. "What sort of ... bigger beasts?" His clawed hands fell to his side.

"Lions are the greatest danger," Cora said, explaining it simply, as though it were no matter for worry. "They get a bit bigger than the sort you would have seen in the north."

"I saw one brought to Reikonos dead, once," Cyrus said. "It was nearly thirty feet long."

"A small one, then," Cora said. "There are much bigger, and other predators of course, as well."

"Gods," Vara breathed, "who would want to live in such a ghastly place?" She cringed as soon as she finished speaking, and Cyrus wondered if perhaps she'd ever let her mouth outrun her sense when speaking to him. *If she has, she certainly didn't feel remorse for it the way she just displayed for Cora.*

Cora, for her part, turned around with a thin smile. "Only the mad, perhaps."

"And you're mad, are you?" Cyrus asked, taking the invitation proffered to ask the question.

"Spend enough time in Sanctuary and you will be, too, Cyrus Davidon," Cora said, her smile faded, and she scarcely met his eyes as she turned to continue leading them along the way to her home.

14.

When they had been under the trees for hours and hours, Cora came to a sudden stop and turned in the path, cloak swishing behind her. If not for the frost stone she had passed him in the waning hours of twilight, he would not have been able to see under the thick canopy of the jungle.

"This is where we stop," Cora said, looking at each of them in turn.

"Stop for what?" Vara asked. There was a gasping sound from Mendicant, who seemed to be struggling to breathe. The air was close in the jungle, heavy with the humidity and heat, even this long after sundown, as though it were kept in by the ceiling created by the boughs and vines far above them.

"For this," Cora said, and her fingers glowed purple as she cast a spell. Cyrus watched her eyes and not the light as it danced from her fingers to stretch over to Mendicant, who stopped panting and stood up straight as it rolled over him, then to Martaina, whose head rocked back gently when the purple light surged out.

"What the hell was that?" Cyrus asked, blinking furiously. He felt as though some strange tiredness had fallen over him for a moment, something beyond the fatigue from the journey. He turned his head to look at Vara but found her frozen like she'd been cast in wax, eyes unfocused and staring straight ahead like there was something ahead in the darkness that had caught her attention.

"I wondered if it would work on you," Cora mused quietly. She glanced at Curatio. "You remain unaffected, I trust?"

"As ever," Curatio said, adjusting the hem of his robes. "You could have made some further mention of it before taking the action, though."

"What action?" Cyrus asked, reaching out to shake Vara's arm. She remained unresponsive, staring off into the distance. "What did you do to us—to them?"

"What she tried to do to us," Scuddar said quietly in the low, menacing voice of a man whose ire had been raised. "was to take our will."

"A man of the desert," Cora said brusquely as though she were gathering her wits about her. "I should have known."

"What did you do?" Cyrus asked, stepping closer to her, cold anger turning the sweaty night cool as goose pimples made their way over the top of his head under his helm.

"She cast a mesmerization spell," Curatio said, holding up a hand to stay Cyrus from any ill-considered action. "In preparation to take all of us under her control with a charm."

"You would have made us your pets?" Cyrus could hear his own voice rise in fury, and his hand fell to Praelior automatically. He heard Scuddar's blade slide out of its scabbard and did not stop him.

"It is necessary," Cora said, still cool as a Northlands night, "in order to preserve the secret path to Amti. Almost no one goes there but with an enchanter guiding them in this way. When the spell is broken, they are left with no memory of how they got to the city. It has kept our people safe thus far from traitors and captives—"

"I don't surrender my will easily," Cyrus said, just barely keeping himself from a poor reaction.

"I have heard that about you," Cora said. "Still, I hope you see our reason for it."

Scuddar's scimitar slid slowly back into its sheath, making a slight screeching noise of blade rubbed against hard leather as it did so. "I do," Cyrus said, letting the sound of the singing sword diffuse a little of his anger. "But I don't have to like it." He chucked a thumb at Vara. "And when she comes out of it, she might well kill you, and I might not stop her."

"I'll deal with Vara's irritation myself," Cora murmured.

"Good," Cyrus said, straightening up as a sizable bead of sweat rolled down his neck, tickling him. "Though I doubt she'll be too pleased with me for letting it happen."

"I can tell her you were ensnared along with her, if you'd like,"

Cora said airily.

"I'm not lying to her," Cyrus said, folding his arms as his vambraces clanked. He shook his head, breathing out of his nose. "Lead on."

"As you will," Cora said and raised her hand once more, the light of a spell diffusing out of her fingers into the night. "I don't have any blindfolds—"

"I'm not Martaina," Cyrus said, glancing back at Scuddar, whose expression was masked, but his eyes were still narrowed. "I don't know one tree from another."

"Then on we shall go," Cora said, though there was no mistaking the tension in her voice as she started forward again. She walked with a slowness that had not been present before, and Cyrus wondered if she thought she was betraying her homeland by bringing them along unblinded.

"You must understand the threat they exist under here," Curatio said, lagging back to walk with Cyrus. Scuddar's soft footsteps were only a few feet back, and Cyrus knew that the desert man was listening to their conversation.

"I understand the threat," Cyrus said stiffly. "I even understand the means they're using to disguise their presence. But she could have said something before—" He cut himself off.

"I expect they're good and desperate now," Curatio said, lowering his voice even further. "That gambit of paying bounties for the dead titans a few years ago? It plainly failed."

"Plainly."

"Now their enemy has grown in strength," Curatio said. "Not unlike the Sovereign had these last few years, until you killed him."

"Vara killed him," Cyrus said absently, thinking it through. *How do you fight an enemy this large when you're so small, so weak ...* "I respect the fact that they're in a corner, but stealing wills is a trick of villains, not the virtuous. There's a reason the Dragonlord didn't hesitate before employing that means on his enemies."

"And you've ordered J'anda to do the same thing on yours," Curatio said with a little sting infused. "In time of war, you do what you need to."

Cyrus digested that for a beat. "She didn't seem too torn up that you couldn't be mesmerized. In fact, she seemed prepared for it."

"Indeed," Curatio said, casting a glance back at Scuddar walking quietly behind them. "It's something of a skill I've developed."

"I haven't developed it as a skill," Cyrus said, watching the healer carefully. "But I can still do it sometimes."

"I've heard that," Curatio said, nodding once, as though that were the end of the conversation.

"How do I do it, Curatio?" Cyrus asked, not taking his gaze off the elf.

"Shouldn't you know that?" Curatio was smiling in the dark, Cyrus was sure of it. "You are the one doing it, after all."

"How did you do it, Scuddar?" Cyrus turned.

The desert man regarded him with careful eyes. "The theft of will is a thing closely guarded against among my people. Great care is exercised in preparing our warriors against being used by a foe in such a way."

"I'd be careful with that one," Curatio said, still smirking, "he's got the bearing of a future Guildmaster already in the way he answers questions."

"Cute," Cyrus said. "No one ever wants to spill the secrets, do they?"

"You're keeping at least one of your own, I suspect," Curatio said slyly, glancing at Cyrus and meeting his eyes for just a flash. "I warned you they would begin to accumulate."

They walked in silence for a while longer, Cyrus's legs beginning to protest the treatment of the day. *Wish I could have brought Windrider.* His mind dragged, the fatigue settled in like an army behind defensive preparations. *Am I much mistaken, or has today been an unusually heavy one for both heat and questions? The only thing I haven't sweated out is the countless little beads of information prompting me to ask inquiries of Curatio and Cora that they'll doubtless pass on even answering.*

"We're here," Cora announced in a greatly subdued voice as she stopped under a tree trunk the size of a large house. Its roots swept around them in all directions, sticking out of the earth by a good twelve feet in some places.

"Really?" Cyrus tried to look around, but the trunk and roots of the tree stymied his attempt. "Right here?"

"Right here," Cora said and rapped her knuckles against the bark. It sounded … hollow?

There was a low sound of footsteps, muffled, that Cyrus could not determine the origin of, and then a door opened beneath them under the layer of foliage, disturbing the ferns and leaves as it came up. Within the square-shaped opening was an elf with fair skin and dark hair, face muddied and marked with dirt.

"Cora!" he said, dropping out of sight with a thump. "We were wondering when you'd come back; I thought for sure you'd be days yet."

"I am here," Cora said, gesturing for Cyrus to enter the darkened trap door. He eyed her for a moment in consideration before he did so, long enough for Scuddar to brush past him and hold up a hand to halt him. The desert man slid smoothly down the ladder, disappearing into the ground.

"All clear," Scuddar's voice came a few seconds later, louder than Cyrus could recall ever hearing it before.

Cyrus followed Scuddar down a crudely made ladder that was tied with strong twine at every step. The craftsmanship was haphazard even for someone used to the shoddy nature of the construction in Emerald Fields. It was certainly a far cry from the beautiful artisanal works of the Elven Kingdom, where even the desks used for the bureaucracy bore carvings on their sides. As he descended, the spare blade he kept under his backplate dug into his spine as the narrow entry tunnel pushed against his back. After a few steps down, the tight space widened, and Cyrus's armor stopped squeezing him.

When he reached the bottom, Cyrus found himself in a simple room with dirt walls. The elf who had opened the door to them stood waiting, wearing an expression of barely contained enthusiasm. Cyrus looked at him and was looked at in return, the elf dancing back and forth on boots made of some sort of animal skin. "What's your name?" Cyrus asked him.

"Partender," the elf said, and Cyrus stopped himself before asking for a surname only through long practice.

"My name is—" Cyrus began.

"I know who you are," Partender said with barely contained glee, and he pushed a dirty hand forward to be shaken, palm angled slightly upward. "You're the Guildmaster of Sanctuary." He took a sharp breath. "You are legend."

"I don't think I'd go that far." Cyrus regarded Partender's angled hand carefully for a moment before seizing it gently with his gauntlet. He gave it a shake and noted the lad twisted Cyrus's hand to match his own angle. Cyrus went along with it, wondering at the slight change.

"It's how they do it here," Curatio said, feet thumping on the ground as he came off the ladder behind Cyrus. "You might want to clear a space for the others."

Cyrus moved back as each of his mesmerized guildmates climbed down the ladder in the same dazed fashion that he'd watched them do everything since the spell had fallen over them. He chafed with anger and felt it tug at his lips, threatening to reveal a furious grimace as Vara wordlessly climbed down the ladder to join them, stepping silently off to the side and standing there, immobile and still in a way he had never seen her before.

He shook his head in disgust as Cora followed them down the ladder, pulling the hatch shut behind them. Cyrus could see that it was made of planks of wood, but that the outside had been covered over in some sort of sewn mesh and decorated with flora to disguise it from even the closest observer. "Can you let them loose yet?" Cyrus asked, chafing at the thought of any of them under the control of another person.

"I don't invade their minds," Cora said, brushing her sleeves off as a small cascade of dirt fell down from the trap door. "I only spin their heart's desire and keep them dwelling in it—"

"That's an invasion of the mind," Cyrus snapped then calmed himself. "Just … take us where we can be rid of it."

"Very well," Cora said a little roughly, as though she were taking his criticism straight to heart. "This way." She nodded at Partender and led them past him into a dark passage at the end of the underground room.

Cyrus followed, heart still full at the sight of Vara struck dumb. He followed along behind her, as though merely keeping in her proximity could somehow help him atone for allowing Cora to abuse her in this way.

They walked down a long and dark passage of dirt packed tight around them. It smelled earthy, reminding Cyrus of Fertiss, of Enterra, of a cave in Luukessia where he'd found a portal, and of Fortin's lair up on Rockridge—places he'd walked under the earth and felt it around him. The air turned subtly cooler than it had been out in the jungle, and less heavy with moisture. He did not care for it, though, and was not sorry to see a light ahead.

They came out in a most enormous cylindrical room at the bottom of a spiraling ramp. It took Cyrus a moment to realize the scale of what he was seeing when he came out of the tunnel. The ramp was carved out of the wood of the tree that they stood within, he realized, and it corkscrewed up inside the tree some several hundred feet, with closed doors all along the spiral.

"My gods," Cyrus said, looking up in awe, torchlight blazing, lighting the place as though it were some keep made entirely of wood. "This is Amti?"

"This is part of Amti," Cora said with a trace of a smile. "Come along." She beckoned him forward and he followed, Vara still beside him, as they climbed the ramp up the inside of the massive tree. He wondered at what was behind the doors they passed every hundred feet or so. *Living quarters, perhaps? If this was a castle tower, that would be them …*

They climbed nearly to the top of the thing where the interior started to taper, and there one of the doors was already open. Cyrus peered into the dark beyond and saw a passage akin to the one they'd gone through in the ground. He squinted, the magic aiding his eyes fading after a space of hours. He thought he could see wood all around in the passage.

"This is one of the boughs of this tree," Cora said with a sense of pride. "And this tree is called 'Narr'omn.'"

Cyrus frowned, trying to translate it in his head from elvish. "The hunter's hearth?"

"The hunter's home would be closer to accurate," Curatio said, sweeping his robes close around him as he stared into the passage. "Have you added more since last I was here?"

"We have four now," Cora said, smiling. "We added 'Blayy'strodd' and 'Tierreed.'"

Cyrus tried again to make those words make sense in his head. "The water … uh, bucket? And the grower's basket?"

"Not quite, but near enough," Curatio said with a smile that felt condescending. His skin looked sallow in the torchlight, very different from how he looked under Sanctuary's torches. "The last is called …

Fann'otte, yes?" He looked at Cyrus. "The mining tower, if you will."

"Save me the trouble of attempting to improve my elvish," Cyrus said with a shrug. He looked at Vara again. "Now can we …?"

"Oh," Cora said and snapped her fingers. "Certainly."

Vara lurched only slightly, as though her footing had suddenly gone uneven, although she hadn't taken so much as a step. Cyrus moved to catch her and grasped her elbow as she recovered her balance. She looked up at him, nearly doubled over, and blinked a few times as her cool blue eyes looked into his. "Oh. There you are."

"Here I am," Cyrus said, concern causing his lips to press closer together than they might normally have. "How do you feel?"

"Quite well," Vara said with a smile, "thanks to you." She blinked and looked at their surroundings, a hint of confusion blossoming on her sculpted features. "Wait … where are we?"

"Amti," Cyrus said as he relinquished her elbow.

She pulled upright again, and her brows knitted together. "How did …?" She cast her eyes about until they settled on Cora. "You …" she said, sounding more than a little irritated.

"I had to mesmerize you," Cora said neutrally. "It is a requirement."

"You could have asked," Vara said, sounding more than a little put out.

"What happened?" Martaina said, brushing brown hair out of her eyes with a calloused hand. She peered through her fingers. "That was a mesmerization spell?" Her voice sounded far away, encrusted in sleep like eyes after a long rest. "I wouldn't mind going back in for another round of that."

"That was the strangest thing," Mendicant said, quietly, dropping a hand to his chest and scratching his claws against his scales, muffled slightly by his robes. "I was … I felt so …"

"Happy, yes," Vara said, not sounding remotely in the realm of that particular emotion. "That's the trick of the spell, isn't it?"

"You don't seem quite as … drowsy as we are," Martaina said, looking at Cyrus and then Curatio in turn.

"Her spell didn't work on me," Cyrus said tautly.

Vara wheeled on him and he saw the fury in her eyes. She looked ready to say something, danger flashing, but it disappeared almost as abruptly, receding like thunderclouds rolling away under the skies above the plains.

"We're going to talk about this later, aren't we?" Cyrus asked, feeling the tension tighten up his insides.

Vara blew air noiselessly between her lips. "Did you ask her to stop it on my behalf?"

"Many times," Cyrus said.

"He was most concerned for you," Cora affirmed.

"But not for us?" Martaina asked, more than a little sour.

"For all of you," Cyrus said, looking at her then Mendicant. "I considered telling her to go to the Realm of Fire, but ..."

"But your natural tendency to lead us into madness won out, of course," Martaina said with her lips in a thin line.

"It always does," Vara agreed, though she did not seem nearly so angry as she had been a moment before. She sighed and shook her head. "I refuse to let my rather pleasant daydream become a source of irritation." She clamped a hand on Cyrus's vambrace right on his upper arm. "Come along then, you, and let's be about this business we came here for."

Cyrus did not protest, and they followed Cora along the darkened corridor. Cyrus let Vara guide him, though he suspected she was not clamping hold of him because she had any idea he could no longer see. *This is her way of reasserting her control over a situation after losing it for a time.* She tugged on his arm a little harder than was probably necessary, but it only hurt a little, so he accepted it with grace as the price for what he'd done—or failed to do.

They came to a point in the hollow bough where a ladder led upward and Cyrus climbed with the others. He passed out into warm, sticky air for a few seconds before the ladder was once again swallowed by a tree branch. All he could see outside was darkness, but for the brief moments he was climbing outside, he could hear the sway of branches, the shifting and rustling of leaves, and the sounds of a jungle at night.

Once off the ladder, he was led forward again to another glowing pinprick of light in the distance. It grew before his eyes until he could see another hollowed tree ahead. Soon enough they emerged onto another carved spiral, leaving Cyrus to wonder how long it had taken to achieve this particular marvel of carpentry.

"Welcome to Blayy'strodd," Cora said quietly as she gestured for them to ascend the spiral ramp. The air was even wetter in here, and had a pungent yet somehow clean odor to it that wafted up from somewhere far below. He looked over the side of the spiral and caught the shine of a reflection down in the center of the cylindrical space.

"The wellspring," Vara said, causing Cyrus to frown again.

"What?" she asked.

"I, uh … didn't quite translate that the same as you did."

"Of course not," Vara said, scoffing as she followed Cora. "I've been speaking the human tongue my whole life. When did you start learning elvish?"

"Around the time he realized his heart's desire was to get you out of your armor," Martaina muttered under her breath.

Vara turned and, rather than the anger he expected to see, there was mischief instead in her eyes, and a smile that curved her lips most curiously. "I like to think I'm worth at least learning another language for. Why, I'm practically a cultural ambassador for my people."

"That's a title I've never heard ascribed to you," Mendicant said without irony. "Though I don't think the others are quite as kind …"

"This way," Cora said, leading them up two loops of the spiral. Cyrus strained, his legs protesting against the hard climb after the long day's journey. He suspected it would not be long until the morning sun made its first appearance, and his body was weary. "Not much farther now," she said.

They stopped outside a door that was carved into the wood, just like all the others. Cora did not bother to knock, instead pushing through; there was no handle. The door swung loosely, mounted to its frame by the most curious metal. It gleamed in the light in a very familiar way, but he was left with no time to study it further, as Curatio harrumphed and Cyrus was forced to move into the room to clear the way for the others.

He found himself in what was plainly a council chamber of some sort. It was very much like Sanctuary's to his eyes, though it was all wood instead of stone, and lacked any hearth. It did, however, have a few torches on wall sconces, already burning. At its center was a small table with only four seats. Three of them were already occupied.

"Cyrus Davidon," Cora said, stepping in to make introductions, "this is our council—"

"Got that," Cyrus said, looking at the elves in the chairs.

They were very distinct individuals, and he took them in with a glance. Two of them were women, one short and hearty, looking at him through weathered eyes and skin, exhibiting what Cyrus knew the Elves called 'The Turn,' when the first hints of age began to show on their faces. Her hair was faint grey, and she wore pants and a tunic that looked like they'd been dirty more than they'd been clean. "Fredaula," she said when she caught Cyrus looking at her, nodding her head even as she regarded him with skeptically indifferent eyes. "Of Fann'otte."

He turned to look at the next in line. She was certainly younger, with hair the color of dark hay, but far, far more wavy. She wore a smile that looked faint but not forced, and her clothing was also tunic and pants with muddied boots. "Mirasa," she said with a nod of her own. "Of Tierreed."

Cyrus's eyes fell to the man. He wore a cloak that was green and strangely familiar. His hair was dark and speckled with grey, though his face showed no sign of age as yet. His fingers were covered in dark dirt, and one of his hands hovered next to a bow that leaned against the table. *He reminds me of—*

Cyrus turned to make a remark to Martaina of his observation, but he found her with her mouth agape, hanging open stunned in a way he'd never seen her before. "So … you know this one, then?"

"His name is Gareth," Martaina said, not taking her eyes off the man, who was watching her in return with something approaching a wistful smile, "and he, like me, was of the last of the Iliarad'ouran woodsmen."

15.

"It is good to see you again, Martaina," Gareth said with a muted smile. Cyrus tried to decide if the man was merely suffering from a severely dampened personality, or if he was trying to keep himself staid in the name of being professional. *Or he could just be a damned elf,* Cyrus thought. He glanced at Vara, who raised an eyebrow at him.

"It is good to see you, too," Martaina said, apparently adopting the understated approach for her own.

"Please, come sit," Cora said, beckoning them forth. The other members of the Amti council stood, making room at the table. Gareth hurried to the side and began to move roughly carved wooden chairs to sit at the table, his cloak—exactly like Martaina's in shade and stitching—sweeping behind him silently.

Cyrus started to assist them in moving chairs when Cora caught his arm with her own, a delicate hand landing on his gauntlet. "Please," she said, meeting his eyes with hers, and he could see ... pain inside them. She guided him to a chair and motioned for him to sit. Gareth slid another next to his and Vara seated herself, her armor clanking against the wood. Cyrus followed her example and the table rearranged itself as everyone sat around it save for Scuddar and Mendicant, both of whom refused chairs of their own, remaining standing behind Cyrus on either side. Martaina, for her part, sat heavily in her own chair, and though her face was staid, he knew by her action that encountering Gareth had affected her in some way.

"So here we are," Vara said, placing her gauntlets on the surface of the table. There was no artisan feel to it, simply a look of utility that Cyrus felt probably encapsulated the difference between Amti and the Kingdom as a whole—*no time for fancy things; they're too busy trying to carve*

78

out a living and survive.

"We thank you for coming," Cora said, placing her hands on her lap, prim and proper now. "And for enduring what you had to in order to keep our secret."

"Well, some of us apparently don't have to keep it," Vara said, giving Cyrus a sidelong look.

"Yes, I'm headed to Kortran right after this to tell them all about it," Cyrus said. "Scuddar and I will have a race to betray the location first, I'm sure. 'It's the eight-hundred-and-fifty-sixth tall tree on your left.' That'll clue those enormous idiots right in."

Cora smiled. "Forgive us for being so cautious. Our threat is great, and we are small in number."

"How many of you are there?" Vara asked.

"A little less than a thousand," Gareth said, shifting uncomfortably in his seat. He glanced at Martaina, found her looking at him, and both of them looked away abruptly. *Looks like this is an uncomfortable meeting for both of them. I wonder if it'll spill out onto the rest of us?*

"You have grown a little, then," Curatio said, sweeping his head around the council chamber as though there were something new to see other than marginally polished wood surfaces and grains.

"Yes," Cora said quietly. "A little."

"Do people still come here from Pharesia, then?" Martaina asked, suddenly upright in her seat.

"No," Cora said. "That road is closed, and has been for years. No one is fool enough to leave the safety of the Kingdom north of the mountains and venture here. They would find it ill to their liking, in any case—there is a silence here, for the most part, especially in the watches of the night, a desperate urge to keep our voices quiet at all hours for fear of discovery. We have little food, only what we can grow ourselves in Tierreed or have hunted for us by those in Narr'omn, especially now that our caravans have halted travel entirely. We have no spices but those we can grow, no outside pleasures or goods save for what can be brought in by a small group like ours, and nothing but fear to inhabit our days." She looked tired at the end of the pronouncement, her auburn hair hanging limp after the day's travel in the heavy heat. "We need help. We need the yolk of the titans off our back, or we will starve into nothingness."

"I want to help you," Cyrus said, letting his first reaction lead.

"But I want to help everyone, so this is not exactly a new phenomenon with me."

Cora gave him a smile, but it looked as hollow as the tree in which they sat. "As the Guildmaster of Sanctuary, I would expect no less from you." She cast a look sideways at Fredaula, who remained inscrutable. "From where does your reticence spring, seeing as—to the point of your guildmate back at your council—you are already at war with the titans?"

"My reticence springs from the fact that we've been at war in one form or another for years," Cyrus said, and he kept the weight of it out of his voice as he talked, even though it felt like tons upon his shoulders. "We've been blockaded inside our guildhall, seen an entire land overrun with death, faced down two different gods, and been in more battles than most people have even heard of. And we've lost … people. People dear to us." Cyrus interlaced his fingers, the black gauntlets squealing as the metal crossed. "Perhaps we are at war again, and I'm a fool not to want to immediately leap in and begin planning a campaign against the largest, most dangerous enemies we've faced—"

"You don't consider Mortus or Yartraak to be the most dangerous enemies you've faced?" Mirasa asked, her dark yellow hair falling over her shoulder. For the first time, Cyrus noticed a small smudge of dirt on her brow. *I suppose she works to grow the crops here as well as runs her tree.* "They were gods."

"There was only one each of them," Cyrus said, "and their armies were of normal-sized creatures, for the most part, largely lacking in magic. These titans were a pox of trouble before they knew spellcraft, and now—speaking from experience—they just gave me one of the hardest shellackings I can recall ever having perpetrated upon me." He undid his chinstrap and rubbed at his face carefully, avoiding pinching himself with the gauntlet's joints. "I don't relish the thought of trying to defeat their entire nation in battle. How many of them are there?"

"They have a fearsome army," Cora said carefully, drawing an irritated look from Fredaula at her frank assessment. "Tens of thousands, I think."

"Damn," Vara whispered.

"We may even be outnumbered," Cyrus said, settling his gauntleted fingers back on the table with a rap. "And who knows how many spellcasters they have at their disposal?" He let out a slow breath. "I have charged into war many a time, some would say stupidly—"

"Only those who know you best," Vara said. "Or at all, really."

He gave her a weak look of annoyance and received a supportive smile in return. "I simply don't wish to commit to a war that I don't know if we can win, especially when I'm not sure if it's even necessary." Cyrus looked around the room. "I mean, really ... why do you stay here? The Kingdom has space to grow, and if you pulled north of the mountains, you could—"

"This is our home," Gareth said firmly.

"The Iliarad'ouran woods were once our home as well," Martaina said, and made it sound like she was reading an indictment from atop a platform in some town square, "but when the time came, you left as easily as if they were not."

"I made a mistake," Gareth said, the sting evident in his high voice. "When I came back, you were—"

"Gone, yes," Martaina said, and her eyes were slightly narrowed. "Because—"

"As much fun as it is for the rest of us to witness this very dramatic, very personal moment," Cyrus said, watching the red spread over Martaina's cheeks as Gareth fidgeted in his chair, "please settle this later." He stared at Gareth then looked to Cora. "You could leave. Back in the Kingdom, you could surely establish a new town somewhere in—"

"No, we couldn't," Cora said sadly. "We're not wanted there, and we don't really believe in Danay's great kingdom in any case."

"Danay's great kingdom," Gareth said with a snort, and Martaina nodded along. "The greatest place in Arkaria to bleed yourself dry for your ambitions while they take every bite of food out of your mouth and reapportion it wherever the king and his advisors desire. Where the lands are all taken by the nobility, and if you want to carve out your own homestead, good luck getting a land grant. For those of us who eschew city life, there is no place in the Elven Kingdom but tending some lord's plantation." He bowed his head and the disgust was plain. "Most of us tried that life and grew tired of it. Better to live free and die here on our own, mostly outside his grasping fingers than be suffocated by his heavy-handed 'benevolence.'"

"Well, that's certainly your choice," Cyrus said, taking it all in. Fredaula and Mirasa were nodding along with every word of Gareth's tirade while Cora had watched Cyrus for his reaction. "But there are other lands in the north—the Plains of Perdamun, for example—"

"Ah yes, the Warden of the Southern Plains offers us a slice of his kingdom," Cora said. "It's generous of you ... but again, it is not our home."

"Your home," Cyrus said, reaching the end of his ability to humor them, "is in the middle of the most hostile habitable land in all Arkaria. You might have better luck settling Luukessia once the titans," he gestured vaguely toward the outer wall of the tree, "have found your place here, because I get the sense that you'll have an extremely short fight once they know where to find you." He lowered his head like a bull on a charge. "The smartest move I can make against an army this superior is to post my own in defense of the Heia Pass and around the portals nearest our settlements to deal with the titans the next time they reach their hand forth to—"

"How long will you be able to do that?" Cora asked sadly. "If they are at war with you, they will come. They will come, yes, to your portals at first, and then, if you turn them aside, which is hardly a given with the size of the forces they could send against you—to portals slightly farther away. They could assemble an army a day's march from Sanctuary for them, and sweep down upon you, climbing your walls with no more effort than you take to scale a stone wall around a goat pen." She stared him down, fierce, eyes awake with anger and passion. "You know what you are facing. You looked Talikartin in the eye, did you not? They are followers of Bellarum, and you should know what that entails—"

"I damned well know what it entails," Cyrus said abruptly, dark and menacing. "I know."

Cora's visage softened, and she looked away. "The hour is late, and the day is gone. You should rest, and tomorrow—or rather later today—we will show you Amti as it is when it is awake." She looked up. "We will show you what we would have you fight for, and you may determine for yourself whether it is, indeed, worth the price we reckon it will cost." She stood and started to usher them from the room. Cyrus let himself be led away, but his head was aswirl all the while as Mirasa and Fredaula led them down the sloping ramp deeper into the tree.

"What is it?" Vara murmured in his ear. Cyrus caught Curatio looking over his shoulder at them, but only a glance.

"We'll talk about it later," Cyrus said, trudging along behind their guides. "In private," he said, though he suspected he need not explain that to her.

They're in a hell of a mess, he thought, trying to keep his boots from echoing loudly in the quiet interior of the hollow tree. He watched Fredaula as she walked ahead of him, head bowed, the perfect image of the silent, steadfast elf. *This is not like the quiet parties of Pharesia or even the subtle noise of Termina. This is a town in silence, enforced and frightened. And Cora was right; they face a relentless enemy, intent on hunting them down. I'm surprised the titans haven't burned the entire jungle down yet just to be finished with the thing ...*

He felt a trickle of cold sweat roll down the back of his neck, and it chilled him almost as much as his next thought. *That day is coming, though, surely. The titans won't stay distracted by the dragons forever—or by us, apparently. They'll come for these people, and it will be a mad slaughter one way or another, just as the God of War would will it ...*

... and when it comes time for the titans to deal with Sanctuary ... he realized rather grimly, *... they won't even hesitate to do exactly the same.*

83

16.

"This is our greatest export," Fredaula said stiffly, almost reluctantly, handing over a chunk of ore. It was a heavy piece, and she laid it in Cyrus's hand with a little extra force, telling him in perfectly clear terms that she was not happy to have to disclose this to him. They stood in a mine several hundred feet beneath the surface of Fann'otte, in a cool, dark cave with rock walls that were occasionally broken by the edges of especially large roots.

He felt the weight and the subtle pressure of it as he stared, puzzled, at the unrefined, shining metal hiding entwined in rock. "Steel? Iron?" He shrugged. "I'm not a smith, so I don't—"

"You should," Curatio said with a smug smile. "You're wearing nearly your weight in it."

Cyrus looked down at the metal again. "This ... this is quartal?"

"Yes," Fredaula said with a hiss of breath, clearly no happier about telling him now than before she'd slapped the ore into his hand. She took it back a little roughly, and it passed under Vara's nose as the paladin followed it with her gaze. "We have the only veins currently mining this most rare metal—"

"What?" Cyrus blinked. "That can't be right. A few years ago I was instructed to seek out quartal, and then the only place it was available was in the Realm of Darkness."

Fredaula shrugged impatiently. "Well, I don't know where you heard that, but it's clear that they were not aware of our secret, for we've been shipping it in small quantities to the Kingdom for almost a century now."

"Where do you think your chain mail came from?" Curatio asked, once again smiling.

"I guess I never asked," Cyrus said stiffly, a bit annoyed. *If Bellarum knew they were mining quartal here, why would he send me to the Realm of Darkness to retrieve the ore from Yartraak's treasure room?* He fingered Praelior's hilt idly. *Unless he wanted me to test my mettle against the God of Darkness's minions rather than simply barter for a chunk of it. It certainly wouldn't take me gathering an army to come here and barter for it ... no conquest, no prize.*

"We had been sending quite a bit to King Danay as our payment for taxes," Fredaula said, still stiff as a tree trunk, "though obviously we are in arrears now."

"I don't expect he'll be rushing to send a tax collector down to make good on your debt," Vara said with a trace of irony. "Would they even know where to look?"

"No," Fredaula said, "but we all have family still in the Kingdom, and the elven law makes clear that family obligations pass in succession, including debts." She cradled the quartal to her side. "None of us wish to be a burden simply because we don't like the king, and we certainly ... reserve a share more for ourselves than we might otherwise have given."

"In other words, you're tax cheats," Cyrus said.

Fredaula's lined face reddened. "It's criminal, what Danay does to the kingdom."

"I'm not going to report you," Cyrus said with a shrug, "merely calling it as I see it. King Danay and I have no love for one another." He started back toward the entry to the tunnel.

"You ..." Fredaula scurried to keep up, "... you've met the king?"

"Met him," Cyrus said, "defended his kingdom, got into a rather heated argument with him. All of those, actually."

Fredaula seemed to soften slightly, her wrinkled face relaxing. "Oh. Well. I didn't expect such a steadfast defender of the kingdom to be ..."

"I defend the people," Cyrus said, boots crunching in the tunnel grit. "The Kingdom and its current monarch can go spit for all I care."

"A noble calling," Fredaula said.

"Yes, it fills him up all the way to his eyeballs," Vara said, and Cyrus caught the hint of a smile at her lips in the way she said.

"We will, of course," Curatio said, sending a darting glance to

Cyrus suggesting he had caught all of Vara's meaning and perhaps was suppressing a comment of his own, "be consulting with our council before making any decisions." Cyrus eyed the healer and received a look in return that suggested he was perhaps stating this as a reminder for all in the tunnel, a small group that only included the three Sanctuary officers and Fredaula. Mendicant, Martaina and Scuddar had drifted down a secondary spur with Cora a few hundred feet back. Miners worked carefully, tapping at the walls with pickaxes. They made way as Cyrus and his party brushed past, bowing their heads slightly and hiding smiles as he passed. *Probably hoping we're their salvation.*

I guess we'll have to wait and see on that one.

Fredaula led them back out of the tunnels and into the pit at the bottom of the tree. Fann'otte did not open directly into the mines; it was hollowed near the bottom, the ramp clear all the way into the roots, and a series of doors on the ramp allowed for carts to be pulled up into the tree proper with their precious ore. Cyrus listened as they opened one of the doors and he emerged into the quiet air of the tree, absent the tinking sound of pickaxes working in time. To his ears it was another maddeningly careful security precaution.

But to these elves, it's perhaps the difference between life and death.

Mendicant, Martaina, Scuddar and Cora waited ahead on the ramp, pausing in the middle of some quiet conversation upon their approach. *This whole place is steeped in silence,* Cyrus thought. *It is the deadest town I've ever seen, perhaps even more bereft of life than the Realms of Darkness or Death.*

Mendicant watched Cyrus's approach and scampered toward him slightly, robes dragging the ground. "Did you see what they mine?"

"I saw it," Cyrus said, slipping into the impromptu circle as Cora moved to allow it to widen to accommodate the new arrivals. "And it is certainly impressive."

"We can come to some accord if you were to deal with this giant problem," Cora said, perhaps a little too coy behind her smile.

"Cora," Vara said, shaking her head, "you should know better than to try and influence us in so crass a manner."

"I doubt it will have much bearing," she said, slightly chastened, though not much given the gleam of her eyes as she looked at Cyrus, "but still … should you rid us of this problem, our gratitude will be made manifest in the form of a ten percent commission to Sanctuary in perpetuity."

"I doubt we'll take it," Cyrus said, looking around the circle.

"It is yours whether you want it or not," Cora said. "We make no demands save for that one—that you will not do this thing without recompense."

Cyrus sighed, and caught a cocked head from Curatio that suggested easy resignation to the riches offered. "Fine," Cyrus said. "I'll put it into consideration with everything els—"

An explosion of sound came from a nearby door, causing Cyrus and the others to jerk their heads around to seek the source. The door slammed open and a peal of laughter filled the air as a child, no more than three in Cyrus's estimation, came bounding out on unsteady legs. An elven man with youthful features emerged from the door and caught the tyke a moment later, scooping the child up and lifting them against his chest. He was flushed and red, and when he saw Cora and Fredaula, he blushed an even deeper scarlet. "I'm sorry," he said.

Fredaula's countenance was dark. "You know better, Arisson. You need to keep the children in that room, safely in the quiet space beneath the earth, at all times."

"I know," Arisson said, in rough resignation. "It's just a—it's tiresome for them, you know, not getting to play outdoors or—"

"These are our laws, Arisson." Fredaula had folded her arms and made an imperious wave back toward the door that the child had sprung through. Cyrus fixated on the fat little face, whose bright eyes were searching over the small group assembled before them. The child's hair was of a length and the features so indistinct he could not tell whether it was a boy or a girl.

"Sweet Vidara," Vara muttered in a low gasp. She broke from the small assemblage and moved toward Arisson and the child, stopping before them as though she were afraid they would turn into vapor if she drew any closer. She stared for a long moment and then, haltingly, started to reach out. She looked to Arisson for permission, and received a nod in return. With that, she pulled free of her gauntlet and reached a bare hand out to stroke the child's ear, which was pointed all the way to the top.

"That's a full-blooded elf baby," Cyrus said as another chill ran through him. "A full elven child." He hesitated. "Unless … are they like … eight hundred or something?"

Vara cast him a withering look. "Don't be an oaf, we mature like you when it comes to childhood and adolescence."

"Right," Cyrus said, nodding. "Because you're thirty-three, not two thousand, and you're," he gestured vaguely at her, drawing another exasperated roll of the eyes from the paladin, "well, you know. Mature and developed and lovely and … all that." He looked to Cora, who wore a tight smile. "How?"

"We don't know," she said, now showing the same sort of reserve that Fredaula had exhibited when showing Cyrus the quartal. "We only know that … well, that it happens now. That here … the curse of the elves has not applied since we were founded." She hesitated, as though admitting something particularly painful. "It is … the other reason we cannot bring ourselves to leave."

"And you hide this fact from the kingdom?" Vara asked, turning furious eyes on Cora. "You keep this to yourselves? You selfish—"

"Why should we tell them?" Fredaula snapped. "Do you know how often the King of the Elves has rendered military aid to us? Humanitarian aid? Any aid? The next time will be the first. We pay our obligations—"

"And cheat," Cyrus muttered.

"—and nothing else," Fredaula said, giving Cyrus a hot glare at his interruption. "They deserve nothing else from us, those infinite pillars of a dying kingdom." She spat, a blob that splattered on the wooden ramp. "Let them die, I say."

"Seems they say the same about you," Cyrus observed.

"They said it about us first," Fredaula said, sullen. "Let their feet twist and jerk with their neck in the noose the same way they would have us hang, that's how we feel about it down here."

"And what if I felt the same way about you as them?" Cyrus asked, catching another deathly glare from Fredaula.

"Then for all I care, you can go hang with your problems, too," she said, her aged skin affecting a darker tint.

"Fredaula," Cora said, gently, trying to steer the conversation back to more civil waters. "Arisson," she said, and the man with the child shuffled silently back to the room and shut the door. She looked back to Cyrus. "You have us at your mercy. The elves will not help us. Neither will the humans, the dark elves, the gnomes, the goblins—"

She looked down at Mendicant, who seemed pensive. "We are on our own, save but for your help, should you be willing to give it." She sighed and looked at the door that Arisson had just walked through. "We will pay any price to survive here, in our home, for your aid, should we be able to give it. If that means … telling the Kingdom whatever you want to tell them, we will pay it." Cyrus watched Fredaula's face harden, but when Cora continued to speak, the older woman kept her peace. "We are at your mercy," Cora said, and she took a breath that suggested she labored with her unease like it was some foe that she had to fight, "for it is either yours or the titans that we will be cast upon," the corners of her mouth twitched upward in a smile that did not remotely come close to reaching her eyes, "and I would rather count on that of the guild of Sanctuary, regardless of who reigns as Guildmaster."

17.

Cyrus stood in the Council Chambers of Sanctuary, staring out the balcony door onto sunlit fields at midday. He took a breath of the fresh air, so different from the stale interior of the trees of Amti with their scent of sap and wood shavings, and—in the case of Tierreed, the tree where they grew their food—the smell of dung and other compost.

"They need help or they'll die," Cyrus said to his companion, his helm left on the table of the council, his hand resting on the doorframe as he leaned against it and stuck his head out into the warm summer day. "Of that much I'm convinced."

"And you ask me for counsel on this?" Administrator Cattrine Tiernan looked at him with undisguised curiosity. "I'm honored. I think."

"You're right in the thick of this, Cattrine," Cyrus said, only giving her a glance before he went back to looking over the Plains of Perdamun. "You have more reason to be angry at these titans than anyone else, and more reason to want to avoid a war with them, as well. When the Council meets in a few minutes, I want you there to render your opinion, whatever it might be."

"I will give you my thoughts," Cattrine said, a little reserved, "though I find them a bit muddled after these weeks of reconstruction." She let a breathy sigh. "Nothing is ever simple anymore, is it?"

"I didn't find it particularly simple before a horde of undead ravaged your homeland," Cyrus said, noting the slight blanch from her as he spoke, "but you are correct in that it does not seem to be growing less tangled as the years spin by."

"We lost thousands, of course," she said, drawing another look from him. "I didn't know if you ever heard the full count. Not that we've got one, just the vague suspicions that come from trying to drag bodies out of rubble and wreckage while simultaneously building enough housing and facilities to feed and accommodate those who lost hearth and home in the attack."

"How many?" Cyrus asked. "Roughly."

"Five thousand," Cattrine said, and at this she looked out over the plains herself, the midday sun hidden overhead by the top of the tower's eaves. She still squinted against its brightness.

"What would you advise?" Cyrus asked, folding his arms against his breastplate, leaning his thick pauldron against the frame of the door. "Vengeance? Justice? Preservation? Risk?"

"You speak oddly, but I think I discern your meaning," she said. "The idea of risking more by engaging these horrible, monstrous *things* in some great war ... putting more of your people as well as mine into a fight ... well, it certainly holds little appeal for me. But the thought of trying to protect ourselves from a foe who means to strike out slyly, secretly, until we are dead? That is a concern, at least, as we go about the business of rebuilding."

"It was pointed out to me in Amti," Cyrus said, "that if the titans mean to deliver destruction unto us, there is little defense now that they have magical means at their disposal. We cannot cover all the portals within walking distance of Emerald Fields or Sanctuary—assuming we could even cover the ones closest to us, which is questionable at best."

"An implacable, unstoppable foe," Cattrine mused aloud, before turning to face him. "Do you ever get tired of facing those?"

"I am tired in general," Cyrus said. "But part of me ... part of me thinks that Talikartin was blustering in what he said to me on the night of the attack. The titans have dragons at their lower gates, and they struck north because it was an easy direction to strike. If they want a full war, they won't be able to gird themselves against the dragonkin and do it, I don't think." Cyrus sniffed, taking in a breath of hot air through his nose. "Or at least, that would be my strategy if it comes down to it—to make them pay such a cost in the north that they have no defense in the south."

"I can see you have given this some considerable thought,"

Cattrine said.

"I always do," Cyrus said with a bitter smile.

"Then let me add my own thoughts to your pile," she said, and any trace of a smile vanished beneath two weeks' worth of fatigue. "The peacemaker, the administrator in me would counsel you to avoid war. We have lost much, and as you said, you don't know how stiff a foe you would be engaging. The war could be long and costly, and we would bear a burden that neither you nor I would care to count the consequences of in blood and our own dear when it was done."

"Close up the gates, then," Cyrus said, staring out across the sun-kissed greenery. Cottony clouds rolled across the skies in front of him.

"I didn't say that," Cattrine said, and now her voice was lower, almost a whisper. "For I have not always been a conciliator, nor an administrator." Cyrus glanced at her and saw darker things in the depths of her lush green eyes. "I know by hard experience that there are some creatures that walk this earth that are so despicable, so monstrous—that they need no provocation, that they simply aim to dominate and destroy all that would not bow to them. They cannot be appeased, and showing any sign of accession to their wishes only prompts them to batter you even harder upon their next opportunity. For some, the rage is soul-deep," she swallowed visibly, "and it will not exhaust itself no matter how many times they inflict their fury upon you."

Cyrus kept his head down as she spoke, pressing his teeth tightly together. "I don't think I've ever told you how happy I am you stabbed your husband in the back and then slit his throat."

"I only wish I'd been able to get away with it years earlier," Cattrine said simply. "I have only seen a little of these titans, but in them I sense another foe who will not bow, will not bend, will not be anything other than broken in their quest to break you."

"Huh," Cyrus said, twisting his lips. "Do you think they'll succeed? They are large, and there are apparently rather a lot of them."

"I don't favor their chances," she said coolly, and she smiled, ever so slightly.

"I—" Cyrus started to speak, but then the sound of a trumpet rang out from far below. "What the—?"

"What is that?" Cattrine asked, staring fixed at something out ahead of them.

Cyrus's eyes scanned the horizon, searching the green and sprawling plains for what she saw. He looked, then looked again, for movement, for shadow, for anything. "I don't see—"

"Not there," she said, and laid a hand upon his chin, lifting his head up. "There."

And he saw it.

"My gods," Cyrus said, and the breath went out of him. It was a shadow in the sky, long and terrible, like a bird given a harsher form, wingspan the size of a small village. It swept out of a bank of clouds as black as if it were a piece of night breaking out of the clear, bright day. Cyrus swallowed hard and his hand fell to Praelior as the shouts of "ALARUM!" began to ring out behind him in earnest. He heard the Council Chamber doors open behind him and wheeled to find Vara standing there with Ryin, Vaste and Curatio. Mendicant scampered in a moment later.

"What the hell is this?" Vara asked, eyes squinted, brow furrowed.

"We were just talking," Cattrine said, looking more than a bit pale, "in advance of the—"

"Not that," Vara said, waving her off impatiently. "What's the alar—" she pointed past them and her hand froze in mid-air. "My gods."

"That's what he said," Cattrine said, turning about to look at the shadow as it glided easily across the sky, directly toward them. "And while I acknowledge that is certainly a frightening thing to see coming toward you, I can't say I know exactly what we're looking at—"

"There's a reason for that," Cyrus said, striding out onto the balcony, boots ringing out as the officers came out behind him. He clutched the railing and leaned, squinting against the bright day to make out what he saw just a hint clearer. He could see the hints of scales, of claws, and of a face marked with teeth, even though it was still some considerable distance off. "After all," he said, motioning to Ryin and receiving a nod, the Falcon's Essence spell taking hold only a second later, "it's not as though they had dragons in Luukessia." And he ran off the balcony and into the open air with his officers trailing behind him. The last sight of Cattrine before he vanished below the stone railing was of her face falling more swiftly than Cyrus himself as he raced to the defense of Sanctuary.

18.

The dragon made a sweeping and majestic turn, baring its full side as it halted its approach and drifted in a slow circle a few miles out. Cyrus watched it as he descended toward the curtain wall below. "Don't run out too far," he shouted behind him to the officers that were in his wake.

"Because of the dragon?" Mendicant shouted back in his raspy voice.

"No," Cyrus said, "because the spell protecting Sanctuary from mystical attacks will strip your Falcon's Essence enchantment and you'll find yourself flailing arms as you come to a rather messy end."

"Good reason," Mendicant agreed after a pause. "This dragon ... this is not a normal thing, correct?"

Cyrus looked back and caught a glance from Curatio, then Vara. "There hasn't been a dragon in northern Arkaria since Ashan'agar broke free, I don't think."

"That you know of," Vaste corrected.

"They're pretty big creatures," Cyrus said. "Seems like someone would have seen one flying around—like that." He waved at the shadows circling back around and heading toward Sanctuary once more.

The wind hit Cyrus in the face as he sprinted down toward the wall. Below him, the keep was emptying and tiny figures were sprinting across the green grounds toward the curtain wall and their assigned siege stations. "Thank goodness we got the last of the refugees out of here," he muttered to himself.

"They wouldn't have been much use against a dragon," Curatio agreed, reminding Cyrus once more that elves heard every damned thing, whether you wanted them to or not. "Do you have a plan?"

"Always," Cyrus said, the wall edging ever closer as he turned his dive even steeper so as not to go drifting out past the spellcraft that protected the bulwarks. The curtain wall was only a few hundred feet away now, and he could clearly see the movement atop it, archers with bows nocked and raised. *That'll do little good*, he thought.

"And that plan is?" Curatio asked, not so patiently.

"Ryin, get the druids to cast Falcon's Essence on the entire army," Cyrus said.

Ryin paled. "That's a … sizable task. It could take a while."

"Well, don't wait too long," Vaste said as they came down on the stone blocks of the wall, "wouldn't want to see everyone get burned crispy, after all. We should save that fate for the pot roasts of—"

"Always with the food," Vara muttered, settling a solid foot above the wall. "Can you think of nothing else?"

"The food is the only thing I feel comfortable talking about," Vaste said, "but I suppose I could work up to discussing my other, more ribald appetites—"

"Please don't," Curatio said, drawing his robes about him. "There are some mysteries which I should care to keep, even after as long as I have lived."

J'anda appeared next to them, staff in hand, a blur of motion. Cyrus balked slightly at the sight of him. *Do I look like that when I'm running with Praelior?* "A dragon, eh?" the enchanter said, stalking up to the edge of the wall tentatively. "I don't know how much help I will be in this; dragon skin is notoriously resistant to magic."

"Then the problem is not just going to be for you, but our entire corps of spellcasters," Cyrus said, watching the enormous shadow sweep over the plains, once more drawing a direct line to Sanctuary. "Good thing we've got a fair helping of mystical steel."

"You realize that thing can cook you in less than a second if it's a fire breather?" Vara asked, landing a hand on his shoulder.

"This feels like a conversation we've had before," Cyrus said with a strained smile. "I can't even make a pretense of throwing a Goliath warrior in front of this one, though. It's all on us."

"Gods," Vara said, rolling her eyes. "How are you planning to handle it? A blind charge across the empty space in front of us?"

"No," Cyrus said, "because of the spell, remember? We'd all

plummet off the wall. We're going to have to fight him within this side of the parapets, which is going to rather limit our action—"

"Or ..." Curatio said, eyes afield, locked on the dragon, "you could wait."

"Now see here, you," Vaste said, all false umbrage, "do you realize who you're talking to? This is Cyrus Davidon, the warrior in black, and he waits for no man, nor gnome, nor dragon, nor anyone but a paladin with excessively shiny armor and hair, dammit. How dare you attempt to disrupt the natural order of things with your suggestions? I think it should be made treason to—"

"That's about enough of that," Vara said, planting a shining gauntlet over Vaste's mouth, the metal dinging against his extended lower teeth. "Why would we wait, Curatio?"

Curatio took a moment to answer, peering out as he did across the fields as the dragon took a moment and swooped in a small circle once more before resuming his advance. He beat his wings, and Cyrus could almost feel the power from even a mile away, holding the creature aloft until he entered a glide, slowly, toward the ground. "Because he has announced himself in his approach rather than simply sweeping in and burning us to cinders, as a dragon on the attack would do. His path is one of leisure, of calm—designed to allow us to see his approach rather than to stealthily charge in and destroy us unexpected."

"You wish to pin hopes on that thing—" Vara pointed at the dragon as it extended its wings and tilted, like a bird coming in for a landing, aiming for the plains a few hundred feet out from the wall, "—and its peaceful intentions? From a dragon? Truly?"

The dragon landed with a thunderous sound of claws digging into the earth, halted its forward momentum and spread its wings, looking as fearsome as any rendition Cyrus had ever seen on countless livery and seals. The dragon posed that way for a long moment before it brought its wings in and straightened up, standing on all fours like some majestic beast. It surveyed the wall with dark eyes, and Cyrus found himself unable to gauge its intent. It held in place for what felt like long seconds dragging toward a minute, and then began to advance on the wall, slowly, still surveying all before it with an inscrutable calm.

"Truly," Curatio said as the dragon drew closer. It was only a hundred feet away now, and Cyrus could see black pupils inset in yellow irises that took up the whole of the eye. The earth shook when it walked, but its steps as it strolled its way up to them were graceful and measured. It singled Cyrus out and moved straight toward him, eyes locked on, giving him an uncomfortable feeling of déjà vu, back to the time when the Dragonlord Ashan'agar had attempted to steal his will by the same mechanism.

Cyrus's hand fell to Praelior and was just as quickly knocked away by Curatio, who gave him a warning look and shook his head, as serious as Cyrus had ever seen the healer. That done, Curatio stepped forward to the crenellations, the teeth of the wall, and stepped up. "It has been a long time," he announced, loud enough to be heard back in the courtyard.

"Indeed," the dragon said, low and ponderous, his speech as slow and measured as his movement. "More thousands of years than I can count, Curatio."

"I have forgotten the number as well," Curatio said, inclining his head to the side. "I assume you have come to our august company seeking a certain someone."

"Indeed I have," the dragon said and looked right back to Cyrus. "I would have words with your Guildmaster, Curatio."

"I suspect he might find a few for you as well," Curatio said, lips pursed as he finished speaking. "May I present to you Cyrus Davidon of Sanctuary, Lord of Perdamun and Warden of the Southern Plains."

"I feel like if he got that printed on his stationary, there wouldn't be room for a very long letter after all that," Vaste said. "Which could be to his advantage, since I'm not so sure our humble warrior is very good at spelling—"

"Silence yourself," Vara said, once more placing her gauntlet over his mouth.

Vaste's teeth clinked against the metal as he placed his lips around her hand and smacked them together. "Tastes like—" She jerked her hand further into his jaws and drew a grunt of pain. "—I was going to say paladin, but now I think I'll go with 'gnome.'"

"At last we meet," the dragon said, coming ever closer to the wall with his head atop a perilously long neck. His skin was dark red, beyond the darkest crimson Cyrus had ever seen, almost black. He reminded Cyrus more than a little of Ashan'agar, whose eyes had been a similarly dangerous shade. "Cyrus Davidon."

"At last," Cyrus said, staring back at the dragon, not daring to look away from his eyes, just the same as he would with any foe. "And ... who are you?"

"Cyrus, may I introduce to you Ehrgraz," Curatio said, stiller than Cyrus could ever recall the healer, "the chief of the army for the dragons of the south."

19.

"I've heard your name before," Cyrus said in greeting to Ehrgraz the dragon, who stood before him unflinching, yellow eyes not leaving his for a moment.

"Not half so often as I've heard yours, I expect," Ehrgraz drawled, sounding almost human in his delivery. He carried none of the raw rasp of Ashan'agar in his speech; his words were smooth and practiced.

"Look at you, legendary man," Vaste said from behind Cyrus, "they've heard tell of your cod swinging even among the dragons."

"If you don't shut your mouth, I will personally use his cod to shut it for you," Vara said, "and I must warn you, after he's been in the armor for a day, it's quite—"

"Okay, thank you, done now," Vaste said. "Please … proceed."

"I can't decide whether it's a good thing or a bad thing that I'm known to the dragons," Cyrus said, still looking at Ehrgraz. The plains behind him seemed to fade away, and all that was left were those eyes, that snout. "But I can tell you I'm not terribly thrilled to speak with you now, especially with you staring at me in much the same way as Ashan'agar did."

"Ashan'agar used forbidden magics," Ehrgraz said, sounding just a little offended. "I trust you wouldn't accuse me of doing something of that nature?"

"I don't know enough dragons to be able to tell what's considered polite conversation among you," Cyrus said, not breaking off.

"No, I suppose not," Ehrgraz said, "being as you've only met two of our kind and you've slain them both."

"So that's why you've heard of me," Cyrus said.

"Oh, I had heard of you long before that," Ehrgraz said, and Cyrus detected a hint of slyness. "But the rest of my people did not know of you before you killed Kalam."

"I hope you're not sore about that," Cyrus said. "Him or Ashan'agar."

"Sore?" Ehrgraz's massive, scaled brow wrinkled just above his eye. "Quite the opposite, in fact. I was there on the day you slew Ashan'agar, watching—"

"I find that hard to believe," Cyrus said. "I feel like I would have seen you."

"You were waking up from a resurrection spell," Ehrgraz said. "I could have paraded myself under your nose in Ashan'agar's skin and you would not have noticed, I assure you. But that is neither here nor there, for it is of the past, and I do not to come to speak to you of the past, but of the future."

Cyrus held himself up to his full height, for all the little good it did. "What did you come to speak to me about, in regards to the future?"

"I have heard," Ehrgraz said, his head moving a little, but never once surrendering his gaze on Cyrus, "that you are considering intervention in the southern lands." His neck straightened high, reminding Cyrus of a giraffe. "I have come to offer you counsel."

"Is that counsel to 'stay the hell out'?" Cyrus asked. "Because I've heard dragons are insular and quite unwilling to suffer the advice of others, so it strikes me as ironic that you would—"

"My counsel is quite the opposite, actually," Ehrgraz said, cutting him off. "You're quite right; most dragons would bury their heads in the ash until such time as the world cracked around them. But I am no such fool, Cyrus Davidon, and do not mistake me for one. I watch your peoples, constantly, carefully, as I watched you the day you killed our former lord. I watch all threats, and I see one now that worries me as few have since the days when the original elves made their pact with us to leave the south alone." His head snaked closer to Cyrus, massive skull coming to rest its chin on the wall. "You know the threat of which I speak. Large and looming, and suddenly capable of more danger than ever they were before."

"Your people are concerned about the titans, then," Cyrus said.

"My people," Ehrgraz said and laughed, rough and loud. "My people worry about nothing, for it is not their task. I head the army, and so they hang the worry upon me instead. No, they go about their business without concern so that I may carry it all for them, and now I find myself overburdened, and trapped in a position where none of them will listen to my rising fears." His wings swept back. "Even now, the sands shift in the south. The idea of the titans learning magic is a frightening one to anyone with sense, but my people lack sense, and worse than that, they have lacked a foe for more millennia than you could count. Peace has made them soft, and even the predations of titans against our lesser kin are cause of easy dismissal. They can't attack Hewat, after all, and they don't dare venture deep into the Ashen Wastelands, so why worry?" He lifted a paw and scratched along the side of the stone wall, causing a grinding screech that made Cyrus blanch. "But you know … you know there is cause for worry, do you not? Do you not see it?"

"I see it," Cyrus said quietly. "It's what to do about it I'm not resolved on, yet. They are many—"

"So are you," Ehrgraz said, eyeing him again.

"They're a little bigger," Cyrus said, "and I don't know how many they have."

"They number more than you," Ehrgraz said.

Nice to hear that from someone in the know, Cyrus thought. "If you're proposing an alliance to stop the titans—"

"I am not," Ehrgraz said archly. "I told you—I came here to counsel. My people want nothing of war with the titans."

"Heh," Cyrus said, not actually finding any humor in it. "I don't think the titans feel the same."

"Nor do they about you, as I understand it," Ehrgraz said, "yet still you ponder." There was a strange amusement in the dragon's scaly face. "They are not nearly the threat to us that they are to you, though."

"But you still feel threatened," Cyrus said, feeling as though he were in some sort of contest with the dragon at this point, though he knew nothing of how victory could be won within it.

"As you have so successfully proven yourself, even you smaller beings can kill a dragon," Ehrgraz said. "We are hardly invulnerable, but millennia of peace have convinced countless of my people that we are. It is a lesson that will come to a rather abrupt and tragic conclusion, and one I work to guard against."

"What would you propose, then?" Cyrus asked. "If we did decide to embroil ourselves in this conflict?" He took a step closer to the wall and laid a hand upon the stone there as Ehrgraz took a step back.

"I would propose you think carefully about it," Ehrgraz said, backing away. "I will return to you in five days. An eyeblink for my people, but we are not working on the timescale of my people, are we?" His eyes narrowed. "No, we move at the behest of titans, whose mortality defines them as yours does for your people." He spread his wings. "If in five days' time you have come to a satisfactory conclusion, then perhaps we will discuss—and nothing more!—possibilities." The dragon drew himself up and flapped his wings, hitting Cyrus with a blast of wind that rattled his armor. "Consider it well, Cyrus Davidon." The dragon narrowed his eyes as he took wing, rising into the sky. "For these sorts of threats are not easily contained, and now loosed, they are unlikely to simply run around you like a river around a stone." He lowered his head as he swept up. "You may not have escaped my notice, but trust me when I tell you that in the south, you are too small to avoid being swept away by the course of things larger than you."

And with that, Ehrgraz took to the skies and flew up into the air, disappearing over the horizon in minutes, far, far faster than he had flown during his approach.

20.

"What the hell was that look all about?" Vara asked as Ehrgraz receded from view, alarmingly quickly.

"What?" Cyrus turned his head to look at her, genuinely perplexed. It was still around them on the wall, the Sanctuary officers quiet and grim after the meeting with the dragon. *Probably stunned into silence*, Cyrus thought. He gave a glance at Vaste, whose lips were puckered tightly and his eyes fixed in the clouds. *Even him? Gods. What times we are in.*

"That look when you stared at Ehrgraz," she said, her blue eyes shining in the afternoon sun, "I've seen it before, on the battlefield, like you're going to grow fists out of your sockets and pummel through his scales."

"Hah," Cyrus said, breaking into a smile. "It's a—it's silly, really."

"What about you isn't?" Vaste asked, leaning over Cyrus and Vara. He caught a glare from her. "Oh, right. The cod."

"It's a thing I do," Cyrus said, giving the troll a sidelong look as he directed his explanation to Vara. "I've done it since … I don't know. Forever, probably. I look them in the eyes and say to myself, 'I meet you.'"

"It sounds very brave, or inspirational, or something," Vaste said, nodding his head.

Vara gave him another acid look. "I was going to say something of that sort, but with actual sincerity." She shifted her gaze, gentler now, back to Cyrus. "I suppose they taught you that in the Society of Arms."

"No, I learned that before the Society," Cyrus said, turning his attention back to J'anda, who was standing quietly a few steps behind them. "Well, what do we think?"

"I think we need to attend our regularly scheduled Council meeting," Curatio offered.

"I meant," Cyrus said, drawing upon patience he didn't know he had, "I wonder what our enchanter thinks of Ehrgraz's openness."

J'anda blinked, eyelids fluttering delicately. "He seemed ... honest enough, I suppose—"

"Did he try to use enchanter magic?" Cyrus asked, spelling it out at last.

"I didn't see any of it from him," J'anda said, shrugging. "But perhaps I wouldn't have, would I, him being a dragon? He seemed to take umbrage when you brought the subject up."

"Dragons don't use magics the way we do in Arkaria," Curatio said, stepping closer. "They consider it to be the work of children."

"So, their children use it, then?" Vaste asked.

"Hardly," Curatio said with an impish smile. "They're too busy hunting and scorching their own food. Do you imagine it's easy to track down any living things in the Ashen Wastelands? I assure you it's not."

"I didn't like that meeting," Cyrus said, shaking his head, deep in his own thoughts.

"Is it because he had a bigger cod than you?" Vaste asked. When every head swiveled to him, he shrugged. "What? I know I'm not the only one who noticed. It was obvious, he didn't even bother to hide it with a loincloth or anything—"

"I didn't like it because there was a lot left unsaid." Cyrus tapped fingers on the side of his helm. "Ehrgraz has been watching me? He's—he's got spies watching the north?"

"Most probably," Curatio said, with his hands behind his back. "He is right, most dragons would consider us beneath their notice. Ehrgraz is no fool, and it does not surprise me that he keeps watch on things up here."

"What do you think he's suggesting in terms of those 'possibilities'?" Cyrus asked, focusing his attention on Curatio. The sun shone down on his black armor, warming him.

"I wouldn't even care to speculate," Curatio said with a shake of the head. "In fact, let me clarify this before you even ask—I do not know the dragons."

"And certainly not well enough to introduce one of their biggest leaders by name, so don't even ask him to!" Vaste said in a faux shout. "Oh, wait, he just introduced you to Ehrgraz personally, didn't he?" Vaste raised an eyebrow and turned to Curatio. "Forgive my sarcasm—"

"Always," Curatio said without expression.

"—but I feel like you're perhaps not being fully honest with us," Vaste finished.

Curatio sighed. "Just because I am familiar with him does not mean that I know him, any more than being somewhat familiar with Malpravus means that he and I are good friends. We had acquaintance in the past, when the elves treated with dragons in days long gone. That acquaintance is long past, and I have no idea what goes on in the land of the dragons at this point." He grew serious. "In short … my ability to help you in this area is hardly comprehensive. Find another tutor."

Cyrus pondered that for a moment, and Vara spoke before he had a chance to get a thought out. "What does that look mean?"

"I think it means he's got a cramp in his buttock," Vaste offered.

"Just a pain there," Cyrus said, sending the troll yet another sour look, "in the form of you." When he looked back to Vara, he said, "Well, I had an idea."

"Figures that would cause you pain."

Vara sent Vaste another searing glance before turning her attention to Cyrus. "What is it?"

"It's a thought, really, though I imagine his look was a little strange because you're not used to seeing it—"

"Vaste!" Cyrus snapped.

"Go on," Vara said, soothingly.

Cyrus turned to J'anda, who stood, placid, still holding his staff. "Well … I was thinking about getting information on the dragons, and my mind came back to where I'd heard the name Ehrgraz before."

Vara placed a hand on his shoulder. "No. You can't be serious."

"Serious? He's *Cyrus!*" Vara's backhand caught Vaste in the nose and made a cracking sound. "Ow. I'll just go bleed quietly over here until I can gather my thoughts enough to cast a healing spell, then."

"Please do," Cyrus said. He felt a tightness inside as he considered the idea again, and it prompted—once more—an outburst of nerves. "We don't really have a lot of solid lines into the dragons, into what they're thinking ..."

"Not anymore, that's true," Curatio said carefully.

"But we still know someone who might," Cyrus said, and he could see by the look on every one of their faces that they knew of whom he was speaking.

"Are you sure about this?" Vara asked quietly, and her mouth settled into a straight line. *She's anxious as well, then.*

"I'm sure we're blind without his help," Cyrus said, settling uneasily upon his course of action. He turned to J'anda. "What do you think?"

The enchanter shrugged lightly, as though it were nothing. "It would not hurt to ask, certainly. I can do it with but a word, if you wish."

"I wish," Cyrus said, taking a long breath. "Please." J'anda nodded slightly, and Cyrus finished his thought. "Ask the Sovereign of Saekaj Sovar if he'd give me—" Vara's hand clinked on his backplate, a little harder than he would have liked, "—give *us* ... an audience."

21.

"So you're going into the dark, huh?" Andren asked, the Reikonos sunshine falling down upon his short-cropped hair. He and Cyrus were walking along the west end of town after having just visited the old guildhall of the Kings of Reikonos. They'd found everything still in order, as always. It was a strange routine to have fallen into, using a check-up on the old horse-barn-turned-barracks-turned-guildhall as an excuse to have a walking chat with his old friend, but they had seemed to do it at least once a month of late, and Cyrus found it always worked as a balm to his occasionally rattled nerves. *It's just nice to get out of Sanctuary and all the questions and long looks from the members every now and again. To go somewhere not hostile, not dangerous.* He caught a glance from a woman in a butcher's apron as she pointed and whispered to a companion as he passed. *On the other hand, maybe it's not so different after all.*

"If Terian will meet with me, I'll go to Saekaj Sovar, yes," Cyrus said, walking slowly down the street. They were reaching the end of the slums and were coming out of the tall eaves that shrouded the valley where the slums were placed. It made the whole section of town dark, torches burning constantly to keep it in even a little light.

"You might be the first person I know who's not a dark elf to go down there, at least without an army at his back like we did a few months ago," Andren said.

"Alaric has been there," Cyrus said. "Curatio, too, at some point, though I got the sense that it was some time back for both of them."

"Well, obviously, what with Alaric being dead this last year now," Andren said, prompting Cyrus to stiffen imperceptibly. "But still, it's a brave thing, going into those depths, knowing it—at least it used to be—a 'death to outsiders' sort of nation. Brave or stupid." He gave it a moment's pondering. "Maybe both, actually."

"If I'm invited, it's probably neither," Cyrus said.

"Yeah, except Terian tried to kill you not terribly long ago," Andren said. "You may forgive and forget these things, but those of us near and dear to your lunkhead arse find ourselves in the unenviable position of doing neither." His face tightened. "In fact, I still desire to give Terian a piece of my mind for that whole business."

"It's all bygones with Terian," Cyrus said, dismissing it as they walked past a glass-windowed jewelry shop that was being gawked at by a young woman in a cotton dress, the air of a middle-class daughter of privilege about her. Cyrus watched her eye several rings until she caught sight of his armored reflection and turned to gawk at him instead. He looked away, trying not to roll his eyes as he did so.

"Yeah, bygones with him, bygones with the girl who slipped into your bed and knifed you—"

"Well, yes," Cyrus said, face suddenly burning, "but that's in the past as well."

"What happened to the bloke who used to walk these streets with me?" Andren asked, clearly rhetorically. "The one who followed the God of War and talked about 'a commitment to battle that no other could match'? I get the feeling he would have dealt with these situations a bit differently, based on what happened with Narstron—"

Cyrus felt a pang of guilt in his stomach at the mention of the name. "That account is settled, too, and you know it."

"Yeah, I get it," Andren said in a bit of a huff, "and I'm not saying that the old Cyrus, the one who screamed and fought until he had to be dragged by ten strong men from Enterra's gates is the sort I would want to catch sight of every day and night in his bitter anger. I'm just saying it might not hurt to bring back a little of that every now and again."

"Blood and vengeance?" Cyrus mused. "You might get some soon, depending on which way we go on this titan business."

Andren was quiet for a long moment. "Well, good. Seems we need a bit of that. Remind people not to muck about with us, no matter how big they are."

"I think that message has mostly gotten across," Cyrus said as he took a turn down a side street. He had paid little attention to where they were going thus far; it wasn't as though Reikonos was a terribly difficult place to navigate. The smell of ale filled the air and he glanced nervously at Andren.

The elf looked back at him. "Don't worry, I smelled it long before you did, and no, I'm not having any."

"Hm," Cyrus said. "Quite the transformation."

"Yeah, you're not the only one who's changed." Andren looked away. "Speaking of … why do we keep coming back here?" He waved vaguely in the direction from which they'd come. "Not that I mind getting a chance to speak to the Man in Black Armor absent all the fawning hangers-on and without his furious wench in tow—"

"I hope you never call her that to her face, because I'd really hate to lose you as a friend."

"Because you'd not be allowed to hang about with me after that?"

"No, because you'd be dead. And painfully, at that."

"Oh. Yeah. Probably." Andren twisted his lips in a look of consideration. "In all seriousness, though—why do we come here? I mean, I remember the history because I was there for it, but you— you've gone from Guildmaster of one guild, a man desirous of increasing his personal power by looting armor and weapons to make him nigh invulnerable—to Guildmaster of another guild, one of the largest, and the undisputed best warrior in the land. Plus, you got your girl finally, the killer woman you've trailed after with a hangdog look for more years than even I can count." He gave Cyrus a knowing look. "Why the trips back through time? You don't long for the miserable old days, do you?"

"No," Cyrus said, shaking his head. "No, it was … it was miserable, you're right." He took a breath. "Though I do miss Narstron. Sometimes …" Cyrus paused, taking stock of his thoughts, trying to piece them together. "Every once in a while, I look back on what happened in the past, and I wonder … if the sacrifices—both the willing and the unwilling … I wonder if they were all worth it." He sniffed, taking in a breath of fresh air into his nose. He caught the aroma of fresh-baked bread and it reminded him of memories long past. "Narstron, Niamh, Alaric, Luukessia … my ambitions and my choices have led us to some dark places." He shook his head. "I wonder sometimes if there was a more … painless way to get there. An easier way, watered with fewer tears."

"Don't go admitting to crying now," Andren said, looking around almost nervously, "you'll sully your grand image."

"We've lost people," Cyrus said, unashamed of his emotions. "We watched—well, I watched—a land burn in its entirety because of my choices. And just last year, I lost a battle that cost us the lives of some five thousand of our guildmates. Most guilds would break at those numbers, but here we are, plowing onward and ready to face death yet again, possibly." Cyrus cringed and watched a woman walk by with a child at her side, little hand in hers, paying him no mind. "At what point does it end?"

"Heh," Andren said. "At what point does battle end? Kind of a funny question for a warrior of Bellarum, isn't it?"

"I'm ..." Cyrus adjusted his helm, rubbing at his forehead, kneading the skin with metal fingers. "We've fought a lot. More than almost anyone but maybe the big three. The idea of sinking ourselves into a long, drawn-out conflict with the titans in the south, one where ... they could attack our guildhall or Emerald Fields at any time?" He shook his head. "This is not the sort of battle I want to embrace. It's not a contest of warriors. Put me on the field against whoever you want—Talikartin, the Emperor Razeel ... I'll fight them all. I'll die, maybe, but I'll fight until the end." He felt his jaw tighten. "But it's not just me anymore, and it hasn't been for a long time. When it was you and I and Narstron, the stakes were lower, the foes smaller, less skilled. Now we're fighting gods and titans and creatures of death ... and it's not just me on the line now. It's the people I care about."

"Oh, wow, you've changed," Andren said, shaking his head. "Oh, gods, what a difference."

"Good or bad?" Cyrus asked.

"Well, I wouldn't go talking this line in the middle of the guildhall in a speech," Andren said quietly, looking around as though someone were listening in. "I mean, it's not exactly the sort of inspiring talk even Alaric would have given, if you know what I mean."

"And I wouldn't," Cyrus said. "I know the expectations; these people didn't join Sanctuary to sit around. Even the ones who believe in our 'glorious purpose' might not stick around if we didn't keep the gold constantly flowing into their pockets the way we have. It's just ... it's an adjustment, moving from General, where all I had to worry about was the fight, to being the Guildmaster, where I have to worry about what happens after the fight." He swallowed heavily. "And I've never had a consequence after the fight like we did after Leaugarden."

"If you're looking for ways to avoid this southern war," Andren said quietly and somewhat stiffly, "maybe you should look to the people whose responsibility it actually is to worry about the titan border."

"The King of the Elves?" Cyrus scoffed. "You heard Nyad. The entirety of Arkaria east of the Perda will sink into the sea before he gets off his royal arse and does something."

"I'm the last person to defend the nobility," Andren said carefully as a child ran between them, howling merrily. He paused to watch him go. "But Danay ... he'll listen to you, and if he doesn't listen to you, he'll probably listen to the woman you're currently bedding—"

"I'm going to miss you when she kills you."

"Feh," Andren said, with a wave of the hand. "I got my own woman to watch my back now."

Cyrus frowned. "You do? Who?"

Andren lowered his voice. "Martaina."

Cyrus felt a rough stab of guilt. "You might want to take a pinch of caution with that one—"

"I know, I know," Andren said. "She's been around the old curtain wall a few times. As have I, I might add—"

"That's not what I meant," Cyrus said, "I was referring to the fact that she's still married to Thad."

"Not so," Andren said, shaking his head. "They're separating even now. She's already moved in with me."

Cyrus looked at him dully. "Are you going to cause drama in my council, Andren?"

"It's amicable!" Andren said, holding up his hands. "We sat at dinner with him just the other night! It's a gentle, necessary parting of the ways." He paused and blinked. "I think he's actually a bit relieved. Tough to satisfy a woman who's lived over a thousand years, y'see, unless you've been around as long—"

"Okay," Cyrus said, shaking his head as he started away. "Well, that's a thought that's bound to haunt me at night—"

"I wouldn't worry, your wench hasn't been around nearly that long, after all—"

"She will kill you. Murderously bloody, that's how it would be, with your head held aloft on a pike as an example to every new recruit—"

"She'd have to catch me first."

"Have you seen her jump? No contest." Cyrus shook his head, eyes falling over the building in front of them, an old wooden inn. He thought it a bit curious, squinting as the overhead sun half-blinded him. He sought out the hanging sign and peered at it, trying to discern the name of the establishment. "Youryn's Tree," he read aloud. The paint was peeling and fading on the sign, looking as if it had been redone quite a while back, and the efforts were gradually wearing off.

"Strange name for a human pub," Andren said.

"Does that sound elven to you?" Cyrus asked, stepping closer, drawn for a strange reason he couldn't even fully define for himself. His palms were sweating, and he looked down the street, a collection of homes that were one and two stories, simple wooden houses, some older stonework dwellings mixed in for variety.

"Sounds like someone doesn't know how to name a damned drinking establishment," Andren groused. "Who wants to drink in a tree?"

"The elves of Amti, apparently."

"They're an odd lot," Andren said. "I mean, I've never had a love of the monarchy, but the extremes they've gone to—"

"They have children," Cyrus said, wandering closer to the pub's door and the sign that hung above it.

"Who doesn't?" Andren asked. "I mean, other than elven men of my age and perhaps younger."

"They have elven children," Cyrus said, stopping just in front of the door to the pub. "Full-blood." He glanced back at Andren, who was peering at him with a hearty frown. "Curse doesn't affect them, it seems."

"Bloody hell," Andren muttered. After a pause, he spoke again. "You're not actually stopping off for a pint, are you? Because I mean, really—years you and I hung about, and now's the time you pick to finally indulge? After I've given up—"

"I'm not stopping for—" Cyrus just cut himself off and looked up at the sign. It was only a half-foot above his face, hidden under the shadow of the pub's eaves. He raised a finger, inexplicably, to the peeling paint. He felt drawn to it by forces he couldn't even understand, and he rubbed it with his gauntlet, causing a small flake to fall and exposing a rather heartier coat of paint beneath it. It exposed the first letter of a word that he was able to piece together by the strategic loss of some of the other chips.

Fish, he read.

Casting a wary eye at the door, he rubbed his thumb against the top of the sign, peeling off a long strip.

"Oy!" Andren hissed. "What are you doing? Knock it off!"

But Cyrus did not, ripping the flakes free and letting them float to the dirty street as he puzzled over the top line of the signage. "Rotten," he read aloud. "The Rotten Fish."

"Congratulations," Andren said, sliding closer and speaking even lower. "You've figured out that the pub with the dumbest name I've ever seen was once a pub with yet an even dumber name. Bravo on that, my friend. Now, can we get out of here?"

"This was the Rotten Fish," Cyrus said, stepping back out onto the street. He looked up and down it, but nothing looked terribly familiar. He stared hard in one direction, then the other, with no luck.

"I think we already established that, yes. Why does this matter?"

"I used to live near the Rotten Fish," Cyrus said, staring back down the street again. He started off at a hard walk, picking one of the directions and just going with it. He made long strides all the way to the next intersection and stopped, glancing from a newer house on one corner to a slightly older house on the other.

"Now that we're a safe distance away from where you committed your defacement of private property," Andren said, catching up to Cyrus more than a little winded, "maybe you can tell me why this matters? You trying to take a sudden trip down a different memory lane? Because speaking from experience, those roads never seem to be in good repair, and that old sod about never being able to go home again? Too true."

"You're right about that one," Cyrus said, looking at both of the houses and feeling nothing. Neither one of them looked familiar. He glanced back down the street toward the Rotten Fish. "I never saw my house again—the one I grew up in—after age six. By the time the Society turned loose of me at eighteen, and I got my freedom, I couldn't find it. Everything had changed." He squinted, but found no satisfaction looking down at the opposite end of the street. "I always wanted to go back—just go back, one last time, but I couldn't—" He sighed. "It's all gone," he said, resignedly. "That's what happens to the past," Andren said, and he placed a hand on Cyrus's shoulder. Cyrus looked at the elf and he nodded his head slowly. "It's true. The past is a shadow, and no matter how much you chase it, you'll never catch it. It's vapor in your hands, a dark tinge that runs across the ground ahead of or behind you, and you'll never do anything more than see a hint of the way things were." He looked around with a heavy distaste. "Come on. You've still got a future, and that, my friend, is almost as tangible as the present."

"I suppose," Cyrus said, and he started back toward the tall Citadel in the distance that marked the direction of the Great Square of Reikonos and the wizard waiting to carry them home. Thoughts of the future did not stop him from looking back, though, nor from memorizing every turn it took to get to the establishment that had been the Rotten Fish in his youth, for he felt certain that at some point in that future, he would return.

22.

"This promises to be a busy day," Cyrus said, snugging the strap of his armor. It was polished to a blackened sheen at the behest of Vara, who stood next to him in the tower of the Guildmaster putting on her own armor.

"I confess that when you asked to have this meeting set, I wondered a bit," Vara said, picking up her helm and putting it atop her head, the noseguard flipped up. "But I suppose it is sound strategy to search out every possible avenue."

Cyrus ignored the stirring within as her choice of words brought up memories of his walk with Andren a few days earlier, and the peculiar search of the Reikonos streets for a place he had long ago left. "I have been accused of charging recklessly into action by some." He gave her a pointed smile, which she returned. "This time, I thought perhaps I'd try something new and seek out different options."

"Well, you've certainly done that in this case," she said, giving him an appraising eye from head to toe. "And I don't think I've ever seen your armor look so close to presentable before. It almost looks like polished onyx."

Cyrus sniffed at the curious smell of the polish she'd used. "What is this?"

"It's a kind of wax they sell in the Kingdom," Vara said, turning to head for the door, her steps crisp. He fell in behind her and they moved as one without even having to think about it. *But then, it's been that way between us for a long while, even when we fought each other we could move in battle together like no one else.* "If you fancy it, I'm sure we could get you some—give the Guildmaster of Sanctuary a new look, something

115

a bit more in keeping with your station."

"A year ago, you would have been the last person I'd thought would be giving me advice about improving my appearance," Cyrus said as they circled the tower stairs past the Council Chambers, "unless it involved getting my face mashed into slurry by troll punches."

"Not so," Vara said, "I have always found you rather attractive. It was your frustratingly stubborn personality I would have preferred to have ground to meal." She flashed him a smile.

"Ugh!" Vaste's voice came from behind the partially closed Council Chamber doors, followed by a sound of retching. "Just go to bed together already!"

"We did," Cyrus called over his shoulder as they descended. "Twice this morning, in fact!" When he turned back, he saw Vara's cheeks flush. "Sorry. He practically cried out for it."

"No, it's fine, anything you throw at Vaste is perfectly acceptable in the spirit of trouncing some of the humor out of that jester," she said, shaking her head. "I was merely thinking about a few years ago, when my mother," she cringed slightly, "said all those things about us rutting together. She had the measure of me then, knew me better than I knew myself."

"You're not the only one who questions how well they know themselves, at least lately," Cyrus said, giving the matter some thought. "Though I admit I'm a bit curious to hear you thinking about it in any depth." He stared down at her as her head bobbed with each step. "*You're* not having some existential crisis that I need to worry about, are you?"

"Nothing of the sort," she said. Her expression was utterly unguarded and held just a hint of worry. "I merely ... well ... it is a little difficult for me sometimes to find myself adjusting to this relationship." She held up a hand. "That sounds wrong. Wait. Let me explain. This has been a surprisingly easy transition over the last months. Things have been ... well, better than I can remember, actually. Much smoother than I would have predicted, given the speed with which we have moved."

"Well, we kind of circled each other in some form of mortal combat for about five years before getting to this point," Cyrus said wryly, "it probably took some of the fight out of both of us."

"You hardly seem lacking for energy," she quipped. "But I think you know of what I speak—liaisons may happen quickly, but the fast ones always burn out the swiftest." She paused on the staircase. "I think what I am trying to say is … this is not one of those occasions. I grow fonder of you with each passing day, Cyrus Davidon."

"I love you, too," Cyrus said without thinking, and then froze as he realized what he said. *Uhh … I hadn't said that to her before, had I?* In fact he knew he had not, though he had pondered it and intended fully to keep it suppressed within until she spoke it aloud first. *There goes that plan.*

"Did you just say …?" she looked at him in wonder.

"I believe I did," he said, a little uncertainly.

She stared at him for a long moment then broke into a smile. "I love you, too, you clod. I wondered when you would develop the courage to say it." And then she turned, and started back down the stairs.

"What, is your mouth suffering injury?" he asked, trailing behind her. "You could have said it first if you felt that way."

"And risk you snubbing me? Never." But she shot him an impish grin, and he could not help but laugh. As they drew closer to the bottom of the stairs, her pace slowed, and he moved to match her. "Do you think …" she hesitated. "Do you think it will last?"

"Having never really been in what you could call a successful relationship," Cyrus said, feeling her tentativeness and reaching for her hand. Their gauntlets clinked. "I suppose I don't know what it takes to 'make it work.' But," he said, forcing a smile through his own hesitancy—it did not take much with her in front of him, "as I said, we've been circling each other for five years. By now I think you've seen the best and worst of me. We've been enemies and friends, and spent a good portion of that time somewhere in between … there's no mystery between us now, Vara." He cradled her smaller gauntlet in his own, wishing that neither of them were wearing the obstructive things. "If anyone knows me and could tolerate me, I suspect it would be you, since we've been together for a few months now and you haven't even thrown a heavy object at my head lately—"

"I'm saving it for a choice occasion," she said, "some particularly dunderheaded act on your part will see something metal whisked at your skull faster than you can say, 'Dall diddly lye.'"

He froze, trying to translate that. "'Earthwork baby doll'?"

"Thank Vidara you're better as a lover than you are at elvish," she said, taking hold of his hand and dragging him down.

"I'd really rather you thank me for that than the Goddess … rather laboriously, later, maybe—"

"Again? Truly?" She gave him a look of exasperation. "Perhaps if we make it through all this day entails, I will consider it."

"That's a 'no,' isn't it?"

"Woe betide you if I find something heavy and metal right now, Cyrus Davidon. It's a good thing you're wearing your helm." She hesitated. "Does it concern you?"

"You throwing something at me?" Cyrus asked. "You've got some strength, but as you pointed out, I am wearing my helm—"

"Our second meeting, dolt."

"The first worries me more," Cyrus said, pensive. "Is that strange?"

"Very strange for a normal person," she said, biting her lip. "But not for you, warrior mine. You are more comfortable with the things you can fight, and you flounder about with the things that you can't."

"I definitely can't fight this one," Cyrus said as they strode off the stairs and into the foyer. The morning sun was casting purple light through the massive stained glass window above the main doors, and Nyad stood waiting for them in the middle of the great seal. The guard was trebled, an enormous circle of uneasy warriors, rangers and all manner of other defenders. He saw Thad standing nearby, watching the whole scene with concern.

"Sir," Thad said, addressing Cyrus in the same formal way he had even before he'd been the castellan of Sanctuary or an officer.

"Thad," Cyrus said, nodding at the red-armored warrior. He spared a thought for the man going through a divorce. *I remember what that's like, and in spite of what Andren said, it can't be an easy thing. Still, he's here, and doing his duty.* "As soon as we leave … close the portal to all traffic. We can walk from the one outside the gates when we return. No need to give the titans an easy in; keep it closed until further notice."

"Aye, sir," Thad said, relaxing only an inch. "I'll see it's done."

Cyrus nodded, then turned his attention to Nyad. He felt Vara drop his hand as she drew herself up to her full height, which was still a head and a half less than his. "Are you ready?" he asked Vara, who still looked stiff in spite of their long, informal conversation on the way down.

"As ready as I can be for this," she said, expression as neutral as he could recall seeing it outside of a battlefield. "And you?"

"If I'm not ready, I will be soon," Cyrus said, pursing his lips. "Nyad ... take us to see your father."

23.

The royal palace of Pharesia was a grand thing both inside and out, and full of the greenery of life that the elves seemed to love with all their hearts. Privately, Cyrus wondered how many gardeners and how much gold it took to maintain the glorious and beautiful heart of the elven kingdom, for it certainly did not look the way Reikonos did, with all its function over form, and its mismatched architecture. It did not even have a royal palace the way Pharesia did, and he could not think of a single building that the humans built anywhere in the entire Confederation that matched the grandeur, scale and expense of the larger buildings that the elves constructed. *I suppose they're built to endure for thousands of years, by people who fully plan to inhabit them most of that while.*

"Do you find this table to your liking, Lord Davidon?" the man way down at the head of the table asked. He seemed to be roughly a mile off. They were sitting in a dining room that should have been bitterly cold, given its immensity and the time of year, but in fact it was warm enough for plant life to be growing all around him. It was something like a conservatory, save for the mammoth table at the center of the room. Greenery abounded, even in the centerpieces of the table, which prevented him from looking directly at Vara. She sat immediately opposite him, delicately eating with the thinnest fork he'd ever seen.

"I'm afraid I can't hear you as well as I might care to, your Grace," Cyrus called to King Danay I, the monarch of the entire Elven Kingdom. He was seated roughly a hundred feet away, at the far end of the table. A host of bowls and plates filled with every sort of meat and dishes beyond Cyrus's imagination covered at least ten feet of the table in front of him. Cyrus, for his part, had a similar grouping of dishes in front of him, far more weighted toward meats and cheeses than the green vegetables that he could barely see in front of Vara across the table. Her feast seemed to blend in with the centerpiece, and he dismissed it with only a thought of disgust. "My human ears might not be up to the task of having a conversation in this place."

The King muttered something down the table which Cyrus did not hear, but it drew a scandalized look from Vara. When he looked at her questioningly, she merely blushed and said, "It is not worthy of repeating."

"Tell me later?" he asked, genuinely curious.

"I said we might as well yell," Danay said, as Cyrus squinted to look at the man, "for doubtless any conversation you wish to have will devolve into that sooner or later anyway."

Cyrus looked at Vara. "That wasn't so bad."

"I also used several elven terms to disparage your parentage," Danay admitted, lowering his voice only slightly. From this distance, Cyrus could not even see his face. "Rather casually, I might add."

"I'd be more offended by that if I knew the terms, perhaps," Cyrus said, "or if I knew my parents better. Though I'm a bit surprised you'd take aim at my father in such a way, given his service to the Elven Kingdom."

Danay chewed loudly on something before answering. "The Hero of Dismal Swamp?" He swallowed loudly. "Who said I insulted your father?"

"I have a hard time getting upset about you insulting my mother given that you didn't know her even half as well as I did," Cyrus said, trying to keep a tight rein on his patience. He couldn't see Danay's reaction to that, but he caught a flash of something from Vara. "Can we merely talk about the south? No degenerative argument intended, I assure you."

"And yet I suspect we will have one nonetheless," King Danay said, "for you are already quite clear on my position in this matter."

"Then you know what I've come here to ask," Cyrus said, staring down the table at him.

"I know you've met with an envoy from Amti, yes," King Danay said, picking up a goblet. "I would caution you, Lord Davidon, not only does every single one of my counterparts in every power and principality know this simple fact, they also are likely aware that you have traveled to Amti and that you are mulling action in the south. Which I would advise you against."

"And that means a lot, coming from a man who just admitted he's spying on my guild," Cyrus said tightly. *Who just admitted he has spies in my guild.*

"I admit it," King Danay said, taking a swig. "And why would I not? Only a fool would have such an army as yours bordering him without taking into consideration that your allegiances may change. You are, after all, not one of my lords on tight rein, but an independent one—"

"Granted that by you—"

"—and by others," Danay finished sharply. "Had I known you would come by those permissions so swiftly after I gave you our claim, I might have hesitated to give it over to you. But no matter now, you are the Lord of Perdamun. You answer to no one and are watched by everyone. And so I know that you consider action in the south. I say again: don't be a fool. It is not a land for those of our stature. Let the titans and the dragons have it."

"You'd pass up on the riches of Amti that easily?" Cyrus asked. "Relinquish the quartal mines without a fight?"

"I have no fight to give," King Danay said, now steepling his hands in front of him. "You know the state of my kingdom. I cannot afford to lose soldiers, and I would lose them beyond numbering if I took my army on a march through the Gradsden Savanna to engage that particular enemy."

"Did you know they've learned magic?" Vara asked quietly.

"Word had reached my ears of that, shelas'akur, yes," Danay said, turning his attention to her. "And before you ask, I do not know the origin of their new skill, and in truth, I don't care. The goblin is out of the cave, as it were, and we are left to deal with the reality of things— the titans are a nearly unstoppable enemy with magic on their side, and I don't wish to fight them."

"You may not have a choice," Cyrus said darkly. "If they come for the pass—"

"Even now," Danay said, cutting him off, "our engineers are burying tons of Dragon's Breath at several strategic points throughout the Heia Pass. If they come north through that route, they will find themselves buried under rock and stone, and a threat to no one."

"They have magic," Cyrus said. "They don't need to come north through the pass. What's your plan to deal with a thousand titans teleporting into the fields outside Pharesia, or smashing through the gates of Elintany?"

King Danay paused for a moment. "We are ... considering this problem."

"Well, consider this," Cyrus said, leaning forward and thumping a gauntlet on the table, rattling the fine silverware and china. "It'll be easier to deal with them with the help of allies—allies like Sanctuary, and possibly others."

"You come straight out of one war that nearly destroyed our world," Danay said, so quietly Cyrus struggled to hear him even in the stark silence of the green-tinged dining hall, "and are so eager to plunge right into another. Truly, I do not wonder that you were the favored of Bellarum."

"I don't want this war," Cyrus said hotly, "but your people are standing in harm's way, and presently—as far as I know—Amti has the only pure-blood elven children other than her," he pointed at Vara, "born in two centuries. Are you aware of this?"

Danay did not stir but his answer came swiftly. "I am."

"And you don't care?" Cyrus looked at him in disbelief. "She's not the last born anymore. Amti could hold the future of your kingdom."

"It would take weaker ears than mine not to have heard the sentiments of Amti's citizens regarding my rule," Danay said stiffly. "And it would take perhaps a stronger man than me to ignore that in the face of all other considerations—the foe we face, the distance away they are, the danger of war with the titans so soon after the destruction of our fight with the dark elves ... I believe it would take nearly human ears to have missed all that."

You royal prick, Cyrus thought. "It wouldn't take human ears," he said instead, "just a frozen heart."

"I think we have reached our end," King Danay said, and a steward stepped up to slide his chair out. The King was clad in his rainbow garb, so bright and beautiful that when last Cyrus had seen it up close, he'd wondered how many years and how many master seamstresses it had taken to craft it. "I bid you better luck in your next meeting, Cyrus Davidon." With a polite nod and a bow, he turned toward Vara. "Shelas'akur. I wish you both ... whatever measure of happiness you might find together." And he stiffly walked out of the dining hall.

"The hell?" Cyrus asked, turning to Vara. "Was he being a jackass because he genuinely can't help, or was there an undercurrent of tension because I'm sleeping with his nation's last hope?"

"I wouldn't care to wager on which was the winning factor in this decision," Vara said, placing her napkin in a balled-up wad on her plate. "But I daresay the decision was made before word of our request for an audience was received." Her eyes narrowed. "Perhaps long, long before."

24.

"This place brings back bad memories," Cyrus said as he stood with Vara in the darkened hall. The mighty wooden throne that had once rested in the Sovereign's chamber was gone, replaced by a dual throne that stood in the middle of the room and looked, to Cyrus's eyes, slightly more approachable than the monstrosity that Yartraak had sat upon. It certainly looked less luxuriant, though now it was as empty as Yartraak's had been when last Cyrus had been here.

"I don't care for the wait," Vara said, looking about nervously. There were guards at the back of the room, barring their exit. Curatio had teleported Cyrus and Vara directly into the Grand Palace of Saekaj, and then left them to be escorted to the throne room while the healer had remained behind in what looked to Cyrus like little more than a broom closet. *A broom closet guarded by half a hundred dark elves with spears and swords*, he thought. *At least Terian learns that much from his predecessor's errors.*

"I heard you had a meeting with the King of the Elves before you came here," Terian's voice rang out from somewhere in the dark behind the throne. Cyrus squinted to see him, but without the benefit of any sort of spell to increase his visual acuity, he failed to discern so much as a shadow. "I assume it went badly?"

"Fair assumption," Cyrus answered into the darkness. "King Danay has some trepidation after the war with your people." He looked at Vara, whose features were barely visible even next to him. *Damnable eyes. Why did humans get the worst eyes in Arkaria?* Vara turned to look at him and he was treated with a blast of her blue irises. *Like those. Those are beautiful.*

"I know how he feels," Terian said from somewhere in the

darkness, though Cyrus could tell by the sound of boots on wood that he was approaching. "I've felt much the same, drawing a circle around myself and placing all the people I care about within it. All else? I would have been content to watch burn, so long as those I counted most dear were protected."

"Is that so?" Cyrus asked, feeling a tinge of sourness on his tongue and in his mind. "You still feel that way, do you?"

"Less and less," Terian said, still invisible in shadow. "But it was how I was in Sanctuary, obviously. How I was as you knew me."

"Until you found a mystical berry tonic that cleansed the selfish asshole out of your soul?" Cyrus asked, losing all patience with the Sovereign of Saekaj and his hiding in the dark.

Terian's laugh echoed in the hall, and he stepped into the light, causing Cyrus to only stifle a gasp by long experience at hiding his emotions. "Something like that," Terian said, making a flourish of his hand that encompassed his entire armor from head to toe. The smile was visible in a way it wouldn't have been had Terian been wearing the armor Cyrus had always known him to wear. *But this …*

Cyrus swallowed heavily, as though he could compel the incredible wash of feelings attacking him to leave him alone simply by hoping for them to. "That's a new look for you."

"We can't all pull off wearing black all the time," Terian said, stepping further into the light. Cyrus stared at him, wondering if an illusion would drop, if his vision would clear, if somehow, some way, he would change his shape back into the old Terian, and not this one …

… this one who was clad in the armor of Alaric Garaunt from helm to boot.

"I wondered where that helm went," Cyrus said, tasting something acrid in his mouth. "Curatio told me not to worry about it."

"You should have asked your lover," Terian said, looking at Vara, his eyes glinting through the thin slits of the helm. "She was the one who gave it to me."

Cyrus slowly turned his head to look at her and found her waiting with an offhand shrug. "He needed it to complete the ensemble," she said simply. "And he was about to be somewhat embroiled in a battle for the fate of his city at the time."

Cyrus looked back at the Sovereign of Saekaj Sovar and noticed at last the axe slung across his back. "Is that ...?"

Terian drew it slowly, hefting it in his hand and swinging it once before reversing his grip and offering Cyrus the long heft. "Noctus, the Battle Axe of Darkness."

Cyrus narrowed his eyes unconsciously. "... So now *you* have a godly weapon, too?"

"Is that a hint of jealousy I hear?" Terian almost sounded like he was crowing.

"More like worry," Cyrus said, "since your last weapon did end up causing me some minor harm, and it wasn't quite so powerful as the current one."

Terian took another step forward, offering him the long handle of the axe. "I meant it when I said it was over on my end, Cyrus. When I got your message inquiring about help, I sent a reply offering this meeting as quickly as I could. My desire to put the past behind us is sincere."

"Put your axe away," Cyrus said, dismissing him with a wave of the hand. Terian spun it in his grip and did exactly as asked in the flash of a second, causing Cyrus a moment's alarm. "Is that ... what I look like when I'm wielding Praelior?"

"Something like that, I suspect," Terian said, stepping closer now that he was unarmed. "So ... you had a run-in with Ehrgraz, yes?"

"He came for a visit," Cyrus said, "and I'm hesitant to trust his word."

"Don't hesitate," Terian said, shaking his head as he removed Alaric's helm—his helm—from his head. "Ehrgraz's word is good. If he offers you counsel or alliance in this, he's sincere. Ehrgraz is like the lone voice of reason among the dragons." He put a hand through his hair, which glistened with sweat in the torchlight. "He's been warning them for centuries that the titans were going to be a threat, but no one wants to listen."

"If they haven't listened to him thus far," Vara said, "why would they start now?"

"I'm at a loss to explain that," Terian said. "I assume he has a plan of some sort." His eyes fixed on Cyrus. "As do you."

"You don't even have to assume that," Cyrus observed. "You know."

"I know," Terian said. "When have you ever gotten close to a battle without a plan? I knew the minute I heard about Emerald Fields that you'd be working on something." He beckoned them toward the throne. "Spill it. What's the idea?"

Cyrus hesitated. "Listen ... I just need your help with the dragon end of—"

"So you don't want my troops?" Terian asked, turning around, lips thin and light blue from pressing together in a straight line as he waited for Cyrus's answer.

Cyrus exchanged a look with Vara. "You just came out of a war—"

"And if the titans decide to come north," Terian said, looking at him evenly, "we'll be in another. Emerald Fields is feeding Saekaj and Sovar at the moment. Much like Vaste, if someone attacks our food, we take umbrage."

Cyrus peered at him in the dark. "You're willing to do this? To fight with us?" *What's your game, Terian?*

"Couldn't pick a better partner, really," Terian said with a shrug. "I don't know many in Arkaria who fight like you two."

"You trying to make up for your attempt to kill me?" Cyrus asked.

Terian made another sweeping gesture at his new armor, and there was an unmistakable sadness in his answer. "Just trying to walk the path."

Cyrus traded another uneasy glance with Vara, who seemed to be experiencing considerably less doubt than he was. "We don't even know if we're going to get involved in this yet—" he started to say.

"Oh, you will," Terian said with a quick nod. "And when you do, let me know, because we'll be right there with you." He stepped up and took his seat on the left hand throne, and now Cyrus saw him sink a little into the padding of the chair. "We don't have as much as we did before the war, but we've got some spellcasters we can bring to the fight, some warriors and rangers, and ..." he reached up and slapped the handle of his axe, "... me, of course."

"You?" Cyrus asked, staring at him in surprise. "You're the Sovereign."

"I'm also the foremost paladin in Saekaj and Sovar," Terian said, smiling just a little smugly.

It took Cyrus a moment to fully comprehend what he'd said, and when he looked at Vara, he could tell she was getting to the conclusion at the same time he was. "I'm sorry ..." she said, speaking first, "… but you meant 'dark knight,' right?"

Terian just smiled and raised a hand at a torch in a sconce some twenty feet away. With a movement of the lips, a small blast of force shot forth from his hand and snuffed the torch, sending it clattering to the ground and decreasing Cyrus's ability to see by a considerable margin. "I said what I meant, I meant what I said," the Sovereign's voice echoed in the hall. "Call on me when you've decided to pursue this thing. I'll be with you, completely."

Cyrus stood blinking while he waited for some further signal. It was only when Vara took hold of his arm and began to lead him out that he realized Terian must have departed. "What the hell was that?" he asked when they were nearly out the door of the throne room.

"A white knight," she said, sounding considerably more relaxed than he felt, "and we should thank our respective gods for him, because if ever there was a clearer sign than that to indicate Terian has changed, I don't know what it would be."

"If he was wearing a tutu and dancing around the throne room?" Cyrus suggested as the throne room doors were opened by the guards. Cyrus caught a dirty look from one of them and he shrugged. "If this is a sign, I don't know what exactly it's a sign of, other than that perhaps some luck has finally broken our way."

"At long last," Vara said, as they were led back through dark and winding corridors to the portal which would take them home.

25.

Cyrus sat at the head of the Council Chamber, all of them assembled around him, looking at the uncertain faces before him, and took a deep breath of the sweet, smokeless scent of the torches as night fell out the window behind him. "And so here we are," he announced, feeling strangely like the previous occupant of the chair.

"Gods, that's a bit of the dramatic," Vaste said. "As though we've strolled up to some momentous occasion rather than being blindsided by a raft filled to the brimming with oversized turds."

"This is a serious decision," Cyrus said, watching the assemblage around the table ripple at Vaste's pronouncement. Cattrine was there, along with all of the officers, their faces lit by the orange glow of the torches. "This will have far-reaching consequences—"

"Can we just beat the holy hell out of these bastards already?" Longwell asked, his lance leaned up against the table next to him, its large and unwieldy head always maintaining perfect balance where he set it.

"They've called down the thunder," Andren agreed. "The great big gits deserve a bit of the lightning, too."

"They have lightning of their own," Cyrus said, cautioning them.

"All our foes have," J'anda said from his place next to Curatio. His own staff leaned against the table like Longwell's. "Save for the dead."

"This is nothing like facing gods," Erith agreed, her blue skin looking almost like a piece of cloth had been cut out of night and draped over her. "Is it?"

"They *might* be as strong as them," Cyrus said, looking at each of them in turn.

"And if your aunt had the appropriate genitals, she'd be your uncle," Vaste said.

"That doesn't make sense," Andren said after a moment's pause had filled the chamber. "If—"

"It doesn't matter," Vaste said, waving him off, "the point is—"

"Wait, we get interrupted by you in the middle of making points all the time," Vara said. "It feels as though there should be some level of reciprocity—"

"I don't interrupt you all the time—" Vaste started.

"Oh, it's all the time," Curatio said, looking particularly bleary-eyed.

"All of it," Ryin said. "Every single—"

"Well, you, of course, yes," Vaste said. "But the rest of you—"

"I can't get a word in edgewise without you dropping some humorous observation into the mix," Cyrus said.

"And possibly you—" Vaste said.

"And me," Vara said.

Vaste looked at her and sighed. "Yes. Okay. Criticism taken to heart; it won't happen again. Now if I may wend back to my original point without interruption—"

"Gonna go with 'nope' on that," Erith cut in with a smirk.

"How have I so wronged you?" Vaste asked, looking near the edge of exasperation.

"We don't have time for you to atone for all your snarky interruptions right now, Vaste, we'd be here not only all night, but all the nights from here until the day of Arkaria's fateful end," Cyrus said. "This war, this one that you all seem so keen to charge into—it will have repercussions." He looked at the faces around the table once more. "This is not going to be an easy fight, and it may not be one that we can win."

"We've won every fight ever thrown at us," Mendicant said with a surprising amount of confidence. "Why should this be any different?"

"Every one of these creatures is of godlike stature," Cyrus said, "and though their strength isn't quite godlike, it's not far behind. Now, with magic as their ally, we can no longer hide before them as we did before. Their power ... it's increased by a very fair margin."

"I'm not afraid of some overgrown, rude beasts that need a lesson in manners," Nyad huffed.

"They could likely march from one end of your father's kingdom to the other and still have plenty enough strength left once there to kill all the remaining trolls," Cyrus warned. "These creatures are dangerous."

"We have allies," J'anda said.

"We have Terian," Cyrus said, "and a handful of elves from Amti."

"We have our whole army," Longwell said, watching Cyrus carefully, his eyes focused on the warrior. "Are you afraid to fight this battle, Guildmaster?"

"Not for my own sake," Cyrus said. "I am hesitant because this is the fight which could hurt us beyond any we've ever been in."

"I doubt that very much," Longwell said, a little hoarsely.

"If I may," Cattrine said, speaking up from her place just past Vara, "I think we all acknowledge that you will face risks, but the greater risk here may be that the titans do exactly what they promised—and bring havoc and destruction all across the north, and here to your very halls."

"It wouldn't be the first time," Vara said darkly.

"Then let's make that the last," Cyrus said quietly, and every head turned to him. He looked them all over, saw the tentativeness there, the wonder at what their Guildmaster was thinking. "They mean to have a war. Let us give them one that will deprive them of any notion that war is a pastime that they ever want to engage in again."

"You mean it, then?" Longwell asked, somewhat skeptical.

"All in favor?" Cyrus asked. A weak chorus of ayes filled the room. "Any nays?" Silence followed. "The defenses of Sanctuary are as good as we can make them. Now we need to embark on solidifying our strategy."

"Which is?" Vaste asked.

Cyrus took a long breath. "I need to consult with Ehrgraz first before deciding, but ... I have an early plan."

"So long as your plan is the only thing early about you, perhaps Vara will forgive you," Vaste said, drawing a look of pure ire from her. "Still, perhaps you might share this idea with us?"

Cyrus surveyed the table, finding undisguised curiosity all around it. "All right," he said in resignation, "here it is—to march our entire army across the Gradsden Savanna and storm the front gates of Kortran, killing every single soldier we come across and mangling the bodies beyond resurrection until we cannot handle one more solitary minute of slaughter." Cyrus watched the faces around the table change from curiosity to dawning unease.

"But you've talking all this time about how tough the titans are going to be," Vaste said. "If they're that tough, they're unlikely to let us just come in the front gate, are they?"

"They are not," Cyrus agreed, "and if that's the case," he swallowed heavily, "then we'll need to fight for every single inch of ground until we can get into the heart of Kortran and inflict more punishment than they can possibly weather ... because if we don't," and now he saw a different look on the faces around him, of horror settling in at the predicament they were now in, "those followers of Bellarum will never, ever let us rest until they've killed us all to the last."

26.

Ehrgraz came out of the sky as promised only a day later, and Cyrus was ready on the wall when the great dragon landed and made his approach. Cyrus had let the alarm sound as usual, concerned that if he didn't, Ehrgraz would take that small concession and see weakness in it. Instead, the entirety of Sanctuary stood ready at the walls with Cyrus as the black and red-scaled dragon made his approach, the ground shaking and dust coming loose of the watch tower to Cyrus's left.

"Lovely day, isn't it?" Cyrus asked as the enormous dragon head came up to rest on the parapet of the curtain wall. The yellow eyes stared at Cyrus and he met them, not looking away, and thinking what he always thought in these situations.

Ehrgraz made a rough noise of plain disgust. "The weather? Do you take me for some sort of human dotard that cares anything about the conditions of sky, whether it rains or not?"

"It's called small talk," Cyrus said, unflappable. "You might want to look into it."

"I call it a waste of precious time," Ehrgraz said, smoke pouring out of his nostrils as he spoke. "What say you, Cyrus Davidon, Warden of the Southern Plains?"

"I'll take your counsel," Cyrus said, "and you can count on seeing us in the south very soon."

The dragon surveyed him, eyes blinking in a way that reminded Cyrus of a lizard he'd once seen crawling the shoots in the swamps of the Bandit Lands. "Very good. What is your plan?"

"What is *your* plan?" Cyrus parried.

"I offer only possibilities," Ehrgraz said, but Cyrus thought he detected a hint of regret in the dragon's voice. "But if your strategy is as sound as I suspect it to be, then I will be able to offer more later."

"I want to come at Kortran from the front gate," Cyrus said after a moment's deliberation. "I want to force my way into the city and destroy it."

"Hm," Ehrgraz said, smoke puffing out of his nose this time. "Very straightforward. Not terrible, as ideas go, but prone to a few problems."

"Like twenty-foot-tall, thick-skinned, spell-casting enemies?" Vaste asked.

Ehrgraz's yellow eyes alighted on the troll. "Yes. Exactly that sort. And more."

"Those aren't problems," Cyrus said, "they're opportunities to convince the titans what a very bad idea it is to continue their war with us."

"Well, then you have many opportunities in front of you," Ehrgraz said, "more than you realize, in fact." He sighed, and a black cloud belched out of his snout. "I can see this is going to require a bit of … education. Yes, I'm afraid that's just the thing, no way around it, really …" He sighed again, this time exhaling a white puff of smoke.

"What the blazes is he talking about?" Vaste asked, again not bothering to lower his voice, his sun-dappled green flesh looking almost yellow in the day's light.

"Setting up a school for us?" J'anda asked, shrugging his thin shoulders. "I don't entirely know."

"Shut up," Cyrus said, turning to look at both of them. "You're making me look bad in front of the dragon!"

"Oh, it takes more to irritate me than the petty carping of J'anda Aimant and Vaste the troll," Ehrgraz said, giving each of them a quite hideous gaze. "You require an education, Cyrus Davidon, and I am the one who must give it to you."

"Teach him to spell his name," Vaste said, apparently taking Ehrgraz's invitation to offend quite liberally. "I think he still struggles with that."

"Come along," Ehrgraz said, lifting a wing up and placing it atop the curtain wall, like a bridge between him and Cyrus.

Cyrus eyed the wing then looked to Vara, whose eyes were wide. "You want me to … ride on your back?"

"I assure you," Ehrgraz said with an air of impatience, "I am no more pleased about being saddled like one of your—what do they call them, your beasts of burden?"

"Warriors," Vaste offered helpfully.

Ehrgraz made a horrible noise, something like shavings being scraped off of metal, and it took Cyrus a moment to realize it was the sound of laughter. "That one was not bad," Ehrgraz said once his laughter died down. Then he looked back at Cyrus. "Come along, then. I know this isn't your first time riding a dragon."

Cyrus started to ascend the wing, but Vara's hand on his shoulder stayed him. "Are you out of your mind?" she asked.

"You've often told me as much," Cyrus said.

"She's got the measure of you," Vaste said.

"You're about to climb on the back of that dragon," Vara said, "with no idea of your destination and no promise as to your safe return."

"If he runs into hazard," Ehrgraz said with a snort, "it won't be my doing. I shan't drop him in Kortran, but will return him to a place of safety when our business is concluded."

Vara looked at the dragon, and then at Cyrus, and her expression hinted at a mind torn. "Go on, then," she said at last. "Go learn what he'd have you know."

"Yes, you go and fill your empty head with new ideas and dragon secrets," Vaste said, gesturing him forward. "Come back to us breathing fire and clad in scales, and teach the rest of us how to do the same, or don't come back at all."

"Does that one get a bit tiresome?" Ehrgraz asked as Cyrus slid down the wing onto his back.

"Constantly," Cyrus said, "but he has his uses."

"I am quite good for the disposal of pie," Vaste called, "also, the soul."

"I feel ready to dispose of my soul quite willingly after just a few minutes in your presence," Ehrgraz said, taking mighty steps away from the wall, "I can't imagine how happy I'd be to part with it after years around you, Vaste. I imagine I'd give it up just for a chance at devouring you completely."

"I'm also tasty, I'm sure!"

"I am tempted to test that assumption," Ehrgraz said, spreading his wings as he moved out of range of the wall and the conversations being held upon it. "The dragons are a taciturn lot, and yours are constantly chattering group. I always thought our ways were foolish, but I begin to appreciate the silence after a short time here." He flapped his wings once, and Cyrus felt the world go unsteady around him as Ehrgraz took them into the air. Another flap of the wings and they were moving forward, wind rushing around Cyrus's ears so that he could not have heard himself even if he'd even been of a mind to reply. Atop the back of a dragon, he found himself soaring into the sky, and his looks back at Sanctuary showed his home receding smaller and smaller until it faded into the distance.

27.

Cyrus rode atop Ehrgraz for what seemed like hours, but was probably less than one. The speed at which the dragon traveled was astonishing, and Cyrus recognized the Heia Mountains when they came upon them. They soared between snow-capped peaks, Ehrgraz keeping them lower to the ground, Cyrus expected, where the air was thick enough for him to breathe. He had been higher, once, and recalled well the thinness of the air.

When they came out of the mountains, the foothills ended shortly, dipping into the thick, lush Jungle of Vidara and then spreading out into the long, loping Gradsden Savanna. At the far end of the jungle, Cyrus could see the glimmering of a mighty lake reflecting sunlight, and beyond that, mountain peaks even higher than the ones he'd just passed.

Cyrus stared down at the flatlands. From up here, the grass didn't seem nearly so high. He caught sight of one of the portals, though he wasn't sure if it was the one they had traveled from to get to Amti. It could well have been, he reflected, looking into the distance and seeing the tall jungle canopy like mountains over the savanna.

There was a smell of greenery now that they were closer to the ground. Ahead in the south, Cyrus could see the rise of the mountainous terrain around Kortran. The city of the titans was in a valley, and though he could not see it from here, he could see other structures before it, scattered throughout the plains …

Cyrus blinked and leaned forward, as though that subtle adjustment would help him see more clearly what he thought he was looking at. "Son of …"

"Yes, you see it now, don't you?" Ehrgraz said, voice rumbling over the rush of the wind. "This is the work the titans have been doing in the last few years. This is the reason the elves of Amti have lost all their convoys of late."

Cyrus stared as they swooped closer, maintaining their height, far above the reach of the creatures that inhabited the structures below. All across the savanna were newly built watchtowers that stood high above the grasses, giving the titans a sweeping view of miles and miles of nearly open terrain. They were legion, these watchtowers, and built big enough to accommodate at least a half-dozen titans at each. And there, in the center of the savanna, was the most worrying thing of all.

"Fortress Returron," Ehrgraz called as he dipped a wing to carry them around the thing in the middle of it all. It was wood, Cyrus could tell that much, with a massive pike wall that reminded him of the trolls' hometown of Gren. "The key to their entire defensive network here in the savanna. Over a thousand titans are quartered in this place, and messengers can run back and forth from even the farthest watchtowers within a matter of hours. Troops can be on the march and reach from one side of the savanna to the other within a day. None of you small people stand a chance here now, and it is their preparation of this fortress which should concern you." Ehrgraz looked back at Cyrus. "They are even now laying in provisions for a larger army, something on the order of six months' worth of food for a force of ten thousand, even though they only currently billet a thousand there." He cocked his head. "Does that concern you?"

"They're preparing to come up through the Heia Pass in force," Cyrus said, mouth dry. He felt the sense of falling even though he was still firmly on the back of the dragon. "They don't feel the need to even try to be sneaky and use wizard teleports. They're not afraid, they're going to come right at us."

"As a disciple of the God of War should, don't you agree?" Ehrgraz asked, but there was some irony in the way he said it that Cyrus did not like. "This is the first test you will face when you bring your forces against the titans. They watch the portals from a distance, and while they might not see a small group such as you took through before, they will most assuredly see coming the army that you will need in order to crush that fortress."

"This is going to be more complicated than I thought," Cyrus said.

"Indeed," Ehrgraz said. "I hope you find it useful, my attempt to cure your naiveté."

"You just saved my army from a hell of a failure," Cyrus said, but now the weight was upon his shoulders and he fell into silence.

"Come now," Ehrgraz said, trying to stir him out of it. "This is not an insurmountable thing."

"No, it's not, it's just …" Cyrus let out a quiet, mirthless chuckle. "It's just another thing on the pile."

"At least your people are willing to fight," Ehrgraz said, "so count your blessings. I stand as chief of the army for a fearsome force that desires to see no use. Even my closest allies feel the restraint of our leaders as the titans continue to grow in strength and boldness, lashing out into our territory. The only reason our enemies go north now instead of south to us is that they know they have nothing to fear from us. I reckon they've grown tired of your people, and see an infinite sea of resources ripe for the plucking in your lands. They will humble your keeps, crush your cities, and feed on the bones of your kind like domesticated, flightless birds for years to come."

"I don't mean to stand around and wait to be plucked," Cyrus said tautly. "And if they think I do, they are about to receive a severe correction to that thinking."

Ehrgraz laughed as he carried them higher. Far below, Cyrus could see titans moving around in the fortress, like insects in an ant mound. Arrows shot toward them, falling before they came even close to the dragon. "You have a fight in you, but you are one of the few now, yes? You northerners have seen war, and now you lack the stomach to face the new threat rearing its head at you after battering at each other for such a long interval—which is not such a long interval to my people, or to your elves, or even your dark elves—but you humans, you last but a flicker of a flame, and have the attention span of these titans."

The words were scornful, but the only thing Cyrus took from them was another reminder about how fleeting his life was compared to Vara's. *Curious that he would intend all that as insult, but I take the sting from the thing most out of my control.* "If we do this thing, the titans will be furious. They'll take all their attention from their southern gates and put it here, on the savanna, leaving you a wide opening and us nothing to pursue once they close ranks."

"Don't be a fool," Ehrgraz said. "The titans may have magic, but they are new to it and their thinking reflects that. There is a portal in the Ashen Wastelands that would give you easy access to their southern gate once it is ungirded. You have no excuses not to make this strike save your heart not being in it."

"Oh, we'll fight," Cyrus said. "The question is—what will it take to get your people to do so?"

"Opportunity and reason," Ehrgraz said, but it was so quiet it was almost left to the wind. "You are about to provide one of those things, and when you are done, we will talk about arranging the other."

"Why not just attack with us?" Cyrus asked. "You alone—"

"I alone would be exiled for participating in your plans," Ehrgraz said, tilting his head to look at Cyrus, quite serious. "Conspiring with you smallfolk in an attempt to bring the dragons into war? My people don't execute our own, but they might make exception for that bit of treason." He snorted fire out of his nose, causing Cyrus to blanch. "My other option, of course, is to stand back and watch the titans destroy you—you tiny people—and then wait for them to renew their strength and come after me and mine. This day will come, I am fully assured."

"You don't think Talikartin will suddenly grow peaceable after conquering the north?" Cyrus asked with a smirk he didn't feel.

"The titans are tyrants, fueled by desire for war in all its forms," Ehrgraz said, giving Cyrus a view of the back of his scaled head. "They follow Bellarum too closely, inculcated in his ways far worse than your Society of Arms could manage even with its best, most fanatic warriors. You have other gods to shape you, moderating influences on your societies. There is no moderation in Kortran, only the billowing forge of war, firing at its hottest, all the time, for a thousand years. They drank deep from this cup of madness, and struck out at whatever was closest ... until Talikartin and Razeel came along." One of Ehrgraz's yellow eyes narrowed as he turned his head slightly to look at Cyrus. "They are men of vision, the sort that come along only once every few generations of your short-lived folk. They are would-be gods who want to make the world over in their image. When they came into power they swept away a regime that they felt did not go far enough in following the ideals of the God of War.

Imagine that for a moment, if you please."

Cyrus bit his tongue at any thought of defending Bellarum. "That's … bound to be an intense … situation."

"Oh, come now," Ehrgraz said, looking back at him. "Surely you can't be thinking of speaking up in the name of your nominal god, can you? I had heard you changed."

Cyrus started to snap then reined it in. *Oh, how you have changed me, Vara.* "I've seen dark things in many places, and evil deeds are hardly the exclusive province of the God of War."

"That is a politician's answer, not the reply of a soldier," Ehrgraz said. "You should choose today who you wish to serve, Cyrus Davidon, because this is not a path that you will want to waver on."

"I don't think I asked for you to be my priest," Cyrus said coolly. "What I believe is entirely my business and none of yours. We have a common ally; that does not entitle you to give me religious advice."

"Oh, I was not giving religious advice," Ehrgraz said as they tilted, drifting, toward the Jungle of Vidara. It loomed large ahead, the tall trees only a few hundred feet below their flight path. "I was merely suggesting that you exercise some thought and consider a different path than the one your people set you upon. Perhaps, instead, you should allow your mind to guide your feet to one that better suits you, perhaps one you were pointed to in earlier days."

Cyrus said nothing, working hard to keep a rising anger from bubbling out. They came lower and lower over the trees, tall boughs stretching occasionally out of the thick-woven canopy of green below. Cyrus could see vines, moss, all the things that stitched the carpet of greenery together and blocked out the sun from the ground below. "Where are we going now?" he asked.

"Your afternoon's education is complete," Ehrgraz said, not turning to look at him now. "I return you to a safe place from whence you can return home."

"You're going to leave me in the jungle?" Cyrus asked as they swept lower, now just fifty feet above the top of the tallest trees. "I can't teleport home, you know that, right? And I'm of little use to you wandering the southern lands alone—"

"Don't be a fool," Ehrgraz said, beating his wings and halting their forward motion in one hard sweep. Cyrus was thrown against the scaly back of the dragon, and then they hung there, hovering, the dragon merely putting forth a minimal effort to keep them aloft as they slowly began to sink toward the canopy below. "I have no wish to remove you, my new ally, from effective action. I merely wish to give you an opportunity to share your knowledge with those who might benefit from it."

"Those who might—" Cyrus looked over the edge of the dragon's back and saw a peculiar sight below. The tree just underneath him was hollowed out and open to the sky above, a ramp circling the inside of the wooden bark visible from where he hovered on the back of the dragon. He looked up and caught Ehrgraz's gaze. "You know where Amti is?"

"I know many things," Ehrgraz said with a toothy smile. "I know, for example, that while they have no wizards at their disposal, with their wondrous and wide-reaching teleportation spells that could carry an entire wagon, they do have two druids, which should be sufficient to bear you back to Sanctuary once your business here is concluded."

"Everyone has spies everywhere," Cyrus said as Ehrgraz drifted slightly lower. He was close to the upper branches now, and Cyrus could see elves staring out him, peering from behind shoots and leaves, tiny bows drawn. He saw Gareth at the lead of them and waved to him as he started to slide down Ehrgraz's leg. "Except me, apparently."

"Yes, you should work on that," Ehrgraz said. "It is not wise to remain ignorant while your enemies and allies gather knowledge around you."

"I'll keep that in mind," Cyrus said, positioning his boot on a massive, scaly foot as Ehrgraz drifted to within ten feet of the topmost ramp. Cyrus could see Gareth watching him from just below, a tight and furious expression on his face.

Cyrus let loose of the dragon's leg and fell, landing a little roughly but absorbing the shock through his armor. His knees ached with the impact, but he grasped Praelior and drew to his feet, the discomfort manageable if not entirely gone.

He looked up to see Gareth pointing the bow at him as Ehrgraz flapped his wings once and rose three hundred feet in a great gust that almost pushed Cyrus back to his knees. It knocked Gareth over just as he raised his bow to take a shot at Ehrgraz, and when he came back up, Cyrus batted his arrow aside as he released. It sailed into a nearby tree with a thunk, and Cyrus shook his head. "Don't do that. It would be an exceedingly bad idea."

"You just led a dragon to our home," Gareth said, ashen of face.

Cyrus did not stop him from drawing and nocking his bow once more, which was a quick enough action that he could only have halted it with the assistance of Praelior. A half dozen rangers followed his action exactly, and Cyrus found himself staring down countless arrows, standing there atop the tree, the smell of greenery and earth all around him.

"I didn't—" Cyrus started but Gareth immediately cut him off.

"Liar! You are under arrest for your traitorous action," he said, fury pulsating through his face, causing his brow to twitch in anger, "and I will see that you suffer greatly for this betrayal."

28.

"Leading the head of the dragon army to our city was not wise," Cora said as Cyrus found himself surrounded by the council of Amti, Gareth over his shoulder with his bow still at the ready. He'd had his men remove Cyrus's helm, but Cyrus had drawn the line at allowing Praelior to be taken. It had resulted in a tense standoff that Cora had broken by conducting them both to the council room, where Mirasa and Fredaula had joined them, the former looking ghostly scared while the latter looked almost as angry as Gareth.

"I didn't lead him here," Cyrus said, exhaling his annoyance as he spoke, "as though I'm some sort of navigational genius who could miraculously pinpoint your city's location from the air. While I appreciate the compliment, perhaps you could accept that the dragons know where you are *because they can see you as they fly overhead.*"

"We should construct a roof for Tierreed," Gareth said from behind Cyrus, rather harshly still. "I warned you it made us vulnerable—"

"Our entire crop will die without sunlight," Mirasa said, fighting back at Gareth with more than a little anger of her own. "How would you have us fed, then?"

"Your farmers will need to be trained by my hunters," Gareth said, coming out from behind Cyrus now, his arrow back in the quiver and his bow at his side, "and we'll cease sowing—"

"Stop," Cora said, putting the end to their argument. "This bickering suits us ill." She turned her eyes to Cyrus. "So they already know."

"At least Ehrgraz does," Cyrus said, shrugging. "I would assume any other dragon flying over would have seen it as well, though it takes a bit of an eagle eye—sharper than mine, anyway—to discern the lone open tree."

Gareth cursed in elvish. "We are fools to have left ourselves so exposed."

"We can't eat only meat," Mirasa said, reddening.

"I'm here to help you," Cyrus said, his discordant statement ringing like a bell that brought all their heads around. "Sanctuary is going to engage in your war, and we've got some allies, including, perhaps, the dragons at some point in the future. For now, though, Ehrgraz has given me an idea of what we're facing, enough to structure a first attack."

Cora stiffened. "So you're going to join us."

Cyrus raised an eyebrow, the faint glow of the nearest torch causing him to see a faint green spot as he turned to look away from it. "I'm going to launch an attack on the titans. You are more than welcome to join us, if you so choose."

Cora regarded him coolly. "You make it sound as if you will be walking across the savanna alone to kick in their gates."

"I lead an army, Cora," he said, not particularly fond of her tone. "They follow. I mean to lead them to your advantage." He looked around. "Why are you not thrilled?"

"This will stir the hornets," Gareth said, looking tense, his fists balled. "Forgive us our reticence, but we fear the sting."

"You live under the constant threat of sting," Cyrus said, getting to his feet and taking his helm back from where it lay on a stand by the door. "I thought you came to us about ridding yourself of it."

"You are the general of these matters," Cora said, forcing a smile. "We are but merely conflicted, that is all. I'm sure your plan is for the best." She looked at Mirasa, Fredaula and Gareth each in turn. "For it could not make things any worse, of that we can be certain."

"It's going to take me a few days to put this together," Cyrus said, looking her straight in the eyes. "Help would be appreciated, but we'll go whether Amti contributes assistance or not."

"You will have as much as we can spare," Cora said quietly.

"Wonderful," Cyrus said, placing his helm back upon his head. "Can you spare a druid?"

"I can spare more than that," Cora said, standing up and drawing her navy cloak about her. "I will escort you back to Sanctuary myself."

She looked to Mirasa. "Find Credena or Iana, will you please?"

"I'll go as well," Fredaula said, standing up and brushing her dirty hands over her grime-encrusted clothes. "We're close to a new vein in the mines, and I have work to do."

"You'd get along well with some dwarves of my acquaintance," Cyrus mused as Fredaula gave him a slight scowl. "Miners. They work the land around Rockridge."

"Sound like cowards, working so far from danger," Fredaula said, the scowl tightening the lines around her eyes.

"They saved the lives of hundreds of people during the titan attack by sheltering them in their dwarf-carved caves," Cyrus said. "One of them, Keearyn, made eighteen trips back down the ridge to find more survivors."

Fredaula blinked first. "Not cowards after all then, perhaps."

"I would say not."

Mirasa disappeared through the door without another word, and Fredaula followed sulkily behind. Gareth hesitated another moment before catching a look from Cora. "Perhaps I'll … see to things as well," he said, excusing himself. He turned away, and for the first time Cyrus noticed a fur pelt hidden under his cloak, wrapping around his chest. It was silvery-white, like wolf fur from the Northlands. He caught Cyrus looking and shut the door quietly without expression.

"I apologize for all this," Cora said, quiet and reserved. "Change is a frightening thing, even when one is hung over a blade."

"You stay where you are, you're going to fall upon it sooner or later," Cyrus said.

"I agree," Cora said, "having been in a similar situation more than a few times myself, which is why I can safely say that your plan can make things no worse in the long term. Those new to this sort of dilemma, well, let's just say it causes them to focus on the immediate at the expense of the long term. Everything feels like a risk, and you start to believe the end is inevitable."

"I don't intend to hasten your end," Cyrus said, "and I mean to move the blade from underneath you."

"That's quite the undertaking," Cora said in a whisper. "How do you mean to do it?"

"I don't … entirely know yet," Cyrus said, taking a long breath, "I just know that this is the first step."

"Then make it a good one," Cora said as the door opened once more and a short woman walked in, clad in a green cloak with druid vestments covered in dirt draped over her shoulders. "Ah, Iana. Would you be so good as to take Guildmaster Davidon back to his guildhall in the Plains of Perdamun, and then remain there as their guest until he has his plans firmly in mind and is ready for us?" The short woman nodded once, and Cyrus stepped closer to her.

"I'm not in the habit of quitting a thing once I've begun it," Cyrus said, giving Cora a last look. "When we embark on this … I won't stop until I've finished it, or until I'm dead."

"I have heard that said about you," Cora said, still in a whisper, smiling slightly, a little mysteriously.

"What?" Cyrus asked.

Cora shook her head, the smile clinging stubbornly to her lips. "You reminded me of a memory. I had a child once in my care who fixated upon things in much the way you describe. Once his mind was made up, even at the peril of discipline, no threat could turn him away from what he'd decided to do." Her smile grew faint. "I hope you won't go at this as stubbornly as a child, intractable in the face of any consequence."

"I'm not a kid," Cyrus said, as the winds of a druid spell started to pick up around him, swirling, "but I'll see it through all the way to whatever end comes to it." And the room vanished around him, Cora's worried smile frozen in his memory as she disappeared into the howl of the spell magic.

29.

"So this is your plan?" Vaste asked, standing with his hand twitching nervously next to the table in the Council Chambers, the parchment map rolled in front of him. "Dear gods, you don't lack for boldness."

"This seems ... I'll just say foolish," Nyad said, looking at Cyrus in wonderment. "Is this not perhaps ... too much ...?"

"We face disciples of the God of War," Cyrus said, the sweet scent of the hearth burning filling the air, the crackles and pops of the fire putting him at ease as the light in the chamber fought against the night outside the windows. "They believe that battle is the greatest thing above all, and that to face it—to face your foes—is the supreme purpose of life itself."

"But you don't believe that anymore, do you?" Erith asked nervously. "Because it seems to me, then, sending an army into a crazy, hopeless battle would be like ... worship for you."

Cyrus gave her a look of slight disbelief. "Have I ever thrown you headlong into insane battle that you had no chance of coming out of?"

"There was that time with the Dragonlord," Andren said.

"The Realm of Purgatory, that first time," Mendicant said.

"That was nerve-wracking," J'anda said, "but not perhaps so much as the invasion of Enterra."

"Let's not forget the bridge," Samwen Longwell said with a measured tiredness.

"Which?" Curatio asked, looking more than a little weary himself, hand propping up his head, all energy gone from the man. "Termina or the Endless Bridge?"

"Well, both, now that you mention it—"

"There was also the God of Death," Ryin said with a raised eyebrow.

"And the God of Darkness," Nyad said.

"That was eerily chronological," Vaste said, peering at the whole table. "But I think I have you all beat, for once upon a time, Cyrus and I faced the Avatar of the God of Death in a temple in the Bandit Lands—"

"Did you not hear me?" Ryin asked. "We killed the actual God of Death, not some avatar that was simply a holding place for his essence while on Arkaria—"

"I think we know by now that I never truly listen to you," Vaste said, "and my story was better, because it was just Cyrus and I, running like mad from Mortus's little shadow, because it was back in the days long before we knew gods were even able to be killed."

"None of those were unwinnable scenarios," Cyrus said, more than a little annoyed. "Merely challenging ones. As this is." He pointed down at the map. "If we do this in half measure, it will provoke a terrible response. If we succeed, however—"

"It will provoke a terrible response," Longwell said, nudging his spear. "But if we do nothing, odds are good based on what you've seen, eventually a terrible response will wend our way. I say we make our terrible response first."

"Well, it certainly looks terrible," Vaste said, and Cyrus gave him a look. "Not impossible, just terrible. If there are as many as you say—"

"A thousand in the fortress," Cyrus said. "According to Ehrgraz. Based on my brief flyover, I'd say he's close."

"Oh my," Curatio said, languidly moving to stare at the map. "Well, so long as we don't retreat, this will certainly not be a half of a measure, not even in titan terms."

Cyrus looked at Vara, seated next to him, deep in thought, and the only one who had not weighed in thus far. "If there are no objections, I'm going to send the messengers to Amti and Saekaj immediately and start getting our forces together for this." He looked around the table. "Anyone?" He stared pointedly at Ryin, who shook his head. "All right, then. We go tomorrow."

"Yay for possible death!" Vaste said with faux enthusiasm. "I always sleep well on nights like this."

"Really?" Andren asked. "Because it's nights like this I miss the drink."

The meeting broke and they began to file out, surprisingly quiet save for Vaste and Andren. Cyrus caught a few hopeful looks from the others, save for Curatio, who merely seemed tired, and Longwell, whose rage appeared to bubble just beneath the surface.

When the doors shut, Cyrus found he was left in the Council Chambers with Vara alone. She stared at the hearth, the flame within, and her expression was inscrutable. "How is it," Cyrus said, jarring her into looking at him, "that the only person who didn't weigh in on my plan of attack was you?"

"I'm certain it's a perfectly wonderful plan," she said, answering a little too quickly for his taste.

"You'd know if you had looked at it or studied it like the others did," Cyrus said. "Vaste called me mad, I think."

"I'm sure he's right as well," she said, still strangely neutral, then she shook her head. "The soundness of your plan does not concern me."

"But something does," Cyrus said, easing into his seat next to her. "What is it?"

"I worry about you," she said, but this answer did not come quickly. "You seem ... more conflicted of late than you were before. You are not the man you once were."

"The man I was before," Cyrus said slowly, "did not have half as much responsibility as the one sitting before you now."

"I don't think it's just that," she said. "I think it's that the man I met in the caves of the Dragonlord's prison all those years ago had less to lose than the one sitting before me now."

Cyrus felt a pained expression cross his face. "I had many discussions like this with Terian for the year I was in Luukessia. He accused me of not believing as I once had—"

"I'm not questioning your conviction," Vara said and she reached out, brushing long fingers against his face. "Or your courage. You have both in as great a supply as your sex drive—that last of which I could do with slightly less of, I might add. I am merely suggesting," she said, lowering her voice even further, "that now, unlike the days when you lived in a barn, you have friends ... You have an entire guild ... and perhaps even me to worry about it." She looked up hesitantly as she spoke.

"'Perhaps' I have you?"

"Perhaps you worry about me," Vara said. "Perhaps you worry about losing me. About losing the others."

Cyrus found himself looking down, stiffening his neck. "I certainly wouldn't care to contemplate that loss too deeply, but I assure you I am still more than willing to commit to the battles before me with everything I have."

"Because now you're the stalwart defender with something to fight for?"

"Look," Cyrus said, cringing slightly as his thoughts made their way out, "this man you're talking about—the old me, let's call him—he's not so much older. I've only been here some five years. I would argue that these worries you attribute to me, these things that hang about me—they're more the work of responsibility and change than fear."

"How do you mean?" she asked, staring into his eyes.

"In the space of five years I've gone from member of Sanctuary to officer and General to Guildmaster." He smiled tightly. "You and I have gone from enemies to rivals to ... well, lovers, in that time." He felt the slight buoying within sag as the last came on him. "We've lost friends. We lost ... Alaric."

"It is rather a lot in a short time," she conceded.

"Sometimes," Cyrus said, shaking his head, "things move so fast I don't even feel like I know who I am anymore. I wake up in the Tower of the Guildmaster with you next to me and wonder for a moment what happened."

"And do you count yourself fortunate in those moments?" she asked, looking slyly at him.

"Absolutely," he said, keeping the smile off his face expertly, "because that tower is just the most comfortable quarters—"

"Oh, you—" she smacked him on the backplate and the clang of metal rang out in the Council Chambers along with their laughter. "I only worry about you because ... of late, you have not seemed like you at all, truly. Since the Emerald Fields, I mean." She brushed a short, stray hair back behind his ear. "You seem a little different is all. The old Cyrus—the one of five years ago—would not have pondered this war so long before committing."

"That Cyrus didn't know war," he said, drawing a solemn breath.

"Not really. He just knew battle. This Cyrus," he clinked his gauntlet against his breastplate, "has known too much of it.."

She leaned in close to him, her breath sweeping across his ear. "You once quoted to me some adept of your Society that said you should embrace war with all the ardor of wooing a lover." She pulled back slightly to look him in the eyes. "I hope you don't lose your fervor for me the way you seem to have lost your love of war."

"Well, with you the destruction is slightly less than—"

"Oh, you are an arse—"

They collapsed into laughter once more, the soft, genuine snickering that seemed to be all that they could manage at this point. He looked into her eyes and pulled a sweaty hand out of a gauntlet, pausing to wipe it upon his sleeve before brushing the back of his hand against her cheek. "I don't want things to change any more."

"Because you're afraid of what you'll lose?" Her blue eyes glistened.

"Because I've already got everything I want," Cyrus said and leaned in to kiss her. The silence of the Council Chamber held fast around them. For Cyrus the world receded as he continued to kiss those most lovely lips, and all else faded away.

30.

They teleported into the darkness of the Gradsden Savanna once night had fallen using druid spells, which gave off no light that might alert the watching titans to their arrival. It took longer to bring the army in this way, but Cyrus favored it, having everyone keep a low profile, well below the grass, as they moved in under cover of night.

"Those of you who can't keep an invisibility spell about you, don't stray from this space," Cyrus said. Nods greeted him. The army was a well-prepared machine ready to execute his plan. "And maintain quiet at all times; this savanna is near-silent at night, and voices carry even with the grass." He held up a lone finger as indication of silence.

"Yet you talk," Vaste said, brushing past him to move into his own formation.

"And I can scarcely stop you," Cyrus said, "better to have the others minimize it, like shifting weight from one side of the scale to the other."

"Mine's a big weight," Vaste said.

"And a big mouth," Cyrus said, turning his back on the troll. He paused and cast a look back. "Vaste ... take care."

"Oh, gods, I'm going to die, aren't I?" Vaste swelled in size. "You put me in the group that's fated for death, didn't you?" He raised a hand over his mouth. "Well, I hope you'll be happy when I haunt your sorry, muscular arse for all the rest of your days. I won't be one of those calm, placid spirits, either, I'll be the kind that issues one of those deathly screams right when you're most intimate with Vara—"

"I might not hear you over my own screaming," Cyrus volleyed back.

Vaste paused. "Ick. Icky. Ick ick ick."

"You'll be fine," Cyrus assured him, and then moved on. The space in which the portal stood was a clearing in which the tall grasses of the savanna did not grow for some reason. Cyrus had long ago stopped pondering the mysteries of magic and its effects, instead focusing on watching the ceaseless motion of the army groups as they were teleported in and then shuffled back behind the portal and out of the zone where the spells carried the newly arrived.

He slowed as he walked past Andren and Martaina, whose heads were close together, Martaina's chainmail coif hanging loose between her shoulder blades. He realized with surprise that he had not seen her wear that piece of armor in quite some time, and as Andren brought a hand around to hold the back of her head, she moved slightly and he heard the links rattle just a little. *That's why*, he thought. *The noise.*

Cyrus walked past Thad almost without noticing him, save for his head was turned in a different direction than the rest of his own army, which was waiting quietly in formation before the red-armored warrior. Thad was looking across at Martaina and Andren with something that looked very much like longing. "You all right, soldier?" Cyrus asked, pausing, and speaking so low that Thad's army couldn't hear what he was saying.

Thad jumped as though he'd been caught committing a crime. "I—no—nothing—uh, sorry sir."

"Thad," Cyrus said, low and reassuring. He traced the warrior's former sightline and repeated his inquiry. "You going to be okay?"

"I'm fine," Thad said, swallowing his emotions in an instant. He puffed up slightly. "I'm, uh—" He swallowed again.

"I've been where you are," Cyrus said quietly, lowering his voice so that no one else could hear them. "It gets easier."

"I'd heard that about you," Thad said, low and gruff, but with a very slight intonation of wonder. "About your—your wife."

"First wife, I hope," Cyrus said, looking around until he found a shining silver helm with blond hair leaking out of it in a golden ponytail.

"Gets easier, does it?" Thad asked, casting his eyes sideways.

"Not at first," Cyrus said, "but yes. It'll burn for a bit, but eventually it'll get easier." He looked at Andren and Martaina, now locked at the lips. "Mostly."

"What happened to your—your first wife, sir?" Thad asked.

Cyrus paused as he felt something lurch within him. "I hear she survived the sack of Reikonos and is back to running her stand in the markets, selling flowers to any who would buy them."

"Have you seen her, then?" Thad asked.

"No," Cyrus said, and he smiled, though there was no joy in it. "I don't have the heart to see her." He placed a hand on Thad's shoulder. "Just hang in there and hold fast to your duty until your heart lightens." He gave a glance at the small army waiting on Thad. "You've got a lot to worry about today, but I know you're up to the challenge." And he started away.

"Uh … what if it never does, sir?" Thad asked, sounding still worried, though perhaps a touch calmer than he'd started out. "If it never lightens, I mean?"

"We'll talk about it after you get some titan blood on you," Cyrus said in a low whisper, motioning his small, precursor army into formation behind him. He watched Andren and Martaina break free of each other and fall in, but Thad was already focused ahead with his own small army on the march, heading slightly left of where Cyrus's was going. *That's the way to do it.*

"Are you going forth and spreading your experience again?" Vara asked as he slipped into position at the head of the army next to her.

"That and my sunny disposition," Cyrus quipped. Nyad stood next to Vara on the other side, and Curatio beyond that. They marched quickly, though not at a terrible pace for Cyrus with his long legs.

They walked in silence through the long grass for hours, the whisper of it brushing Cyrus's armor and being trod under the boots of the small army group that followed him. The gentle night wind rolled through, causing the stalks to wave above Cyrus's head. He fell into the quiet that permeated the night, losing his own thoughts as he marched in time, each footstep in a cadence he lost measure of after a time, until he felt like all he had ever done was march, and it was all that was in his future as well.

Who are you? he wondered. *Guildmaster? General? Warrior?* He flicked his eyes sideways and was rewarded with a glimpse of Vara, cheeks red with the exertion of the march, hair shining where it flowed from underneath her helm. She already had the nose guard down, obscuring her face, but he could have traced every line by memory if he had a charcoal pencil with which to work and a little parchment. *Lover?*

Friend?

Are these the things that define me? He looked down and saw his armor, dark in the night, like a shadow out of place in the eve. *Or is it this? This is how they know me in Reikonos, in Pharesia. The warrior in black, known by the armor my father left behind?* He let out a low breath that felt almost like a joyless laugh. *To be remembered for what my father gave me rather than anything I did …*

The soft crunch of the ground underfoot persisted with each countless step. Cyrus let the compass Vara held be his guide, watching the metal spin in the curious device as they stalked through the night. It was the work of hours, and soon enough he heard a boisterous laugh from somewhere in the distance. When it came through, he held up a hand to stop his small force, waiting and listening.

"What is it?" Cyrus murmured quietly, looking sideways at Vara, who was stiff, her ears hidden under her helm. "What are they saying?"

"They're making a very crude joke, I believe," she said, eyes moving as she considered what she was hearing. "Typical soldiers."

"But they don't know we're approaching?" Cyrus asked, a little more urgently.

She listened intently again then shook her head. "I don't believe so. All I hear is casual conversation. No alarm, no watchfulness—just talk and the crackle of a fire below the tower."

Cyrus smiled. "Well, that's good. Whoever's down there won't be able to see squat in the darkness, not with that big light spoiling their night vision."

"Take care," she said, with a hand upon his shoulder in caution, "we don't know how acute titan eyes are."

"No," he agreed, "but I know how cute yours are. Your ears, too—"

She rolled her eyes and made a *pfft!* noise with her lips, but he could see that she was pleased with the compliment. He motioned the army forward, and they continued their advance, this time toward the faint spot of light ahead of them through the grass. It grew brighter and more visible as they made progress, and soon enough Cyrus could see the tower above. Here was where the nerves kicked in, and he watched to make sure that the army spread the way he'd ordered, passing between blades of grass without touching them wherever possible, giving them only the lightest suggestion of contact, as though nothing but the wind were moving through the savanna.

It took the better part of an hour to make the final approach, so obsessed was Cyrus with not tipping their hand. It took a sort of maddening patience that he didn't normally possess, and as soon as he was able, he locked his eyes onto the top of the watch platform and did not remove them from the titan atop it, keeping careful watch on the beast several hundred feet above him. It was an enormous platform, one designed to give the already-tall titans an extra boost to thrice their normal height. Cyrus estimated the tower was some forty feet in the air, a construction of mammoth logs and strong rope.

There was only one titan atop it. With a careful motion to his army to halt once more, Cyrus began a long creeping approach along the side. For the last hour he'd noticed that the titan on watch had not looked in any direction but straight ahead. *He'll pay for that*, Cyrus thought.

Cyrus circled quietly around the camp, coming out at the rear and getting a quick look at the titans now sleeping around the fire. Only one was awake on the ground, and three were dozing, one of them very fitfully only feet away from the grass where he surveilled them.

"Easy pickings," came a voice from beside him, and Cyrus nearly jumped as he turned to see Martaina there, edging close to him. "Terrible watch protocol, with the fire and low numbers of guards."

"I agree," Cyrus murmured, almost afraid to speak. He watched the lone titan on the ground lean against one of the support posts for the tower. "Well … that could be useful …"

"Wouldn't count on it," Martaina said softly. "Even if we could somehow kill him in one good stroke, which is hardly a foregone conclusion, it wouldn't do much but unsteady the watch tower and tip the one above that they're under attack, giving him a perfect chance to shout his alarm all over the savanna. Maybe someone hears him and maybe they don't, but …"

"Right," Cyrus said, nodding slowly. "Not a good chance." He gave her a sidelong look. "Go back around and bring the army here. No point in coming at their front."

She gave him a raised eyebrow as if she wanted to argue. "You just going to sit here by yourself until we get back?"

"Well, I'm damned sure not going to charge out into the middle of them to try and silently kill them myself," Cyrus said, "though I appreciate your assessment of either my skill or my insanity."

"Be right back," she promised almost noiselessly, and she whispered off through the brush. He did hear the chainmail coif rattle just slightly as she did so, confirming in his mind his earlier guess. *But hopefully not loud enough for a titan to hear it over this gusting wind.*

He sat there on the edge of the titan camp, waiting, watching. The lone waking titan on the ground began to pace every few minutes, walking back and forth under the tower, letting out a mighty yawn at one point. His footsteps did not quite shake the ground, but Cyrus felt them where he waited, the blades of grass twitching just slightly at the force of the steps.

Cyrus felt an internal pressure, like something squeezing him, compelling him forward. *I could kill those things, couldn't I? They can't all be as strong as Talikartin. I've killed them before. Go at their knees, drop them down, open their throats ... not a quiet business, though, unfortunately. That's a mark in the favor of waiting.*

It was almost like an itch under his scalp, the desire to charge forth and unleash havoc. He drew slow breaths, calm in and chaos out, until the desire passed. Soon enough, he heard motion, not nearly so quiet as Martaina, and out of the grass came Vara at the head of the army. Cyrus moved his gaze back to the titans, but they continued their rounds seemingly unaware of the small force just behind them.

"I need Falcon's Essence," Cyrus said, low, and let the word be passed rather than shouting it out like he normally would, "Vara too, and all of group A." He looked at the even smaller sliver of his army that comprised group A, and after a moment, they all began to float, though he felt his feet leave the ground before the others. "We go at the count of five, so ready yourselves." He turned to face the camp, and held a hand aloft, all his fingers extended. One by one, he lowered them as he counted off. *5 ... 4 ... 3 ... 2 ... 1—*

And he led the quiet charge into the camp of the titans, almost soundlessly as they raced in to kill their foes in the still night.

31.

After all the long waiting, Cyrus found the rush of true wind against his face invigorating. He did not spare the speed of Praelior, not this time, and circled the encampment in a rush, slitting the throats of two of the titans swiftly before the rest of his army caught up with him. The noise he unleashed in doing so was not quiet, a choking, gasping, gurking noise that caused the sentry under the platform to spin to see what was happening.

Cyrus was already on the move upward, though, trying to ignore the titan below as best he could. *The others will handle it*, he thought, ignoring the instinct to rush back down. Instead he circled in a hard spiral up the tower, running on imaginary stairs. He paced his climb perfectly, ensuring that he came even with titan's platform around the creature's back.

A small cry of surprise split the night, causing Cyrus's target to jump in reaction. It did not cause Cyrus so much as a moment's hesitation, however, and he plunged Praelior into the titan's knotted flesh under the back plate the creature wore to protect its vital organs. It looked rather like a finger-sized dagger plunging into a creature that size, but the titan grunted in pain as Cyrus ripped the blade back out of the leathery skin and continued upward just a little further.

The titan jerked in pain at his attack, as though he'd been stung by an insect instead of a full-sized sword. *This is the problem with titans and dragons, it just takes so many hits to kill the bastards when they're not lying there waiting for their throats to get cut.*

Cyrus watched the titan spin his head toward him, jerking as he saw the black-armored warrior right in front of his nose. Before he could cry out in shock, Cyrus buried Praelior directly in the joint of his jaw, drawing a muffled grunt of pain and a reactionary swipe at Cyrus, who dodged the blow easily by stepping backward. The titan's eyes alighted on Cyrus, fury gleaming within them. "Rogh rawr!" the titan said, clutching his jaw with one hand as he leaned forward to attack Cyrus again. Cyrus merely took another step back and let gravity take its course.

The titan swiped too hard, reached just a little too far, clutching into the night with extended fingers and nothing else. He hit the small wood beam that circled the platform as a guard rail and kept going, the strength of his momentum carrying him over the edge. He tried to scream out in fear as he fell over, but it came out muffled once more as he struggled to open his mouth.

The titan fell to the earth with a significant thump, landing on his shoulders and head and then sagging, moaning in the night, arms flung wide and his eyes shut.

"Ahh!" another titan below shouted, though not too loudly. Cyrus ran down swiftly, passing Vara as she halted her own upward momentum and turned to join him, the rest of group A in tow.

"I'd tell you to slow bloody down," she said as he darted past, "but it would seem you're doing all the work, and I don't mind that at all."

"Just like—"

"Do not say—" she warned, the rest of her reply lost to the wind as he left her behind.

Cyrus rushed back to ground level to find one of the titans that had been sleeping was now quite awake, though bleeding heavily from a botched attempt to cut his throat. He studied the creature, watched the bluish blood pumping out from beneath its left hand, and he shook his head. "Wrong side of the throat to start on, people," he said at a normal volume. He cast eyes behind him and saw a few of his finest warriors pulling the titan that had been on guard to the ground. It had only a hand up in the air, and a faltering one at that, coming under the attack of half a hundred blades.

That situation in hand, Cyrus threw himself toward the titan bleeding from the neck, darting in a zigzag pattern toward the creature. It followed him with dull eyes under a heavy brow, peering at him with a hint of fear. *You know death when you see it, don't you?*

The titan made to swing a fist at him, but its motions were slow and clumsy, and the first swipe missed wide of Cyrus, and indeed wide of where he had been during his entire run. The titan's bleary eyes failed to track him, and so he moved in and cut the artery with a quick motion, moving around a thumb to do so. When he finished, he jabbed Praelior into the voice box and gave it a swift slice before throwing himself backward to avoid reprisal.

None came, and the titan made only one further attempt to speak, a gagging sound, ululating deep in the throat, before it slid slowly sideways to the earth and relaxed into death's grip.

Cyrus surveyed the raw chaos of the watch post with reluctant pride. "Any deaths?" he asked, back to speaking normally.

"Not on our side," Vara said from a few feet off. She looked to have been doing some surveying of her own, and her breastplate's silver was still immaculate, bearing none of the glistening red that glinted on his in the firelight. She inclined her head toward the titan that had fallen off the platform. "I think that one's still alive, though they're working on it now."

"Indeed," Cyrus said, watching the group that had carved up the other sentry falling upon his. They had him surrounded. A few climbed atop him like tiniest children on an adult, and were stabbing furiously at any square of flesh they could find. Cyrus cringed at the image, trying to shake the thought of it out of his mind.

Vara's gaze mirrored his own, and she puckered her lips. "It is a bit odd to see, isn't it? Like a rebellion of infants slaughtering the grown-ups?"

"I was thinking the same and finding it highly disturbing," Cyrus said, focusing on her. "We need to pull down the watch post and add it to the fire."

"Don't you think the other posts will notice that?" she asked, nodding at the large wooden structure. "It's rather large."

"Probably," Cyrus said, taking a few climbing strides up as he looked out over the savanna. To the east and west, he could see more watch fires. The ones closest to them, in the north, were already glowing brighter. "But it's what I told the others to do. The purpose of this isn't just to piss off the titans, it's to destroy the mechanism by which they're enforcing their dominance here. Let them haul tons of lumber out to rebuild all we take; we'll just come and do it again if they don't guard carefully."

"But your very plan hinges on them becoming so upset as to

increase their guard," Vara said. "Wasn't that the purpose of all this? To draw them out the front door?"

"If the dragons can fulfill their end of the bargain, yes," Cyrus said, staring out over the ocean of darkness across the savanna, the grass gently swaying below him. She stepped up to his side. The sounds of dying titans far below had faded into the night, and now he could hear his army working at disassembling the tower—quietly chopping at the ropes that held it all together. "What if the dragons don't intervene?" Her voice was quiet, hushed. "What if Ehrgraz can't get them to do what you hope he will?"

"Then this strategy is even more important," Cyrus said quietly, meeting her eyes in the dark, barely able to see the glistening blue save for by the power of a spell, "because if we don't get the help we need, we're going to have divide and conquer them." He looked south, where he knew, somewhere far ahead, was Fortress Returron, and beyond that, somewhere in the dark, Kortran. "And with these titans … it's a hell of a lot to divide and conquer."

32.

After they were done with the tower, the army moved on once again, swiftly and silently through the tall grass. They walked for a further three hours, maintaining a fast pace, with stops every twenty minutes for a short break and to allow Vara and Martaina to listen carefully to the wind. Each time they were rewarded with a quiet that indicated no guard patrols were moving, which was as Cyrus expected.

"The titans haven't gotten used to having the Eagle Eye spell at their disposal," Cyrus said after they had reached a point just below a hill that he'd noted on his map after his flight and confirmed with Cora through a few messages carried by her druid. "Either that or they don't have enough spellcasters to spread it around."

"If I were planning a war, I don't think I'd care to hinge it upon that belief," Vara said. When Cyrus looked at her blankly, she went on. "On them having few spellcasters, I mean. I'd assume ignorance first, and that they can adapt at any time."

"That's always how I plan," Cyrus said. They sat between tall blades of grass, the small army spread out around them, huddled in silence as they ate conjured bread and jerky brought in their small packs. "I assume the worst."

Vara made a face. "That explains the first several years of our acquaintance."

"It was certainly a hostile series of encounters," Cyrus said with a smile.

Vara started to make a reply and then stopped, and he could sense her ears twitching. "Small footsteps—one of the army groups, but they're coming out of the west."

Cyrus directed his eyes toward the grass to the west and stood, putting his hand on Praelior. Soon enough, he heard it, too, and waited, until a familiar, bucket-shaped helm peeked through the grass. Terian grinned, his mouth and chin exposed to the world. "We should really have set up a sign and countersign; who knows what loathsome characters could have come strolling into your camp—Malpravus? Goliath?"

"You," Vara said, but it lacked much sharpness.

"Terian," Cyrus said with a slight smile pulling at one side of his mouth. Terian strolled into their makeshift camp, an army of dark elves trailing in his wake, a slightly larger group than the one Cyrus had with him. Though they were armored poorly compared to Sanctuary's group, they seemed heavy on spellcasters. Cyrus took it all in, and when Terian got close, he nodded at a thick cluster of enchanters that moved together, their robes looking particularly fresh. "I didn't think nations were allowed to have this many spellcasters at their disposal under League law."

Terian's lips puckered and he reached up to scratch the back of his neck. "Well, Saekaj's Leagues are in a slightly different place than the rest of Arkaria's, in that they answer to the Sovereign."

Cyrus took that in, but Vara beat him to the follow-up punch. "You're saying that the other Leagues don't answer to their nation's authorities?"

"Nope," Terian said with a shake of the head. "They answer to the gods." He made an almost apologetic shrug. "Which, I mean, technically, answering to the Sovereign—well, it used to be the same thing …"

"That's interesting," Cyrus said and meant it. He watched the slow mingling of the Sanctuary group with the dark elven forces, an uncomfortable melding at first, the sides looking slightly standoffish or shy. "I have to admit, Terian … it's a relief to see you." He caught the curious look from the white knight. "I mean, I saw your fires on the horizon when your people took out the watch towers we'd assigned, but a part of me didn't dare to hope you'd actually be here until now."

Terian let out a low guffaw. "Hope? I imagine it's not an emotion you're used to associating with me at this point."

"But once, yes," Cyrus said, and he smiled ever so slightly, "and lately, again."

Terian planted a hand on Cyrus's shoulder, reaching up to do so. "We'll keep working on that." He looked around, his new helm snug upon his head, the axe on his back sticking far up into the air as though he were bearing a pole to hold a standard behind him. "Where's the rest of your army? Things are looking a little spare around here."

"Well, they didn't have quite the short jaunt that we did," Cyrus said, turning his head to look to the east. "We sent some to another portal closer to their targets, and of course we had some help out of Amti—"

"Which has arrived," came a quiet voice from only a few paces behind Cyrus. He turned and saw Gareth, nearly blending in with the grass. Cora appeared at his side, her spell of invisibility dropping like water sloshing off her. Cyrus saw other elves, cloaked in what looked grass cloth, their movement in the still night the only thing to give them away.

"Cora," Terian said warmly.

"Gods," Cora whispered, taking a step toward. "Terian, is that you?"

"It is I," Terian said, and she took halting steps forward until she embraced him, wrapping her arms around the armor. "I suppose I'm not as easy to recognize as I used to be."

"You look very distinctive," Cora said, pulling back and taking him in with a glance, "but, you are correct ... you no longer look like the old Terian." She tapped his pauldron, now smooth, though weathered. "It would appear you found an impressive chrysalis for your transformation."

"I had one given to me," Terian said with a muted smile, "at a cost most dear."

"General," came another voice from behind Cyrus. He turned once more to find Odellan approaching, footsteps as silent as Gareth's, though his armor was covered in scarlet liquid, the blood tracing lines in the intricate designs. His helm was slightly off center as well, the wings pointed just a touch to the right.

"Odellan," Cyrus said, acknowledging him. "I take it you were successful?"

"We destroyed our target," Odellan said, easing into the small circle forming. He looked at Gareth and Cora, and gave each a nod before taking in Terian with a careful, considered look. "Isn't that the armor of ...?"

"Did you succeed in your mission?" Cyrus asked Cora and received a nod in return.

"It was a bit of a strain," Gareth said, voice a little rough. Cyrus glanced around and saw Martaina standing a ways off with Andren, her eyes on Gareth.

"I suppose you're used to hunting smaller game," Cyrus said, turning his attention back to the ranger of Amti.

Gareth made a rough snorting sound that was near-silent. "Have you seen the beasts of these savannas and the jungle?" When Cyrus shook his head, Gareth went on. "The predatory cats we hunt are one and half times the size of a titan. They can swallow you whole." He looked toward the hill just south of them, the one that stood between them and Fortress Returron. "Our only advantage there is that they're solitary creatures." He looked back at the assemblage. "Titans hunt in packs."

Another few minutes passed in quiet conversation, and another few army groups trickled in, their leaders making their way to the circle of officers and leaders for the expedition. Cyrus listened to the conversation, Vara standing still next to him, only the occasional look passing between them. The arrival of Samwen Longwell, his spear tip bloody and crusted in dirt along with Curatio, white robes covered in red splotches, signaled the end of the waiting. Cyrus looked to the sky and saw no hint of dawn, which gave him a very slight relief.

"Looks like it's time to begin," he said, tracing his way to the center of the circle without hesitation. When he got there, he paused, reflecting. *I'm in the middle of leading an expedition that includes all the forces that Amti and Saekaj can spare, with their respective leadership here, listening to me.*

And five years ago I was sleeping alone in a horse barn, in a bed barely big enough for me, with Andren and Narstron not ten feet away, broke, utterly desperate, and with not a follower to my name other than those two. Now I speak to the leaders of nations and command larger armies than anyone else. He caught a glimpse of Vara watching him, and she quietly gave him a smile of encouragement, as though she could read what he was thinking.

Oh, how the wheel does turn. And swiftly, at that.

"You've all seen the plans," Cyrus said, "so I won't belabor the point. The tasks are assigned, and I know you all well enough to be sure you know your parts." He saw a nod from Terian and got a more subtle one from Gareth. "When we go over this hill, everyone needs to take their positions slowly and quietly. You are all in charge of your own divisions, and they must move perfectly in synchronization for this plan to come out a success. If even one of our groups should move out of turn, or go before the attack is called, we risk the safety of this entire combined army." He took a deep breath. "We have only a few precious hours until dawn, and we have another stop to make after this. Let's get going." With a sharp nod, he dismissed them and strode forward out of the camp, his force falling into line behind him without need of a word being spoken, the Guildmaster of Sanctuary on march with his army.

33.

Cyrus waited under the last cover of grass, an even hundred yards separating him from the outer wall of Fortress Returron, the immense structure looking like a forest transplanted out of the south beyond Kortran, the trees the size of the ones around the Iliarad'ouran woods. They had clearly been harvested, had the boughs skinned off, been smoothed slightly, and driven hard into the ground to make a great wall around the fort. Stationed at six equidistant points around the wall were towers of the sort that had been built out on the savanna. Cyrus counted two titans per tower, on watch and in varying states of sloth. The two nearest him were laughing, and to his left, almost near the back gate to the south, the two atop that tower appeared to be sleeping on their feet.

"Druids," Cyrus said, "you know what to do." He felt his feet lift off the ground a moment later. He had held there a moment to give the others time to get into position and make ready. Now he floated up and looked to the south. The watch tower fires were burning brighter against the sky than they had appeared to when last he checked. *So, we're ready, then, so long as the ones to the west are burning ... and I have to assume they are.*

"Forward," he hissed and sprang forward out of the grass at a dead run, heading straight for the wall ahead, not daring to use Falcon's Essence to rise, not yet.

Cyrus ran, pumping his legs and letting the strength of Praelior take him ahead of the others. *The longer the army is exposed on this run, after all, the more likely the titans see us and start to sound the alarm ... and we can't have that.*

When he reached the wall, with all its rough-cut timber, bark still patchy and present, he started to run upward in a spiral once again, just below the tower. *I hope the others caught the sight of my motion ... they should if they were watching at all, and they'll be moving on all six now ...*

He reached the topmost section of the spiral and came up behind both the titans. One of them, the one nearest him, had his head down, peering at the ground. He started to speak, and Cyrus sprang forward and rammed Praelior into the exposed base of the titan's spine.

The titan did not even cry out; he had no chance to. Instead, his weight took over and he slid off the point of Cyrus's blade, toppling against the wooden rail and slumping to his knees, limp as a boned fish.

The other titan looked left to watch his companion's fall, somehow missing Cyrus's dark, shadowed movement in the corner of his eye. Cyrus, for his part, did not fail to take advantage. He moved in haste and shot forward to jab Praelior into the titan's exposed temple. It prompted a sharp cry as the pain started to hit home, but before the titan could fully react, Cyrus stabbed once more, and deeper this time, running his blade along the front of the skull in a hard line, dragging his sword down just above the nose.

The titan jerked, spasmed, and lurched backward. He hit the rail with his lower back and made a scraping noise as the metal armor met wood. Then the titan went over backwards, unbalanced, and Cyrus watched him land on his head and shoulders, his neck breaking at an unnatural angle.

"Showoff," Vara whispered as she joined him atop the tower. Others from his group were moving up now to stand with them. There was movement on the tower directly opposite theirs, and Cyrus squinted but could not discern what was happening, merely that one of the titans was already on the ground and another seemed to be swinging wildly at something he could not see. "Terian," Vara said, nodding in that direction. "He's making mincemeat of them with that axe of his."

"Good," Cyrus said. He let his eyes trace over to the nearest tower to his left, where the titans still stood, but they faced inward now, toward the interior of the fortress, and a small figure stood between them. He peered over and realized it was Cora, plainly in view of her enemies. "She's charming them," he realized as the titans moved to climb down the ladder into the fortress.

Cyrus made a quick sweep of the fortress with his gaze, confirming everything he'd suspected about it from a distance atop Ehrgraz. Two enormous barracks were built across the southern wall on either side of the gates, big enough to quarter a few thousand titans each, he guessed. The building against the northeast wall had the flat, bulky look of a storehouse, without much in the way of windows. *Burning that will put a crimp in the titan supply lines.* He shifted his gaze to the northwest corner, and there he found a smaller building. In the middle of the fortress was muddy, open ground. *Parade grounds,* he thought. *And that smaller building must be the command post—and possibly the officer quarters,* he thought as he let his eyes dance to the building connected to the command post.

"Well, what do you think?" Vara asked, her gaze darting about to each of the towers where fighting was still—quietly—going on.

"I think I had the right of it from my first impression," Cyrus said, nodding as much to confirm for himself as for Vara. "The plan is sound."

"Well, good," she said, "because it's about to be executed."

"So are the titans," Cyrus said grimly, and with a last look over the Fortress Returron, he charged over the walls, and saw the rest of the army, at the six points around the fortress, mirror his motion as he led them into war.

34.

"Fire the corners!" Cyrus shouted, breaking the quiet he'd imposed on them before. Here in the heart of the savanna it would not matter, surrounded as they were by their enemies already. Cyrus heard the noises of alarm in the barracks, the sound of a titan army stirring to wakefulness as he charged down into the parade grounds.

Cyrus had scarcely made it to the ground when his order was taken up. Flame spells sprang up at the doors to the nearest barracks; he looked and saw the same happening at the other barracks. *This is the tense part; if the buildings burn, it will be both good and bad, and it's hard to say which it will be in greater measure until we see how it all plays out ...*

The door to the nearest barracks was ripped open first, and a half-asleep titan stumbled near-naked through the flames of a waiting wizard spell. He screamed, agony piercing the night as the fire burned his knotted flesh. Cyrus got a good look at him shirtless before the fire ate at his skin, and it was just as thick and nubbed as the faces of these creatures. *Scars from training, or natural skin growth? In either case, it certainly makes them tougher in a way that does us no kindnesses.*

The first titan burned, skin sloughing off as he danced forward, screaming loud enough that Cyrus might have thought the heavens themselves were descending upon them. The titan fell to its knees, blackened muscle exposed on his forearms and face, all his tangled hair gone, consumed by the fire spell that was even now being replaced by another. They were to go in cycles, the wizards and druids, covering each of the major entrances and preventing titans from escaping.

Cyrus looked toward the southern horizon, but was stymied in his gaze by the wall of wood. *We can only hope that our other forces have arrived at their targets, because if this gets seen by the sentries at Kortran's gates* ...

The flames burned all comers, catching the titans alight as they streamed through the threshold of the barracks. The screams were loud, punishing to Cyrus's ears, but provided all the distraction he needed as the titans began to come out from other exits as well, half-clad and furious, running shirtless and armor-free into the fight. They came in numbers too many to count, the titans so tall as to strain Cyrus's perspective and make him feel like he were trapped in another world.

Cyrus led on his front of the attack, rushing toward the command post and catching a titan with a long, ripping strike across his calf as he used his superior speed to rush past and attack the next in line. They wore no uniforms, caught next to naked while sleeping, and while this one had a blade in hand, he appeared not to know quite what to do with it. He made a thrust at Cyrus that was easily parried.

Cyrus came at him toward the neck and was forced to back off as a hard backhand struck him a glancing blow, rattling his helm and armor and making him take a shuddering step back on air. Cyrus readjusted his attack and looped around, the titan following him with angry eyes under knotted cheeks. Cyrus feinted toward him and the titan swung with all his might, missing and exposing his back. Cyrus rushed in and planted Praelior behind the creature's ear, drawing a sharp grunt that cut off after a moment and led to the titan pitching forward into the dirt.

Flames danced all around, the fires on the parade ground and blocking the main doors of every building in the fortress growing higher and higher by the moment. They'd spread to the thatched roofs of the barracks and Returron was becoming a hellish spectacle reminiscent of the time that Cyrus had seen the boiling oil pits in the Realm of Death lit afire. *Please, oh, please let our people have killed the Kortran sentries,* he offered in silent hope.

When he swept his gaze around to survey the field, he found war lit by firelight. A titan was howling on the ground, a pack of three wolves tearing at his legs, ripping them open. The master of the animals, Menlos Irontooth, was plunging his sword into the titan's lower back all by his lonesome, his long beard and frightening, angry visage filled with a battle fury that might have exceeded that of his wolves. The titan was swatting at him ineffectually, and Menlos withdrew his short blade to battle the probing hand, delivering defensive strikes to the titan's palm every time he brought it around for another swipe.

Cyrus turned his head at the sight of a flash and saw Ryin Ayend blasting forth with coursing lightning that was drawn to a titan wearing his breastplate. It hit the metal and sparked, causing the titan to jerk, his feet planted to the ground like they'd been nailed in by long spikes. The lightning ran up and down the enormous beast with each bolt thrown from the druid, and the creature's fingers danced and twitched as he fell to his knees, then slumped onto his face, limp, eyes open in death.

Cyrus dodged an incoming strike by instinct alone, bending at the waist as he flipped, Falcon's Essence keeping him aloft in his maneuver. His opponent came at him with a balled fist, furious and calloused as if he had practiced his punches on a boulder until each knuckle had outgrowths of rough skin enough to make it appear doubly bony. The punch sailed over his head, and Cyrus realized dimly that had it hit him, it might have killed him. The titan's movement carried him through, and Cyrus caught him in the armpit with Praelior, driving it into the skin and up to the quillons. As he pulled it out, a rush of foul air and a slight spritz of blood sprayed him in the face. The titan's breath went out of him and he bent double. Not waiting for him to succumb to his wound, Cyrus delivered Praelior's edge to the back of the massive neck with a fury, hacking it thrice before the head came off entirely.

Cyrus spun, looking for his next foe, and caught a glimpse of Longwell in the firelight of the parade grounds, two titans coming at him. He jabbed one straight in the belly with his spear, the long haft braced against his side. It landed in the titan's liver and the beast stopped, grunting in obvious pain, his face lit with the horror of his wounding. It started to bend at the stomach, as though to control the agony surely writhing through its belly, but Longwell pulled the spear out and spun, catching the next titan charging him under the chin with it as it stooped to swipe at him. The tri-pointed blade lodged under the jaw and the mighty mouth came up, revealing the center point of Longwell's weapon sticking out of the middle of its tongue like a stake planted in its mouth. The dragoon withdrew his blade and spun once more, this time delivering the weapon to the exposed heart.

The titan sank sideways, curling up to die without a fight.

"This is how we do it!" Vaste's cry caused Cyrus to pivot. The healer ran up to a titan that was distracted, half a dozen arrows jutting out of its face like a porcupine's quills, Calene Raverle plucking away at it with her bow. Vaste ran right between its legs, raised up his staff, and shouted, "LIKE A CHIPMUNK!" before striking a mighty blow into the titan's groin.

The titan's reaction was immediate, all thought of the arrows and their shooter forgotten, he clutched at his crotch, falling to his knees as Vaste scrambled out of the way. Calene Raverle placed three solid bow shots right into the eyes, and the titan fell dead, his pain forgotten.

"This is chaos," came a small voice from next to Cyrus. He turned and looked down at Mendicant, quivering in his robes only a few feet from Cyrus. "Utter and complete."

"We tend to bring it with us wherever we go," Cyrus said dryly, "like we carry it in our travel trunk, I suppose."

"Indeed," Mendicant said and shot a spell of ice across the battlefield where it came to rest on a titan's face, encrusting him from chin to forehead as he was reaching down to strike at Odellan, whose back was turned where he stood perched in the middle of the battleground. He spun at the sound and leapt up with the aid of Falcon's Essence to smash the titan in the face, shattering the ice and part of the creature's cheek with it. Cyrus caught a glimpse of skull, muscle and bone, along with bare eyes, bereft of the cover of lids, before the titan fell to the ground.

"Where are the titan healers? That's what I want to know," Cyrus said, moving slightly to the side to give Mendicant a clear shot as he hurled another spell past Cyrus and into a cluster of titans running from behind the barracks. The spell burst in a cloud of green that filled the air with a noxious toxin, and when the titans emerged, they came out as green in the face as if they'd been painted by it, and all three fell to their knees within ten paces, only to be finished off by a raging army of dark elves.

"In the barracks, I would hope," Mendicant said, gathering his robes back around his tiny figure. "Burning to death." The robes were streaked with mud that was visible in the light of the burning buildings. The fire had consumed the roofs of the barracks and the command post. The storehouse, however, was only partially lit, and while Cyrus wasted a second pondering what to do about it—

"Look out!" Mendicant cried, but it was too late.

A titan burst through a first-floor window twenty feet away from Cyrus, fully committed to his charge. Cyrus took him in with a glance as he flew forward, buttoned up with his armor on, not only the chestplate but the gauntlets as well. He flew through the air in a fury on course directly for Cyrus. The warrior froze, the speed of the titan carrying him unerringly forward.

35.

"Arnngraav, urnkaaav!" Mendicant cried. Cyrus's mind tried to make sense of the exhortation even as he watched, still slightly stunned, as the titan dropped precipitously toward him. He had Praelior tightly clutched in his hand and was ready to spring to the side when a burst of flame the size of a steed bellowed forth from behind him and struck the giant full on, causing him to raise his gauntlets to defend his face.

The titan's maneuver failed. The flame shot past his weak defense, striking him full in the eyes, in the nose, the chin, and lighting his coarse beard on fire. He landed on his elbows just in front of Cyrus, sliding forward as Cyrus stuck out Praelior and jabbed, reflexively, into the titan's closed eye. He pushed, hard, and the titan jerked only once before dying, laying his cheek in the mud and moving no more.

"That was ... a bit hairy," Mendicant said from behind him. Cyrus turned to the see the goblin looking more than a little discomfited. He'd seized his robe by its front and was clutching it with clawed hands, carefully kneading the material between his fingers.

"Aye," Cyrus said, watching the wizard with care of his own, "but we made it through, you and I." He pondered for a moment then asked the question on his mind. "When you shouted at him, was that—"

Mendicant's scaly skin flushed a deeper shade of green, almost imperceptible in the dark. "Please don't tell anyone I did that."

Cyrus's eyes narrowed. "That wasn't just a goblin curse, was it? That was—"

"Shhhhh," Mendicant said, raising his hands in a panic, eyes wide and lit by the fiery backdrop around them. "I wouldn't—please don't

177

say anything, I don't want to be declared heretic—"

"Your secret is safe with me," Cyrus said with a smile. "It was an accident, but keep in mind that we regularly associate with people in our guild who have committed actual heresy. I doubt anyone will get much up in arms about you speaking a spell aloud while trying to save your Guildmaster—a dumb warrior with no use for magic—from a leaping titan. If they even knew about it—which they won't," Cyrus said with a smile, holding a single finger up to his lips.

"Thank you," Mendicant said with undisguised relief. "Truly, Lord Davidon, you are—"

"Please do not pour ever sweeter compliments into his ear," Vara said, strolling up to them. A quick glance confirmed for Cyrus that the battle for Fortress Returron was well and truly over. Every one of the structures ringing the wooden wall was fully engulfed in flames, fire pouring out the windows, roaring to the skies higher than five titans. "It makes him ever more insufferable to deal with, his ego expanding like the fortifications these grotesque creatures have placed across the savanna."

"My apologies, Lady Vara," Mendicant said and scampered away without another word, his robes trailing behind him.

"What was that all about?" Vara asked as they watched him retreat to stand by Nyad, who was some distance off in a small circle next to a dark elven spellcaster with a long white ponytail.

"Mendicant just saved my life," Cyrus said with a very slight smirk. "He's struggling with it."

"I used to struggle with that very dilemma," she said seriously. "More than a few times I found myself wishing I hadn't."

Cyrus waited a beat. "But you're glad you did it now, right?"

She gave him a smirk of her own. "Most days."

"'Most days'?"

"Come along, Guildmaster," she said, taking him by the hand, her gauntlets clinking with his. "This fight is over, but we have another on the horizon, and the light of morning is drawing ever nearer …"

Cyrus took one last look around, surveying the chaos they had wrought. The beams of the nearest barracks were plainly exposed, the roof burned away. A look at the second barracks found it already collapsing in upon itself, fire blooming heavenward. *No survivors there,* he thought. He gave one look back at the storehouse and motioned to

Larana as he passed her on his way out of the camp. She nodded once, his command understood, and he saw the brightness of her flames as she cast them at the last building in Fortress Returron.

"All right, Sanctuary," Cyrus said, lifting his hand and raising it up, sure that his command were being obeyed even without needing to look back to see, "let's go make a hostile visit to Kortran." He took a final look at the flaming wreckage of Fortress Returron and its thousand-titan garrison. "It's time we teach the titans to keep their big, knotty noses the hell out of the north."

36.

"That was so much fun," Terian said, falling into stride next to Cyrus at the head of the combined army. Cyrus had judged Terian's manpower to be somewhere in the ten thousand range, noting more than a few women in the dark elven army as well, warriors and rangers mostly. The Sovereign of Saekaj let out a deep sigh. "I've missed this."

"I suppose leading a nation doesn't offer many opportunities to go out and destroy things," Cyrus said, looking sidelong at Terian.

"Not as many, no, now that we're at peace." He straightened up in his armor. "But that's not exactly what I meant. I could lead an army anytime, I've certainly got one now." He waved vaguely behind them. "And a pretty good one, at that, though they need some more training, and our spellcasters are almost all young." He settled into a solemn march for a few paces before expounding further. "I mean I miss ... this." He cast a look over his shoulder at the Sanctuary army. "This feeling. Being here, not just by myself marching with an army, but—"

"I know you what you mean," Cyrus said, and looked back over his shoulder to see Vara nodding along, surely listening, only a few paces back. "Sanctuary was always a different sort of place. I'd applied to other guilds before, you know, before I took over the Kings of Reikonos, and it was always—stiff, formal ... you know."

"They kept you at arms' length," Terian said, nodding. "You never felt like you belonged."

"Yeah," Cyrus said with a nod, grass crunching beneath his feet. "That's it exactly."

"You were blacklisted by the Society of Arms, Cyrus," Terian said, pursing his lips as if in pain. "I don't know if anyone ever told you—"

"No." Cyrus said, shaking his head. "That can't be right. I graduated—"

"And they blacklisted you immediately after," Terian said. "That's why you couldn't get accepted to any of the guilds you applied to before Sanctuary. Grinnd brought me the record himself; it went out to every League in Arkaria."

"Why?" Cyrus asked, his surprise coming out in a whisper. "I—I made it through the gauntlet they made me run." His voice rose with his emotions. "I passed every damned challenge they hit me with, and I—"

"I know," Terian said. "There was no further detail in the instruction, just, 'Cyrus Davidon is not to be admitted to any guild, or they shall suffer a loss of—' I forget exactly how they said it, but they made it sound like whoever took you in wasn't going to get invited to any more tea parties."

"Must have been some good tea," Cyrus said, a strong strain of bitterness running through his words.

"Well, it all worked out, didn't it?" Terian asked. When Cyrus looked at him with a half-irritated glance, Terian went on. "Think about it—what if you'd gotten into a bigger guild before you came to Sanctuary? You might have ended up in one of the big three at this point, and you'd be—I don't know, an officer, maybe? Probably a really good one, or, depending on how the war treated you, maybe a dead one—"

"Maybe," Cyrus said, feeling a hard stab of disappointment. "I didn't … gods. That explains a lot. So much, really. I thought maybe …" He rubbed his forehead, nudging aside his helm to do so.

"I'll admit, the whole thing makes me curious, too," Terian said, nodding. "Unfortunately, my Society of Arms head is pretty new at his job, and the old one died in the war, along with most of the staff, so …" He shrugged. "Sorry I can't give you more."

"Well, that certainly explains why I didn't find a guild I could 'belong' with until Sanctuary invited me to join," Cyrus said. "And like you said," he felt a hint of great consolation, "if I'd taken any other path, I probably wouldn't be walking here right now."

"I know exactly what you mean," Terian said, now suddenly all too serious. He turned his head back toward the south, and they continued their march through the night with the rustle of the wind at their backs.

37.

The gates of Kortran were enormous, but hardly an actual gate. It was, instead, a massive stone arch tall enough to accommodate several titans stacked atop one another. When Cyrus and his army approached, it was without fear, for the very obvious sentries posted at the gates had been slain, some eight of them, and all around them lounged a mixed army of Sanctuary and dark elves, standing in near-silence under the star-filled sky at the base of the mountain pass to the titan city.

Standing in the shadows of the arch and visible only after they drew closer were five additional titans. Cyrus did not worry, since they were merely standing there, only a few arms' lengths away from the army, but he did not truly relax until he reached the opening of the pass and saw, up close, the blue-robed enchanter standing beneath the mighty creatures. His back looked slightly hunched, but he still carried his staff, leaning on it for support. "Ah," J'anda said, taking in Cyrus's approach, "there you are. I feel as if I have been waiting all night."

"If your staff is anything like my sword," Cyrus said, "it makes the passage of time seem too slow."

"I'm still getting used to that with my axe," Terian said, casting a look at Cyrus. "I, uh … wouldn't suggest you try using it in bed."

Cyrus did not reply, but a thunderous response came from behind him, unbidden. "You clutched your axe in an intimate moment with your wife?" Vara asked, voice a low hiss in spite of the force of her question. "You idiot!"

"I didn't think it through all the way," Terian said, his deep blue skin darkening. "It sped up my reaction times on, uh … everything."

"Plus, you were clutching a weapon in the bedroom," Vara said.

"Hardly the most ideal or exciting marital aid."

"Depends on the marriage," Terian said with a barely suppressed grin. "I can imagine that it'll be ideal in yours."

"Wait, he's married?" Cyrus asked, feeling as though he'd been lost several turns back in the conversation. "When did that happen?"

"Years back," Terian said, dismissing him out of hand. "Try to keep up."

Cyrus shook off that thought, standing under the archway and staring down the winding path into the mountainous valley. Kortran was somewhere ahead, hidden here in terrain so rugged that he could not see any other route through save for the road or Falcon's Essence. "Huh," he said.

"Work through your shock at his marriage later," Vara said, causing Cyrus to snap his head around to look at her.

"I—what? No, I was thinking that I bet the titans don't guard their northern approaches with bowmen even after this," Cyrus said, inclining his head toward the city somewhere below, ahead of the turns in the road. "They're very inflexible in their thinking thus far. I suspect they have towers set up in the mountains to the south to block dragon approaches, but I don't remember seeing any from the brief look I got into the south mountains when I was on Ehrgraz's back." His lips twisted in a smile. "If we manage to pull this off, we might still have an opening into Kortran." He paused, wavering. "Albeit one with an exceedingly long travel time."

"Indeed," Vara said, "well, keep that one in your pocket for later." She brushed her lips against his for a bare second. "For now, focus on the matter at hand, yes?"

"That didn't help," Cyrus complained as she pulled away from him, but she did not look back, and he watched her cross to Belkan Stillhet, who stood with his own army group, which had been tasked with eliminating some of the eastern towers. He stood next to Scuddar, who had a group of his own, and Thad, whose earlier nervous glances at Martaina seemed to be stifled at present. The warrior looked calmly straight ahead, a satisfied smile on his face and his armor a darker crimson than usual.

"Women are quite the mystery, aren't they?" Terian asked, causing Cyrus's head to whipsaw around.

"I'm still stuck on the thought of you, married," Cyrus said. "You, the man who visited whorehouses more frequently than he visited the latrine."

"I'm proud to announce that I evened that number out with my morning movement."

"It's not morning yet," Cyrus said, unable to hide his smirk. He looked at the assembled army making their way forward in loose lines, the last elements trailing out of the grass, and he held up a hand to silence them. Quiet fell, even among the dark elves that had never before seen him. "Down this path lies a sleeping city of titans. You've seen them by now, and you know the danger they represent." He cast a look back down the strange path and realized something surprising. *There used to be boulders down there—they're gone. Titans must have realized they give cover to us little people.* "This is a foe that thinks themselves prepared for us, that makes ready to come into our lands and wage war upon us." He felt the lines of his face harden. "They think us food, like hares or chickens, something to make supper with. Make no mistake, they would feast on our bones, and those of our families, and every other person in the north." He cast a sidelong glance at Cora, who stood next to Larana and wore a slightly perturbed look. "And everywhere in between," he added hastily.

"The purpose of this strike is not merely to damage their capability to land such an attack," Cyrus said, "it is to make them question why in the Realm of Death or Fire they would have thought it was a good idea to even ponder such a thing. I mean to make them fear us, fear us all. Let them find us a morsel unpalatable for their consumption, even more unpalatable than we find the idea of them flooding into our towns and cities." He glanced at Terian. "Or else we'll all be living underground soon enough." He raised his hand and beckoned them forward, down the path to Kortran.

"Nice touch," Terian said, falling into line beside him, "I think it appealed to the greatest fears of my Sovarians, the idea that we'd have even more people squeezed down there with them."

Cyrus looked back and saw J'anda's pets striding forth at the sides of the army. One of them had a strange shape atop its shoulders, and it took him a moment to realize the enchanter was riding the titan, legs spread around its neck, holding his staff high to urge it onward. "That's a hell of a thing," Cyrus muttered.

"I've seen weirder," Terian said, and nodded to Cyrus's left. He turned and saw Fortin striding down the path, eyes forward, his face even more furious than usual. "Like that, for instance. Good morning, Fortin."

Fortin's head swung around to take in Terian. "Good day, pretty thing."

Cyrus tried to decide what exactly Fortin meant by that and failed utterly. "You look ready for battle, Fortin. I trust you had a productive slaughter in the savanna?"

"I killed several titans with my bare hands," Fortin said, lifting his rocky fists up. They still looked a little damp, and the blood was unmistakable. "I look forward to killing more. Their skin provides a challenge, being so thick, but I find it to be a nice, rough surface to scratch against." He looked down at his fingers. "I have honed claws upon their flesh."

Cyrus looked at the rock giant's hands, and, unmistakably, it looked as though the craggy skin had given way to sharper points at the end of each finger. "Does that ... did that ... hurt?"

"It felt joyful," Fortin breathed, and Cyrus almost wanted to take a step back from the giant at the euphoric tone. "Once this is over, I will rip the heart from one of my foes and hold it aloft, showering myself in his lifeblood as it courses out—"

"Stop," Cyrus said, shaking his head. "You just ... I was an adherent of the God of War, and that might be a little too much for even me."

"'Was'?" Terian asked, sounding like he was teasing. "Didn't I warn you about losing your belief in things?"

"This is not—" Cyrus stopped mid-explanation and waved a hand at him. "Never mind."

They came around a bend in the road, the last bend, and before them was laid out the city of Kortran, haven of the titans. Cyrus's eyes ran around the edges of the place. A ring road circled the entire city in a long ovoid. The path ahead of them joined on the narrow end, and to his right the mountainside was carved in beautiful reliefs, with stone entries to any number of grand doors. When he looked to the left, where the road curved to the other side, the mountain there held only two entrances, but enormous statues and dual arches gave both the doors there a feeling of great importance. Sandwiched between the mountains on either side, and in the midst of the ring road, situated in a rough sort of indent in the earth, sat Kortran itself. Many of the buildings looked to be carved directly out of the rock, but others had been built with thatched roofs and wood. Some of the structures looked new since last he'd been there, and the whole place had a more crowded feel. Watch fires burned in the night, and titans were visible down in the city streets from where Cyrus watched on high. He counted himself fortunate that no moon hung overhead to light his passage or illuminate him to his waiting enemies.

"On the mountainside over there," Terian said, pointing to the dramatic entries on the left side of the curved road. "The dragons say that the Emperor's palace and the titans' greatest temple lie over there, separated from everything else because of their importance. Their god first, their leader second."

"A temple to Bellarum?" Cyrus asked, brow furrowed. "Sounds wrong. He's supposed to be worshipped in battle."

"And yet, there it is, if the dragons are to be believed—and I suspect they are."

"Which is which?" Cyrus asked, peering at the entries.

"The dragons aren't clear on it, and so the wurm brothers didn't know," Terian said with a shake of the head. "It's not like they come here, after all, it's all just rumors from prisoners that Ehrgraz has interrogated." He glanced at Cyrus. "Surprised he didn't tell you himself."

"He didn't give me as much as you might think," Cyrus said, staring at the city before them. "Mostly counsel on what lay before Kortran; I got the feeling his main concern was to piss the titans off, stir them up, and that he thought the key to that was wrecking everything they'd set up on the savanna."

"Guess he didn't count on the grand ambition of Cyrus Davidon carrying you quite this far, eh?" Terian asked with a smirk. "I suppose he doesn't know you well enough."

"I suppose not," Cyrus said, considering all he was seeing for only a moment before issuing his orders. "We're going with plan B."

"Excellent," Fortin said in a low voice.

"Do you even know what plan B entails?" Terian asked, leaning to look past Cyrus at the rock giant.

"I know it involves me prying the most sensitive pieces of flesh off more titans," Fortin said. "I recently discovered that they keep their genitals between their legs, and it has resulted in considerably more screaming and terror than I was ever able to yield before—"

"Oh, gods," Terian cringed, "I don't know if I even wish that on the titans."

"They're pretty big," Cyrus said, "if we don't attack their weak points we're at a real disadvantage."

"Still, ow," Terian said.

"All right," Cyrus said, cautiously, as they reached the ring road, clouds rolling in overhead and blotting out the starlight, "we have a job to do." He started toward the left, following the road as it curved around, fixing his gaze on the space between him and the temple in the distance. Sentries were obvious there, but no guards were present between the two. *How far off will they be able to see us?* He tried to count, but amongst the entryways into the mountain were columns, plenty large enough to break the outlines of the titan guards.

They drew closer and closer, the quiet of the sleeping titan town below a lulling feeling. *Could they really be this arrogant?* he wondered. After a moment's reflection, he came to his conclusion. *I probably was, back when I believed in the promise of constant battle offered by the Society.*

His feet crept over uneven stones, and though he tried to do his stealthy best to mask them as they came around the curve, his efforts were middling at best. He looked back at J'anda's pets, and only hoped that their approach would mask the sound of the smaller forces cloistered around their feet. He looked back and saw the entire army trailing behind him, some thirty thousand or more, still filtering down the mountain pass into the valley. *If it comes to an all-out fight, we're going to make it a good one.*

He made a motion to halt, and everyone did. His eyes searched until they found Ryin Ayend, and Cyrus beckoned him forth. "Falcon's Essence," he mouthed, and was rewarded once more with the spell that helped him compensate for lack of stature in these fights with beings on whom he only reached the knee. When he had seen the spell cast a few more times, he started forward once more, followed immediately by Terian and Vara, Fortin only a few paces behind them.

They crept between the columns, striking swiftly and quietly. Fortin came upon the first, overtaking Cyrus, ramming his hand into the guard's mouth as he turned to gape at the surprise appearance of a fighting force at his side. The rock giant removed his hand a moment later, with a great and horrid tearing noise, and half the titan's face came with it. Disgusting, watery gasps in the night were the only hint of the titan's passage from life as Fortin lowered him, gently, to the ground below without a further sound.

They took out the next three almost as silently, save for the flopping noises the massive creatures made when they died. By the time they reached the first entry to the mountain, Cyrus was once again covered in fresh ichor and quite sick of it. He motioned for part of the army to keep going, cleansing the second entry, and J'anda sprang forward with his small squad of titans to oblige. He wore an unmistakable look of satisfaction as he rode past on a titan's shoulders, and Cyrus moved to enter the first great hallway to the mountain's interior.

The tunnel was not well lit and looked only big enough for two titans to walk side-by-side within. It seemed to stretch long into the darkness, however, the torches ensconced on the walls unlit.

"This is the temple, right?" Terian whispered next to him. Vara, on his other side, gave them both a look that indicated they should shut up. "They'd keep the palace entry lit all night, wouldn't they? But a temple ..."

"Disciples of war should make their prayers always," Cyrus answered by rote. "Whatever the hour, just like to any other deity."

They followed the tunnel, and ahead Cyrus could see the darkness did not break. Even with the spell cast upon his eyes, he struggled to discern anything more than the vague lines of the tunnel walls and ceiling up to the point where they seemed to cease. Beyond that, he could see nearly nothing, just a blackness that hung in the air like smoke over a fire.

"What is that ahead?" Cyrus asked, and he watched Vara peer into the darkness. "Any idea?"

"I think it's an open space with no light," she whispered back. "This is a cave, after all. Perhaps you should ask the expert on these."

"It's an open space, yes," Terian said, staring confidently into the dark. "I can't see much other than carved rock, though, and it's enough of a distance that the purpose isn't entirely clear to me yet."

They advanced, Cyrus casting a look back to be sure his army was still in close attendance. They were, and he caught a flash of Andren's face as the healer shot him a thumbs up. Cyrus gave him a nod then let his gaze fall to Longwell, whose spear was up over his shoulder, that look of weariness mingled with caution present on his face.

When he reached the edge of the tunnel, Cyrus paused, letting Terian look out. "Huh," the dark elf said. "Well."

"Well, what?" Cyrus asked in a hushed voice.

"Well, it's the temple," Terian said, but there was more than a small amount of tension in the way he said it.

"I don't care for your tone," Vara said, staring at him through narrowed eyes.

"You're going to care even less for what I have to tell you next," Terian said tightly, and then he sighed, deeply. As the dark elf's breath faded, Cyrus heard something else. Deeper. More resonant.

Louder breaths.

"We're not alone," Cyrus said as he caught the first hint of Vara stiffening in reaction to the sounds. Terian just shook his head, almost sadly, and lifted a hand in the air before casting Nessalima's light and illuminating the room around them.

They stood at the entry to a floor filled with bones and sand, spots of blood and rotten flesh discoloring everything and giving the room a ghastly smell that Cyrus noticed only now. The space before him was enormous, bigger than Sanctuary's foyer, and it reached considerably higher up into the mountain, farther than Terian's spell could light it.

Forty feet up from the ground, the stone had been carved into a tier that circled the killing floor upon which they stood. There was another ten feet further up, and another, stairs carved into the mountain's insides that stretched far above them in an ever-widening cone. There were seats in each tier, and with cold surprise, Cyrus finally realized the purpose of the 'temple.'

"The only way to worship the God of War in a temple," Cyrus said tightly, letting his eyes fall on the top tier as someone lit a brazier far, far above him, and then another, and then another as the light made its way down, handed by the processions of titans that were already waiting, hidden, above them.

"As well you should know, Cyrus Davidon," a voice called, one that sounded like it took amusement in every misery it could, drawing Cyrus's eyes to a stand far to his right. There, sitting in the very first tier was a titan, his head adorned with a crown made of a dragon's skull dipped in gold. The cloak perched on the shoulders of the titan was green dragonskin, and the scales stood out as more torches were lit around the arena. The breastplate worn by the beast was a hard metal; it looked like quartal even to Cyrus's inexpert eye. "As any adherent of the God of War should know."

"Emperor Razeel," Cyrus said, resignation flooding through him as the first of the titans reached the edge of the last tier and vaulted it, jumping down into the arena to stand before him. At the head of them was Talikartin the Guardian, his silver armor shining in the torchlight, and his scarred face stretched wide in a smile that told Cyrus that he had been waiting for this moment.

38.

"I think they call this an ambush," Cyrus muttered, looking at the titans arrayed against him. The arena was slowly filling, and it looked as though it had room enough for thousands. The smell of death filled his nose, and he clutched carefully at Praelior, drawing his sword and holding it before him in preparation for the battle to come.

The sounds of fighting outside reached his ears over the movements of the titans within the arena. "The battle is joined," Vara said, and Cyrus caught the hint of worry in her voice.

Cyrus swept only one look behind him, and saw no fighting in the tunnel. *It's all outside, and those lot are on their own; there's nothing I can do for them right now.* With the lone look he dared to give, peeling his eyes from the titans for mere seconds, he noted Curatio, Andren, Fortin, Martaina, Belkan, Odellan, Longwell and Scuddar all close at hand, at the fore with him. *I have to hope that some of the others I trust most are with the army outside, leading them against whatever mad battle they're currently facing.*

"I don't think much of leaders who send their subordinates into battle while they watch," Cyrus said, turning back to taunt Emperor Razeel. "I don't think Bellarum does, either."

The titans that had been creeping closer to Cyrus's war party halted as though someone had yanked the collars of all of them, save Talikartin, whose grin seemed to widen just a bit. Every eye turned to Razeel, who stood abruptly and clutched one of his rough hands against the edge of the first tier. "And I suppose you think I should take instruction in the art of war from a whelp such as yourself?"

"I think when a man of any size calls a warrior a coward, he probably deserves the most forceful possible answer," Cyrus said. He caught a glimpse of Terian's hand still glowing with Nessalima's light.

No cessation spells on this place, which means we could still run ...

Razeel peeled the golden dragon skull off his head and tossed it behind him. It rattled against the wood of his seat, and then the tall Emperor unfastened the cloak of dragonskin around his neck and vaulted over the edge of the first tier to join his soldiers. His face matched his voice, full of malice and anger, with a hint of delight in his eyes in anticipation of the upcoming battle. He looked to Talikartin. "If you defeat Davidon, save his corpse for me. I wish to bite his head off before you consume his body. His armor will make a fine plaything for our younglings."

"And my sword will make a mighty nice toothpick," Cyrus quipped, staring at the Emperor of Kortran. He waved Praelior in the air. "Or possibly a letter opener, assuming you read?"

"Only a weakling taunts when he can hurt," Talikartin said, easing closer to Cyrus, a hundred titans at his back.

"Only a gutless idiot would hold back from charging a clearly smaller, physically inferior enemy," Cyrus shot right back. And before Talikartin's face could do much more than twist in rage, Cyrus charged right at him. Everything seemed to explode into action at once, titans leaping forward as Cyrus sprinted toward the fight. "Get Razeel and Tali!" Cyrus shouted, and saw Vara following a few steps behind Terian, who was just at his back.

"If you think killing their leaders will make this lot calm down," Vara shouted back over the bellowing roars of countless titans, "I have a fine lakeshore property to sell you in Saekaj Sovar!"

"Actually," Terian said, "we do have the Great Sea, although parceling out lakeshore isn't something we've looked at yet. Maybe when I get home ... might be worth a look—"

A titan darted into Cyrus's path, moving quickly and yet still slowed by the power of Praelior in his hand. A knotted face with mouth yawning open in front presented itself, and Cyrus dodged, maneuvering up over the creature's shoulder. He struck its nose at he went by, ripping open a nostril and turning the howl of rage into one of pain. The titan had no time to respond, however, for Terian sailed by in Cyrus's wake and chopped right into the side of its neck like he was swinging to fell a tree, his attack geysering a slow blast of blood out as they both moved on.

"You're pretty good with that thing," Cyrus said, consciously speaking faster, knowing Terian would catch it.

"Have you gotten used to slowing down your speech when talking to people without a godly weapon?" Terian asked, speaking just as quickly. "Because it feels like having a conversation under water sometimes, and I just want to reach in and drag the words out of their mouth so I can respond."

"I actually use my sword to give me an extra margin for thought during troubling conversations," Cyrus said, shrugging.

Terian's eyes burned on him. "I always thought you were a little too witty at times, and others such a dunderhead."

Cyrus dodged an overhand strike from a titan, catching it with Praelior on the titan's wrist and cutting until he hit bone. Moving on, sneaking under the arm and around the back, he poked his blade above the titan's buttock and kept running, withdrawing it and watching a small spurt of blood tell him he'd hit something important.

"That's right, keep softening them up for me," Terian called from behind him. Cyrus heard the satisfying sound of an axe hitting home, breaking bone and drawing a sharp grunt from a titan over the sound of howling, enraged voices that echoed in the arena under the mountain.

Cyrus looked back to reply and completely missed the titan reaching for him from out of his blind side. The grasping fingers wrapping around his midsection were a rude awakening to his distraction, and he snapped his head around as the titan pulled him toward a furiously open mouth. They were squeezing, but his armor was holding the mighty grip at bay, keeping it from crushing him like grape.

The mouth drew closer, and it didn't take Praelior-enhanced time to think for Cyrus to realize that the titan meant to bite his head cleanly off. *Well, that would kill me*, he thought as his stomach dropped. *And I doubt they'd get my head back in any condition for a resurrection spell … and probably not within an hour, either …*

A buzz of spellcraft shot past Cyrus struck the titan in the face, hurling his head back with a snap. He bellowed, but the force of the spell's impact caused him to lose his balance, tipping over and landing on the arena floor with a hard clatter, rattling against the bones in the dirt.

The smell here was fierce, and Cyrus took the opportunity

presented to jam his sword into the back of the giant creature's hand. It drew a scream, and more importantly, caused the titan to relax his grip. Cyrus stabbed him again, then brought his legs up, using the Falcon's Essence spell to create a foothold on air and propel himself up and away from the fallen giant, climbing the invisible steps the spell provided more quickly than any staircase he'd ever climbed.

He went higher than a titan's head before pausing to take stock of the situation. The battle was well underway, titans storming around the arena and finding plenty of Sanctuary forces to occupy their attention. Cyrus watched Belkan deal a stabbing blow to a titan that was running past him, dropping his foe to the ground and pursuing with an attack to the exposed back of its neck. Belkan's swordsmanship made up for his lack of speed, and it only took one hearty stab to render the titan dead.

Odellan shot past Cyrus just below, circling a titan as though he were a fly, striking swiftly, a dozen cuts already opened on the raging titan's rough face. Blood streamed down into its eyes and it swung blindly, hitting one of its fellows and leveling them as Nyad peppered the falling titan with multiple fire spells to the face. Cyrus caught a glimpse of skin dissolving, black smoke pouring off its face as its hair caught fire and traveled up until it reached the creature's helm. Its flailing hands knocked aside the metal cap, and it spun wildly, trying and failing to get away from the fire that was scorching it. Cyrus saw that it was dead without knowing it quite yet. It fell a moment later, its fight ended.

Cyrus focused his attention on Talikartin, picking him out ahead. The titan war leader was swinging wildly at Terian, who circled without landing a blow in the seconds Cyrus watched. He started forward to join the fray, but lightning passed underneath him and caught a titan full in the face as it leapt up to attack him. The blast caused it to draw its hands down to react to the sudden pain, and its attack fell far short. When Cyrus flicked a look to the origin of the lightning, he saw Larana dart away, casting a massive fire spell that she hurled into a knot of three titans. It became a swirling inferno, a tornado of fire that seemed to draw all three of them in as surely as if they were falling into a crevasse at its center.

Cyrus sprang toward Talikartin, who was watching Terian carefully, the two of them trying to gain the measure of each other.

He was committed when a familiar cry from his right tore his attention away.

Vara.

He swung around to see the paladin in the hands of Emperor Razeel, clutched tightly in his grip, her sword knocked away. The Emperor squeezed her and the sound of her armor creaking reached even Cyrus's ears. The battle seemed to pause as everyone drew a breath, and Cyrus felt rage and acute terror rip through him with the force of a sword blow.

"I see I have your attention," Razeel said with a fearsome grin. He brandished Vara as though he were holding a trophy, and she hammered uselessly at his fist. "We see now what you prize above all, hollow man. You are nothing but armor and a sword, no true believer in war." Razeel's knuckles went white as he squeezed Vara tighter. "I wonder if you will still care so much for her in pieces?"

And before Cyrus could move, Razeel thrust Vara up to his mouth and clamped his teeth down on her arm. Vara shrieked in pain as the Emperor of the titans found the joint of her armor, and the world around Cyrus seemed to hold completely still as fear and fury raged impotently inside him.

39.

Razeel laughed through clenched teeth, and the sound of Vara's armor straining under the power of his bite filled the air in the arena. The smell of death and gore was heavy in this place of sacrifice. Time slowed to a stop as Cyrus watched helplessly from a distance.

Vara, for her part, cut off her scream as soon as she realized she was doing it, and Cyrus locked eyes with her across the wide gulf of sand and bone between them. The braziers lit in the viewing area cast the whole arena in a burning orange light. When Cyrus looked into Vara's eyes, he saw—

He saw—

Fury?

Her lips moved almost imperceptibly as Razeel clenched down tighter, and Cyrus remembered that while Vara did not have Praelior to give her exceptional speed, she did possess armor with more than a little enchantment of its own, rather than a sword to give her aid—

Vara's force blast spell sprung forth from the hand trapped in Razeel's mouth. When not trapped, Cyrus had seen her use of the spell bowl over countless men, growing in power from a merely stunning force when he had first seen it to something now approaching lethality. He knew, for his part, that he would not have cared to be on the receiving end of it ever, but especially not at this point in her evolution as a spellcaster.

Unleashed inside the mouth of the Emperor Razeel, the force she let loose was trapped with nowhere to go. Cyrus watched the Emperor's eyes widen just a hint as he felt the first impact inside his mouth—

-and then his head exploded in a blast of blood, bone and tissue that reminded Cyrus of a fountain erupting after long disuse, disgusting ichor spraying up and out in every direction. A silence fell over the arena as Vara dropped out of Razeel's now-lifeless grip. She hit the ground and rolled, springing to her feet as the white light of her healing spell danced over her, her armor stained with the evidence of her kill. She swept her sword back into her hand and dodged the Emperor's corpse as he toppled like a felled tree, the rattle of his armor against the bones on the arena floor a thunderous sound, echoing into the silence. "Idiot!" Vara said, a curse spoken in relief and anger.

"That's not gonna be something you can heal with a spell," Terian said dryly, breaking the spigot of silence wide open and unleashing a torrent of titan fury.

The titans moved in a complete lack of battle order, a frenzy unleashed by the rage of seeing their leader killed. Cyrus tore his gaze from Terian and Talikartin to Vara, who now had the attention of every single titan in the room. "Shit!" Cyrus breathed and broke into a dead run toward her, trying to beat the flood of titans heading her way.

Cyrus stabbed blindly as he scrambled to reach her, flying over the shoulders of countless enemies. He aimed for the neck but did not watch to see if he hit, paying more attention to his running than his swordplay. Vara, for her part, was already somewhere in the swarm below, bereft of a Falcon's Essence spell. He could no longer see her under the crashing wave of titan backplates and helms, he could only try and carve his way through the onslaught to her.

She just killed the Emperor of Kortran.

She'll be fine.

I dearly hope.

Please ... let her be fine.

He swung hard on the exposed back of a titan neck, breaking a vertebra but failing to end the beast. The titan, did, however, stumble hard to his side, knocking over a wave of titans pushing against him. Cyrus counted it as a victory, albeit a small one, and then jabbed his sword more carefully on his next attack against the back of a titan's head, planting his blade between the spinal joints and causing the titan to drop with barely a grunt, tripping those following behind as the beast was rolled over like a spinning log underfoot.

There were at least eight titans between Cyrus and Vara, in his estimation, and the sweat was stinging his eyes as he made to close that gap. He caught a flash of crimson robes beneath him and saw Scuddar In'shara standing off with one of the titans, drawing it away and engaging it in single combat with his scimitar. It looked like a ridiculous mismatch, but the man of the desert was holding his own easily, his blade spinning as he moved, dancing out of the way of attacks and inflicting more than a fair amount of damage of his own, parrying every strike of the titan and drawing more blood with each exchange. The titan's arms were red to the elbows, and it roared at Scuddar as it came on once again, this time losing a finger in its attack.

Cyrus had no more time to watch, however mesmerizing Scuddar's fighting style might have been. He charged forward, watching as arrows flew beneath him, spanging off the helm of the titan immediately beneath him. He saw Gareth atop the shoulder of another titan for just a second, drawing and shooting as it did a double take at his appearance. The elf leapt as the titan moved to deal with the ranger's menace, and the titan ended up smacking himself on the shoulder hard enough to cause him to cry out. Gareth, for his part, had leapt to the shoulder of the next titan in line, his flawless balance keeping him upright as he drew again and fired. *Without a Falcon's Essence spell?*

That elf is crazy.

Cyrus ran on, encouraged by the realization that there was, at least, some help. He reached the front of the line, nearing panic, and had his sword in the wrong hand to even strike a blow at the last titan as he breezed past, running on air. Instead, he caught the nape of the helm, the flowing bit of steel that protected against attacks to the back of the wearer's head. He slapped its edge as he went by, knocking the helm forward. The front, normally designed to rest on the titan's forehead, fell down to cover his eyes as Cyrus ran past, not stopping to deal a deathblow.

He paused as he looked down at the spectacle below. A wave of emotion hit him as large as the titan advance, relief of a sort that was as unexpected as any titan ambush.

Vara was attacking the knee of a titan below, the one he'd blinded, holding back the advance on this front. The titan stumbled, all those behind him halted as they butted against his back. Cyrus moved with fleet feet, avoiding the inevitable fall of the creature. It was still blinded by his handiwork as it came down to its knees, and Vara leapt to finish it with a practiced cut across the throat.

Others were coming to the side, though, and this was the most surprising sight of all, Cyrus thought. Fortin held that line, somehow having cut through under the ranks of the titans to Vara's side, with another standing just behind him. Andren stood in the rock giant's shadow, a short sword in his hand and a wary look on his face. When he saw Cyrus he waved quickly with the sword, beckoning him down.

"Looks like you've got it under control here," Cyrus said as they backed closer to the arena wall. The tier above them was empty in the Emperor's box, and Razeel's corpse was off to the side, still headless. *Terian was right; no healer can fix that.*

"Don't use it as an excuse not to help!" Vara cried as a titan fell next to her, tripped by the corpse of her last kill. She buried her blade in its temple, and it roared, so she struck it again. This time it fell silent and stayed that way.

"Do you need a healing spell?" Andren asked, waving a hand at him. Light danced from his fingers and a curious tingle ran over Cyrus's body. "Just in case."

"I'm fine," Cyrus said, turning to face a roaring titan as it leapt over the fallen bodies of the last two comers. When it landed, Cyrus found himself face-to-breastplate, as inopportune a place to be as any, so he ran higher as he saw Vara go low, spearing it with her sword in the side of the hip while Cyrus distracted it and drew a furious backhand that missed him so closely the wave of air that followed in its wake spun him around, disorienting him.

When he came back around, Cyrus swung at the face lunging toward him. He caught it below the eye with Praelior, withdrew the sword, and went back again, this time at the eye itself. Landing it prompted a howl, and the titan started to sink. Cyrus planted his blade squarely in the middle of the forehead as it dropped. It moaned like a troll as it died, falling backwards, probably breaking its knees as it folded over.

"This is getting out of hand!" Vara shouted as another came forth. Cyrus was too quick for this one, however. He went for its face; it flinched and started to dodge back, dragging its head away and leaving its beefy neck exposed at a forty-five degree angle. Cyrus swung and was rewarded with the familiar splash of red spray and the titan fell over exactly like its comrades.

The battle.

Oh, Bellarum, the battle.

Perhaps I have missed this.

As the titans before him scrambled over the growing mound of their own dead to mount another attack, Cyrus used the spare seconds to look back toward the entry to the arena. The tunnel still seemed jammed with the Army of Sanctuary, but hints of the war that must have been going on out in the city beyond were suggested by the ripples of motion through the forces Cyrus could see.

He caught a glimpse of Larana weaving through the air still hurling spells, and Curatio standing his ground, a bright blaze of lightning blasting from his fingers, rendering his face in flashes of white. "What the hell, Curatio," Cyrus muttered. "Not even trying to hide it anymore."

There was a roar from within the tunnel, and Cyrus watched a thousand bright lights flash into existence. It took a moment for his mind to interpret what he was seeing. *Wizard teleportation orbs?* The flashes of the spell energy taking hold as people seized the orbs and disappeared in a burst of light began a moment later and ran through the tunnel. It seemed to move in lines, until the entirety of the army up to the corps fighting around Curatio disappeared.

"What the—?" Cyrus breathed, blinking in astonishment. *I didn't call the retreat! What's going on here?*

Titan feet appeared at the farthest reach of the tunnel that Cyrus could see, following fast behind a small figure running at top speed ahead of them. Cyrus noted the flash of robes and realized it was Ryin, sprinting with an alacrity Cyrus was not used to seeing from the druid, the hem of his robes whipping behind him. He did not stop until he reached the knotted circle of Sanctuary defenders around Curatio, at which point he turned and held a hand up to his throat, voice coming out amplified by some spell that Cyrus did not know.

"KORTRAN IS BURNING," Ayend's voice sounded, "OUR ARMY OUTSIDE HAS WITHDRAWN SAFELY, THOUGH ONLY BARELY. THE ENTIRETY OF THE TITAN ARMY IS NOW SWARMING THE TUNNEL." He locked eyes with Cyrus and the electricity he communicated was as potent as one of Curatio's bolts of lightning.

The entire rest of the titan army? Coming here? Cyrus swallowed heavily as the action slowed for a moment. *That explains the retreat; without heavy spellcaster support our normal armies can't stand against that.* He swept a gaze over the arena and saw more than a little fresh blood in the gaps between titans where he could see sand. *Hell, we've got some of our best here and we're still having a time of it …*

"Sound retreat!" Cyrus called, bellowing out over the carnage of the battle. "Let's get the hell out of here while we can!"

A scream of rage followed Cyrus's order, and he swung his head round to find Talikartin still swiping ineffectually at Terian. The guardian yelled something, a shout of some word in the titan language that Cyrus did not understand, and a ripple ran through the scene of the battle.

"Cyrus!" Vara cried. "Get down here, now!"

He spun to look at her, catching sight of Terian diving for the ground as well, running in a steep dive to join them. Cyrus did not think, did not ponder, merely acted, and ran as swiftly as he could toward Vara.

He was only ten feet above the ground when the titan cessation spell draped itself over the battlefield and stripped the Falcon's Essence from him.

Cyrus hit the ground with a hard thump as Vara left it in a leap. He watched her sail through the air gracefully, once more striking down an attacking titan with a swipe of her sword so perfectly aimed that the titan did not even manage a riposte. She used his breastplate as a springboard to return to the ground, landing only a few feet away as Cyrus struggled back to standing.

"You all right?" Vara asked, tugging at his arm and helping him return to steadiness.

"Not really," Cyrus said, back to a balance a moment later. He looked at the formidable odds arrayed against them, and realized that without Falcon's Essence, he could no longer even survey the full battlefield of the arena. He was limited by the mob of titans in front of him, so numerous that they blotted out any view of Curatio or the rest of the Sanctuary force still standing.

If they're still standing.

With a breath of horror, the full weight of what had happened slammed home on Cyrus as the next wave of titans moved in on him and his small party. *With a cessation spell over the battlefield with the tyrants, we're trapped here among them.*

No fire to burn them.

No lightning to drive them back.

And no teleportation to get us out of here … alive.

40.

How do you find a wizard with no vestments? Cyrus wondered as he drove his blade into a swiping hand, cleaving two fingers loose and causing the titan attacker to stagger past Cyrus. He nicked the back of the titan's leg as it passed, and it tripped into the hard stone wall of the first tier, the clang of its helm upon impact ringing through the air over the clamor of battle.

If I were aloft, I could just look for the big bastards chanting under their breath, he thought, moving to finish the titan that he'd just knocked over. He aimed for the neck as usual and was rewarded in the same way as always, though this time he mostly managed to dodge the stream. He did not, however, manage to duck under the panicked titan's hand as it reached to staunch the flow of its lifeblood, and the clipping strike sent Cyrus spinning into Andren.

"Oof!" Andren cried as Cyrus slammed into him, knocking them both to the ground. Cyrus was the first to recover, pushing up on one arm. "Watch where you're going!" Andren said, looking more than a bit put out.

"Thanks for the soft landing," Cyrus said, adjusting his helm slightly before turning to get back to the battle. "Let me know if you see any wizards."

"These titans all look the bloody same!" Andren called as Cyrus watched Fortin tear the knee off a titan and then smash the bone into the jaw of the very same enemy, like a small shield.

"Exactly my problem," Cyrus muttered, finding himself with a brand new challenger as he staggered to the left to cover their flank while Vara dealt with a titan that came right up the middle at them. *No vestments, no robes. They all seem to be wearing armor, at least all that I've seen.*

He plunged a sword through a slow-moving titan's knee and did some kneecap removal of his own, though his was incomplete and left hanging, unlike Fortin's. "Is the cessation spell still on us?"

Andren's answer came back a second later, nearing panic. "Yes!"

"Okay," Cyrus said, taking on his next challenger as Terian came staggering out from between the legs of the titan at him. The dark elf swung his axe and sent the titan stumbling. Cyrus narrowly avoided being caught under the enormous thing, the creature's hip clipping him as he dodged its shadow.

"Sorry," Terian said, sweeping into place next to Cyrus. "But it was either take him down or wait for you to do it while the next one behind took a free shot at me." That very titan swung at Terian and he met it with an overhand chop that split the titan's hand in half. "Hope that wasn't his dominant hand, or he's going to be so irritated at me when he gets back to the barracks and has some alone time—"

Cyrus lunged forward and plunged his sword into the titan's exposed abdomen as it clutched at its wounded hand. Blood dripped down, and the smell of disgusting rot, fouler than nearly anything he'd smelled before, told him he'd struck its bowels. He dodged sideways, ripping with Praelior as he moved, and the titan fell on a growing pile atop their last kill. "I don't think that's going to cross his mind later, strangely."

"Still no sign of healers for these bastards," Terian said, "not that I'm complaining!" He paused, striking again with his axe against the hip of a titan passing to attack Vara. "Please, please, don't answer my complaint, fates."

"Now you believe in fates," Cyrus muttered, scrambling back from a particularly aggressive titan attack. "It's almost as if you lost your faith in the God of Darkness."

"Can't imagine what would have prompted that," Terian said dryly, laying his axe into the back of the knee of the titan attacking Cyrus. "Maybe it was that I got to know him entirely too well to respect him anymore."

"I have a similar problem, I find," Cyrus said with a muted smirk.

"I—" Terian began.

A fearsome bellow from Fortin drew both of their attentions, and Vara's as well from where she plunged her own blade into the face of a titan coming at her. She came to the ground, breathing heavily, the toll of killing the massive things now obvious. Cyrus looked past her and found Talikartin moving on the rock giant, finally through the crowd and coming to attack.

"Death is coming for you, foes of Kortran!" Talikartin called, his expression one of rage mingled with joy, some hybrid Cyrus could recall perhaps feeling himself on early battlefields, some strain of vindictive anger crossed with the thirst for bloody revenge and abject excitement as battle played out before him in thrilling spectacle.

I'm fighting giants and winning. Their blood soaks me. The war roars within me, and the fight goes ever on.

Isn't this what I've always wanted?

Fortin screamed again and charged at Talikartin. The rock giant came up to the titan's waist, planting a craggy fist right into his hip. Talikartin grunted and blanched from the impact, bending slightly at the middle from the force. He brought around a punch of his own in reprisal, however, and Cyrus watched it land against Fortin's face, knocking the rock giant back a step of his own.

Rather than let Fortin recover, Talikartin pursued. He hit Fortin again, this time in the chest, and the sound of air rushing out of the rock giant's lungs was like a bellows being pushed in a smith's shop. Talikartin struck again and again, raining hard blows down upon the creature that stood so short against him. The power of the strikes was unquestionable, and Cyrus could hear the cracking of rock.

Fortin staggered, striking out blindly in an attack that hit Talikartin in an undefended thigh. It tore his trousers but did nothing to the skin beneath, and the titan reached down and seized Fortin by his small neck, lifting him into the air. It looked like a labor for Talikartin, but the titan did it, slowly levering the rock giant up until he could grasp him with his other hand, grabbing him around a leg.

Within his grip, Fortin struggled, but it was a futile effort. The rock giant looked dazed, some of the fight taken out of him by the ruinous blows. "You are strong," Talikartin said, staring into Fortin's eyes. "I am stronger," he said with a rush of hatred, and he lifted Fortin up and brought him back down again, slamming him over his knee—

Fortin broke cleanly in half at the waist, black fluid pouring out of either side of him as Talikartin tossed the split pieces. One hit the wall of the arena and bounced near Andren, the other came to rest at

Talikartin's feet.

The titans around them roared in appreciation at the battle they had just witnessed, and Cyrus did not realize that he had been holding his breath until he made to let out a cry of outrage and had no wind with which to do it.

"Uh oh," Terian said.

"We're a bit screwed, here," Andren opined.

"DIE!" Cyrus screamed, and he charged across the dirt arena floor, vaulting over the femur of something massive and using the other end of it to stage a leap at Talikartin, who waited with great satisfaction.

Cyrus had telegraphed his jump too much, he realized belatedly, rage feeding him poor strategy. Talikartin saw him coming, his trajectory obvious, and there was little Cyrus could do once in the air to alter it. The titan still stood, smirking, waiting, and moved only slightly so that Cyrus would impact upon his breastplate—

When Cyrus hit the quartal breastplate, he had already prepared himself for the impact. He huddled up and let his right pauldron lead him. It struck, the force of impact transmitted through the armor, through the chain mail beneath, mostly dissipating somewhere between the two. Cyrus hit the padding hard, the nearly immovable wall before him that was Talikartin forced a step back from his impact.

Cyrus dropped to the ground some ten feet, absorbing the impact again through his knees. He felt the pain and used Praelior to help ignore it, hoping that somewhere down the line he might get a healing spell to fix whatever minor problem he'd just caused himself. Now he was at Talikartin's feet. The titan had probably meant for him to be here, but also probably intended him to be a bit more stunned. Talikartin himself was stumbling back a step, arms trying to balance his unwieldy frame.

Now Cyrus found himself in a curious position. Talikartin wore thick metal boots, unlike the rest of the titans, but they only stretched to just below the knee, and Cyrus stood a tiny bit higher than that—

He rushed in and stabbed Talikartin in the knee like he'd done to so many other titans, not even worrying about simply going deep; he dragged his sword around as he ran in a circle like the titan's calf and shin were some maypole that he was trying to wrap festively.

Well, I certainly brought out a different color, he thought as he opened it up.

Talikartin staggered again, his balance utterly failing before he had a chance to recover it. He went down, falling to the ground on his back, rattling as he landed on something. Cyrus heard the shattering of bone but was under no illusion it was Talikartin's. He saw plainly a piece of something's rib cage jutting out from under the titan's shoulder as he ran up the breastplate to the titan's stunned face.

"EVERYBODY DOWN!" Another magically aided voice boomed out over the arena, this time obvious as Curatio's. Cyrus swept low, jumping off Talikartin's breastplate, halted by the force of the suggestion. He used the titan as cover as a flash of orange too bright to be the braziers in levels above filled the air.

Snakes of fire swept over Cyrus's head, darting less than ten feet above where he crouched at the side of Talikartin. They swept lower as he cowered there, watching magic fiercer than any he'd ever seen before writhing as though it had life of its own above him. The flames coursed with energy, popping and cracking, showering him with something akin to sparks from a flint, and Cyrus needed only sweep his eyes around once to see corpses of titans caught aflame, burning around him as the sky on fire began to recede.

What the hell was that?

"AHHHHHH!" Talikartin's howl prompted Cyrus to move. Cyrus sprang to his feet, stumbling away from the titan, who sat up now that the flames had receded, his face burnt to a crisp and his armor glowing from the heat of the magic that had just been used.

A flash of blue burst in front of Cyrus as wizard magic sent a teleportation orb to him. It hovered in front of him, winking into existence like some grand joke. Cyrus scanned the arena to find every titan contained therein either on fire and screaming or dead and aflame. Most of them were not taking it nearly as gracefully as Talikartin, at least those few still alive.

"Cyrus!" Vara screamed at him, and Cyrus spun around. She stood with Terian and Andren, blue orbs in front of them all, the healer crouched over the portion of Fortin that had landed near him. Cyrus watched as he grabbed the orb of teleportation in front of him and disappeared with half of Fortin's corpse into the wizard spell.

Cyrus sent a last look toward the tunnel entrance as he sprinted toward Talikartin's feet. He caught sight of Curatio there, hunched over, a half dozen defenders still around him. Cyrus waved a hand and saw them start to fall back, a wall of titans just behind them in the tunnel. He blinked and looked closer, and saw J'anda atop the shoulders of one. With a look back at Cyrus, the enchanter saluted, and then disappeared into the light of a spell of his own.

"I will kill you for this," Talikartin said, and Cyrus turned his head to look at the titan even as he vaulted over Talikartin's legs and came to rest on the upper body of Fortin. The rock giant's red eyes stared up dully, black liquid pooling beneath him and streaming down his lips like magma. "For this insult."

"You come at me, I come right back at you," Cyrus promised, meeting the eyes of Talikartin. They were hazy, slightly burned, but not so badly that they would not heal naturally. It looked to Cyrus as if Talikartin's scarred skin had spared him the worst of the burns inflicted on the others. "We can do this dance forever—or at least until one of us is dead."

"It will be you," Talikartin mouthed, cracked lips bloody as he forced his way to his knees. He grasped at his own breastplate and the sizzling sound of flesh burning against hot metal filled the air. "I will do whatever it takes to destroy you and yours utterly, completely. This war—is not over," he said, and with a growl he raised a hand to strike at Cyrus.

Cyrus caught the glimpse of Vara and Terian disappearing in the flash of teleportation, and he knew that Curatio and the others had already left. For a split second he considered fighting back, on his own, in the arena of war in the middle of Kortran.

To the death.

To the end.

The way I was always meant to.

But as his eyes met the dead ones of Fortin with a glance, Cyrus stooped and wrapped his arms around the dead rock giant, seizing the blue light of the teleportation spell. He felt the world of war disappear around him, as though burned away by some magic, and found himself hugging tight to half the corpse of a rock giant on the floor of his quarters, and he let himself take a peaceful breath at last.

"I would say that was a rather successful sortie." Vara's voice surprised him, and he pushed up to all fours to find her standing before him in the Tower of the Guildmaster.

Cyrus just shook his head, looking down at the dead rock giant. *I'll need a healer for him. Need to get the rest of him back to Andren.* He sighed, exhausted. "I don't think I would call it that at all."

"We killed Emperor Razeel," Vara said. Dawn was breaking over the horizon, the sun coming up in the eastern sky, an orb of red setting the world afire. *Soon it'll burn, all right,* Cyrus thought.

"*You* killed him," Cyrus agreed, but reluctantly; not for the credit, but for the rest of the thought that followed.

"Yet you seem … dispirited." She cocked her head at him, curious at his despondent reaction, surely.

"We failed," Cyrus said after a moment's pause, and let that sink in. "If we'd killed Talikartin, maybe—but we didn't." He knocked off his own helm and let it rattle across the floor.

"What are you saying?" Vara asked, coming a knee next to him. The sweat dripped down her face along with the blood, and he knew if he sought out a mirror, his countenance would be just the same.

"This isn't over," Cyrus said, shaking his head. "Not even close. Not by a long, long ways."

41.

"You went all the way to Kortran and struck at their temple?" Ehrgraz's voice was harsh and furious, smoke pouring out of his nose. "You are a special sort of fool, Cyrus Davidon, and when I say that, it carries some weight, for my own people are the most complacent group of fools on Arkaria who sit and wait for death to come for them. You are not that sort of fool, no, you are the sort that seeks death out all on his own—"

"I didn't wait around for them to come out and meet us," Cyrus said. It was a few days after the battle, and the hot summer winds still swept around the Plains of Perdamun as Cyrus stood upon the wall looking into the furious yellow eyes of Ehrgraz, who had swept in on the morning wind. Cyrus had a suspicion based on the dragon's somewhat controlled demeanor early on, that he had already heard of the attack on Kortran, calmed himself and was now becoming enraged once more at the further hearing of it. "I—"

"You were supposed to draw them out of the front gate," Ehrgraz spat, sending sparks out from behind a forked tongue.

"Well, I did that," Cyrus said, arms folded in front of him. "And you didn't say not to attack Kortran, I might add."

"I assumed you would not be foolish enough to dig your own grave," Ehrgraz said. "Apparently, I was in error."

The warm wind stirred Cyrus's hair across his forehead, and he glanced around. Vaste was not present this time, thankfully, nor anyone else save for Vara, who stood back at the other end of the parapet, listening but not involved in the conversation. "You got what you wanted. The titans are currently filling the Gradsden Savanna from one side to the other."

210

"Is that so?" Ehrgraz asked, eyes flashing. *As though you don't know.* "We've tried to send scouting parties to the portals in the intervening days."

"How many attempts?" Ehrgraz interrupted.

"Two," Cyrus said coolly. "They barely made it back alive. The portals are watched. This has been confirmed by the elves of Amti—"

"Let me also confirm it for you," Ehrgraz said. "They have increasing garrisons standing guard around every portal in the area, and archers waiting to bring down anyone such as yourselves who can't fly high enough to avoid their gaze and their arrows."

Cyrus did not blink, but only through careful practice holding things in. "I suppose that strikes our next plan, which was to conduct a long-range attack back into Kortran—"

"*Back?*" Ehrgraz's wings spread out in what looked like some combination of shock and outrage, his jaw flapping open. "Why in the name of the demons of old would you go back? Have you not done enough to try to kill yourself?"

"I figured if we killed Talikartin—"

"If!" Ehrgraz huffed. "Yes, indeed, if you had! I, for one, am amazed you succeeded in killing Razeel, and it seems that only his own incompetence allowed you to do it." He shifted his gaze to Vara. "Personally, I would have ripped your head off first, were I him, but I suppose I view you as dangerous rather than dinner."

"You know a surprising amount about what happens in Kortran," Cyrus said carefully.

"And you know surprisingly little about it considering what you attempted." The dragon made a low rumbling noise in his throat. "Did you lose anyone in the effort?"

"A few," Cyrus admitted. "Probably two dozen, all told, mostly to titan attacks that smeared them into a state where they couldn't be healed or resurrected." At this, he felt the plucking of regret within him. "Not as many as we killed of theirs." He paused, trying to find a clever approach for his next question and giving up when the route was not apparent. "If you know so much about what happened in Kortran, why don't you know who is teaching them magic?"

"Why would you assume that I learned what I know about the events in Kortran from the titans?" Ehrgraz asked, looking far too satisfied for Cyrus's liking.

"Because the titans were the only other ones there," Cyrus said, annoyed.

"And how do I know all I know about you, Cyrus Davidon?" Ehrgraz's eyes flashed. "You think I get that information from my spies in Kortran? I don't."

Still another person who suggests that we have spies in Sanctuary. It shouldn't surprise me, given the size of our guild, that there might be a leak or two. He hardened his face. "For all your rustle and rattle about spies and wisdom and foolishness, I have yet to hear a suggestion from you about how best to proceed."

"Nor will you," Ehrgraz said, drawing his wings in close to his body once more, "so long as you continue to consider idiotic plans like launching some foolhardy long raid into Kortran." He paused. "What would your aim be? What end, other than yours, obviously? You say to kill Talikartin, but you have failed in this task repeatedly. What would be different this time?"

Cyrus bit back the angry answer that bubbled up from within. "This time ... I'd intend to make it so he wouldn't see us coming."

"Ohhh," Ehrgraz said, seemingly amused. "Now this is a fascinating thing. Do you mean to suggest he was supposed to see you before?"

"I meant to punch him in the nose before," Cyrus said, "to bloody him good and have him know it." He blinked away from those yellow eyes. "Next time ... I just want him dead, and I don't care if he knows it's coming before or during. He's too dangerous to live unchecked."

"Now we enter interesting territory," Ehrgraz said, "wherein the Guildmaster of Sanctuary considers assassination a valid option." He made a sound like a chuckle, but rougher, and his wings spread once more.

"Do you see a better option?" Cyrus asked, his cheeks burning with a slight shame.

"You don't know what I see," Ehrgraz said with something akin to a shrug of his massive, scaled wings. "But I will say this much—the cause is perhaps not as hopeless now as it was when I arrived, and for that I am heartened."

"Because I'm willing to murder this titan, suddenly things are better?" Cyrus asked, frowning at Ehrgraz. "How does that make any kind of sense?"

"Because perhaps you are not the fool I thought you were when I came here today," Ehrgraz said, lifting into the air with a powerful sweep of his wings. "I find hope in that, personally." He looked at Cyrus with careful eyes. "We will speak again ere too long." And with a sweep of his wings, he flew into the sky and was gone in a matter of seconds.

42.

The Council Chamber was still and silent, the quiet hanging oppressively in the air above them. Cyrus sat in his seat and dared to move only his eyes in surveying all those around him. It was the full complement of officers, along with Cattrine once more. She still looked tired, though perhaps less so than she had when he'd seen her before.

The one who looked most tired was Curatio. Since the arena, the healer had shut himself up in his quarters for long stretches of time, and even when he emerged he seemed changed, wearier, his complexion faded and his posture stooped.

"I liked killing the titans," Longwell said, rattling his lance slightly as he adjusted it where it leaned. "I make no bones about it. I wouldn't mind killing more." The resentment practically dripped off his features, and Cyrus made a mental note to speak with the dragoon later about his gradually darkening demeanor. "I only wish we could have hung in the fight longer before we had to run."

"That was a very near thing," Odellan said, his winged helm catching the sunlight on the table and causing Cyrus to blink away. It seemed perfectly positioned to hit his eyes, and he moved just an inch to his left to find relief, the green spots in his vision fading. "I wouldn't care to have to run that particular expedition again, personally, for I would fear that a repeat engagement would not find the luck on our side as it was last time."

"Luck nothing," Erith snorted. "I heard about what happened in the arena." She nodded at Curatio across the table. "If you hadn't had a badass heretic on our side, you'd have been trapped with no hope of escape."

"Yes, well," Curatio said, waving a hand lightly in dismissal, "let us not tread too heavily on said heretic, for these sorts of things are very taxing."

"I wouldn't care to be caught behind again, that's sure," Andren said, nodding. His short hair stuck out in a few different directions, and Cyrus wondered if perhaps he simply didn't know quite what to do with hair that short. "And Fortin may have come out of it all right in the end, but I'll tell you right now that joining him back together and resurrecting him? Nasty work. He almost killed me—"

"I, for one," J'anda said, his staff in hand, "didn't find the fight too taxing."

"You were riding on a titan's shoulder the entire time," Ryin said.

"But I was in several minds, charming my pets," J'anda said, "and it was all terribly easy for the most part. I could do it again. The titan minds, though," he shook his head, "terribly simple. You can probably imagine."

"I don't think I'd care to," Mendicant said, shuddering from where he sat, face barely visible above the table edge. "I was outside when their army started stomping through. It was not …" He breathed a rattling breath. "We lost—"

"I know," Cyrus said, nodding slowly. "We're not going back to Kortran." He caught a look from Vara out of the corner of his eye. "Not yet, anyway."

"Oh, good," Vaste said, much more mildly than usual.

Cyrus waited, as did the rest of them, for further comment, but it did not come. "Uh … Vaste?"

The troll looked up from where he was staring at the table. "Yes?"

"Where's the ill-timed barb?" Ryin asked, staring across at him. "Where's the jibe? The jape?" The troll stared back at him blankly. "The—"

"I know what all those words mean, you cockeyed dunce," Vaste snapped. "If I had anything particularly humorous to say, don't you think I'd say it?"

A shocked silence persisted for a moment afterward, broken by Cattrine. "This is serious, then," she said, her long, thin fingers laid out on the table in front of her.

"Why do you think they're guarding all the savanna portals?" Vaste asked sullenly. "It's not because they're looking to have a massive harvest of long grass, I can tell you that much."

"They're afraid of attack, obviously," Ryin said.

"No, they're not," Vaste said with a shake of his head. "Not really. Not against Kortran, not again. They're afraid of sorties. Of raids."

"How do you know this?" Cyrus asked, frowning.

"They're afraid we'll hit their supply line again," Vaste said simply, sagging back in his chair. "Because what we did to the fortress and the storehouse? That was the real pain we inflicted. I mean, other than killing their Emperor. That certainly pissed them off, and I say brava to Vara for her part in angering our already angry enemy." He clapped his hands together once. "Also, before you ask, that was not a joke, a jape or any other j-word of the same rough meaning."

"They're coming to the pass, then," Cyrus said, staring at Vaste. "If you're sure that's why—"

"That's why," Vaste said quietly, not an ounce of humor in him. "They're rallying for it, and they don't want any more ... interruptions."

The silence sank in once more, and Nyad was the one to speak this time. "What ... what do we do?" Her voice was small and terrified.

"You might want to ask your father for permission to move our army through his lands," Cyrus said, with a heavy air of resignation. He caught every eye in the room. "Because without Sanctuary at the fore ... the elven army really doesn't stand a chance of holding them out of the north."

43.

Who are you?

Eyes of red haunted Cyrus, pursued him, snapping him awake in sweat-sodden sheets, wrapped around him like they were entrapping him, smothering, holding him down and strangling him to death. He gasped for breath as though they had choked him, and when the first torch sprang to life in front of him it was a shock to his eyes as much as the vision of the pale elf lying next to him, her hand delicately touching his shoulder. "Cyrus," Vara murmured, more than a little sleep in her own voice. The silken slip she wore to bed hung off her shoulder, and her hair was loose around her face.

Cyrus breathed in the sweet torch smell as the hearth on the far end of the room sprang to life, the fire bursting into it and lighting the room. The balcony doors were all shuttered, making the Tower of the Guildmaster feel smaller than it did when they were open to the plains below, moonlight shining on the green grass. Cyrus's breathing was still ragged and rasping. He rolled to let his feet touch the cold stone floor, sheets sloughing off his naked body.

"Are you all right?" Vara asked, rolling over to place a hand on his back. He didn't quail away from her touch, but the vision in the nightmare had been so vivid, so irrationally frightening … and now he couldn't even recall what it was.

"I'm …" Cyrus took another deep, calming breath, letting it all flow in. "… I have no idea."

"If you're all right?" Vara moved to sit next to him, her creamy thighs sliding off the bed to hang next to his over the edge. Her feet were so small, so delicate, compared to his. She placed a light arm around his shoulder and brushed his other with her hand, leaning her soft cheek against him. "I think, physically, it is fairly obvious you are all right."

The panic of the nightmare had receded enough to allow Cyrus to see the humor in what she spied. "Huh. I, uh … guess so, in that regard."

"However, don't count on me being quite awake enough to go in for that, seeing as we already rutted once tonight," she said, pressing her warm skin close against him. "Did you have the nightmare again?"

"I did," Cyrus said, nodding sharply. "I think."

"Which one? Leaugarden or …"

"The other," Cyrus said, shaking his head, turning it enough to see her gazing at him through sleepy blue eyes. "The—I don't even remember what happened other than awaking to a—just a feeling of …"

"Of what?" she asked, running soothing fingers across his shoulders and back. It tickled just a bit, but in a wholly good way.

"Like I don't even know who I am," Cyrus said, rubbing at his eyes.

"Oh," she said. "Well. That seems to be coming up quite a bit lately. Not quite as often as—"

"Yeah, yeah."

She held herself tight against him. "I know who you are, even if you don't."

His shoulders straightened at her words, and he looked her in the eyes. "Who am I?"

She looked right back at him, the faintest smile on her lips before she spoke. "You are … my little moppet."

Cyrus closed his eyes. "Please … don't ever say that where anyone else might hear it."

She chuckled lightly. "I'll keep it entirely between us, I assure you." She ran fingers through his hair, and he caught the scent of the soap she used, sweet and slightly fragrant. "From whence does this desperation to know yourself spring?"

"I don't even know," Cyrus said, shaking his head as she threaded her fingers through his hand and placed it upon her thigh. When he looked down, almost expectantly, she sighed and moved the hand into the air, as if to disabuse him of any possible notion of things going in that direction. "I mean, there are obviously things on my mind, conversations I'm having with others, with you, with myself about the changes going on, but I wouldn't think it would come out this way in some sort of deep, frightening ..." He groped for words.

"Crisis of identity?" she asked, tightening her grip on his fingers and bringing his knuckles to her lips with a kiss. "You've had two nightmares about it now. It would seem your mind is trying to tell you something."

"Tell me what?" Cyrus asked, tensing his shoulders, afraid of the answer he might get.

"I don't know," she said. "Something about what you're doing, perhaps." She hesitated. "Something about what you're willing to do, maybe."

He looked away. "You're talking about the conversation I had with Ehrgraz."

"Assassination is not something I ever recall us discussing," she said quietly.

"We still haven't," Cyrus said, hiding his eyes from her. "It was just ... me thinking out loud to Ehrgraz—"

"Yet you sent scouting parties into the savanna," she said, no accusation to her words. "You planned the long-ranging strike, a knockout punch past their defenses?" She uncoiled her fingers from his. "What were you thinking in terms of an endgame? Not another fair fight with the titans and all their armies, I assume, and yet you said very plainly to me that this would not end because Talikartin was still alive. That leaves—"

"Killing him however we have to, yes," Cyrus said, feeling caught. He expected her arms to sweep away from him in revulsion, her warm skin and cool silken slip to push against his side as she made her getaway. He dared to look, just a glance, really, at her.

"What?" she asked.

"I'm surprised the noble paladin isn't retreating from me."

"Even if the crusader in me wanted to," Vara said with a sigh, "the woman in me is taking precedence at the moment. I feel as if she's usurping my will and my very limbs. It's quite exhausting, being this divided. I can only assume my paladin self is still asleep." She smiled lightly.

"You're joking about it," Cyrus said, now looking at her with a little less shame, "but you know Alaric would never have sanctioned this. He would never have dreamed—"

"You might be surprised what Alaric would do if pushed into the corner we find ourselves in," Vara said evenly. "I watched him kill Partus with a single spell, unseen, for merely insulting and threatening me. With what we are against, even Alaric might consider desperate measures."

"I have a hard time believing that," Cyrus said, and now he hung his head low for a different reason. "I think of him as this looming shadow that hangs over every decision I make, judging me silently for my failures, which are growing too innumerable to count."

"What is this self-pitying drivel?" she asked, and now she did pull away.

"We lost people in the attack, Vara—"

"We were an army on the march," she said stiffly, like he'd insulted her. "Death is a possible consequence, especially when the foes are as dangerous as the titans are. Anybody not aware of that danger and willing to face it would not have joined our army or the armies of Saekaj or Amti. Certainly not the latter two, given the scarcity of healers with the resurrection spell." She brushed hair back over her ear, giving her blond locks a lopsided appearance. "If you want to bludgeon yourself into senselessness for every death that happens in this particular war—which you did not start, by the way, much as you might want to take responsibility for everything under our sun—this will be a heavy toll on you. Responsibilities of leadership, I didn't think I needed to tell you, include the death of your soldiers, your guildmates. It has happened in the past. It will happen again."

"But when I think of Alaric," Cyrus said, the fire burning inside him, trying to get out in his words, "I wonder if he ever felt the desperate pain of it like—"

"Of course he did," she snapped. "Do you have any idea how—" She cut herself off. "No, I suppose you wouldn't have, it was after you went to Luukessia." She focused her eyes on his. "While you were gone, after I had regained some of my composure following … all that happened in Termina and the Realm of Death and afterward, I offered to go with Alaric to pay a call to Niamh's family … to tell them she was dead." She straightened. "He informed me he had already gone, while you and I were off to escape the assassins. He did it himself, and the look he gave me when I asked about it … told me everything I needed to know about what happened and how he felt about it." She ran a hand, once more, across his face. "Alaric faced it, too. He felt it, too. You are not alone in this responsibility, and the only way to ensure you never have to face it again is to break all ties with Sanctuary, renounce your position of leadership, and hide away in some dark corner of the world where no one will find you." She paused, then a ripple of amusement made its way out. "Though I wouldn't expect that to work, because wherever you go, I will find you, and if you run, warrior, I will administer the most shockingly painful kicking of your arse you will ever experience."

"That sounds … borderline exciting."

She slapped him on the chest. "There will be nothing titillating about it, I assure you—"

A knock at the door interrupted them, and both their heads swiveled at the sound like it was the herald of an approaching attack. "Yes?" Cyrus called without thinking, and the door at the base of the stairs opened before he could so much as gather the sheets around him. Vara rolled back over the bed and snatched them out of his grasp, covering herself and leaving him quite exposed.

Calene Raverle emerged from the stairs a moment later, a purpose in her walk. "Sir, our scouts in the Heia Pass report approaching titans, and—" She seemed to realize he was naked partway through the delivery of her message. "Oh, gods!" she said and threw a hand up as she averted her eyes.

"Sorry," Cyrus said, rolling to try and grab the tangle of sheets away from Vara, who had them clutched against her tightly. "Give them to me!"

"No," Vara said, looking quite outraged. "I'll be left exposed!"

"What do you think I am? Aren't you elves supposed to be more—you know—worldly and sensual and open to—"

"I am not open to displaying my body like some Priestess of Life—"

"You showed me your naked backside when you still loathed me—"

"I'm rapidly doubling back toward that feeling just now—"

"And you're at least wearing something under those sheets, unlike me—"

"Whose fault is that? No one told you to come to bed as naked as a plains dog, and with much the same look in your eye—"

"Uhm, excuse me," Calene said, head still tilted away. "The, um, titans are approaching the Heia Pass, and it's a two-day ride to reinforce them since the portal at the savanna end is—"

"Yes, thank you," Vara said, sitting up and letting the sheet drop, her slip still fully covering her more effectively than many dresses Cyrus had seen worn in Reikonos. "We're both fully aware of the strategic and tactical planning considerations involved here." She paused, looking a little indignant. "And I assure you, we will both be down momentarily, so if you could go and sound the alarm ..." She held out a hand to shoo off Calene, but the ranger was not looking at her, nor Cyrus.

"Okay," Calene said, easing blindly back toward the staircase. She used her foot to feel for it without sight. "I will, just ... uhm ... get ... going, then ..."

"Why don't you just turn around and go," Vara suggested irritably.

"Right," Calene said, and fled down the staircase with all haste. She paused at the bottom and hesitated, her hand on the doorknob. "You know, I really respected you before, but even more now."

"Don't swell his head," Vara said, "it's already quite oversized."

"I wasn't talking to him," Calene said, darting a look at them and then snapping her head back as if she'd been burned. "I meant you. I mean—" she waved a hand in their direction, "with ... with that, and all ... I mean ... goodness ... I don't even know how you can manage to walk normally after, let alone keep up on the march—" She stumbled through the door and closed it with a slam behind her.

"What a nice compliment to you," Cyrus said as the noise of the door shutting faded, and the sound of Calene's shouts of "ALARUM!" rang out below them.

"That's not going to help the ego at all," Vara said with a sigh as they both fumbled to escape the bed, rushing to their respective armors.

44.

The ride south through the Heia Pass was long and arduous, though harder on the horses than their riders, in Cyrus's estimation. They did not stop for sleep, only water and the occasional break, and kept at it, at a canter, almost the entire way. By the time nightfall came at the end of the first day, Cyrus had grown weary of the rocky outcrops that had hung over him for the entirety of the trip. They reminded him of the gargoyles on some of the newer, grander structures in Reikonos, lurking overhead like ill omens.

There was much conversation, though all of it was muted. The majority of the convoy of Sanctuary riders was, in fact, spellcasters. Cyrus was one of the few warriors and rangers along for the fight; they already had a sizable contingent of troops at the end of the pass, and Cyrus's thoughts seemed to be ever on them as they rode.

They reached the crest of the pass the night after they left, but it was so dark and moonless that even when they began their descent, there was no chance of observing any battle at the southern mouth of the pass. Fires were visible there as distant spots and little else, though Cyrus could not tell if they were watch fires or the flames of battle, of wagons burnt and fortifications lit.

"Take heart," Curatio said, riding alongside Cyrus as they descended beyond the sight of the mouth a few hours before dawn. "The titans have quite a ways to go before they reach this side of the mountains."

"But it won't take them as long as it takes us," Cyrus said, consumed with his thoughts and a wave of guilt. Thoughts of amusing jokes and japes with Vara had left him once they'd teleported north of the pass. The entire ride had been uneasy and filled with worry for what he would find at its end. "We might meet them in the dark, even—and what would that herald for our guard force at the other side?"

"That they have gone on from this world," Curatio said, staring straight ahead.

His words plucked at the uneasiness in Cyrus as though it were a string of a musical instrument, reverberating inside him. "You're awfully cavalier about that, Curatio."

"No," Curatio said, after a moment's thought, "not cavalier. It would be a tragedy, of course, and one I would not wish to witness. But ... if I may, I think I perhaps hold a different perspective on this, being somewhat longer lived and having seen many of these wars."

"And what perspective is that?" Cyrus asked, almost afraid of the answer. "That we short-lived creatures are like insects to you, as fleeting in our existence as one of those little flies that only lasts the day and no longer?"

"No," Curatio said, shaking his head, expression pure contrition. "I didn't mean to give you that impression, as though I am some overarching being like the gods, only concerned for the biggest picture, unworried about smaller works and the brush strokes on canvas as small as a handprint. Every life is its own painting, you see. Some finish before the first daub is applied, some last longer and necessarily require more space to make their mark. Each has its own glory, though. Sometimes a single stroke conveys more meaning than one the size of a mural, grand and soulless and ultimately empty of any feeling." He shook his head again. "No. No, this sacrifice would have meaning, just as all do. But it is not in our grand power to be able to do anything to affect its outcome. Even casting Falcon's Essence on every horse and straining ourselves by running up mountainous ascents would buy us—perhaps—two hours at the expense of further exhaustion."

"Aye," Cyrus said, trying to follow all the myriad directions the healer had carried him in with his brief statement. "Your perspective is different ... and perhaps a bit, uh, rambling."

Curatio laughed. "Sometimes I find it hard to get it all out in a suitable time frame for you shorter-lived beings. I could say my piece for decades, pour it all out—but no one would stop to listen for that long."

"You talked about the small brush strokes of life," Cyrus said, catching a thought casually tossed out by Curatio and finding it seized his imagination. He nodded his head into the darkness, indicating the path forward, and somewhere out there, its terminus. "Yet ... we seem constantly embroiled in larger events. I suppose I find it hard to imagine concentrating on the mundane after wars and scourges and titans and gods." He paused, and the thought of peace rolled through him, a pleasant shock to the system after a long ride, and the thought of some country home where Vara waited while he worked a plow in the warm sun. It was a lovely contrast to the bite of the cool night air upon his skin.

"It is easier than you think." Curatio smiled in the dimness. "There is the wide world, of course, which I have seen in its glory and possibility. But there is other life—that which takes place inside your own front door, with a different kind of infinite possibility. Where but a gesture," the healer said, almost longingly, "and the actions of a single night can spur hours of study. Where every day can be spent focusing on that which truly matters."

"Curatio," Cyrus said quietly, "we're riding into this pass so that we can stop the titans from coming north and destroying everything—everyone—we care about. How can you say that doesn't truly matter?"

"Cyrus," Curatio said, "suppose you fought for the next five years, as hard as you could, and effected great change of the sort you would wish upon all Arkaria. At its end, you stand triumphant, all foul institutions such as slavery have been destroyed, cast into the pit of history. You win, Sanctuary is preeminent, you are the undisputed greatest warrior in the land, and everyone nods their head as you pass." He shot Cyrus a sidelong look. "It is not too far off where we are today, minus our present menace of course. You could stand as the ultimate warlord, the one who united the land under a banner of fair and just governance—"

"I don't want that responsibility," Cyrus said.

"Of course not," Curatio said, a little too quickly. "But assume you did, and that you did great good with the mantle. But at the end of it all," the healer subtly turned until he found Vara, riding with Nyad and Erith, the three of them engaged in some hushed discussion, "you were left without ... her." He looked back at Cyrus, and the expression in his eyes was tired, but spoke of many lifetimes' worth of experience. "What good would it do you to save the world but lose all you fought for? What would be left of you at that point? What would you even be?"

Cyrus opened his mouth to answer but found none to be satisfactory.

"To have all you hold dear yanked away from you while gaining the whole land ... it would be a terrible irony, I think," Curatio said. "I have known more than a few men and women who sacrificed all they held important upon the altar of their ambitions. Take care that you do not do the same, for the yield on that particular crop is naught but bitterness, and I assure you it is inedible, at best, poisonous at worst." With that, Curatio lightly whipped the reins and his horse surged forward a little faster.

Cyrus rode on Windrider's back in utter silence for a moment, then steered his horse toward where Vara still spoke with Nyad and Erith. As he grew closer, the whispers became audible, and he heard Vara's voice, stiff with her unwavering annoyance. "... No one with dignity would partake in such unnatural sexual practices."

Erith giggled. "It's really not that unnatural, in fact."

"Hm," Vara said sternly as Cyrus hesitated on the outer ring of their little circle. "Apparently it is as I have always suspected; there are some things so low that only a dark elf will stoop to them."

"It's not so bad as you make it sound," Nyad said, utterly assured. "You get used to it after a while, though I suppose with what you're dealing with, it might not ever—" She halted mid-sentence, snapping her head around at the look on Erith's face to find Cyrus watching them, eyebrows halfway up his forehead. "Oh. We were talking about you."

Cyrus felt his brow struggle to fold double, and he started to pull Windrider away. "Do ... do I even want to know?"

Vara looked completely irritated, eyes narrow and flat, mouth a line so thin and fixed that he wondered if she might ever smile again. "Say nothing if you ever wish to—"

"Whoa," Cyrus said, pulling Windrider's reins to lead him away from the conversational circle, "like after all these years I don't know when to keep my mouth shut." He steered the horse a short distance away and nearly stumbled across Vaste, riding along, a tight smile perched on his face. "What are you grinning about?"

"Oh, was I grinning?" the troll asked, running a finger experimentally over his bottom teeth. "Yes, yes, I suppose that looks a bit like a grin. That does happen from time to time when I hear immensely hilarious things."

Cyrus cast a look over his shoulder to find Vara dealing a heated reply to something Erith had said. She looked as though she were about to fall off her horse, wagging a finger at the dark elf. "I am now certain I do not want to know what they're talking about."

"Buggery, actually," Vaste said, drawing a slightly shocked expression from Cyrus. "Since it's not about goats, I'm rather enjoying listening to it."

Cyrus felt the heat of Vara's gaze on his back and turned slightly, confirming that she was looking at him with a somewhat dangerous glare. "I feel like I should get even farther away until this settles down."

"What is it you do again?" Vaste asked.

Cyrus frowned at the troll. "I'm the Guildmaster, idiot. You should know, you helped elect me—"

"Not that job. The other one, the one you went to your League for."

"A warrior?"

"Yes, that," Vaste said, sounding slightly exasperated. "What is it you do?"

Cyrus frowned and answered by rote, using words he'd learned long ago at the Society of Arms. "A warrior's job is to stand in front of our foes and take the abuse aimed at us—"

"A fact I am well aware of," Vaste said, now smiling more broadly, "and often use to explain your relationship with Vara."

"… What?"

"Oh, face it," Vaste said, looking ahead with a rather immense amount of self-satisfaction, "you like your opponents the way you like your women—merciless. And speaking of …"

Cyrus regarded him with undisguised curiosity until he heard hoofbeats approaching in a steady cadence from behind him. He turned, expecting Vara, but found Martaina Proelius instead. She brought her horse alongside his, and when Cyrus turned to say something to Vaste, he found the troll galloping ahead to catch up with Curatio. "Do you have a moment?" Martaina asked, drawing Cyrus's attention back to her.

"This is the most unusual and blazingly fast series of conversations I've ever had," Cyrus said, feeling slightly disoriented. She looked at him with utter befuddlement, and he shook the thought away. "What can I do for you, Martaina?"

"I have a personal matter for you as Guildmaster," Martaina said and looked around before lowering her voice and leaning in. "I was wondering if you'd consent to marrying me."

The world seemed to pause around Cyrus. "I'm ... uh ... with Vara ..."

"Not marry me yourself," Martaina said with an air of impatience. "Marry me to Andren in your capacity as Master of Sanctuary."

Cyrus gave that a moment's thought. "I ... uhm ... don't know that I have that authority, and ... also ... have you talked to Andren about this yet?" *The disorientation is not getting better. This long ride is probably not helping ...*

"We've discussed it," she said in a clipped tone.

"Aren't you still married to Thad?" Cyrus asked, feeling an urge to put a wet cloth upon his forehead and lie down for a space of time. *A very long space of time, if possible.*

"Our marriage was never recorded by any government," Martaina said, "only performed by the Priestesses of Life."

"Don't they ... work for the elven government?"

"There's a tax of gold on the stamps for official documents," Martaina said, rather brusquely. "I wouldn't pay it, so we're not accorded marital standing in the kingdom. Thus ..." She waved a hand.

"Your union is at an end," Cyrus said with a nod. "And more easily than mine was, at that." He massaged the bridge of his nose with metal-clad fingers. "I don't know how to perform a marriage ceremony, having only been to my own, and being somewhat, uh ... unsteady at the time—"

"You were drunk at your own wedding?"

"Out of pure joy and nervousness, yes," Cyrus said, and Windrider seemed to shudder with laughter before letting out a whinny beneath him. As though he needed to explain to both elf and horse, he went on. "I ... was marrying someone that I hadn't known for very long, and I wasn't really used to being with people ... or dealing with people in anything other than combat ... or instructors talking to me about combat ... It was a very difficult time for me," he finished a bit lamely.

"No judgment here," Martaina said, though she appeared to be hiding amusement under a very thin veil. "There is a text I've chosen, something akin to reading a part in a play. The ceremony of the Iliarad'ouran, recounted in an old book of Korinn's History of the Third Age of Elvendom—"

"If all I have to do is read," Cyrus said, eyeing her for a hint of deceit or anything further that she might be hesitating to mention, "I suppose I can do it, though I ... I'm surprised Andren didn't come to me for this himself." He searched out the healer and found him plodding along atop his horse, eyes partially closed, looking like he was fully asleep. "He certainly looks enthused about the nuptials."

"He's on a long ride," Martaina said with clipped annoyance. "Give you a few more hours and you'll be nodding off in the saddle as well, and just in time to fight a battle with titans three times your height."

"Thanks for that warning," Cyrus said sourly. "I might have forgotten otherwise and gone for a nice nap as soon as we arrived, all thought of titans as gone as a good dream when you wake." The smell of horses and unwashed riders hung heavy in his nose. He parted from her with one further thought. "How do you think Thad is going to react to this?"

"Him, I haven't talked to about it," she said, and now she rode off, "for what I do does not concern him in this regard, and he is at the pass in any case." She showed her unease at this last, and when Cyrus tried to discern her feelings on the matter, the conclusion he came to was that she was slightly more fearful of her former husband's current safety than she was of his approval for her new marriage.

His head still whirling, Cyrus rode on through the night, the dawn coming. Not a titan was yet in sight on the dusty trail through the Heia Pass. And yet still he found no comfort.

45.

The camp still stood at a small, flat gap just north of the southern terminus of the Heia Pass when they arrived, and yet still Cyrus felt no relief. At the last hill, he had stood upon one of the elven watchtowers and looked out on the slice of Gradsden Savanna visible over the last two peaks that heralded the end of the pass, and the sight which greeted his eyes was not a happy one.

A titan war camp stood a few miles ahead on the plains, stretching as far as he could see, more troops than he could count without climbing high into the sky. Tents big enough to house all of Sanctuary's keep were visible, billowing in the warm savanna wind behind the smaller tents that were merely large enough to engulf a reasonable-sized barn.

When they rode into their own camp, there were muted cheers of relief from all within, lined up as though to watch a parade. Cyrus caught sight of elves in their intricate armors, unit standards from some of Danay's northern armies flapping the breeze. The army of Sanctuary's forces were apparent as well, though they did more to disguise their relief at the arrival of reinforcements.

Thad was one of the first to greet Cyrus as he rode up, dismounting and watching an elf in leather armor hustle forward to take Windrider's reins. The horse whickered at the elf but allowed himself to be led off.

"Have you seen?" Thad asked without preamble, looking more anxious that Cyrus would have liked.

"I saw," Cyrus said with a nod. Belkan Stillhet ambled up beside the young warrior and elbowed him aside without mercy. Thad, looking slightly discombobulated, faded back into the crowd as the old warrior took his place with a generous spit at Cyrus's feet. "You seem calm about it."

"Calmer than some," Belkan agreed, motioning Cyrus forward.

Cyrus looked back and watched Vara dismount her horse rather stiffly as he walked ahead with Belkan. She gave him a wan smile, her ire clearly passed somewhere in the night. "What do you think the hold-up is?"

"Provisioning, maybe?" Belkan shrugged his broad shoulders, old pauldrons clanking as he did so. He walked toward a line of troops milling about underneath the last rocky chasm that surrounded the trail before it flattened out into rolling foothills out of the mountains. "Once they start moving, they'll need a lot of food to feed that army."

"They can conjure bread now," Cyrus said, taking large strides forward. "And water. It shouldn't be a concern to them."

Belkan snorted. "You see titans eating a lot of bread, do you? I picture them tearing into meat constantly."

"I don't," Cyrus said, looking out past the foothills. The enemy camps were nowhere near as visible from here, but he could see the tops of some of the larger tents, like pointed mountain peaks in the distance. "Can you imagine how much meat that would take? How much grazing land? What sort of herds?"

"I saw a mountain goat from around those lands once," Belkan said quietly, staring out at the savanna with him. "They're taller than you, hoof to back. I hear they keep them up in the high peaks, out to the west of Kortran."

"Well, that answers the meat part, I guess," Cyrus said, chewing his lower lip. "It's not as if they spend any time sowing, that much is sure."

"That much is sure," Belkan agreed, and he turned his back to the savanna, looking inward at the camp and the army within.

"What's on your mind, Belkan?" Cyrus asked.

Belkan shook his head. "Got a lot of people spread out all over the place, Davidon. I don't like it."

"I'm not so fond of it myself," Cyrus said. "But we have to guard the portal nearest Emerald Fields, and keep those scouts watching the others near—"

Belkan spit again, and for the first time Cyrus realized there was dark tobacco in the stream of saliva. He shuddered a little bit, and

Belkan clearly noticed, for he smiled in amusement. "Your father didn't truck with this habit of mine, either." His face darkened. "But he listened, dammit, and you should, too. No good is going to come of this."

"You think we should pull back?" Cyrus asked, looking out at the savanna again. "Leave this defense to the elves?"

"Pfft," Belkan said, "elves can't win this." He shook his head. "I just don't like being spread this thin, is all. Sanctuary doesn't even have a good castellan in place right now because Thad and me are here with all these young and impressionable pieces of titan luncheon." He made a humming noise, but lower. "I didn't like fighting the trolls, but this is—it's worse."

"You'd know," Cyrus said, feeling that stir of discomfort come back. "Belkan ... we're not going to walk away from this fight. You know that, right?"

"At my age, Cyrus," Belkan said, "you get a little tired of fighting sometimes. At this point, I'd just like to sit in my armory for a while and get things back in order. You seen the mess in there?"

"I have not," Cyrus said, reaching down to touch Praelior's hilt. "Haven't needed a sword in a while."

"Now you've got a spare, as well, I hear," Belkan said, clinking him on the spine where his reserve blade rested below his backplate. "I recall you walking in my armory with a bronze weapon you picked up off the ground in a dragon raid, and now you're standing here with mystical rings under your gauntlets, sword of a dead god on your belt, and some mystical short thing hiding behind you in case you—I don't know, decide to get really angry and need something for your other hand."

Cyrus felt a smile force itself out from beneath sullen lips. "I have been known to wield two every now again when things get a mite ... touchy."

"You've changed, lad," Belkan said, making it sound like a curse, "and not necessarily for the better. I'll always remember you knee-high to me. Now you're knee-high to a titan." He made a rough bark of a laugh. "You're doubting yourself, aren't you?"

"Hard not to when you've got enemies like this coming for you." He pointed at the most obvious tent in the distance, the pointed top bearing a flag, barely visible.

"Enemies are enemies. The bigger they are, the more they bleed before they die, that's all."

"I think you got that expression wrong," Cyrus said.

"I like mine better," Belkan said, waving him off. He finally turned back around to look at the pass. "Whenever they're ready … they're going to come rolling in like one of those hurricanes that works their way up the Bay of Lost Souls every now and again." He scowled and looked at Cyrus. "You ever been around for one of those?"

"No."

"It's a hell of a thing," Belkan said, staring off into the distance. "Rattles the windows like it'll tear the latches. So much rain you swear the chimneys will drown the fires in it, but they don't. Like Tempestus himself is leading the storm's vanguard ashore, and he's got the angriest warriors in any realm with him to help make the stir." He shook his head, coming out of what looked a little like a trance while he spoke about it. "It's not a cracking good time, and I suspect we're going to see it from these titans once they get their supply lines in good order."

"How long do you figure?" Cyrus caught a scathing look from Belkan. "Come on. You've lived through more wars than most of us can name. Give me your best guess."

"A week," Belkan said, puckering his lips before letting out another spit. "Maybe a month. Then that storm's gonna come tearing right up this pass, because these big idiots," he waved a hand out to the savanna, "they don't know any better. If they were smart they'd use Falcon's Essence and come over the peaks on us—"

"Oh, gods," Cyrus said.

"I already posted sentries against that," Belkan said with a grim smile. "My point is, though … it won't be long, and we'll be—I'd say up to our necks in them, but … really, it's more like in over our heads, isn't it?"

"Over our heads sounds right," Cyrus said, and he finally broke from looking at the savanna as a late afternoon breeze came whipping through the pass behind him. It gave him a surprising chill even though it was mild, almost warm. "It sounds like exactly where we stand, in fact."

46.

A week passed with sight of nothing but titan tents and titan patrols, moving occasionally up into the foothills before marching back to their camps. Cyrus got little rest, sleep being elusive even in the tent that he was sharing with Vara. She watched him with careful eyes when he thought deeply, as though she were afraid to break silence for fear of him losing the one idea that would save them all. At other times they spoke and acted normally, as though they were in the Tower of the Guildmaster and all was right with the world.

Cyrus often took to walking during the sleepless night watches himself, patrolling among the soldiers on the last hilltop and then wandering back into the camp, sparing a few kind words for the sentries that were up on the peaks above them, and then making his way back to the tents in the night when he realized that the attack was not coming, not yet, not on this watch.

It was on one of these patrols that he found Thad watching in roughly the same spot where he had had his conversation with Belkan only a few days earlier. The warrior was looking for himself, focused on the night fires in the titan camp over the foothills. The sky was alight with the burning flames, though not a single fire was visible from where they were. Cyrus had seen them, though, from the other stations, and they were so numerous as to make him worry anew.

"Guildmaster," Thad said as Cyrus stood there with him. "General. I always think of you that way, first."

"It's what I've been known as for longer," Cyrus said in quiet acknowledgment. A peal of laughter from somewhere behind him reminded him that there were still others taking comfort in this camp, doing their jobs and finding some measure of relaxation when their day was through. Cyrus looked at the red-armored warrior. "How are you doing, Thad?"

"I'm fairly well, considering we're standing at the edge of the world I knew," Thad said, nodding at the pass walls a hundred feet to their left and right, sheer rock forming a canyon. "I only ever heard tell of the southern lands, you know. Wasn't sure I really believed half the things I'd heard about creatures so large they defy the mind to come up with a scale for them."

"It's a bit of an adjustment," Cyrus agreed, crossing his arms over his breastplate. "Takes the eye some time for the mind to digest a morsel this big."

"Aye," Thad said. They paused for a moment. "I took in what you said before, about marriage. You were right. It's gotten easier, especially with all we've got going on down here at the moment."

"Good," Cyrus said, suddenly stiff, unsure of what he should say after his conversation with Martaina about her impending nuptials. It caused a sudden tightness in his stomach. "I'm glad you, uh … that it was helpful for you."

They stood there for a while, just staring out into the blessed quiet, until Thad broke the silence. "I've got a question for you."

Cyrus stared out across the empty, rolling foothills beyond, and realized it was not possible for him to stiffen his muscles any further. "All right," he said, wondering exactly how much discomfort the impending inquiry would cause him.

"That was your father's armor, wasn't it?" Thad nodded at Cyrus's black metal encasement.

Cyrus stood there, frowning. "This is what you've been thinking about? My armor? Now? Here? With this going on?" He swept a hand out to indicate the savanna beyond the hills. "And with, uh—your personal, uh …"

"Well, I—yes, I mean—uh …"

"It was my father's armor, yes," Cyrus said, bemused by the query. *That could have been so much worse.*

"Well, that wasn't really my question," Thad said, feet shifting on the dirty trail, the grains of sand crunching beneath his boots.

"Okay," Cyrus said slowly. *Uh oh.* "What is your actual question?"

"My armor's from the Gatekeeper," Thad said, looking down, "in Purgatory, you know? He gave us mystical steel back when we first started to conquer the place—"

"I was there, I know this." *Where the hell is he going with this?*

Thad nodded at the scuffs dotting his breastplate, nicks in the red where the steel showed beneath it. "I've had mine for going on four years now, you've had yours for as long as I've known you, and to my knowledge you've never repainted it."

Cyrus blinked a few times, trying to figure out where the warrior was taking him with these inquiries. "… And?"

"So it's beyond mystical, isn't it?" Thad asked, sounding like a little bit of life had been poured back into him.

Cyrus looked at his black armor. It looked dusty, that was certain, but it always seemed slightly dull, even after he'd just polished it. He frowned as he stared down; he certainly hadn't ever painted it, and it wasn't dented or dinged to speak of, it merely looked worn, like it had been through considerable daily wear for longer than he had worn it. "Maybe," Cyrus said, wondering for the first time if the warrior might have a point.

"I mean, you got hit by Mortus and Yartraak," Thad went on, "and it doesn't even have a ding to show for it." There was a lively quality to the warrior's voice, like a child in excitement. "So here's what I was thinking—"

"That wasn't it?"

"—is…what happened to your father's sword?" Thad finished, with a smile on his face. "Hmm?"

The frown deepened on Cyrus's face. "I don't …" He tried to reach back in his memory, trying to picture a house. He could see the fire in the hearth, could recall a rug of some animal skin that lay before it. He remembered his father's rough hands, pushing upon his head, and arms like steel when they wrestled, his father laughing heartily as Cyrus had done everything he could to break the grip. He remembered a man in black armor, clad in it up to the helm—

"Do you remember it?" Thad asked, as though he could read Cyrus's very thoughts.

"I don't," Cyrus said, puckering his lips, twisting them as he tried to think. "I remember—there was a black scabbard?" He tried to picture it, but it was as fleeting as smoke on a strong wind, he could imagine his father in the armor, standing by a wooden door. When he tried to focus harder, his father's image turned to his own, looking into one of Sanctuary's mirrors. "I barely remember him in his own armor anymore. My mind keeps replacing him with me. The sword itself…" He tried to picture it, but it was like trying to grasp water with his fingertips.

"Was he tall like you?" Thad asked, sounding a little hopeful.

"I think so, but you'd have to ask Belkan," Cyrus said, resolving to do much the same the next time he saw the armorer. "On both counts. He was the one who made sure my father's armor got to me at the Society."

"When did they give it to you?" Thad asked.

"Not until I was big enough for it," Cyrus said. "Sixteen? Maybe seventeen? It wasn't as though I had a place to store it until I left, anyway, so I slept in it."

"Aye," Thad said, and now he seemed strangely aloof. "That I recall. I suppose you would have had to."

"Yeah, I—" Cyrus stopped as a strange, ululating yell came howling down from somewhere above. It was taken up by the watch on the hilltop, and he froze, staring out at the savanna, trying to see the top of the tents. They had been mere shadows against a darker sky before, but now his eyes failed him, and he saw nothing but the orange horizon where the fires still burned. "They must be moving."

The shouts confirmed it a moment later. "Titans on the march! Titans on the march to the pass!" The call was taken up and carried into the night, and all through the camp, a sleeping army began to awaken.

"I guess this is it," Thad said sadly.

"This is it," Cyrus agreed, and instead of the thrill of battle he'd felt in the arena of the titans, he felt a clawing dread. Not fear, and certainly not fear for himself, but rather a tired acknowledgment that battle was coming, and that it would be long and hard. Cyrus drew himself up to his full height and adjusted his armor. "Thad, get the army ready." And as the red-armored warrior ran off to do as ordered, Cyrus began to marshal himself to do much the same, to prepare for another fight that he was unsure his army would be able to win.

47.

The titans began their assault with a roaring charge toward the gap of the pass in the canyon south of the camp. It was the kind of formation Cyrus relied on, a tight spot in which to fight, barely big enough to bring their armies in walking a few side-by-side. *Like a bridge, it's a narrowing of the way, and until these idiots figure out how to use Falcon's Essence to change their whole world, I'll take their ignorance and use it to my advantage*, Cyrus thought.

The night was lit with thousands of torches. The smoke was not the sweet scent found in the Sanctuary fires, but an oily one. Above, on the cliff faces some three hundred feet up, Cyrus could see the archers in position, Martaina leading them on either side. Cyrus doubted their efficacy in this particular battle, but he could hardly see another use for them, and they were out of danger unless the titans began throwing spells or rocks up at the cliff edges. *Perhaps they'll distract, perhaps Martaina herself will get a couple kills, but for the most part, archery is flinging toothpicks at these creatures.*

The sky had begun to weep in a light trickle, no sounds of thunder. It spattered on Cyrus's pauldrons and onto his cheeks, where the rough beard growth had taken root over the last few days without a razor or washing water at hand. *Could have had Vara do it with her sword, I suppose.* He looked at her and found himself smiling at the notion. She stood in a line a few down from him, and, sensing his amusement, turned her head to catch him. She cocked her own, giving him a quizzical look. "What?" she asked mildly.

"I'll tell you later," he promised.

"Yes, and I'm sure that'll be so very amusing, should we survive this momentous occasion," Vaste said, very loudly.

"Oh, Vaste," Cyrus said, "when will you stop doubting my brilliant leadership and just—"

"Leap foolishly into everything you suggest?" Vaste asked. "Listen. I'm always with you, even in the stupid moments. Like this one. But to think we'll just drive the titans back without consequence is shockingly naïve, I would say."

"A rather mild retort for you," Vara said, staring into the distance. "Usually your insults are ... well, insulting."

"I usually have more to work with," Vaste said. "Here, I'm fighting against the blinding terror of facing creatures over twice my size at every moment."

"Stand back," Cyrus said. "Let me take the punishment for you."

"That hasn't worked with Vara," Vaste said, drawing an irritable look from the paladin, "and I doubt it will work with beings that can step over you and come smash me."

"One can hope, though," Cyrus said. "That it would work, I mean. I don't hope you'll get smashed."

"I feel much better now that you cleared that up."

"Perhaps now would be a moment for one of your inspirational speeches," Vara said, whispering down the line to him.

"I think not," Cyrus said. "Vaste always interrupts those until they lose all meaning." He eyed the troll.

"What, are you not so subtly asking me to shut up?" Vaste asked. "Because I'm not sure that's physically possible—"

"Vaste," Vara said sweetly, "dear troll. If you interrupt my beloved's speech this time, I will regale you with tales of Cyrus's sexual prowess in exquisite detail from now until the end of my days. If you are fortunate, that will be a short time. I am, however, capable of outliving you, and thus you may have your twilight years to look forward to, interspersed with phrases such as, 'firm buttocks,' 'enormous, python-like—'"

"I will shut up now," Vaste said. "And possibly forevermore."

"That was easy," Cyrus said with a frown. Vara nodded her head at him, and he took a few steps forward before raising his voice. The bulk of the officers stood before him—Curatio, J'anda, Thad, Erith, Andren, Nyad, Vaste and Vara. Longwell remained at the Emerald Fields with a small army of a thousand, while Mendicant and Odellan were maintaining the defense of Sanctuary in addition to running the scouting parties posted at half the portals in southern Arkaria.

"Friends," Cyrus said, calling out into the night, the rain still spattering his shoulders lightly, "I stand with you now at the southern edge of the wild. Beyond us sits the grimmest threat that Arkaria has known these many years—titans with magic. A warlike people with a fury and now the force of spellcraft to back it. Well, they may be capable, but they are not terribly bright, much like the trolls." He watched Vaste's yellow eyes pop open a little wider, and a scowl settled on his face, but he did not speak. "And much like those terrible, dull creatures, we will take the dignity from these beasts as well.

"For they are not a threat to be taken lightly," Cyrus went on, noting a small vein popping out in Vaste's forehead. *Probably thinking how wonderful a pun 'lightly' would make.* "And we do not take them as such; they are the gravest threat we have seen, and we will hold this pass against their predations, making it understood that they are not welcome here in the north. This is our land, and we, the creatures they would subjugate like rabbits, will not take another helping of their fury. We will return it with more of our own. Their height will not avail them any more than it did the troll menace, and soon enough, we will all be sitting around a fire, talking of the days when we drove these wretches before us." Cyrus paused and heard a small roar of approbation, before stepping back to the line.

"I don't feel that was one of your best," Curatio said, frowning.

"See, I think my added commentary keeps him sharp," Vaste said. "This was all just one big attempt to link the titans to my people, which is truly stupid, because we all know the titans are dumber than the trolls."

"Who said you could speak?" Vara asked. "Have I told you about the time that Cyrus—"

"Aghhhhhh!" Vaste shouted, covering his ears.

"—with my lady flower—"

"AIIIIEEEEEEEEE!"

The first spell hit a moment later, a blast of ice so poorly aimed it struck the side of the cliff far to Cyrus's left. It did, however, have the fortunate effect of stopping the back and forth between Vara and Vaste, and for that, Cyrus found himself supremely grateful. Shards of ice sprayed down upon them before cracking and bringing down chunks of the canyon wall only a few moments later. That side of their line moved quickly, pushing forward as the glacier-sized block crashed to the ground.

Cyrus spun about after the ice fall, catching a glimpse of the first ranks through the rain. The initial titan line of attack was only a hundred meters ahead, marching through the rain in a disciplined formation. The next spells came harder, and Nyad threw up a cessation spell around them that dissipated their fury against it like water sloshing off a rock barrier.

"That's a lovely plan," Vaste said dryly, "but when they get over here in the next ten seconds or so, I suspect our people will need healing spells."

"If I didn't do this now," the princess of Pharesia said with an aura of annoyance, "our people would be dying under the impact of fire and ice right this minute, no wait required." She gave him a haughty look. "And if you don't like it, perhaps I can share some of my sexual exploits with you."

"Please do," Vaste said, causing Nyad's cheeks to flush red and a slight smile to appear on her lips. "We can make an evening of it."

The first titans came crashing along just then, and Cyrus strained against the ground before remembering that with the cessation spell, there was no Falcon's Essence to be had. "Nyad!" Cyrus called, and made a slashing motion across his throat.

"Yes, I'm sure you'll die in no time against these things," Vaste said.

Nyad, for her part, dropped her hands, the spell light disappearing as she did so. Cyrus looked around for a druid but failed to find one, and his time ran out with the arrival of the first titan boots to come stomping out a few feet ahead of him.

Grimacing in pure irritation, Cyrus moved out to meet them, unwilling to merely stand there and provide a convenient target for the smashing. Now the titans wore plate metal boots, all of them, another development he found annoying. *And likely fatal one to many of our number.*

Cyrus dodged a titan kick and slid past one of them to plant his blade under a kneecap. A howl cut through the rainy atmosphere, and he dragged the sword through the middle of the joint with immense effort. The titan swayed, screaming into the night, and then fell over, his leg nearly cut from his body.

"Plenty more where that came from!" Vaste called. Cyrus spared only a glance back to see Vara performing one of her mighty leaps through the air. She landed on a titan's chestplate but for a second, plunged her blade into the small indentation where his collarbones met. As he gasped, she thrust a hand right up to his eyeballs and unleashed a force blast spell. He hit the ground back-of-the-head first, his lower body strangely unmoved by the spell magic. He trailed blood as he went, Vara's sword remaining firmly in her hand as she came in for a landing on his carcass, driving the point into his neck.

Two titans came at Cyrus and he fought back against both of them in a rolling dodge and stick attack. He avoided one's strike, stabbing into the thigh of the other as he came up. As that one reacted in pain, Cyrus used his Praelior-charged reflexes to come at the other, driving his blade into its hip with a leap. The titan froze in place with the pain of his thrust, the sword wedged between bones and its muscles all contracted. Cyrus dragged the blade ninety degrees along the same axis, chopping into the joint as much as possible before he got out of the titan's way and let it fall. Then he returned to his original foe and brought it the rest of the way down from its knees with a leaping attack against the side of its neck.

"Cyrus!" Curatio's voice was a magic-aided bellow in the night. Cyrus turned to see that the Sanctuary line was well and truly infiltrated, the titans stepping over the front rank and into the thick of the army. Screams were coming loudly now, all running into one another, the cry of the titans in furious battle rage, and the screams of the wounded as well. Cyrus's feet lifted off the ground as a Falcon's Essence spell took hold on him, and he did not bother to look for the caster, instead running back to his own lines with wildest abandon, the last man out in the middle of the titan advance. Even Vara was back now, driving her blade into the legs of titans that were swarming into the camp, tearing down tents and stomping through the latrines.

Cyrus stabbed through a few necks on his way back to his lines, now high enough to do so with spell aid. *This is the view of a bird, truly*, he thought as he punched a titan right behind the ear, staggering him with the strength of the blow. His enemy pitched over, landing on at least two warriors below, one of whom struggled out from beneath the breastplate with a look of pain upon his face. Before Cyrus had a chance to call for a healing spell for the man, a titan came along and stomped with a metal boot. A splatter of blood squirted out in two directions on the dusty ground, like wine spilled. When the boot came up again, Cyrus knew there was no healer in Arkaria that could repair what had just been done to the soldier.

With more than a little anger to spare, Cyrus attacked the titan responsible. The creature wore an expression of angry glee, rumbling his amusement at his small triumph. Cyrus ran by and drove his sword in at the joint of the jaw, ignoring the extra strength it took to push the sword through the knotty titan flesh and cartilage. He yanked forward and ran, cutting half the giant's jaw off and ripping straight through the lip on one side. It reached up to touch its wound, but failed to restrain its own strength, inadvertently thrusting fingers into the deep cut that Cyrus had just made. The titan fell to its knees, and within a second of its landing there, Vara leapt up to deal a deathblow.

The camp was a mess now, the first rank of the army completely in disarray. Elven soldiers were fleeing, running back toward the hillside where the second watchtower was mounted. Cyrus frowned, a pained look. *This is not going the way I'd hoped ...*

He spun and started to re-enter the fray as a titan swatted at him. Cyrus put his sword out, but it was too late. The blade buried itself in the titan's palm, but Cyrus was flung into a canyon wall, slamming to a stop and falling onto the air. The Falcon's Essence spell caught him, holding him some twenty feet up, as he tried to gather his wits back around him.

The titan advanced, malice in its eyes. *A warrior who can smell the kill*, Cyrus thought. He still had Praelior clutched in his hand, and as he started to get up, the titan raised a hand once more—

And then howled in pain.

Cyrus looked down to see Belkan in his thick armor, plunging his blade into the titan's shin again and again, sliding in the muddy ground as he repositioned to attack the Achilles heel of the beast. Cyrus blinked, and the titan shifted its balance enough to move its foot—

And it kicked Belkan to the ground.

The old armorer rolled some ten feet, as dazed as Cyrus had been when the last blow had landed on him. Before Cyrus could get to his feet, he watched the titan warrior go after the newest blood it could find, dealing with the active threat that had just hobbled it, like any good warrior of Bellarum would.

And as the plated boot smashed Belkan into the ground, the sound of armor crunching under weight sounded like a thunderclap to Cyrus's ears. When the boot came back up ...

... Cyrus knew that Belkan was dead ... and that there was no hope at all of resurrection.

48.

"NO!" Cyrus screamed above the chaos. He came at the titan responsible in a raging fury, spearing it through the ear after knocking its helm aside enough to cut through. He rammed his sword into the canal eight times in a row before the titan started to slump, and he followed it to the ground with furious swipes, driving his blade into the temple, over and over, the rain now hammering at him as titans swept by like eddies in a sea.

When he came back to himself, Cyrus spun around and saw more foes at the gap of the canyon entry than it was meant to hold. The mere sight enraged him, and suddenly he felt the pulsing desire for battle that had not been present before. He wanted to put blade to titan throats and cut away with a will, to slash and hack his way through the beasts at neck level until he was practically drowning in their blood.

This is how it was meant to be, he thought as he drove forward, kicking a titan in the chestplate hard enough to stagger him back a step. Cyrus did not rest on his laurels, however; he drove up from beneath and slaughtered the titan with three sharp cuts to the jugular.

I was meant to bathe in the blood of my foes. To fight for empire, to carve a kingdom of my own. Might makes you right, and weakness is nothing to be celebrated. Force of arms will carry you where gentle words will not. The titans ... they understand this.

How have I forgotten it?

Leaving behind the place where Belkan had died, Cyrus drove forward in his own mad attack. The titans had become used to seeing the smaller people falling back under the pressure of their advance. Cyrus screamed and came at them more quickly than they were used to seeing. Some raised their hands to guard their faces in panic. These he stabbed in the armpit, guiding his blade straight to their hearts. Some scowled, shouted, and came at him. He cut their fingers from their hands and stabbed them in the eyes, ripped open their throats, turned aside their angry blows by dodging and countering, bellowing his own war cry into the night all the while.

A fire spell blew past him narrowly, spending itself against the ground in an inferno of heat that turned Cyrus's head around. He swallowed heavily when he saw it land, consuming a titan and three Sanctuary rangers when it landed. Another followed indiscriminately a moment later, this one hitting ineffectually against the side of the canyon.

Ahead Cyrus could see the titan responsible, hand glowing as he cast magic with no energy remaining. His nobby skin was already showing the signs of the strain, and then he heaved another powerful fireball, once again with poor aim. *They must teach that in the Leagues …* The fireball hit just below the cliff's edge, sending two rangers scrambling back.

Cyrus scanned the edge of the cliff; almost all the rangers were gone now, and none remained at the mouth of the pass. Frowning, he stabbed through a titan coming at him, and cast his look back. The main line, if he could even consider it that, was some several hundred meters behind him, titans swarming all in the midst of the scrambling fighters. The elves had broken, and only a veteran core of Sanctuary fighters was keeping the titan advance even remotely in check—himself included.

"Dammit," Cyrus muttered under his breath, turning eyes once more to the pass. *I could hold it. Myself, maybe a few others—we could hold it against the titans until—*

With a start, he jerked, remembering exactly what they were meant to hold against—and until. "Sonofa—" He sprinted back toward the Sanctuary front line, running high above the heads of the titans as he did so.

"Oh, hi there," Vaste called as Cyrus spiraled down to them, cutting through a titan on the way. It fell sideways, providing them a momentary bulwark against the advance. "Glad you could join us here in the fight for our lives."

"Where is the elf in charge?" Cyrus asked, stopping roughly ten feet above the ground.

"I'm glad you came back to ask," Curatio said drolly, "because I was about to send Vara to come get you." He jerked a head back toward the watch hill only a hundred meters behind them. "I think you know where the commanding officer of the elves has gone."

Dammit. I was right. "This isn't going well," Cyrus said.

"No, that's not how you do it," Vaste said. "When you make these blatantly obvious statements, you either have to do it with a very sarcastic delivery or else append something extremely amusing to it."

"Such as?"

"I ..." Vaste paused, then jabbed his staff out to hit a titan in the knee as Thad did the same to the other knee. "Put me on the spot, why don't you? I do this all the time, you know, you'd think by now you'd have enough to select from without making me create an illustrative example up out of thin air, like I'm some sort of joke-teller by magic alone. It doesn't work like that."

"They're not stopping!" Vara shouted, coming back within range of them after covering the left flank. "Except, of course, those few that we manage to hit in the groin. They stop rather quickly." She looked at Vaste. "That's how you do it."

"I bow to the mistress," Vaste said, not actually bowing.

"They killed Belkan," Cyrus said, repelling a titan's attack with a flurry of blows of his own.

"They've killed a number of us and an even larger number of my father's soldiers," Nyad said, lifting her staff into the air as she cast a fire spell straight into the face of three advancing titans. "We only need hold a few more minutes, and then—"

"And then what?" Vaste asked. Cyrus jerked his head toward the cliff walls ahead of them. "Oh. That."

"Yes, that," Cyrus said, sweeping his sword around. "That, which we are waiting—"

A heavy explosion ripped through the night, its flash casting the pass in white and then orange light as the mouth of the canyon burst with the fury of Dragon's Breath. The titans caught between the teeth of the pass disappeared in the fire and then the cloud of debris that followed as a second explosion rocked the night, this one from the opposite side of the pass. Another blew, further up one side, then another, a rolling series of explosions that climbed the face of the mountain where the King of the Elves had placed barrels of the alchemical mixture.

Before the smoke at the entry had cleared, a deep rumble had started. Cyrus looked up and saw where the barrels of Dragon's Breath had been planted, deep scars were now gouged out of the rock face and the dust swirled around them. Below, huge chunks of mountain ripped free and fell into the entry to the pass and the canyon.

Cyrus could not see because of the dust, but he knew that there were at least a hundred titans swallowed under the fall of the rolling detonations and the sheet of rock turned loose from the mountainside. He fought the next titan, and the next, but now they were no longer endless; now there were only a couple hundred.

The fight went on until dawn, wizards poised to evacuate them at the first sign of reinforcements coming over the top of the debris field where the pass had been closed. They never came, and when the first light broke, Cyrus found himself staring over a field of dead and dying, with the remains of plenty of titans, elves and men to make all sides equally miserable as to the outcome.

49.

Cyrus smelled the familiar scent of dinner cooking when the magic of the teleport spell vanished around him. The fires were flickering at the open doors behind him. The light of day shone down and from where he stood, Cyrus could see people moving about on the Sanctuary grounds. They were unhurried, languid in their pace, and he wondered exactly how they could seem so relaxed when he felt anything but.

"You made it back," Odellan said with sharp relief, standing in circular guard with other warriors, their spears now lifting into the air, the possibility of threat firmly resolved. "We hadn't heard anything and were wondering—"

"The titans came through the pass last night," Cyrus said, inflection flat. Vara stood at his side, her head bowed. "The King of the Elves ordered the pass sealed if they swarmed, and his officers carried out his orders." Cyrus tried not to pour any bitterness into it, but it seeped out regardless. There was no way to regard their stinging defeat, even after so short a battle, as anything other than what it was. "We had to stick around for a while to make sure they didn't come over immediately, but ..." Cyrus shook his head. "Our army is falling back to the portal at the northern terminus of the pass. We'll take our turns defending it while we wait for the titans to make their next move." *And they will,* he did not say, but the air was heavy the answer anyway.

"How did we fare ... in terms of losses?" Odellan asked, his voice a little lower now.

"Over a hundred," Cyrus said roughly even as he caught sight of motion just inside the doors of the Great Hall. "Excuse me."

He shouldered past Odellan after the figure he'd seen watching him from just inside the hall. The clink of Vara's boots followed him as Cyrus entered the hall, the smell of food permeating the air even more heavily here. He cast a look back at Vara, who nodded, and moved to shut the doors to the Great Hall.

Larana was nearly back to the kitchen, but she halted in place, a small cauldron clutched in her hands, while Vara shut the doors. He had never studied her in great detail, but he noticed her now; bushy brown hair that hung in frizzy lengths, as though she had never once tried to control it with a ponytail as Vara did. Her eyes were downcast and dark, what little he could see of them by the light through the stained glass windows against the far wall. She seemed to huddle there in her light robes, as if she were anticipating death coming toward her, unable to move out of its path.

"Larana?" Cyrus walked closer to her, hesitating to approach, as though she might strike at him. She did not answer, merely stared, mouselike, at him. "I have to talk to you," he said, tentative. "There's something I need to tell you."

Still she said nothing, huddling with the cauldron in her hands. She turned ever so slightly toward him.

"Belkan," Cyrus said. "In the battle just now, with the titans ... he ..." He lost his words. "I'm sorry. He didn't make it out alive. There was nothing ... nothing I could ..."

She turned away from him, her head bowed, shoulders slumped. The cauldron hit the nearest table with a thump, as she got it out of her hands just in time. Her back still turned to him, she trudged, one slow step after another, back toward the kitchens.

"If there's anything ... I can do ..." Cyrus started, and at that she stopped, leaning heavily against one of the tables, turning enough that he could see her in profile. She had very little chin and a small nose, and her hair covered most of it. Her eyes darted toward him, and he could see tears in the corners. "Let me know." He began to turn away.

"Thank you," she nearly whispered, and somehow it halted him where he stood.

Cyrus froze in his turn, wavering, caught between what he wanted to do and a question burning on his mind. "Larana?" he asked, and turned back to her. She looked at him quizzically, the tears plain in her eyes, and he somehow found it in himself to ask. "I hate to even bring this up right now, but ... I meant to ask your father before he died, and there's no one else I could …" Cyrus paused, nearly having to push the question out as though he were dragging it to the edge of his lips and flinging it into the abyss beyond. "Do you know what happened to my father's sword?"

Larana hesitated, head still bowed, though she looked at him with eyes caught between curiosity and tears. "No," she whispered, "I'm sorry."

"I'm the one who should be sorry," Cyrus said, mentally remonstrating himself for his ill timing. "I'm the one who asked a question in your grief." He nodded respectfully to her once and began his retreat in earnest. "If there's anything I can do," he repeated and fled toward Vara, who had a curious look of her own as she opened one of the doors for them to pass through.

"Reckon we're on our own for supper tonight," Andren said, a little mournfully, as Cyrus came out of the Great Hall.

"You could always fix something," Vara said with a healthy amount of acid. "Though I would avoid anything that involves a brandy sauce."

"I'm not much of a cook," Andren said. "Tended to buy my food off street vendors before I came here."

"Yes, you got everything off the street, didn't you?" Vara said as she and Cyrus moved toward the stairs.

"Hey, I resent—"

"Andren, find someone to help make dinner," Cyrus said, in no mood for argument.

"Uh, I'll check with Vaste and see what we can come up with," Andren said, shuffling off as Cyrus stormed the steps, the foyer disappearing from view in seconds.

"What was that about?" Vara asked as soon as they were up a few flights of the spiral staircase.

"I don't want Larana to have to worry about dinner in her current—"

"Not that," she snapped as a ranger passed them, trying his hardest to blend into the wall. "What was that about your father's sword?"

"Something Thad brought up just before the attack," Cyrus said, "something I'd never thought of before." He clanked a gauntlet against his armor. "Two gods have struck me, and my armor doesn't show any damage."

She frowned, ascending alongside him. "Well, it doesn't exactly look new, either, though, does it?"

"Worn is not the same as god-struck," Cyrus said. "It should be destroyed for every hit I've taken." He rapped his knuckles against his greaves. "I saw what happened to Belkan's armor being stepped on by a titan." He shuddered slightly. "If this were normal steel, it would be flat as unshaped metal. Instead, it may look old, but it shows no sign of damage, nor need of repainting." He stared down at it. "It doesn't even appear to be painted at all."

"Well, that's not exactly a shade found in nature—"

"It's like night itself!"

"Have you ever seen a night? You think it's that shade? Even the Realm of Darkness wasn't as inky as—"

They paused in their argument as two spellcasters eased past them, casting sidelong, nervous looks.

"Maybe the dark looks different to elven eyes," Cyrus said, trying to stop the quibble before it became something more.

"Perhaps," Vara conceded. After a waiting another moment, she proceeded. "So, because your father had some potentially mystical—"

"Mystical would have taken a god's hit a little better than steel, but ... I think this is more." Cyrus looked down at his breastplate, at its metallic surface. "Quartal, perhaps?"

"Quartal is very distinctive," Vara said, sounding a little skeptical. "Look at your sword and your chainmail. I suppose, under whatever black ... enamel ... or whatever coats the armor, there may be quartal, but it does not exactly carry the glimmer. In any case, you presume that your father's sword would be similarly enchanted?"

"I don't presume anything," Cyrus said as they went past the Council Chambers. "I merely wanted to know what happened to it. Belkan made sure the armor passed to me; I just want to be certain that I'm not missing a sword I should have." He lowered his voice as they came to the final set of stairs, up to the door that opened into the Tower of the Guildmaster. "It's all I have left of him."

Vara came in and shut the door behind her. She stood at the base of the small set of steps that led up into the quarters, back pressed against the door, hair slightly messy where a few strands had broken loose from her ponytail during the battle. "I always hear you talk about your father. Why don't you ever talk about your mother?"

Cyrus halted just out of the channel of the stairs. "I don't remember much of her," he said. "She didn't exactly leave a large trace, either; my father was a hero of the war against the trolls. He won the battle of Dismal Swamp, after all. Hard to compete with that when you're stuck staying at home, watching a kid."

"You must remember something," Vara said, easing up the stairs. "She died after your father, didn't she?"

"I remember her eyes," Cyrus said. "Very faintly. They were green. I remember some of the smells of the things she cooked, like her meat pies. It was a pretty traditional Reikonosian delicacy. We had them in the Society regularly, but it was never the same. Larana's are close, I think." He shrugged. "Not much to talk about other than her cooking, which is why I suppose I don't talk about her." He blinked as another thought occurred. "She passed on her rage at the trolls to me. Bitter about my father's death, I assume."

"That is a shame," Vara said, eyes touched with sadness. "To have so little time with either of them. At least your father made an impression." She nodded at him, armor and all. "And you walk his path, of course."

"I wanted to be like him," Cyrus said quietly. "The instructors at the Society … they didn't want to talk to me, but whenever they discussed the history of the troll war, they would say my name." He smiled faintly. "Well, they would say my last name, anyway, and they'd say it with a reverence for my father that they never once showed for his son, sitting in the same damned room with them. It was always a bit mysterious how it unfolded, that battle, because—well, almost no one survived. But the word got out that he'd done something amazing in it."

"I cannot imagine what you have gone through in your upbringing," Vara said, and she leaned against him, armor against his. Her breath was warm in his ear. "To have done what you did … to be so reliant on yourself … it has made you strong."

He turned his head to look at her. "You think it made me strong? I think it made me weak, always turning inward rather than asking for help when it would have made life simpler. Do you know how hard it was for me to start to trust after the Society?" She shook her head. "It was a hell of a journey, let me tell you. Consider yourself fortunate that Imina and Narstron did some of the heavy lifting in that area."

"You don't think I would have liked you had I met you earlier?" she asked. "If we had crossed paths when I was a young officer of Amarath's Raiders and you were applying to any guild you could find taking applicants?"

Cyrus chuckled. "I actually applied to the Raiders at one point. It was a short visit."

She looked pained. "You didn't make it past the foyer, did you?"

"I did not," Cyrus said with a chuckle. "The look they gave me told me everything about what they thought the moment I walked in. I wasn't escorted out, but I was politely asked to leave and given the impression that if I didn't do it in haste, I'd have been tossed momentarily."

"If only they'd known," she said a little sadly, "what they were missing."

"I don't think it would have worked out very well for me," Cyrus said, feeling a little sadness settle over him. "If they'd taken me, I mean. Because then, I would have been there when—"

"Oh," Vara said, and her hand came to hover over her stomach involuntarily. "Of course. The purge of the righteous."

"Is that what you called it?"

"I called it much worse than that," she said, pulling away from him. She walked slowly toward the freestanding mirror in the corner. "The great stabbing in the back, the day of the traitorous wretches, and other, more creative and profane names that require a better grasp of elvish than you possess—"

"I'm really good with the profanity. It's your subject and verb agreement that trips me up. Also, conjugation."

"Yes, well," she said, turning back to him. "Those were dark days."

Cyrus nodded. "I think I feel a little darkness seeping in here lately."

"It's not like it was there," Vara said quickly.

"No, I didn't mean it was—" Cyrus sighed. "I just meant things have taken a grim turn these last few months."

"Indeed," Vara said with a slow nod. "We went from being a guild on the rise, walking with a confidence in our step from winning the dark elven war for the rest of the world—a guild so ... I don't want to

say overconfident in the ascendancy, but certainly feeling our oats …
to … well, now." She shrugged. "We're down. There's no denying it,
and not much point in trying. But down is hardly defeated, at least not
for good."

"I can't figure out why the titans haven't come at us harder,"
Cyrus said, shaking his head. "This should be over by now. They
could have come north at any time, with magic at their disposal."

"As you said, they are rather one-dimensional in their thinking,
and magic changes the rules remarkably in battle."

"I never liked counting on my opponents to be stupid," Cyrus
said, starting to unfasten his armor. "No, they'll get smart sooner or
later, and when they do, we're going to be looking back on these dark
days as positively sunny."

"I don't fear it," Vara said, taking off her gauntlets. "Not with you
in charge."

He smiled. "How did you go from hating me to saying such kind
things?"

She strained at that one, and he could see the sarcasm threatening
to spill out as she rolled her eyes, then she brought them back under
control as she looked at him. "They say there is a desperately thin
veneer between love and hate. Honestly, I still waver back and forth
depending on the conversation."

"Ah," he said, bringing her close again. The smell of sweat was in
her hair, on her skin, but it did not bother him. He kissed her lips and
found them sticky with dried perspiration. It was only a peck, just a
few seconds, and then she pulled away. "What?" he asked.

She sniffed the air. "You need a shower desperately."

"Hey," he said, scowling, "you're no sniff of rosewater yourself.
I've been waiting on the line of battle for days and—"

"Well, you're not waiting any longer, and there's a shower right
over there," she said, pointing to the small room tucked into the
corner of the tower between two balconies. She slipped off her boots
and then blanched like she'd been hit. "Perhaps a bit of that for both
of us, then."

"Together?" Cyrus suggested slyly.

She rolled her eyes once more. "Why not?" she asked, as though it
entailed great sacrifice on her part. Armor clanged against the stone
floor as she slipped out of hers and he from his.

"What do you fear?" Cyrus asked when they were nearly naked, and he saw her muscles tense at the question, standing out on her back as the long scar that stretched just to the side of her spine reddened.

"Nothing when I'm with you," she said, standing up straight, turning to face him with only her light cloth trousers still hugging her waist. He could see the scar on her belly now, similarly angry red against pale flesh.

"Nothing at all?" Cyrus asked, watching her carefully.

"When I'm with the greatest warrior in Arkaria," she said, just a little too breezily, "what is there to fear?" With that, she slipped the light trousers from her waist and let them fall to the floor. She stepped out of them and walked seductively toward the shower. "Are you coming?" she asked as she disappeared behind the frame. A second later, he heard water rushing through the pipes and spattering on the stone floor within, gurgling in the drain.

There was something in her answer that he did not care for, that he did not understand, but he let it rest, and followed her into the shower. The water, however, felt strangely cold in spite of the company.

50.

"So what's the next big idea?" Ryin asked, more alert than he had looked during the last Council meeting. He didn't seem quite as weary, though the druid still had an air of concern about him.

"I don't even have a sarcastic one at this point," Vaste said, "which I know will surprise you all."

"What's got you so grim?" Vara asked, brow furrowed as she looked at the healer.

The room was dark, the light of day barely shining in but the torches extinguished. It was a curious situation, the magical light of Sanctuary not quite doing its job, though Cyrus was a bit torn on whether the torches were really needed. The room was just a bit dim after all, not dark as night. All the officers were present save for Odellan, Mendicant and Longwell, each of whom were on duty in the various places the Army of Sanctuary was presently stationed.

"Well, we have lost some lives lately," Vaste said. "And we've got people still out there trying to hold things together, maintain scouting so titans don't come running up on us in the middle of the nights and crash through our gates before we can get roused to go die at their hands—I mean fight them."

"You really think the titans are going to come here?" Erith asked, looking more nervous than Cyrus had ever seen her.

"It certainly wouldn't be the first time," Curatio said quietly. The healer looked more pensive than usual today, but also tired in a way that was becoming surprisingly common, as though some sleep spell were being passed around among the officers, draining their vitality.

"We'd make it the last, though," Thad said with more than a little bravura.

"Because we've done such a smashing job of beating them back at every turn thus far," Vaste said, nodding sagely.

"Your sarcasm does not help the situation, troll," Vara snarled.

"I actually wasn't being sarcastic this time, either," Vaste said, shrugging. "Think about it from the perspective of the titans. They attack Emerald Fields, and while that was not our most smashing success ever, we made them retreat, vestigial tails between their legs. When next we met, on their turf, we destroyed their entire savanna watch operation, invaded their city and killed their emperor. Now we've destroyed the Heia Pass and left more of their dead rotting there than our own." He looked around the table. "From our perspective, it's disasters from start to finish. But the titans aren't us, and they aren't used to the decreased danger that having healers with resurrection spells brings. They're used to fighting and dying with every war. From their perspective … we're dishing out a lot more punishment than we're taking."

Cyrus frowned. "That's … not a bad point."

"Try not to sound utterly shocked," Vaste said.

"I *am* utterly shocked," Vara said, leaning her elbows onto the table, "but I agree with the troll."

"I am glad that the elf agrees with me," Vaste said, drawing a look of irritation from Vara. "Oh, sorry, was responding in kind to your condescending remark inappropriate in some way?"

Vara's eyes glistened like ice in the sunlight. "Last night in the shower, Cyrus and I—"

"Okay," Vaste said, throwing up his massive green hands, "I surrender, I yield. You have the equivalent of a verbal godly weapon, and I am no match for it. Please don't tell me any naked tales of the man in black armor."

"I wouldn't mind hearing some more of them," Erith said.

"This is an important meeting," Andren said, slamming his fist to the table with exaggerated emphasis. He held a straight face for almost five seconds then turned to Cyrus. "Would you mind finishing that story for me later? Just a bit of talk between the boys, you know," he said in explanation to the rest of the table. "It's the privilege of being old friends—"

"Yeah, we're not discussing that—any of that—anymore," Cyrus said, feeling a discomfort inside like he'd swallowed boulders.

"Yay!" Vaste said.

"In Council," Cyrus said, giving the troll a sidelong look. "If Vara wants to torture you in her own time with ... uh ... whatever details of our private personal lives that she wants to make public," he drew a stinging look from her, "uh ... that's fine."

"Not so yay," Vaste said.

"If nobody else has anything to say on this—" Cyrus began.

"What do we do when the titans come over the mountains into the Elven Kingdom?" Nyad asked. There was a hint of plaintive concern to her voice. "Now they're not isolated to any one particular avenue, with the pass closed. They could come over anywhere—walking over the Bay of Lost Souls, or coming up the coast on the other side—"

"I know this is going to come as a surprise to all of you, given it's me speaking," Ryin started, "but ... am I the only one who wonders how we can simply ... end this?" Now he looked almost as tired as Curatio. "I am frankly to the point where wiping out every man, woman and child in Kortran is an idea I'd entertain, in the style of the conquerors of old." He paused, as though the words he spoke reached his own ears. "Though not an idea I'd condone."

"We'll make a wild, savage pillager of you yet," Vaste said. "And I admit, the druid speaks reason. I am of the opinion that the titans will not be stopping without very, very good cause, and while I certainly think, as I stated earlier, that we've inflicted some considerable damage on them, we haven't drawn the sort of blood that will make them stop."

"What next, indeed?" Curatio asked, and now it was almost as though a competition was going on between him and Ryin to see who could sound the most tired. "They strike at our people, we strike back at theirs. We invade their lands, they invade ours. This is poised to go on forever, with blow and counterblow. One almost wonders if Ryin's unthinkable solution is the only one."

"But we're not actually going to do it, right?" Vaste asked. An uncomfortable silence filled the air. "Right? I mean, we didn't even do that to the trolls—"

"The trolls stopped when we scared them," Cyrus said, unable to pull his eyes off the table. "When we hurt them bad enough. Much like Vaste and Ryin, I find myself wondering what it will take to make them let go of this particular bone of contention." He looked at Curatio. "When the titans attacked Sanctuary before, Alaric didn't go after them, did he?"

"No," Curatio said. "He was rather more preoccupied with mourning and ... other details."

"Oh, a mystery!" Vaste said. "I heard a mystery. It's been a while, but I just heard one, dumped out unceremoniously upon this table like a naked elf!" He caught a hard look from Vara. "I didn't say a female elf, yeesh, don't be so presumptive and quick to take offense."

"There's not that much mystery to it," Vara said, the anger subsiding. "And it was a little like what you suggest, Vaste, in that Alaric brought me into Sanctuary within a day of Raifa dying. I believe he and the small complement of remaining members were somewhat busied in the time that followed seeing to my health."

"Oooh," Vaste said, "all right. Not quite as exciting of a mystery as I thought it'd be, but I'll bite. Where did Alaric find you?"

She stared at him flatly. "Where Archenous Derregnault and Amarath's Raiders left me to die."

"I heard that happened in the Trials of Purgatory," Thad said, frowning.

Vara froze, looking somewhat caught. "It did."

"Lucky Alaric just happened to be wandering through, then," Cyrus said, noting the peculiarity of her reaction. "Especially since Sanctuary wasn't able to beat the trials until years later."

"I told you I sensed a mystery," Vaste said, "and here it is, meat on this bone that everyone else thought was bare. I can smell them, I tell you—"

"That's your upper lip and possibly your underarms," Vara said.

"How did Alaric get into the Trials of Purgatory?" Erith asked, wrinkling her nose like she could smell, if not a mystery, then something.

"I presume he had a wizard take him there," Vara said archly, but the effort she was putting into holding back her feelings was obvious to Cyrus.

"To what purpose?" Andren asked. "Why would you go there unless you were trying to do the Trials? I can't imagine it'd be to have a friendly chat with the Gatekeeper, charming fellow that he is—"

"Alaric and the Gatekeeper seemed to know each other," Thad

said.

"Alaric seemed to know everyone," Andren said, scratching his head.

"As Alaric is dead, I suppose we have no one to ask," Ryin said.

"Unless our resident paladin knows more than she's telling us," Erith said.

"There are quite a few things I'm not telling you at the moment," Vara said, "including my opinion of your intellectual capabilities, which is—"

"Vara," Cyrus said gently. "You can tell us."

She cocked an eyebrow at him. "Can I? Very well, then. What secret have you been holding back, Cyrus? Surely you can share it with everyone here." She paused then pressed again. "I know you've got a secret. Something you're holding back even from me. Something you don't want to say aloud, even. It's on your face even now, how your chin is wavering just the slightest bit." She nodded at him in a challenging manner. "You tell your secret, I'll tell mine."

"Hold—" Curatio started, lifting a hand.

Cyrus felt her provocation and was strangely moved by it. It wasn't pride that spilled over him, but a sudden desire to simply let it out and be done, to not have to worry about hiding it anymore. "When Yartraak was about to strike me down, I saw a vision of Alaric in the Tower of the Guildmaster." Cyrus drew a long breath in the silence and let it out. "It was so real ... I think he's still alive." He locked eyes with her.

"If Alaric is alive," Ryin said quietly, "why isn't he here?"

"I don't know," Cyrus said.

"And why's he appearing in visions only to you?" Andren asked, looking a bit miffed. "I've got questions for him, you know. Like you're some kind of favorite son—"

"Perhaps Cyrus was simply delusional from being battered around by a god," Vaste said, a little too quickly for Cyrus's taste.

"Perhaps he was simply delusional from being Cyrus," Nyad muttered. When everyone looked at her, she reddened. "Well, I mean, all this can't be good for his ego."

"That's exactly what I've been saying," Vara spoke under her breath.

"So what is it? Your truth?" Vaste asked, pinning Vara with his own look. "He spilled his secret. Now time for you to spill yours."

Vara looked at Cyrus, and he got the impression of a woman trapped. Still, she did answer. "I once asked Alaric what he was doing in Purgatory, and his answer was very much in line with him. He swore he would tell me some of it right then, and the rest at another time later."

"Come on, come on," Vaste said, "what's the part he told you?"

She hesitated. "Do you recall the sequence of portals in Purgatory that the Gatekeeper has told us any number of times not to walk through? The ones at the very end?"

"Yessssssss?" Vaste said, voice rising expectantly.

"One of them is a gateway to a place," Vara said slowly, "where for a short time after permanent death, one can reclaim a lost soul."

It was so quiet in the Council Chambers that Cyrus would have sworn that even the popping of the absent fire would have sounded like barrels of Dragon's Breath going off in the Heia Pass.

"Excuse me?" Nyad asked, a look of horror stitched on her face.

"That's ... troubling," Vaste said, and his expression reflected it and more.

"You're telling me that behind the Trials of Purgatory, which we can beat at a will," Thad said, "there's a gateway to a place where we could reclaim our lost—our dead." His eyebrows were low, mouth open at a furious angle. "The dead we've been losing over the last few weeks—months—years? Those we lost before that, even?" He poured a little hope into the last question.

"There is some cost," Vara said quietly, now looking more cornered than ever, "that he did not explain to me. It is not a simple thing, this ... this task, however it happens."

"Can we also just reflect on the fact that Alaric apparently beat the Trials of Purgatory himself in order to get to this back gate?" Erith asked, blinking. "Unless you were stabbed at the entry?" Vara shook her head. "Wow. By himself."

"He was not by himself," Curatio said, stirring to life after a long silence. "I was with him."

"The two of you?" J'anda asked, eyes widening. He had remained silent throughout the entirety of the meeting thus far. "Alone? Against the entirety of the Trials? The golems? The eel? The Siren of Fire? The—"

"Yes," Curatio said, "I am aware of the Trials, having bested them myself." He looked stiff, rigid, as though he had become rooted in the chair. "And Vara is quite right. There is a price associated with that particular portal. It does not lead anywhere ... good."

"We've been in the Realm of the God of Death," Vaste said, "when a whole mess of trapped souls burst loose and came screaming down upon us. You're intimating that this is something worse?"

"You have heard of the God of Evil, yes?" Curatio asked, the fatigue infusing his voice.

"Hard not to," Vaste said. "His work is so very widespread."

"Well, this is his work as well," Curatio said. "There is legend of a last gift to mortals from the God of Good, something handed to them to give them hope—"

"The ark," Cyrus said, drawing a flash of surprise from the healer. "Scuddar told the story over in Luukessia," he explained. "It made an impression."

"Well, the legend goes that the God of Evil made a similar contribution, and that the other gods were so ... put off by his efforts," Curatio said, "that they made every attempt to contain it. Where the ark supposedly brought hope to people, this gift stole it away under false guise. So, yes, you can supposedly retrieve your loved and lost dead for a period of time after the resurrection spell does not work, but at some considerable cost."

"Like ... as bad as a soul ruby cost?" Cyrus asked.

"Arguably worse," Curatio said. "Where a resurrection spell steals some small memories as its exacted price, this ... *process* ... shall we say ... steals them all. The person you bring back has no memory of you at all, no memory of their life before, and is essentially a blank canvas." His head sagged as he bowed it. "We set off that day to retrieve Raifa from that place, but came across someone else in dire need." He nodded very slightly at Vara. "She, too, was past the hour of healing for her wounds, and cursed with a dark knight spell that would have prevented her from healing herself. Faced with the choice of abandoning Vara, this stranger we had stumbled across, in order to bring Raifa back, Alaric ..." Curatio sighed. "He did not hesitate. Not even in the face of the Gatekeeper's taunting, not even against counsel telling him that we had come this far, to not be foolish and sacrifice his cherished love helping some poor soul who didn't appear to stand any chance of survival." His eyes darted around the table. "Some of you saw my … my moment of doubt before we left for Luukessia. Where I doubted Alaric, doubted his intentions. I feel a fool for forgetting that moment in Purgatory, and a thousand others like it, when he held true to the mission of Sanctuary above all else." He looked solemn. "That is how you know who a man is—not in his decisions in the best of times, but in his decisions under greatest strain, when the things he cares for most are ripped from his grasp without mercy."

Curatio sighed, loud and long. "By the time Vara was well, Alaric did not pursue a vendetta with the titans, and they did not come through the pass and challenge the elven defenses again. The fear of the dragons set in on the titans, I think …" He waved a hand. "A fear they don't seem to have any longer."

"Wow," Vaste said, leaning back in his chair, ample belly looking like it would strain out of his robes. "That was like a buffet of secrets. I don't think I've ever had so much in the way of secrets come out at this table before, except maybe that time when Alaric threw his sword down after we killed Mortus. I almost feel too full for lunch." He rubbed his stomach while the others sat in silence. "Come on! Alaric, may be alive, or else our Guildmaster delusional! The realization that Alaric and Curatio were a team of badasses so powerful that they could take apart the Gatekeeper's little pet labyrinth like it was nothing?" He made a *pffff!* sound. "They didn't even need us when we started going through there a few years ago. Chew on that for a minute. The rest of us are struggling to survive, and they're out there doing what it takes hundreds of us to do by themselves." He looked at Curatio and saw a hint of something else there. "Right?"

"Close enough," Curatio said, waving a hand at him. "I think … it best I retire." He slid his chair back from the table. "If anything else is decided, be kind enough to inform me in the morning."

"Curatio," Erith said, "it's the middle of the afternoon."

"I am old," Curatio said, weaving toward the door, looking as if he meant it, "and I require a nap." He opened and closed the door in near silence.

"Is Alaric really alive?" J'anda asked, leaning across Curatio's empty chair to look at Cyrus.

"I don't know," Cyrus said, now feeling slightly pinned himself. "It was awfully real, what I saw that night in Saekaj, as the Sovereign—Yartraak—was choking the life out of me. More vivid than any daydream or delusion I've ever had."

Vaste nodded at him. "So you're saying you've had a lot of delusions, then? Enough that you feel you can tell the difference between those and ... uh, this?"

"I'm not prepared to gamble my life on it," Cyrus said, "but yes. I think he's alive, somewhere." He saw a furtive glance from Vara, watched it slide off of him and back to the table, and mustered up a near-finish to his thought, one that was steeped in doubt and guilt. "But I don't know why he's not here."

51.

The Council broke, and even Vara prepared to leave the chambers in advance of Cyrus. He stopped her with a word. "Vara."

She looked back into the darkened Council Chambers as Erith passed her by. "Can we talk later?" she asked. "I find myself ... perhaps in the mood for a nap of my own."

"Sure," Cyrus said, and watched her go, the slump of her shoulders obvious even through her shining armor.

"Cheer up," Andren said, making his way to the door. "We can go on a walk to Reikonos if it'll make you feel better?" He paused at the door. "Maybe look for your mysterious house again? Eh?"

Cyrus started to say no, but something about the thought of Andren's proposal held him up. "Maybe," Cyrus said. "Yes. I think ... yeah, that sounds like a—"

The door next to Andren thundered open, slamming wood against stone as its hinges reached full extension and started to spring back from the force. For a moment, Cyrus thought perhaps the alarm spells of Sanctuary had gone off, warning of foul deeds afoot somewhere in the keep, but he saw the dark-armored figure with the lance tucked over his shoulder a moment later, and relaxed almost imperceptibly until he saw the look on Samwen Longwell's face.

It was dark as the Council Chambers; darker even, perhaps, thunderclouds on the broad brow of the last King of Luukessia. He stalked into the room with a furious purpose, every motion relaying obvious anger. "How could you?" Longwell asked, thumping the haft of his lance against the floor with every step like a walking cane. He did not appear to need its support, but it channeled his fury into the stone and echoed through the Council Chamber with all his anger.

"Watch your tongue with your Guildmaster," Andren said, coming back into the room and slamming the doors behind him. "Perhaps show a bit of courtesy, too, to the man who's done more for your people than anyone els—"

"I am here," Longwell said, so harshly he cut the healer off with his fierceness, "because of my people. Because of what just reached my ears about the Heia Pass." He snapped his head around. "How many Luukessians died in the defense of that place?"

Cyrus regarded him coolly, trying to think his way through the situation before him. *He's plainly agitated. There's a burr deep under his saddle; best not ride him too hard right now.* "I didn't break down the list of casualties by their place of origin, Samwen."

Longwell's eyes flashed at the use of his familiar name. "Well, I had a glance at it when it came through at my station in Emerald Fields. I counted forty-five." He edged up to the table, butting his chest out. "Forty-five men of Syloreas, Actaluere and Galbadien—"

"Of Sanctuary, I think you mean," Cyrus said, trying to remain calm, channeling Alaric to the best of his ability.

"Of Luukessia!" Longwell practically shouted. "And you threw them into death!"

"Come on," Andren said, scoffing, "half the damned guild is Luukessians, Longwell. You can't expect them not to die when we have losses—"

"What I expect," Longwell said, his own voice dropping into icy ranges Cyrus associated with wizard spells, "is that my people aren't going to be the shield vanguard for every stupid fight we get into."

Cyrus raised an eyebrow. "Defending the pass against the titans— defending the new Luukessian homeland against them— that's a stupid fight?"

Longwell flushed scarlet. "Did you have to put them up front?"

"I had to put the best fighters up front, yes," Cyrus said, giving him a steady, even stare, but trying to put some compassion into his voice as well. "Just the same as at Leaugarden, when I had to use the cavalry dragoons to—"

Longwell exploded before he had a chance to finish. "And that's another thing! Using us as your spear to do your dirty work, the hard work, even when—"

"Hey!" Andren shouted, silencing Longwell for once. "I didn't see any of 'your' men flinching away from doing their asked duty. I didn't see your dragoons hesitate to charge when ordered—when you ordered them, by the way, because I recall you being right at the fore in that fight." Longwell jerked his head as if struck. "This is a guild where we fight, and right now we're holding the line to defend your Emerald Fields, man! You were bucking for battle not that long ago, in fact, looking like you'd enjoy tearing a piece or two off titan flank with your teeth. What happened to that bloke?"

Longwell turned slowly back to Cyrus, all the fight drained out of him. His pale face was hollow of expression, and his lip quivered in a way that Cyrus had never seen from the dragoon. "There are so few of us left," he whispered. "So very few. And with ... Emerald Fields, and Leaugarden, and now ... now this ... and more could ..." He choked a little.

"Samwen," Cyrus said, trying to hold himself up as a stone wall though his legs felt heavy bearing the burden of his body at the moment. "We are going to do everything we can to protect your people. But your men aren't—the ones we've sent to Leaugarden and the pass—they're not farmers." Cyrus felt the sag of his lips as emotion weighed them down. "None of us are. We're fighters. Soldiers. We go to war. And this ... this fight with the titans, it's reminding me what real war is, without the safety of the armor of magic and healing and resurrection spells."

"There are just ... so few ..." Longwell pitched back, his rump hitting the chair nearest him, and he landed on the floor with a short bounce. "So few ..." Now the hot tears were running down his face.

Unsure what to say or how to say it, Cyrus walked over to the dragoon and knelt next to him, placing a strong hand on his shoulder as the last living King of Luukessia wept openly in the middle of the Council Chambers.

52.

"That was a bit of downer," Andren said as he walked the streets of Reikonos off the square with Cyrus at his side. The healer's stride was lighter than his bearing, and evening was already starting to settle on the world. Autumn was in full effect, the cool breeze blowing through the streets, the few trees in the city shedding leaves that whipped along down the dirt and cobblestone avenues.

"He's had a rough run of luck," Cyrus said, adjusting his belt, feeling for Praelior's hilt instinctively. They had waited with Longwell for quite some time, until the dragoon pulled himself together, wiped his eyes, and offered Cyrus a half-hearted apology before he made his retreat.

"That's the truth," Andren agreed as they took a turn down a shop-lined street, glass windows glinting in the last light of day as the sun moved into the west. "Martaina told me that he's quite the weepy fellow when, uh ... engaged in the business, you know."

Cyrus frowned. "No, I don't know. What are you talking about?"

"You know," Andren said. "He and Martaina ... in Luukessia ... they ..." The healer arched his eyebrows.

The answer hit Cyrus like a titan fist. "Oh! Oh, gods! I didn't need to know that about your paramour."

"Well, you were with her over there," Andren said. "You must have known she did a bit of dabbling."

"I tried very hard not to discuss it with her more than the once or twice it came up," Cyrus said, quickening his pace as though he could leave this particular conversation behind if he walked fast enough. "Why is everything so focused on sex of late? It feels like every conversation tends that way sooner or later."

"Stuff of life, mate," Andren said with a twinkle in his eyes. "What else is there? Battles, sex, food—I mean, that sounds like a warrior of Bellarum's whole bag right there."

"There's more to it than that," Cyrus said, shaking his head. "There's got to be. That's a hollow life, my friend."

"Well," Andren said cautiously, "some people go in for the drink—"

"More than that," Cyrus said.

"Such as?"

"I don't know," Cyrus said, trying to look at the buildings they were passing. Shops were giving way to some houses, broken by businesses, taverns and the occasional small lot for farming, or communal ovens. "Love? Companionship? The bond of the brotherhood and sisterhood of our guild—"

"Bleargh," Andren pronounced with a finger shoved down his throat. "You're getting a bit sappy as you're hovering toward settling down—again, I might add, as if you failed to take away a single lesson from your first marital experience."

"Says the man who's about to tie the knot."

Andren's eyebrows arched upward in surprise. "Say what?"

Cyrus froze in the middle of the street. "She told me you'd talked about it."

Andren frowned, clearly befuddled. "Who? Martaina?"

"No, Aisling," Cyrus snapped back. "Of course Martaina.

"Hey, it could have been that dark elven minx. Based on the number she did to you, though, I'd be a bit warier in my approach, maybe try and—"

"Martaina came to me and said she wanted me to perform a marriage ceremony for you," Cyrus said. "For the two of you. Said you'd talked about it."

Andren gave it a moment's thought. "I suppose we did at that."

Cyrus waited for the reaction. "And?"

Andren just shrugged, the shadow of a nearby house disguising some of his expression. "Okay."

"Okay, what?"

"Okay, I'll marry her."

"What?" Cyrus could not avoid the tug of disbelief. "Just like that?"

"Well, yeah," Andren said. "I didn't know she was serious." He broke into a goofy smile. "It's kind of an honor, being asked by a woman like that, you know? Clearly she has plenty of options available, and she wants to marry me. I'm flattered."

Cyrus stood there, thinking that one over. "That's a ... unique perspective."

"You don't live as long as I have without gaining an appreciation for a good compliment," Andren said, starting down the street again. Cyrus had to hurry to catch up once he'd recovered his wits. "I mean, after all, she's got her pick of all these men in Sanctuary, she could maybe go for that bloke in Amti—"

"Gareth?"

"That's the one," Andren said lightly. "I guess they grew up together or something? Anyhow, it's really quite flattering to be chosen out of all those."

"I suppose," Cyrus said, inclining his head as he fell back into step alongside the healer.

"Kind of like you with Vara," Andren said. "When are you going to chain that little lady down?"

Cyrus's mouth fell open. "I ... don't know."

"You want to, don't you?" Andren prodded. "Eh? You've wanted nothing but her for years, really. So why wait?"

"Because of reasons," Cyrus snapped, though he could not think of a single one.

"Oh, yes, the reasons," Andren said, straight-faced, nodding. "The reasons being you're afraid she'll say no."

Cyrus froze again, and Andren began to outpace him. "Are you calling me a coward?"

"In battle? Gods no. In love ... well, if the boot fits ..." The healer looked down at Cyrus's feet. "Those are mighty big boots, I might add. Probably difficult to find in the right size."

"Well, they were my father's," Cyrus snapped, "so I suppose they're rather one of a kind."

"Much like your elven paladin, the shelas'akur," Andren said with a twinkle in his eye as they approached an intersection. "Might want to—put her on or—or something," he started to get flustered, and finally gave up. "Just marry her already."

Cyrus bit back the hard reply that he wanted to spout. "I'll consider it," he said instead.

"Swallow your pride, idiot," Andren said, looking around the intersection before nodding at the tavern that had been the Rotten Fish. "If she says no, just realize it's her pride talking, and that makes the two of you even more perfect for each other." He broke into a jog as he crossed the empty intersection, heading toward the pub.

Cyrus hurried to catch up, the sight of the pub causing him to divide his attention between the discussion they were having and the reason he had come here. "Your advice is noted."

"Yeah, you file that away for later," Andren said. "Where are we going here?"

"This way, maybe?" Cyrus pointed down the street. "I don't know that I have a hope of finding my actual house, since—I think the last time I saw it, the roof was caving in. It could be rubble, or more probably, long gone by now. I just want to see if anything looks familiar."

"Mmhmm," Andren nodded. "And how's that going so far?"

"All the houses look different," Cyrus said, "same as last time." The thatched roofs all blended together, and Cyrus frowned the further they walked from the pub.

The smell of night and the city was in the air, the smell of horse dung and baked bread heavy in Cyrus's nose. The autumn breeze of evening whirled around him, finding the cracks in his armor and cooling him where he'd sweated earlier in the warmer plains air. The houses were becoming shadowed now, a few souls still sitting outside here and there, watching the passersby. They took one look at Cyrus and did double takes, or let their jaws hang open.

"Not exactly inconspicuous, are you?" Andren asked.

Cyrus did not bother to answer. The distance they had gone seemed incredible, too far, really, and he was about to give up when his eyes perceived a gap in the houses ahead. He quickened his pace, half-expecting to find a field where farmers had a small patch here in the city. It was a simple space between houses, after all, but as he got closer he noticed the remains of the stone fence that had once parceled the lot, and the hints of a foundation that remained visible even though whatever had stood atop them was clearly long since gone.

Cyrus paused outside the fence and stared at the empty lot. A house had stood here once, he was sure of it. But to see it vacant now, and clearly for some time—it was a most curious thing in a city where housing was practically fought over.

Cyrus looked left and then right, to the houses on either side, and he saw movement in the dark, the light of a pipe flaring in the shadows at the entry to the house next door. Cyrus picked his way over, slowly, keeping his hands obviously visible. "Good evening," he called, announcing himself in case the person behind the pipe was the suspicious sort.

"Evening," a scratchy female voice greeted him. The woman stepped out of the shadows, and Cyrus immediately guessed her to be in her fifties. She wore a scarf over her head, along with simple work trousers and a shirt. She had the look of a laborer, and the weariness of a long day was apparent in her posture.

"I'm sorry to bother you," Cyrus said, placing his gauntleted hands on the stone wall that separated him from the woman. "I was wondering how long you've lived here?"

The question seemed to catch her by surprise. "Oh, long enough, I suppose," she answered, and he realized she was trying to count it out rather than being intentionally deceptive.

"Long enough to remember the house that used to be here?" Cyrus pointed at the vacant lot next door, and the woman's brows surged up.

"Not that long, no," she said, shaking her head. "That house was falling to ruin when I showed up, and it got hauled off brick by useful brick within a year of me coming here from the other side of town."

"Ah," Cyrus said, feeling a pinch of regret. "So you don't know who used to live there?"

She shrugged. "Not really. Some of the older lasses from this street might know. Joenne, across the way, perhaps." She pulled her pipe out of her mouth, pointing its stem at the house across the street. Cyrus turned to look, but not a light was on in the windows. "She's out of town at the moment," the woman said. "Visiting family in the Northlands."

"So how long have you actually been here?" Andren asked, furrowing his own brow in concentration. "By the count of years, if you remember exactly?"

The woman puffed her pipe as she gave it some thought. "I

reckon I've been here ... twenty years now?" she finally decided. "Since I bought this place from that elven dame."

"Hmm," Cyrus said, still feeling the pinch of disappointment. "Thanks for your—"

"What elven dame?" Andren asked. "Do you recall her name?"

"Like you know every elf," Cyrus said under his breath.

"Well, I might," Andren said with a shrug.

"Mmmm," the woman said, taking another draw of the pipe as its red light flared with her intake. "What was her name? She was a stately one, seemed like the sort who'd act like she was better than you—you know, like elves do—"

"I have heard that about them," Andren agreed. He nudged Cyrus with his shoulder, lightly. "He'd know. He's about to marry one."

"I am n—" Cyrus gave him a dirty look.

"Corinne?" The woman asked, drawing Cyrus's attention back to her before he realized she was trying to recall the name of the elf she'd bought the house from. "No, that's not it ... Cora. That's it. Cora. That was her." The old lady nodded, seemingly sure, and took another smoke.

Cyrus, for his part, sat there in the street, his hands on the stone fence, skin gone cold, tingles working their way up the crown of his skull.

"Well," Andren said with immense self-satisfaction, "as it turns out, we both know her. What are the odds of that coincidence?"

"So low as to not be coincidence at all," Cyrus said, the chill wind wrapping itself around his skin like a blanket. "In fact, I would say it's well-nigh impossible."

53.

When Cyrus returned to Sanctuary, dusk had passed and darkness had fallen. He made his way through the grounds, around the ancient walls of the keep, the stones glistening in the dark from specks of lighter sand grains catching the reflection of the watch fires around the curtain wall.

He found her out in the garden, atop the bridge, staring down into the dark waters below. The pond was scarcely a few feet deep, but with the moon overhead and the watch fires burning, he could see her reflection where she looked down into the water as he approached.

"Hey," he said, announcing himself. She did not look up, merely continued staring, her hands firmly planted on the stone railing that kept her from falling into the water below.

"Hello," she said, a bit distantly compared to how she'd been of late. He sidled up next to her, planting his own hands against the railing and leaning. "I expected you ages ago, honestly."

"I hope you're not insulted that I'm late," Cyrus said. "I wanted to give you some space, honor your wishes and all that."

"I assure you I am not offended," she said, leaning over to him and giving him a kiss on the cheek. "Merely lost in my own contemplations."

"About Alaric?" Cyrus asked, though he already knew the answer.

"About Alaric," she agreed. "About where he might be if he is in fact still alive."

"Well, when last I saw him he was in the Tower of the Guildmaster," Cyrus said with a quiet smile. "But I expect you and I have, uh, explored every surface of that place over the last few months, and I don't think he's hiding in there now." Cyrus paused.

"Though if he is … he's had quite an eyeful."

"Indeed," Vara said. "It's a curious thing, isn't it? The idea of searching for a man who can go as insubstantial as the mist. It rather boggles the mind when trying to decide where even to start."

"I figure if he wants to be found," Cyrus said, "he'll let me know where to go. Until then," he swept a hand toward the walls in the distance, and a hoot of laughter echoed in the night from atop them, "I have the responsibility he left."

"I helped give away his armor to Terian," Vara said, her face pinched.

"Which is strange because when I saw Alaric, he was wearing it," Cyrus said with a shrug. "But then again, that was before Terian had it." He frowned. "Maybe we should ask the Sovereign of Saekaj Sovar his take on the matter."

"Curatio gave him the armor," Vara said with certainty. "I pilfered the helmet from the shrine once I heard what he was doing." She nodded toward the small structure just past the bridge.

"And why did you do that exactly?" Cyrus asked. "I'm a little fuzzy on the logic there."

"Terian was in need," Vara said, and there was not a trace of doubt in her tone. "He was trying to make right a long series of wrongs, and he was without armor as he headed into a crucial battle. Whatever Terian did that caused us to cast him out, after Saekaj and Yartraak, I was convinced that he was making every effort to strive for the redemption he spoke of." She lowered her voice. "Under those circumstances, I felt Alaric would want him to have the best possible chance at success."

"Well, it seems to have worked out well," Cyrus said. "He's as changed a man as any I've ever seen."

"It's a curious process to watch it play out in reverse," Vara said, her face a little haunted. "I watched Archenous go from paladin to dark knight right under my nose, losing his soul to the reckless desire for power." She flicked her gaze to him. "You asked me earlier what I fear? I fear that. I have seen in you, since the beginning, the same threads of ambition that he wove into purest darkness. I have counseled you all along to walk the right side of the path, to steer away from vengeance, turning you from warrior of Bellarum to the nearest thing to a paladin without magic that I could." She stepped closer, and placed a bare hand upon his breastplate. "I have watched you struggle under burdens that would crush lesser men, watched you make difficult choices that others would have made more simply, expediently, and utterly wrongly. You took the harder path, and I admire you for it." She bit her lower lip lightly. "But still ... I fear. I fear what you would become if you chose the path of the warlord that everyone has always accused you of wanting to be."

"I'm not a warlord," Cyrus said, his throat dry. "I'm a Guildmaster."

"You're the Lord of Perdamun," Vara said, "unchallenged by any government in that title. You need but reach out your hand and this whole land would be yours, a territory that would stretch from Prehorta down to the Waking Woods, all the way to the Bay of Lost Souls and around to the Perda. You could be a King with but a command, and the peasantry that remain here would accept gladly the thought of protection that would come from so strong an authority."

"Don't I have enough trouble running a guild at this point?" Cyrus asked. "I mean, I can't even get Vaste to shut up for more than five seconds unless you threaten him with lewd stories about our romantic interludes—"

"I know you jest," she said, but there was seriousness laced all through her stiff bearing, "but I see you caught between being the Warden of the Southern Plains, with a desire to protect all under your tent, and the man who would strive to fix every problem in the world the way he solved those of the goblins, the trolls and the dark elves."

"Well, I'm up against a problem now that's bound to keep me from exercising those imperial ambitions anytime soon," Cyrus said, not really sure what to say but to quip.

Vara nodded in clear discomfort at his answer. "You don't fear what you would become?"

"Not with you here beside me," Cyrus said, and he leaned in to kiss her. She hesitated just a moment, then reciprocated, and she filled his arms as they got lost in each other—

And then a giant pillar of water doused them both, rushing down Cyrus's collar as it fell with more volume than any rain he had ever seen, a steady gush as though the pond had leapt forth over the bridge railing and attacked them. Cyrus sputtered as the water splashed through his armor, soaking his underclothes. Vara let out a scream of protest at the sensation, and once it had drained away, they stood there staring at each other as quiet footsteps broke the silence behind Cyrus.

He spun to find Curatio standing there, wearing something approaching a smirk on his tired face. "Good evening, you two. Did I interrupt something?"

"What the hell sort of spell was that?" Vara asked, her outrage bleeding out through the chattering of her teeth.

"As with most I know, a heretical one," Curatio said with a smile. "Would you like to see it again?"

"No," Cyrus said, the steady drip off his armor louder than the steps Curatio had taken approaching them.

"Did you come here just to dump cold water on us?" Vara asked, spreading her arms wide and slinging excess dampness off her vambraces. Liquid spilled out from where her gauntlets were missing, heavy at first and then slowing to a drip.

"Not at all," Curatio said, the smile disappearing. He looked straight at Cyrus. "Ehrgraz is here. He approached quietly in the night and asked a sentry at the wall to speak with you. Scared the poor bastard out of his mind; thought he was alone, and then suddenly, a dragon's face was in his, making a polite inquiry." The healer shook his head. "He says ..." The elf's eyes narrowed as he delivered the message, as though suspicion hid behind them, "... he says it is most urgent."

54.

Ehrgraz was waiting in the night, lurking just outside the curtain wall, eyes catching the light of the watch fires as they glowed like hot coals. He tracked Cyrus's approach with fervent intensity but said nothing until Cyrus was nearly upon him. "Cyrus Davidon," Ehrgraz said, locking eyes with him. "So kind of you to grace me with your presence at last."

"You should have sent a messenger," Cyrus said, folding his arms in front of him as Vara settled in next to him, Curatio a few paces behind. "I would have scheduled you an appointment."

Ehrgraz's nose flared red in the night as fire appeared to rise out of it. "I do hope you're joking."

"I'm here, aren't I?" Cyrus managed a tight smile at the dragon as the wind whipped in out of the east. "What can I do for you?" Beads of water ran down his skin from where Curatio had drenched him, and the wind gave him a bit of a chill.

"I have come to propose something to you," Ehrgraz said, speaking more slowly than he usually did.

"Propose away," Cyrus said, suddenly conscious that Vara was very close to him.

"I want to bring the dragons into your little war," Ehrgraz said.

"So do it," Cyrus said, cutting him off.

"If only it were that easy," Ehrgraz said, his patience strained slightly judging by the tone of his voice. "But there is a way."

"Not an easy one, I assume?" Cyrus asked, now warier than before.

"No," Ehrgraz said softly. "Not easy at all. For either of us."

"Make yourself plain, Ehrgraz," Cyrus said. "What do you want from me?"

"I want you to attack Yonn'revenn—the Dragonshrine."

Curatio gasped and Cyrus turned to look at the healer, who recovered quickly. "Are you quite out of your mind, Ehrgraz?" Curatio asked. "You want us to attack your most sacred place?"

"I don't *want* you to attack it," Ehrgraz said slowly, with a hint of regret. "I *need* you to."

"How does us attacking your shrine help get your dragons into the war against the titans?" Vara asked. "It seems to me that doing such a thing, if you view it that strongly, would invariably lead to you declaring war against *us*, not the titans."

"And there is the difficulty," Ehrgraz said. "You must not be seen to do it. It must appear as though the titans are responsible." His wings moved in the dark, shadow against the plains ground. "I am not talking about some mean attack upon the outside, or some ineffectual slap at one of its defenders, either. It must be an attack, true, damaging and utterly abhorrent." He lifted up, placing a clawed hand upon the edge of the curtain wall, bringing his enormous abdomen up as he did so. With his other claws he brought a small pouch, roughly the size of a gnome's head. "You'll need this if you're to succeed."

"What is it?" Cyrus asked, plucking the leather bag from Ehrgraz's grasp. It was sealed, like a coinpurse.

"It is an alchemical compound of ancient derivation," Ehrgraz said, narrowing his eyes. "And I do mean ancient, from the days when the demons of old still walked the world."

"The ... what of what?" Cyrus asked.

Ehrgraz made a sound of disgust deep in his throat. "You short-lived races!" he grumbled. "Not you, Curatio, naturally."

"Naturally," Curatio said, nodding. "In the days before the War of the Gods, there were fiercer things roaming Arkaria. The ancients, at the height of their empire, brought these dangers to heel in what they—and we—called 'the taming of the land.'"

"They wiped out the demons of old," Ehrgraz said. "As best they could, at least." He chuckled. "They did a poor job of it, though, or rather limited, at least."

"Ehrgraz," Curatio said, "you have asked us to attack your greatest temple, and—if that powder is what I assume it is—to desecrate utterly the greatest icon of dragonkin."

"Yes," Ehrgraz said quietly. "I have, haven't I?"

"Why?" Vara asked. "That is ... I assume it's a rather provocative step."

"Probably almost as devastating to my people as killing the last born elf would be to yours," Ehrgraz said, and while it might have come off as a threat to other ears, to Cyrus he merely sounded sad. "Because none of them *see*. So rooted in the past are we that we take no heed of the future, which the titans are shaping even now to their liking. They are moved by forces more dangerous than my people can imagine. Their will to conquer all should not be underestimated."

"This thing you ask of us ..." Cyrus said. "I'm not sure we can do this."

"You are fully capable of it, I assure you," Ehrgraz said. "It is left to you to decide whether what you fear from the titans will drive you as far as it has driven me." He raised his wings and flapped them once, leaving the ground. His wings caught the light of the watch fires, the braziers illuminating the undersides, the bony extrusions that held together the flapping, light skin that helped propel him aloft looking like canvas with a torch in front of it. "I, for one, hope you come to the same conclusions about these dangers as I have, for the alternative does not bear thinking about, a titan empire that will sit astride your north." He flapped his wings again and rose higher, out of sight in the darkness within seconds, leaving Cyrus, Vara and Curatio alone on the parapets, pondering what a dragon feared.

55.

"This is the worst idea of any idea that has been presented in or around our halls at any point in time," Curatio pronounced into the still night after Ehrgraz's departure.

"Vaste should dance naked every day during dinner," Vara said, drawing shocked looks from both Cyrus and Curatio. "Mine is worse, no?"

"It's a near thing in my estimation," Cyrus said.

"It is not a near thing," Curatio said, hotter than the watch fire burning only a few feet away from them. The healer's voice crackled in the night. "He intends for you to lead an offensive against the dragons under deceptive terms. To have you fool them into thinking that the titans have destroyed their greatest shrine." He cocked his head. "Do you know what happened to the last person that meddled in that place?"

"How would I?" Cyrus asked.

"Because you rode him into the ground," Curatio said, voice brimming with fury, "after Ashan'agar was exiled from their company. Dragons do not kill one another; it is their highest law. Even Ashan'agar did not commit murder on his own when he marshaled and defiled their temple. But now, Ehrgraz would have you do it and you would jump heedlessly into it without thought."

"I haven't said yes yet," Cyrus said.

"You didn't say no immediately," Curatio said, "which is almost as bad."

"Why are you pushing so hard on this?" Cyrus asked, his own ire rising. "Without a thought, you dismiss it? Curatio, we are desperately in the swamp on this fight with the titans."

"And you will sink us further into the mire should you undertake this course of action."

"When you're already in the mire over your head," Cyrus said, "I don't notice much difference whether I drown by an inch or by a mile." He stepped closer to the healer. "They are coming, Curatio. They're coming, and we likely will not be able to stop them, not by the numbers."

"Think about what you're saying." Curatio pointed a finger at him. "This is not just desperation, it is madness. It is treachery. Deceit."

"It is necessary," Cyrus said, not backing off.

"Is that what a paladin would say?" Curatio asked, looking over Cyrus's shoulder. He turned his head to look, but Vara remained silent, looking somewhat stricken in the glow of the fire.

"I'm not a paladin," Cyrus said, drawing the healer's gaze back to him. "And this is not a noble war. It began with a cowardly attack by superior forces against a town of civilians under our protection simply to spite us."

"And you answered it in kind," Curatio said, and Cyrus felt as though he'd been struck. "Yes, that surprises you, I'm sure, but Kortran is not all titan warriors and arenas. They are not some monolithic evil. There is argument among them, surely, even now, but Talikartin and the death of their Emperor is a knife in their side which worshippers of Bellarum will feel obligated to avenge." He lowered his voice. "How you win this war is as important as winning it, because what you do here, now, will affect who *you* are for all the rest of your days."

"The only thing that matters in this war," Cyrus said, feeling the rage trickle through him, "is winning it."

Curatio's head rocked back slightly. "A familiar sentiment, and an old one. But not yours originally, I think."

"This enemy is not going to stop at the sea, Curatio," Cyrus said. "They don't have a weakness like the scourge." He pointed at the central tower of Sanctuary. "I had to listen to Longwell today bleed his feelings out because of the loss of more of his people. He's frightened at the position of Emerald Fields, so close to the titans." Cyrus shifted his finger to point south. "How about the elves of Amti, living on borrowed time in their trees, forced to hide from the world because of their fear? And the elves? Your own people? You think they'll survive the titans coming north?"

"You see a reflection of all your failures here," Curatio said, glancing past him at Vara, "and so do I. But where you are wrong is the means you are considering. When I stood with the Guildmaster of Requiem at the twilight of the ancients, helping him defend the humans of Arkaria against that night of fire and destruction, I warned him against despair. I see in you the same seeds of fear and darkness, that desperate desire hold back a tide that you fear will consume everything you hold dear. But it will do you no good to win this fight and lose your soul, Cyrus." He stepped closer and lowered his voice. "Being willing to do whatever it takes to win, even assassination and duplicity are perfectly acceptable considerations for an adherent of Bellarum." He pulled back, looked Cyrus straight in the eye, and did not waver as he spoke, "But not for the Guildmaster of Sanctuary."

"What if there is no other way, Curatio?" Cyrus asked. "Do you see another way?"

"Can you see the River Perda in the darkness over yonder?" Curatio waved his hand to the south. "No? Just because you cannot see it, does not mean it is not there."

"What good does it do," Cyrus asked, "what virtue is there … in being a defender of the people who fails to defend the people?"

"I do not know," Curatio said, voice down to a whisper. He turned, slowly, tentatively. "But I know you have not failed yet." With silent steps, he retreated into the night.

Cyrus watched him go, waiting, and when Curatio was gone, disappeared into a tower to climb down from the wall, he turned to look at Vara. "What do you say?"

She hesitated, but her true reply burst forth when she spoke. "You know, Alaric would never have—"

The rage and frustration that had bubbled in Cyrus throughout his talk with Curatio burst free like a volcano. "I'm not Alaric!" His voice echoed in the night, bouncing off the wall, making his proclamation over the plains. When it faded, he spoke again, this time whispering. "Do you wish I were?"

"No," she answered immediately and stepped closer, placing a hand upon his shoulder in reassurance. "But I wish that he were here."

Cyrus swallowed the brief surge of bitterness that welled up in him and let the regret take over before he spoke. "So do I," he said, as he looked out on the dark, moonless plains. "So do I."

56.

"When I said I'd entertain almost any plan," Ryin Ayend spoke into the torchlit Council Chambers early the next morn, "and included that whole bit about women and children being slaughtered … I was being rhetorical. It was a bit of hyperbole, really, to highlight how desperate this situation has become." The druid placed his palms flat on the table, the room so quiet that Cyrus heard the flesh press against the wood. "And yet you found something almost as morally dubious, and here we go merrily down that path."

Cyrus looked to Curatio at his left, but the healer said nothing. He rested his elbow on the arm of his chair and lay slumped with his cheek against it, dangerously close to falling over should anything disturb the balance upon which he leaned.

"I, for one," Vaste began, causing Cyrus to cringe inside, "find that old sod about desperate measures absolutely applicable here."

"What old sod is that?" Erith asked with a frown.

"'Desperate measures are the most fun,'" Vaste said, "'for when someone is desperate, you get to find out who they truly are.'"

"Must be a troll saying," Erith said, "because I've never heard that."

"Can't be a troll saying," Andren said, "it's far too wise for that."

"You know, before everything went to shit up in Gren," Vaste said a little hotly, "we were occasionally capable of good, even great, things."

"Far be it from me to suggest otherwise," Odellan said, "having been to war with against your people and having seen what desperation did to them twenty years ago and more recently, last year." He looked around. "But to the point—an attack on dragons. Are we really discussing this?"

"We've fought dragons before," Andren said, waving a hand. "With less numbers, even, than we've got now."

"Kalam was no picnic," Vara said, "and we caught him napping. Meanwhile, Ashan'agar nearly killed more than a few of us when he broke loose of his imprisonment, and would have done much more damage had Cyrus not goaded him into riding up into the sky while he worked out a careful plan to deprive the bastard of his life."

"Yes, it was a careful plan," Cyrus said, nodding sagely, "in fact I even started working on it a year earlier when—"

"This stinks of revising history to fit your ego," Vaste said.

"Agreed," Vara said tightly.

Cyrus smiled. "Can't blame me for trying. But that dragon had a powerful ability to charm people just by looking in their eyes—"

"Yes, you Alaric'd him, it was brilliant," Vaste said, covering a fake yawn with one hand. "Now, back to this plan of yours—"

"Ehrgraz's," Cyrus said.

"Fine, back to this dragon plan," Vaste said. "How do we know it's not a trick? We show up, we kill dragons, we deface their shrine, Ehrgraz comes in bellowing and kills us all in a blast of fire hot enough to render my succulent bones and meat completely inedible, which would be a great tragedy for all, but mostly for me."

"That is a valid point," Cyrus conceded. "But I don't think he's betraying us."

"No one ever thinks they're being betrayed until it happens," Nyad said. "Case in point, there was that time you got stabbed in the back last year—"

"Hey," Cyrus said, "nobody saw that coming."

"I saw it coming," Vara said.

Cyrus gave her a sour look. "Fine. Do you think Ehrgraz is betraying us?"

Vara thought it over. "I don't think so, no. But he need not betray us for this plan of his to go horribly wrong. There is much he has not yet deigned to inform us about how it would be carried out."

"That's true," Thad said with a nod. "It doesn't take much to go wrong with a dragon fight for people to die in large numbers."

"You don't have to tell me that," Cyrus said, mildly aggravated. "I've stood in front of them before during fights. All I want to know is if anyone has a better plan. Because now is the time—"

"Find a pile of turnips and hide in it until this whole thing blows over," Vaste said. When he had every eye in the room upon him, he shrugged and elaborated. "Nobody likes turnips. I presume the dragons are at least sensible enough to be alike in that regard."

"So our alternatives at present are to attack the dragons," J'anda said, "or to hide in discarded vegetables." His fingers clenched his staff. "I know which I pick."

"Ooh, is it the vegetables?" Andren asked.

"No," J'anda said, "I don't like turnips, either."

"Far be it from me to suggest treachery is ever the best way to deal with anything," Nyad said, "but I share Cyrus's concern that the titans coming north is merely a matter of time. If they conquer the Kingdom, the rest of Arkaria will surely follow shortly. Even a combined force of all armies would have great difficulty standing up to them on the march with magic at their disposal."

"That seems personally motivated at least in some small measure," Erith said.

"And if your Sovereignty was under threat to be overrun with—I don't know," Nyad said, blushing, "gnomes digging into your tunnels and invading, I think you'd be personally motivated to help them, too."

"I know I'd be the first to volunteer to help in that case," Vara muttered.

"This titan threat's not going away," Longwell said, breaking his silence. "Not without us doing something." He shook his head. "If this gets the dragons in the fight and gives us a chance … well …" He lowered his head. "I'm sorry, but there are lives on the line here. More than a few. Probably the entirety of the north's, in the long term." He blinked away. "And in the short … the last survivors of Luukessia. And that's a personal motivation for me, in case anyone wants to call it out." He flushed.

"I've got an idea," Vaste said, snapping his fingers, "we pit the scourge against the titans." He waited, but all that greeted him was horrified silence. "Okay, fine. The dragons it is."

"All in favor?" Cyrus asked, and he watched the hands rise one by one, as though this were too solemn an occasion to trust to a voice vote. Curatio's was the only one not raised, though none were raised high. "And so it is," Cyrus pronounced, and the chamber stayed silence, "we battle with dragons."

57.

"I wish you all the best with your bold endeavor," J'anda said, tipping his head to Cyrus, "and I will see you in just a few short days."

"I like how you chose 'bold' instead of 'crazy,'" Cyrus said. "I've gotten no shortage of the latter since we started planning this, after all."

The foyer of Sanctuary was packed, the strike army Cyrus had assembled to undertake the mission to the Dragonshrine filling it nearly from one side to the other. He figured there were somewhere on the order of a thousand people, but there seemed to be room enough to pack plenty more into the spaces if he had felt compelled to bring more.

"I do not feel the need to tread where others do," J'anda said with a glimmer in his eyes that reminded Cyrus of the old him, the enchanter as he had been before Luukessia, where he'd drained so much of his own life that he'd aged well before his time. "I'm sure you will be fine."

"I worry more about you," Cyrus said.

"Do not worry about me," J'anda said, shaking his head. "With Mendicant and Ryin to help me, I will be fine. You, on the other hand …"

"I have plenty of help," Cyrus said, turning to look up to the balcony, where the other officers waited for him, watching the spectacle of the army below as final farewells were said. Cyrus had chosen carefully, and it was happy coincidence that he'd found little need to include many Luukessians in the army. The majority of them were cavalrymen, after all, and they had no need of that where they were going.

"But you don't have me," J'anda said, shrugging lightly. "At least not—"

"I'll miss you, too," Cyrus said, and clapped him lightly, once, on the shoulder before moving toward the balcony stairs. "See you in a few days."

"Indeed you will," J'anda said, nodding as he turned about, his massive staff preceding him, and headed for the stairwell.

"Are we ready, Guildmaster?" Curatio asked stiffly as Cyrus joined the officers up top. From here, he could look down and see the great seal of Sanctuary that perfectly coincided with the teleportation portal mounted under the floor.

Cyrus looked the healer up and down. "Are you sure you want to come?"

"I would be remiss if I did not," Curatio said, more than a little stiffly. "I am the Elder. I have responsibilities."

You had responsibilities as acting Guildmaster, too, Cyrus thought but did not say. *That didn't keep you from hurling the medallion down last year.* "Odellan?" Cyrus asked, and the elf stepped forward. "Are we ready?"

"Your army awaits, Guildmaster," Odellan said, giving a stiff nod over the balcony.

Cyrus strode to the rail and watched the last farewells exchanged, and loved ones and companions moving out of the center of the army's loose grouping. "What do you think? Do I need a speech?" he asked quietly.

"Let's go kill some dragons!" Andren shouted, and the call was taken up in the foyer with several thousand raised voices. "Nope, I think I got it for you."

"All right, then," Cyrus said and nodded to Nyad. The elven princess stood back a little ways from the balcony, looking a little peaked. "Take us to the Ashen Wastelands, Nyad."

"Aye," she said and steeled herself visibly. The light of a teleport spell burst from her hands and cracked around them, carrying them off in a cascading light storm of fury.

When the light faded from Cyrus's eyes, he was greeted with strangely familiar dark skies. Clouds filled the horizon from end to end, grey as any day he'd ever seen, and near enough to night as to make him wonder how it had been mid-afternoon only a moment earlier.

He took a step and felt the soft ground envelop his boot. He glanced down and saw ash, indeed. He took another step experimentally, and the ash came up almost over the toe. "Well, this is going to be a long walk."

"Six days," Vaste moaned, stepping up to look out over the horizon with Cyrus. "Why couldn't the dragons have built a portal nearer to their most sacred and holy shrine?"

"Because that would have doubtless opened it up to assaults of the sort we are about to perpetrate," Odellan said, stepping up beside them.

"Yes, but it would have been so much kinder to my tootsies," Vaste said, pointing at his feet.

"All right, Army of Sanctuary," Cyrus said, making his usual motion, "fall in."

They walked through the rest of the day, treading in ash, mountains barely visible both before and behind them on the horizon. Cyrus could see nothing to their left or right, to the east or west, and could scarcely tell direction but for the faint hint of the sun somewhere beyond the clouds.

The air carried the stink of something burnt, and coughing was a common thing to hear from the army behind him. Cyrus led the way until the darkness grew so complete that they could not go any farther, and they halted for the night, eating cold provisions and bread conjured before the night grew dark enough that spell light would have lit the wastelands and alerted dragons to their presence.

When they bedded down, they buried themselves in ash in the way that Cyrus had once seen a child on a beach cover herself over. In the night they heard the shrieks of dragonkin, of drakes and wurms, wyverns and other lessers of their sort. Cyrus heard the flap of wings overhead once, as did, he suspected, everyone else in the army.

They slept poorly, and continued their march the next day covered in ash. Their target was plain upon the horizon, and they scarcely needed Curatio to guide them once they knew what they were looking for. Cyrus stayed at the fore, his black armor grey from its coating, reminding him more than once of Cass Ward.

After three days, the silence began to feel oppressive. No conversation was carried out above a whisper, per the orders of Cyrus and Ehrgraz, when he had laid out the plan. "Echoes carry in the wastelands," Ehrgraz had said, "and the last thing you need is to draw attention to you small people by talking in big voices."

Cyrus had acceded to the dragon's wishes, and now he saw the wisdom in it. Fewer dragonkin passed in the day, and always the army halted when they were sighted, dropping and hiding among the piles of fallen ash. It was easy to blend in, and after three days, Cyrus almost believed Vara's natural skin tone was a deep grey.

"This is a bit much, isn't it?" she asked when they ate lunch.

"Whatever it takes, right?" he replied, but saw her face fall as he said it.

On the fourth day, they crossed an acidic stream, clogged with the dusty grey ash that filled the land. It held a putrid smell, and as they crossed it, Cyrus wondered at its toxic properties. It seemed to run toward the sea that he knew existed far, far off to the west, but he did not hold much hope that it would become much cleaner at its mouth.

On the fifth day, the shrine on the horizon seemed so close they could almost reach it if they ran. Cyrus kept the pace steady, but not quick, and he could feel the restlessness growing in his army as the time passed and the miles grew long.

"They want to be done with this grim land," Odellan said to him as they started to settle for the night. "The army grows sick of the march."

"Aye," Cyrus said, nodding. "This isn't exactly like anything we've ever done before, is it?"

Odellan smiled, cradling his carved helm on his lap with one hand while he held his bread in the other. "It's always a new adventure with Sanctuary, isn't it?"

"Like I said when I asked you to join," Cyrus said with a faint smile. "Though I doubt you knew what sort of adventure you were in for."

"No, indeed not," Odellan said with a low chuckle. "And to think I had figured killing the God of Death was an unusual week for you. If only I'd known ..."

"You would have run away and joined a mercenary company?"

"I don't think so," Odellan said with a shake of the head. "I probably would have run twice as fast to join Sanctuary." He grew serious. "There is no one doing as much to defend the Elven Kingdom that I swore loyalty to as Sanctuary is, whether they see it or not." He waved at Nyad, who was already covering her robes in ash in preparation to lie down for the night. "I mean, you have the King's heir as one of your officers, and we're about to attack dragons in a somewhat mad effort to redirect the attention of the Kingdom's greatest threat." He shook his head. "I might be doing more to uphold my oath here than I ever would have as an Endrenshan, or even an Oliaryn of the Elven Kingdom."

The night was long and quiet, the stillness almost maddening after nights of drakes and wyverns flying over them constantly. Cyrus was prepared for this, he thought; Ehrgraz's notice about the zone of desolation around the temple assuring him that there would be no traffic, no patrols to discover them this late in the expedition. It was still a hard night, even with Vara close at his side, their armor pressed against each other, yet separating them.

The dawn of the next day was barely one at all, the sun slipping behind the sea of clouds that covered the sky before Cyrus even noticed it. Rising, he found the shrine the largest point on the horizon, and only half a day's journey at that.

"Come on," he said, still keeping his voice low, and he pressed the army forward.

The ash clung to them, hung in the roof of Cyrus's mouth, and no matter how many times he spat and washed it with water, more seemed to flood in through his nose. He wondered if he would ever be rid of it, even after leaving this place far, far behind.

The shrine drew ever closer, and yet like an object just out of reach of the fingertips, felt impossibly far away. The noon hour came and left, and Cyrus's mind made him believe that he was no closer than he'd started the day. The shrine was clear, though, strangely familiar architecture wrapped around a steep-sided volcano, the top smoking, adding its own small contribution to the ash that filled the wasteland.

"I had a friend," Curatio said, "an elven craftsman, one of the old ones, like me—he assisted the dragons in building the temple structure around the volcano." Curatio pointed. "The dragons ... they liked elvish architecture, but their claws don't allow for great detail in building. Their eyes appreciate it at a scale they can't hope to deliver on their own."

"Why is this place so important to them?" Cyrus asked, trudging along in ash.

"You have to understand," Curatio said, his hood up and grey as everyone else's in this expedition, "the dragons believe differently than we do. Their focus is on nature and the elements, the elemental powers of earth that correspond to each type of dragon that is out there." He looked slyly at Cyrus. "You didn't think they were all fire-breathers before this, did you?"

"I knew they weren't," Cyrus said with a shake of the head. "Or I'd heard it, anyway. I guess I never gave it much thought."

"There are fewer of them than you would think," Curatio said. "Of the old kin, anyway. Their bastard offspring—drakes and wyverns and such—they're the footsoldiers of the dragon army. The type we're about to face ... they're the real thing." He shuddered.

By the time the dark began to fall, and Cyrus called the halt, they were within a mile of the shrine. Even in the dark, he could see the colonnades, the three tiers of the immense structure that wrapped around the volcano at its heart. The first two reminded him just a little of the Coliseum in Reikonos, but the last looked like claws reaching up the side of an egg where it jutted out of the second level, cresting a few hundred feet below the volcano's exposed peak.

It was another poor night of sleep for Cyrus, this close to the goal and forced to wait until the morning. Vara slept silently in his arms, apparently not nearly as worried as he. The ash in his mouth was beginning to remind him of the smell of dry death, choking him every time he thought he was about to fall asleep.

And then the morning came, and after a silent breakfast that felt strangely like it might be their last, Cyrus marshaled his army and marched them under the great arch and into the most sacred shrine of the dragons to make war.

58.

The wide first floor was empty, a maze of columns and silence that left Cyrus listening hard, even as he watched Vara do the same before she shook her head, flakes of ash falling out of her hair, which was no longer gold. The smell of burning was heavier here, and Cyrus followed the map in his head as laid out by Ehrgraz, circling around the first floor of the dragon shrine. It took the better part of an hour for them to find the massive staircase, but once they had, it only took a few minutes to ascend the mountainous steps with Falcon's Essence as their aid.

In the hallway above, Cyrus took stock of his surroundings. The corridor was gargantuan, stretching up above him, the size of several dwellings stacked atop one another. The perimeter looked out through the wide columns that had been visible from outside, but the interior was not the rock of the volcano, but rather square lines of carefully laid blocks, layered to create living quarters in this place for its inhabitants. Cyrus could see the great door to the nearest of those ahead, but it did not open like a traditional door, with a knob and hinges to allow it to move to one side. This one opened up, hinged like a contraption he'd once seen in Reikonos to allow dogs to pass out of houses, a cutout door at the base of a larger one.

This was no door for a dog, however, being big enough to fit a house through. Cyrus led the way over to it, exhibiting a confidence he did not feel. When he reached it, he stood with one hand placed upon it, the elven craftsmanship obvious in its attention to even the small details. The door did not scrape the ground, and there was barely enough room between it and the floor for Cyrus to place his boot in the gap.

He took a breath, deep in, letting his anxiety flow out. He did not dare speak for fear of warning the inhabitants of these quarters of their arrival before he came crashing in with his army. Instead, he waited for them to assemble behind him, and when it was done, he beckoned forward a few strong men, and they lifted together, holding the door up long enough to allow the army to fill in, for others to take up the burden, and then Cyrus came back to the fore.

The room they found themselves in was a natural wonder, made of smooth rocks that looked as though they'd been taken from a mighty river and layered one atop the other. Their natural shapes made the floors and walls uneven and rough, and Cyrus felt unsure in his footing. In the corner of the room slept a dragon in the middle of a small pond. It moved, rustling, and the sound of splashing followed, a small wave of water cresting out of the nest of the water dragon.

Cyrus held a hand up in front of his lips, listening to the water splash and ripple from the dragon's last movement. He made his way over to his quarry, as quietly as possible, boots clinking lightly against the uneven stone floor.

He had barely made it halfway there when the dragon did more than stir; it rose out of the water and spread its wings, eyes sprung open and taking him in with all his followers. It was smaller than Ehrgraz, and when it opened its mouth, the dragon language came pouring out along with drips of water big enough to fill a pot.

"Hello, Wellsheverr," Cyrus said, noting the surprise in the dragon's eyes as he used the name that Ehrgraz had given him. His army filled in behind him, and he felt a hope spring up, a confidence that this would be the first victory of many today. "Time to spring some leaks."

Cyrus started forward in a charge, but his hope died as a blast of water shot from the dragon's mouth hit the ground just before him. Without warning, without a chance to prepare himself, Cyrus lost his footing and was swept away, flung through the air without grasp on anything, until he hit something—a wall, perhaps—and unconsciousness overwhelmed him.

59.

"You really stuck your head in the dragon's mouth this time, meathead!" Erith's voice screeched in Cyrus's ears as he wakened, soaked, the ash washed from his face and down into his eyes, burning them. He coughed and the ash came out in great clump in his spittle, along with more liquid, causing him to retch further.

"I don't feel so well," Cyrus said, pushing against the hard stone he was lodged against as a cacophony reached his ears. Water pooled in one of them and drained out of the other, running down his cheek to drip off his chinstrap.

"You just got hurled across a room," Erith said, thrusting a blue hand in his face and giving his eyes something to focus on. "Did you expect it would feel like a gentle roll in the hay with a she-elf?"

"Clearly you've never been with a she-elf," Cyrus said, taking her hand and nearly pulling her down as he got up. The world swam around him, color and lines blurring. His eyes focused, and he realized that the world wasn't really blurring …

… the room was flooding.

"Shit," Cyrus breathed as he watched Wellsheverr spray a mighty geyser of water out of his mouth, sending a half dozen Sanctuary warriors flying with the force of his attack. Odellan stepped out in front and shouted loudly enough that the dragon paused to focus on the elf, and then sprayed his mighty blast right in Odellan's face.

The elven warrior ducked as the blast hit, knocking him back a few steps, but ultimately, leaving him on his feet, albeit hunched over. "Nicely done," Cyrus breathed.

"Yeah, well, you might be able to do better yourself if you weren't standing over here gawking like a dark elf on his first time in

Reikonos," Erith said and slapped him on the pauldrons, knocking him forward a step. "Get back in there; you're healed. What are you waiting for? An invitation?"

Cyrus took a breath, hesitating a moment more, and then he charged forward into the rush of knee-high water that was already flooding the room, rushing for the exit. He slipped a few times as he fought his way through, but never enough to fall.

Wellsheverr was blasting water against Odellan again, though this time the elf was circling away, running on air as the dragon chased him with the spray. The elven warrior was a step quicker, though his breastplate and greaves were now absent the layer of grime and ash that had settled on them over the last few days, dulling them. Now, the elf looked like himself once more.

"A eritan yaghrah iune glaymorre!" Odellan shouted as he darted toward the dragon's head. "Unataara, glaymorre!"

Cyrus's mind struggled to put that one together as he watched the elf plunge his blade into the dragon's left eye, dodging the spray to do so. "'I take from you now your … cheese? Give me your cheese'?"

"You really are awful at elvish," Vaste said, causing Cyrus to look to the side to see the troll cradling his massive head in his hands. "I'd hate to see how you'd mangle trollish."

"I speak it very well," Cyrus said, dodging past as Odellan recoiled from the dragon, retreating into the air, "it's not hard to understand grunting and pointing."

"Oh, ha ha."

Wellsheverr had stopped spraying water, and the rush was subsiding, finding its level as it ran toward the exit. Now the dragon stood on its hind legs in the enormous chamber, trying to thread its long, thin neck to strike at Odellan, who clearly bore the brunt of its displeasure. Odellan, for his part, dodged another snap of teeth bigger than Cyrus's hand and circled around to bury his blade in its remaining eye. With a scream, Wellsheverr dropped back to the ground, a flurry of spells bouncing ineffectually off his scales.

"I wonder what pioneering genius of battle Odellan learned that strategy from?" Vaste asked with a healthy dose of irony, and loud enough that Cyrus could hear him even as he ran toward the cascading battle. Warriors and rangers were milling about, struggling to position themselves where they could hack at Wellsheverr's legs.

"Or what idiot, perhaps?"

Wellsheverr opened its mouth, and another blast of water began to spray out, blindly this time, but someone was ready for it. A crackling burst of lightning hit the spray so quickly that Cyrus could only tell what was happening thanks to Praelior's enhancement of his speed. The lightning surged into the dragon's mouth and down into the water pooling around them as well.

The pain was immediate, causing Cyrus's muscles to spasm hard, giving him a headache that was sudden and persistent, just behind the eyes. He saw a similar effect fall over the rest of Sanctuary's army, a sudden doubling over of everyone in the room that had their legs in the water, a full-brain pain of the sort Cyrus recalled having once when he had eaten snow from the ground in a northern pass too quickly while trying to sate his thirst.

A thud shook the room as Cyrus pried his eyes open again. Wellsheverr had fallen over, now resting on his side, tongue hanging out of his mouth, scales cleanly torn from his legs.

"Oh, well done," Vara said acidly from a little in front of Cyrus. He saw her clutching at her own head, and then she waved her hand, which glowed with healing magic. "That bloody well hurt."

"But it hurt him more," Odellan said, comfortably above them all, and, Cyrus reflected, probably not suffering from a headache brought on by the lightning strike. "Being responsible for his death and all."

"We were killing him just fine without needing to resort to striking the entire raiding party with lightning whilst we're all knee-deep in water," Vara snapped. The water was actually receding now, either draining into the pool where Wellsheverr had nested or running out the door.

Cyrus turned to look and found the door slightly open, a few bodies caught in the crack at the bottom. He frowned. "When did that happen?"

"Probably while you were tumbling through the air," Vaste said, easing closer to him. "Wellsheverr's water blast looked like it hurt."

"It didn't feel good," Cyrus said, turning his neck experimentally. "Go resurrect those people, will you?"

Vaste looked flatly at him. "I'm going to need a druid, too."

Cyrus blinked. "Why?"

Vaste sighed. "Because there are more. Ones that didn't get

trapped in the door, that got washed out it instead, and if they followed the level of the floor—"

"They're in the ash below," Cyrus said, coming to the reluctant conclusion. "All the way down."

"That's right," Vaste said with a nod. "I'll also probably need Andren and Erith. An hour isn't much time when you have to climb down and sift through wet and muddied ash—"

"Do what you have to," Cyrus said, waving him off toward the door. "We'll recuperate here for a bit."

"Yay, we killed a dragon," Vaste said lightly as he walked away. "Five more to go."

Cyrus looked at the corpse of Wellsheverr as the water ran by him, now only up to his ankle. The raiding party was quiet, subdued, with the sound of muted conversation, hushed whispers, all around him. They were looking at the dragon, who, in spite of commanding one of the milder elements, had put up a considerable fight.

Cyrus found a stone that protruded slightly out of the water, and sat upon it, watching the rush and the chaos, and the recovery from battle, and wondered exactly how much of a toll the next fight would exact.

60.

"You look like a man with doubts," Curatio said, his robes a mess, bags firmly entrenched under his eyes and made darker by the ash. He gathered the hem of his robes about him, still dripping water and smeared with ash, as he sat down next to Cyrus.

"You knew it'd be like this," Cyrus said.

"Of course," Curatio said, matter-of-factly. "This is hardly my first run-in with dragons, nor indeed, even with these dragons."

"You know these specific dragons?" Cyrus asked, staring at the rest of the Sanctuary army, milling about next to the corpse, carving scales as souvenirs, cutting pieces off the tongue. He shook his head at the ghastly business being done there, but knew there was nothing for it. Dragon parts fetched a pretty penny in the markets of Reikonos. *And we're always seeking gold, aren't we?*

"I did," Curatio said. "These are the very dragons that killed my friend who worked on this shrine." He folded his arms in front of him.

Cyrus pulled his head around in surprise. "Killed him? Didn't he build this place for them? At their request?"

"Indeed," Curatio said, expression utterly flat. "But there is no gratitude like dragon gratitude, I suppose." He turned his head. "They view us all as lesser creatures, beneath their notice nearly, except when we are useful. Ashan'agar was not unusual in these beliefs. Ehrgraz may act civilized, but he is no friend to our kind, either. We are a convenience to him, and one which he will not hesitate to discard in the future when we cease to be of use."

"So you think he's betraying us, then?" Cyrus asked.

"I don't know," Curatio said, now looking tired. "But I doubt it.

We're still of use, after all."

"Another grim reality I don't want to deal with," Cyrus said, lowering his head and his voice. "I was almost starting to feel guilty about coming here to—well, to do what we've come to do."

"Commit murder?" Curatio asked. "I wouldn't feel too terrible about it. Indeed, I don't. That's why I am here, though I disagree on this course of action most strongly."

"Indeed you do."

"This is not going to be an easy fight," Curatio said. "For any of us." Cyrus caught his gaze, and the healer's weariness faded for just a moment. "You should prepare yourself now by asking yourself how far you're going to be willing to go to see it through."

"Curatio," Cyrus said with a subdued smile, "I've dragged an army across the Ashen Wastelands for a week with the intent of killing dragons and desecrating a holy site. I think I'm in this all the way up to the hilt."

"Very well, then," Curatio said and gathered his robes as he stood. He started to walk away, then turned back. "When you were in the Society of Arms, and they taught you to kill … what would they have said if you plunged a blade into someone up to the hilt and they still lived?"

Cyrus looked at him evenly. "You either bury your arm in them up to the shoulder or pull it out and do it again to finish the damned job."

Curatio smiled, but his face was tight and absent any joy. "I had a feeling you would say that." With a bow of the head, he went to see to the recovery of the wounded, leaving Cyrus to prepare for the next in a long string of battles.

61.

Cyrus could feel the cold seeping out of the next dragon's quarters several hundred feet before they reached the door. There was a ghastly chill in the air that called to mind the frozen Realm of Life, where every spot of green had been covered over with snow and ice. The chill seeped through Cyrus's armor, finding the cracks and drawing to mind comparisons with the frozen room in the back of the Sanctuary kitchen. He stopped to shiver and beckoned Nyad forth. As they grew close to him, he whispered, "We'll need fire spells. Continuously. Let your people know."

"I will," Nyad said, nodding firmly and then slipping back toward the ranks of the spellcasters. The grey sky hung out beyond the columns of the shrine's outer exterior, still heavy and forbidding.

With a grunt of reluctance, Cyrus turned his eyes to the door and motioned forward a few of Sanctuary's warriors. They pushed it open enough to pass through, and once more Cyrus led the way. Once more, he found a sleeping dragon in a corner, though this time the nest was of ice rather than water.

It had piled snow in a circle ten feet high around its abdomen. Cyrus wondered idly if the snow was fresh or if it had been in here for a period of years. It had little smell to it other than a cold winter's day, infusing its way into his sinuses and making him crinkle his nose.

"What's this one named?" Vara asked, suddenly at his elbow.

"Gren'averr," Cyrus said, so softly he could scarcely hear any sign of his own voice.

He crept forward on crunching snow, a thousand others making their way in behind him. The bitter chill was heavy, like a gremlin of cold climbing its way into the cracks of his armor. It felt like it was stabbing gently at him, icy claws trying pry him out of his skin with burning intensity. He exhaled and the air in front of him clouded into mist with his breath.

Cyrus was almost to the dragon when it awoke, prompting him to dash forward. The Falcon's Essence spell landed on him as he sprinted forward, and he took to the air as the long neck flew up and the eyes sprung open with alarm and rage.

Gren'averr was a shorter beast than its brother, with scales as white as the snow it inhabited. When it took a simple breath, Cyrus felt the winter wind whip around him as surely as if he'd been teleported to the Northlands without warning on the coldest day of the year.

Gren'averr did not waste time with any taunts, if he even knew the human language. He merely opened his mouth and breathed ice, turning the air around him into daggers of cold.

Cyrus moved fast enough to avoid the winter breath, but ice crusted up his back as he charged sideways to avoid the attack. Gren'averr did not follow him, instead directing his attack at the army still coming at him from behind Cyrus.

Cyrus whipped around, turning in the air when he realized the dragon's stratagem. *Thought he'd chase me, but apparently I haven't pissed him off enough to take his eyes off the army charging him down ...*

The wintery attack hit the first rank of the Sanctuary army and spread over them like ice rolling slowly up spilled water on a frigid morning. Cyrus watched fifteen of his finest dusted with cold, frozen in place, their armor their only defense against the instant freezing—

And then he saw someone hit with the breath of ice that was not wearing armor at all.

Nyad had a fire spell glowing in her fingers, ready to fling it, as Gren'averr's exhalation hit her. She did not even have time to flinch before it rolled through her hair, blowing it back as it turned her pale skin a deathly white. It covered her over completely in mere seconds. Cyrus watched it all with the benefit of Praelior in his hand, the entire spectacle slowed down to a horrible, lethargic pace, until Nyad, the heiress of the entire Elven Kingdom, was nothing but an ice statue.

A warrior, his armor frozen over from Gren'averr's attack, staggered sideways at exactly that moment. He collided with Nyad, his footing lost on the ice slicking the floor below, his upper body hopelessly entangled in her outstretched arms, and the pair fell to the ground, the warrior coming down hard upon the ice princess.

She shattered like glass dropped out of a window's frame, into fragments no bigger than a simple icicle, and Cyrus almost felt he could hear her scream in the sound, but it was nothing more than the howling breath of a winter dragon, screaming in triumph at the death of the elven wizard.

62.

Shock ran through Cyrus's limbs like cold tingles twitching at him, compelling him into action. He ran at the dragon's face in a pure sort of rage, and Gren'averr dodged away, twisting his long neck to protect his face from Cyrus's attack.

Cyrus found he did not care, that an eye was too easy a target in any case, for this particular bastard of a dragon, and he plunged Praelior hard from the hip into the dragon's scaled neck, twisting it as he drove it in.

He was rewarded with a cold wash of blood, a shade of orange that he couldn't have guessed at if he'd been forced to. Gren'averr bucked and recoiled at his attack, twisting his head back down to snap at Cyrus, but Cyrus was already rolling to the side. Gren'averr's head presented itself perfectly to him as he brought it down, and Cyrus jabbed the blade into the joint behind the dragon's jaw, neatly skirting the scales and knocking two of them loose with the force of his attack.

This drew a shrieking from the winter dragon, not unlike the one he'd emitted when he'd caused Nyad's death, but more pained this time. Cyrus pulled his sword back and noted a crust of icy ichor on the surface, then plunged it in again and pushed upward this time. Orange blood dripped down the dragon's neck, staining his pristine white scales as he tried to twist to look at Cyrus, but reaching his full extension and failing.

Cyrus dragged his blade around, cutting a jagged path between scales as he ripped his way through dragonskin. Gren'averr ran his head around slowly, twisting and drawing still more orange liquid out of the gaping wound as he tried to attack what ailed him. With every

foot further he cut, Cyrus watched the strength fade from the
dragon's motion as it fought helplessly to try and strike at him until it
started to sag, and finally, when he had almost reached the back of its
neck, went limp and dropped to the icy ground beneath him, a great
cloud of snow arising on either side as he landed.

"Sonofabitch," Cyrus said, staring down at the dead dragon.
Gren'averr's tongue did not hang out of his mouth like his brother's
had, and for a moment Cyrus considered running down and ripping it
with his own hands in hopes that some small, ebbing part of the
dragon's life still existed enough to feel it before it perished forever.

"Well done," Vaste called up to him. Cyrus stared down at the
troll, who wore a wide smile. There was a thick crust of ice on the
armor of the warriors at the fore, but Cyrus could not see any other
bodies, and already it looked like the victims of Gren'averr's assault
were being pried from their frosty entrapment.

Cyrus drifted down slowly. Vara was lingering not far from where
Nyad had perished, looking at the ground carefully, Curatio at her
side. Simply in the way they were moving, the stiff way they carried
themselves, he was certain that they knew.

"What are you so damned grim about?" Vaste asked as Cyrus
reached the floor. "We'll have the frostbite cleared up with some
healing spells in a few minutes, no problem."

"Come with me," Cyrus said, beckoning him forth as he headed
for Curatio and Vara. He motioned toward Andren, whose fingers
were glowing with the light of a healing spell. "Get the other officers,"
Cyrus called, and with a nod, Andren moved off to fetch them.

"What the hell is going on over here?" Vaste asked as he and
Cyrus came up to the spot where Vara and Curatio were quietly
standing their vigil. "You look someone died—" The troll paused.
"Oh. Oh, gods. Someone died, didn't they? Some poor, unfortunate
warrior whose name none of us even knows—"

"Vaste," Cyrus said, voice low and hushed. "It was Nyad."

The troll's eyes flickered, his lids closing and opening rapidly. "I'm
sorry?"

"Nyad was up front to cast fire spells to keep the cold at bay,"
Cyrus said, his voice low, as Thad, Longwell and Odellan trotted up.
He knew each of them was catching his words as he threw them out.
"She was hit by the dragon's breath, and … she got tripped over by

one of the warriors at the fore."

"Who was it?" Vaste said tightly. "I want to remember this clod's name. Forever."

"It doesn't matter," Cyrus said. "It was an accident. Gren'averr did it, not the warrior."

Vaste clutched a mighty hand together. "If he weren't already dead, I'd kill him."

"You could resurrect him if you feel that strongly about ... whatever it is," Andren said as he and Erith joined the circle. "What are we mad about?"

"Nyad is dead," Vaste said in a voice that suggested he was without life of his own.

"And there's no way to ... piece her back together?" Odellan asked, looking as ashen as the lands they had just traveled through.

"There's not enough left of her to properly fill a coinpurse," Vara said with a muted savagery.

"Good gods," Erith said. "Nyad? Truly. We're not just ... joking or something?"

"Do I look as though I'm in a joking mood?" Vaste asked, menace in his voice giving it a quiver. He half turned, and in his profile Cyrus saw danger, his anger on a thin leash. "What do we do now?"

"We go on, of course," Thad said, frowning. "We're not done yet."

"We just lost the heiress to the Elven Kingdom," Vaste snapped at him. "Continuing is hardly a foregone conclusion."

"We go on," Cyrus said, and every head snapped to look at him. "We gain nothing by leaving now. It certainly doesn't honor her sacrifice, and we have ... people counting on us." He set his jaw.

"Fine, then," Vaste said in a voice that suggested it was anything but. "I'm going to go pound on the dead corpse of that ice dragon with my staff for a while. Let me know when we're ready to kill the next one." And he spun and left before anyone had a chance to respond.

The rest of the Council stood in shocked silence for a moment after that then began to break up, separating into smaller groups. Cyrus could hear the hushed voices, the quiet surprise, the disbelief as the word started to spread beyond them and into the army.

"Are you sure about this?" Vara asked, under her breath, from just behind his ear.

"No." Cyrus did not turn to face her. "But we're going on anyway." The chill in the room felt suddenly unbearable, and he was filled with a desire to say anything but, to take her in his arms and have a wizard cast them home, where he could strip off his armor and throw it to the ground along with his sword, leaving it all behind forever. He did not say this, though, but he was certain Vara could hear it anyway.

63.

When they went charging into the next room, they found a dragon very much awake, and very quick to respond to them. This dragon, called Groz'anarr, was brown-scaled like the earth he represented, and even before he came at them, he swung his spiked tail into one of the boulders piled around his quarters and sent it rolling into the ranks of the frontline warriors charging at him. Cyrus dodged it, watching it spin past and slam into the armored forms behind him, drawing screams of pain as it struck and rolled through, chewing bodies under it as it went.

Gods, let their armor protect them, Cyrus thought as he sprung off the ground with Falcon's Essence as his aid.

The smell of earth was thick in the chamber, like fresh upturned dirt and rock dust. *It would have been nice to have Fortin for this one,* Cyrus thought, but knew that leaving the massive rock giant out of the expedition had been the most expedient course.

The flat, blunt face of Groz'anarr wavered, then decided on Cyrus as his target. He took a breath as Cyrus drew closer, and when he opened his mouth, a stream of rocks as wide as Cyrus's thighs came shooting out as though propelled from a trebuchet. One of them clanged off Cyrus's armor, spinning as it ricocheted. It left a numbness where it had struck, not so hard as the punch of a god, but most certainly noticeable and definitely fatal without armor as protection.

Groz'anarr saw the impact of his attack and switched targets immediately, directing his breath toward the advancing Sanctuary horde. He sprayed into a field of warriors advancing at a run, and Cyrus watched them bowled over as surely as if the dragon had sent another boulder through their number. Cyrus, for his part, advanced toward the dragon's head, heedless of the danger.

Spells were impacting all along the dragon's flank as he turned sideways to snap at Cyrus. The dragon moved quickly, but not so quickly that Praelior did not give Cyrus advantage. He dodged as the dragon halted its breath and snapped at him. Cyrus landed a swipe against its nose as he passed, and it bucked its head and smacked him in the back as he ran past it, dragging Praelior into the side of Groz'anarr's face.

The dragon's attack was offhand and somewhat lucky, but it did not stop Cyrus from being staggered nonetheless. It knocked him off balance, sending him stumbling on air, knees wobbling and trying to catch himself. He failed and hit the air in an ungainly face-plant, spared injury or pain by virtue of the Falcon's Essence spell. Cyrus fought back to his feet and turned his head to look, anticipating another dragon attack.

Warriors were crouched around Groz'anarr's legs now, hacking away at his scales to some effect, mystical swords carving swaths of damage with their blades. The dragon paid little attention to this, however, as his head was engulfed in a swarm of arrows like nattering insects in his face. A few of them stuck out of the wound Cyrus had made, and Groz'anarr swung around to direct his attack toward the rangers below, stomping away from the warriors at his belly.

"No!" Cyrus shouted, getting to his feet and propelling himself into motion, chasing the back of the dragon's retreating head. The beast's long strides carried him past and through the scattering frontline warriors, toward a patch of green cloaks crouching near a series of boulders, Martaina in the front.

The bombardment of arrows did not slow as the dragon drew nearer the rangers, slinking along like a lizard with his belly near to dragging the ground. "Scatter!" Cyrus shouted, but it was too late.

Groz'anarr unleashed his breath of rocks only thirty meters from the formation of rangers, and few enough bothered to seek cover. Cyrus watched Calene Raverle dodge behind a boulder, but she was one of the few. In some he saw the steadfast defiance, the courage that sprang from wanting to face down their foes. On one elf, he watched the movement of lips throwing out some curse, and in a few others he saw surprise as the first rain of rocks came down and the rangers finally began to react.

Martaina was at the fore, and she moved at the last second, throwing herself to the ground. The blast of rocks struck her on the hip as she dove, and Cyrus saw blood, though whether it came from her or the rangers behind her, he could not tell in the chaos that followed. Screams filled the air, filled his ears, and he saw at least one head completely destroyed, splattered as surely as if a titan had landed a foot upon it. Another ranger seemed to dissolve into red as if a strong wind had blown him apart, and yet another, a dark elf, exploded in dark blue, his chainmail falling to the ground as if uninhabited.

"NOOOOOO!" Cyrus screamed, slamming into the dragon's head with nothing but rage. He hit the scales at full sprint, his Praelior-enhanced speed and reflexes allowing him to strike with the force of a boulder dropped off a cliff. Groz'anarr's long neck dipped from the impact, then slammed down to the ground as Cyrus's momentum carried him forward. Scales burst free from the back of the dragon's neck and flew through the air like tossed rocks, and while Cyrus staggered, he came back to his feet as Groz'anarr's head wobbled back up.

This time, he faced the dragon head on, and in a flash he saw Nyad in his mind, the icy statue, shattered forever, and it spurred him on in another charge. Cyrus ran at Groz'anarr's face, ignoring the mouth and focusing on the punch-drunk eyes. He saw the dawning awareness just before he hit, the late-term attempt to simply open its mouth and swallow him, and he corrected for the lazy motion, slamming shoulder-first into the dragon's nose, knocking asunder more scales and not even bothering to plunge Praelior into flesh as he shoulder-charged the bastard.

This time Cyrus did not give ground; he merely slammed into the dragon's nose and held his position, letting the force of impact run through him as though he were a wall. The dragon's face gave against his anger, and Groz'anarr's neck snapped back some twenty feet while Cyrus held his place in the air. This time the dragon's eyelids fluttered.

Cyrus howled with rage and charged again. He knew that Groz'anarr, in his present state of near-unconsciousness, would not be able to avoid his attack. This time he caught the dragon under the chin. His head snapped back harder this time, the sound of breaking bones running down the thin neck. Groz'anarr's head fluttered like a leaf for a few seconds, and then dropped without ceremony to the ground, landing on a boulder, deep purple blood oozing out from under his head. His eyes were fixed, a deep green, staring straight ahead, unmoving.

"Sacred shit," the unmistakable voice of Calene Raverle said from below him. "Our Guildmaster just beat a dragon to death."

"He is not dead," Curatio said from somewhere below. Cyrus's eyes found him with the healers, standing short next to Vaste's immense bulk. At the mere statement, however, Vaste started forward in determination, long strides eating up the distance to the dragon's head, where he drove his staff through the dragon's almost unnoticeable ear, with its trickle of purple blood, slamming through the canal and burying it almost up to the crystal at the tip. The troll then stirred the staff around like a brew in a cauldron, his muscles straining and the effort showing on his face as he flushed a deeper green before he ripped the staff back out of the canal, covered entirely in purple gook.

"Now he is dead," Curatio pronounced somewhat flatly.

"Martaina!" Andren's shout drew Cyrus's attention back to where the rangers had been attacked. He stalked over to where the healer already crouched over the fallen body of Martaina, who clutched at her hip, which was bleeding profusely.

"I'll be fine," Martaina said, face tightly suffused with pain.

"Of course you will," Andren said soothingly. "You're so tough—"

"I mean I'll be fine once you heal me!" Martaina spat. "What are you waiting for?" She writhed and grimaced, blood spurting from between her fingers.

"Oh, right," Andren said and thrust his hand aloft, spell light flickering from it. Within a few seconds, Martaina had ceased her writhing, soothed and settled, and then she went stiff, her eyes flickering around the area where she had fallen.

"How many did we lose?" Cyrus asked, low, taking the last few steps to stand by where she lay.

"I count six," Calene said, coming out from behind a boulder. She nodded with her head to where armor and cloaks lay, remains so obviously destroyed by the dragon's breath spread before them among a few other wounded.

"Damn, that could have been you," Andren said under his breath. "But it wasn't," Martaina said stiffly, and Cyrus could hear the familiar guilt of a surviving commander in the way she said it.

"Martaina!" Thad's voice echoed as he pushed through the crowd thickening into a line around the site of the ranger fallen. "Oh, thank the gods." His hand fell to his chestplate, where the red had been scraped from his armor.

"Should we even bother to have an officer meeting about this?" Vaste asked in Cyrus's ear, whisper-quiet. Cyrus had not even heard the troll's approach.

"To what purpose?" Cyrus asked coolly.

"I don't know," Vaste said sarcastically, "maybe to discuss the sheer number of people we've lost today? To consider, for perhaps sixty seconds before charging foolishly ahead, whether the price we are paying is going to be even close to worth it? Or we could just have a talk about other ideas that could have become inspired by these losses, alternatives to this mess we find ourselves charging headlong into?"

"Do you have any ideas?" Cyrus asked, and waited for the troll to shake his head. "Anything to stop the advance of the titans?"

"There is no titan advance, Cyrus," Vaste said, the anger in his voice threatening to burst out of a whisper. "Perhaps we should reconsider and come back when there is."

"It'll be too late," Cyrus said, shaking his head. "Once they figure it out, the north is done."

"If we keep going, we may be done," Vaste said.

"We're not done," Cyrus said quietly.

The troll waited for just a moment before replying. "Well, maybe we should be." And with his bit said, he walked away, slapping his staff into the eye of Groz'anarr as he did so, as futile—and as understandable—a gesture as Cyrus could imagine.

64.

The next dragon lay up the stairs, on the top level of the temple. It took the battered Army of Sanctuary almost an hour to make their way up to that dragon's chambers, Cyrus carefully following the instructions given by Ehrgraz. He knew what rested behind the door before he came to it, but held out his hand for a quiet regroup a few hundred meters from that door, not willing to face it without a break first.

"What are we up against next?" Vara asked, settling next to Cyrus on the hard stone floor. It was flat and surprisingly cold to the touch, when Cyrus took his gauntlet off to wipe the accumulating perspiration from his palm.

"Weck'arerr," Cyrus said. "A poison dragon."

Vara frowned. "Poison? How poisonous is this thing?"

"Corrosive, supposedly," Cyrus said. "The way Ehrgraz explained it, his breath can burn through flesh in much the same way as fire, but slower."

"That sounds like a wicked sort of alchemy," she said, shaking her head. "I have heard of similar solutions created by potion, but to imagine a dragon with that sort of substance at his command defies my imagination."

"We face creatures several times our size," Cyrus said with a sad smile, "dragons that live in cities and shrines, even gnomes and goblins and trolls, things that are so much different. Hells, you and I are a human and an elf, and while we mostly look alike save for our ears—"

"And I am much prettier than you."

"—and that, of course, but there are differences." He still smiled

314

at her wistfully. "Even the closest related of our races is dramatically different. Our world is a … peculiar place, I would say, filled with wondrous and horrid creatures."

"That was quite the little speech," Vara said, eyeing him.

"Well, I didn't get to give a motivational one before we came here, so I suppose the need to fill the air with my words leaked out in the form of dull introspection instead."

She leaned against his arm and held still for a moment before she asked her question. "Do you want to talk about the deaths?"

"Not now, no," Cyrus said, meeting her gaze and finding earnest concern in those blue eyes, bright as a sky he had not seen in a week. "But later, I'm sure I will."

She nodded once, then stood, shuffling past Scuddar In'shara, who sat only ten feet away, his robes gathered around him, Calene Raverle sitting across from him, the two of them saying not a word, but looking at each other intensely. "Stop it, you two," Cyrus said, drawing the attention of both of them, "your staring contest is quite disturbing to those of us watching."

"It's a tradition of the desert," Calene said with youthful jubilance that did not match Cyrus's current mood. "Staring into the eyes of your battlefield compatriots before a fight. Builds trust."

"If you don't trust him yet," Samwen Longwell said, plinking the end of his lance into the rock next to where Cyrus sat, "I don't think staring into his sun-yellow eyes for a space is going to do much more other than perhaps blind you when you look away." He paused, looking down at Cyrus. "How are you doing, Guildmaster?"

Cyrus glanced away from Calene and Scuddar to return Longwell's eye contact. "Hanging in there. And you?"

Longwell squatted down, his armor squealing as he did so, dropping the grip on the haft of his spear to its base. Cyrus watched the tip waver, but it did not once threaten to fall even once. "Better than you, I'd wager."

Cyrus smiled wanly. "And why should I not be in finest form, Samwen? Am I not a warrior, bred for combat, here in the middle of most inspiring battle?"

"I was wrong in what I said to you when last we spoke." Longwell lifted the lance up a half-inch and tapped it back down again. "It was unfair, and it was unkind."

"It was inconvenient," Cyrus said, looking away, "as most truthful things are. Your people have suffered—"

"My people volunteered to join Sanctuary," Longwell said, looking straight ahead, "to earn their keep. And Sanctuary has paid them well, seen them through, helped give us a home. For me to complain about the sacrifice war entails was foolish, minimizing the sacrifice that the dead have made. It was a willing one, and for me to say what I said cheapens it, as if those men didn't have a will of their own to do what they did." He turned his head. "Nyad had a will of her own. The rangers in that room back there, they had wills of their own as well. We all do, and we're here."

"You're here because I've led you here," Cyrus said darkly. "I use your trust in me to compel that will to action. That's leadership."

"But we embrace it," Longwell said. "We choose to follow."

"And I choose to lead," Cyrus said, "but I don't choose to lead you into death; death happens in spite of my best intentions, or maybe even because of them." He turned his head to look at Longwell as he spoke. "We face dragons and titans, and they can kill us in a way that we don't normally face on the battlefield—"

"Begging your pardon, sir," Longwell said, "but we faced an army at Leaugarden, and they killed more people than anything I've seen since the scourge killed almost all my people." His lips remained a tight line until he spoke again. "War is an uncertain thing. Leadership is an uncertain thing as well. You do the best you can. Better than most, I'd say."

"What if my best isn't good enough?" Cyrus asked, letting a question slip out that he might not have dared let anyone else hear. It rang with uncertainty and with pure honesty as he stared into the eyes of a man who should have been a king.

"Well, then I guess we're all up shit creek," Longwell said with a muted smile as he stood, "because there damned sure isn't anyone else who could do any better, I assure you." He tipped his helm to Cyrus and went on his way, walking with a confidence that he had not shown only a few days earlier.

65.

Weck'arerr was sleeping, his snores as loud as the shouts of a rock giant going into battle. As he entered the chamber, Cyrus froze at the sound, afraid the dragon was already alert and ready to attack. The attack did not come; instead Weck'arerr simply extended a wing momentarily up from the nest in the corner, stretching in his sleep. Cyrus did not relax, but rather crept on quietly.

The floors were smooth and flat, but in the corner, over the sound of Weck'arerr's prodigious snoring was a low bubbling, like lava. Cyrus saw it as he grew closer, a pit of acidic green sludge that bubbled as though it were at a low boil. He drew closer, stepping up to the dragon, only twenty feet away now, feet off the ground as he came in closer, moving not quite silently as he—

Weck'arerr snorted in his sleep and turned again onto his side, his light green belly not as dark as his scaled back. He lifted another wing straight into the air, revealing the soft tissue strung between the bones. They were covered in the pungent acidic mixture that filled the poison dragon's nest, dripping down onto the body and sizzling as they hit scale and rolled off like beads of water. It had a harsh, metallic smell, and it made Cyrus want to plug his nose with whatever he could find.

Cyrus made his way to where the dragon's head was tucked under his front shoulder. His nose was slightly submerged, the solution bubbling even more where his head was planted, air burbling from beneath the dragon's lips. Cyrus pondered his course of action, deciding where to strike first. The back of the neck seemed a ripe target, with the possibility for an instant end to the fight. Taking the eyes would also similarly put things on an uneven footing, though not as surely as the strike to the spine.

He ultimately decided on the quickest, most expedient path, and positioned himself just above the nape of the dragon's neck. He raised his sword silently, and brought it down—

Just as Weck'arerr rolled to the side.

Cyrus planted Praelior squarely in the side of the dragon's neck, trying to adjust to the unexpected movement but failing. He struck off some half-dozen scales in the process, but missed the artery that he had aimed for. Some blood was drawn, yellowish like Scuddar's eyes. Weck'arerr's own eyes sprang open and his head lifted in fury. Cyrus struck again, running a jagged cut along the side of the dragon's face, skipping along the jawbone and ripping another ten or so green scales off the beast.

Weck'arerr roared in pain and outrage, taking in the whole army and Cyrus in one glance. Cyrus could read the emotion on the dragon's face, transfusing into anger as he opened his mouth to belch forth toxicity. Weck'arerr wavered between Cyrus and the army beyond, and instinctively, Cyrus leapt in front of the bastard's mouth, stabbing him in the discolored, light green gums and cutting a tooth clean out of its mouth as the dragon roared and sprayed him with green liquid.

It covered Cyrus's face and armor, blinding him instantly. His skin burned, nerve endings screaming in pain. Cyrus held onto his sword, clenching it tightly as the corrosive spray ate into his face and eyes, and he struck blindly at where he knew the dragon had been only a moment earlier, not ignoring his pain but channeling it into a rage of his own. His reward was a scream, the hint of resistance that told him Praelior had hit scale or tooth or bone, and he stabbed back once his strike was through, ignoring the sensation of his very flesh peeling off his face.

A healing spell brought warmth and feeling back to Cyrus's face, and his sight was restored long enough for him to catch a glance of blood and skin and a toxic green hissing on his breastplate and below. His armor looked as though it had been dipped in Weck'arerr's bed, but he felt nothing beneath it to concern him, just the sense of residual burning from where the healing spell had left him phantom pain.

Weck'arerr stood before him, jagged cuts on his lip and nose, and

Cyrus struck at him again as the dragon spat another burst of bile directly at him, a spray large enough to cover him completely. Cyrus's vision once again vanished. The pain followed a moment later, as though someone had taken a torch and thrust it into his helm's open face, rubbing it into his eyes, against his forehead and nose, burning them off completely. Stray searing bolts ran across his scalp, and the smell of disgusting acridness disappeared as his nose was once more burned completely off by the acid bath.

In spite of this, Cyrus struck twice more into the face in front of him, staggering ahead blindly, sensing the dragon reeling away from him by the sound of his screeches. He swung again and missed, then struck once more as he raised his blade and speared it forward.

The next healing spell hit him and threw the pain back some distance, leaving a little more than the normal residual pain. Cyrus realized that some of the acidic liquid was trapped between his helm and his skull, and the scent of chemicals burning his hair drifted into his reconstituted nose. He ignored the feeling like a claw rubbing against his scalp and drove himself into the face of the dragon again as it recoiled away from him. He plunged his blade under its jaw as it tried to lift its neck higher, and then it jerked down, yanking him toward the toxic nest below. Cyrus caught his footing on the invisible platform the Falcon's Essence spell provided and extracted Praelior from where it was stuck, plunging it into the roof of Weck'arerr's open mouth just as another splash of the dragon's breath belched forth.

Cyrus lost his vision again, but more slowly this time as his face was inclined downward when the spray came out, his body half-lodged in the dragon's mouth. One moment he was looking at brown-stained tongue, the next his face was once more alight with what felt like the hottest fire spell Cyrus could imagine. Through it all, he stabbed and stabbed, upward, as teeth clanked futilely against his armor and Weck'arerr breathed more acid to no effect.

Cyrus made one last strike as his strength started to fade, driving the blade up and punching through bone. The teeth clinked against his armor, but more weakly this time, and suddenly he was dragged down inside the mouth of his enemy. Cyrus's sight returned with the wash of the healing spell just as the dragon's mouth hit the ground, and he lay there, stunned, even as shouts grew closer and light flooded in. Strong hands propped open the dragon's mouth and tugged him out, his armor dragging along the front teeth, breaking them with a crack as his backplate hung up on them.

"Gods, you idiot!" Vaste shouted, his face clouded above Cyrus. Cyrus's eyes still burned, as though he'd dipped them into something hot. Water splashed in his face from a skin held above him, forcing Cyrus to close his eyes. Another healing spell ran over him, and this time his vision cleared completely. Someone pulled his helm off as Cyrus tried to force open his eyes again, bleary, and another splash of water rushed over him and down into his helm. He could hear the sizzle of the toxic brew as it washed out onto the stones below.

"All of you, back away!" Vara said, in a tone that brooked no argument. "Officers!" she snapped. "Get over here!"

Cyrus tried to sit up but felt a troll foot land on his breastplate. "You can take part in this from right there," Vaste said. "No need to strain your already clearly impaired faculties."

"I'm ... fine," Cyrus said, managing to finally open his eyes. There was a circle of the officers around him, Vaste standing just above him, tree-like foot still planted in the middle of his chest like he wanted to take root there.

"You are out of your gods-damned mind," Vaste said in a hushed whisper.

"The elves can still hear you, probably," Thad said, shuffling from side to side on alternating feet as he stood uncomfortably in the circle.

"To hell with anyone listening," Vaste said. "Did anyone else just see what I saw? Because I'd wager some of the members did."

"Saw what?" Cyrus asked, trying to stand again as Vaste planted all his weight on Cyrus. "Saw me go toe-to-toe with a poison dragon? Good. They should know I'm not above standing in the middle of the fight."

"It seems to me there is a difference between standing in the middle of the fight," Curatio said quietly, "and thrusting yourself heedlessly into certain danger."

"My armor could take the breath," Cyrus said, not remotely relaxing where he lay. "Others couldn't."

"Damnation, man," Andren said, and Cyrus caught a glimpse of him, face as white as sheep's wool. "Do you know even know what happened to you there?"

"I fought him," Cyrus said, jerking his head at the carcass of Weck'arerr, staring dully at them from a few feet away, mouth wrecked and blood pouring out from where his rescuers had ripped him from the grasp of the dragon's teeth. "We won. Yay for victory."

"He burned your face off," Vaste said with a little acid of his own. "Three times. I counted, because—well, because do you have any idea how that looked? I mean, I was surprised, because I honestly thought it would be an improvement, but it wasn't. At all. It was horrible."

"I did what had to be done," Cyrus said.

"This is a familiar song," Curatio said.

Cyrus clutched Praelior tight in his hand and bucked Vaste's foot off his chest with a concentrated effort. The troll staggered a step back, and Cyrus got to his feet before the troll could recover. "Then I hope you enjoy the chorus," Cyrus said with a little bitterness, "because you're probably going to hear it again after the next dragon, too."

"Cyrus," Erith said quietly. "You just got into a fistfight with the earth dragon, and you threw your face literally into the dragon's mouth with this one. We're concerned about you." She looked at Vara. "We are, aren't we? All of us?"

Vara said nothing.

"Well, most of us are," Vaste said, "because to the untrained eye, it's starting to look like our esteemed Guildmaster has a death wish he wants to play out right here in front of us." He held his gaze steady on Cyrus. "Is that right? Because the next dragon, if I'm not much mistaken, is going to give you a wonderful opportunity to prove us right, if we are."

Cyrus felt the bristle of cold tingles down his back, the hot phantom pain still upon his scalp where the acid had been healed away. "The next dragon is fire, yes."

"And are you planning to go nose-to-burned-off-nose with him as well?" Vaste asked. "Because I can tell you how that will end out before we even get there."

"I've done it before," Cyrus said as coolly as if Gren'averr had frozen him and not Nyad.

"This is insanity, Cyrus," Andren said. "You shouldn't have to face these things alone. You're not a one-warrior army."

"I think that I have to be in this case," Cyrus said, holding up

Praelior. "Because the alternative is to let him turn his attention to the rest of you, and let the consequences—and the death—fall wherever they may."

"Or we could—here's a brilliant idea—leave." Vaste folded his arms. "We've done our part—"

"Our part is not done yet," Cyrus said, the fury rising.

"You're out of your damned mind," Vaste said, "I'd say the acid got into your brain, but you were acting irrationally even before that—"

"This isn't happening," Erith said, shaking her head. "I'm dreaming this."

"I think this is tending a little toward a nightmare, really," Odellan weighed in, looking solemn.

"How many deaths since I put myself out front?" Cyrus asked, spinning in a slow circle to face each of them in turn. "I let that earth bastard turn away from me and we lost six. Gren'averr attacked our army, and we lost Nyad." He slammed his palm into the center of his breastplate and it clanged loud enough that Vara flinched. "I got their attention, their focus on me, for these last two, kept them attacking me, and how many did I—did *we*—lose—" he corrected himself at the last second.

A silent pall settled over the officers. "Cyrus," Curatio said, looking as if some of the life had drained out of him. "You can't blame yourself for—"

"This is not a discussion we're having right now," Cyrus said through gritted teeth. "If you don't want to be in this fight any longer, I invite you to have a wizard send you back to Sanctuary." He looked at each of them with angry eyes. "The rest of you," he said, raising his voice to let it roll over the army, "fall in. We have two more dragons to kill."

He ignored the shocked silence as he pushed his way past Thad out of the officers' circle, the warriors the first to fall in behind him, hurrying to catch up. He lifted the door out of Weck'arerr's acid-stinking quarters and squeezed out, following the circle around the shrine to his right. The grey skies between the columns taunted him, the first hints of blue in days showing between them.

The clouds of ash seemed thinner up here on the highest floor, as if they'd ascended to near the peak. Cyrus suspected they were only halfway up the volcano based on his observations from outside, before they'd begun their climb. He stalked on along the circular corridor that opened to the sky outside, but the breeze between the columns did not reinvigorate him. He only turned once, to take stock and see if anyone was still following beyond the warriors at his immediate back. The officers were there, a ways further back, Odellan and Thad almost right behind him, along with Scuddar and Longwell. He caught a hint of a green-robed shape lurking behind one of the warriors and snapped, "Larana—back with the spellcasters." He watched until she shuffled back in the formation, head bowed under her cowl.

Cyrus saw Vara about a third of the way back, her face still and settled, like she had been carved into statuary. *This is the way it has to be*, Cyrus thought as they approached the next door, the massive wood structure hanging from the ceiling like it had been carved out of the largest tree Cyrus could imagine. He felt his breath catch in his throat as he walked up to it, and had a brief flash, wondering if it was in fact death's door he stood before. His nerves stirred, prickling at him, but duty pushed him on regardless.

This is what needs to be done.

This is the only way.

I am the only one who can stand before the might of these things.

His mouth was dry and filled with bitterness, like he'd fallen on the earth outside and it had filled him up to the overflowing, dripping over his lips and absorbing every last ounce of moisture.

If I have to die to protect my people … so be it.

He hesitated only a second before the door and began to lift. Other warriors came forward to help, Odellan sneaking in at his side, Scuddar next to him, Longwell balancing his spear as he brought his shoulder low to help lift.

The door opened with a squeal that tore through Cyrus, and he did not hesitate now, ducking under the open door and stepping into—

—into—

—light?

The world changed around him in a single step, the grey sky outside the shrine replaced by something brighter, by a blue so rich he would have sworn he had never seen its like in all his life. Cyrus took another step and his boot clapped against hard stone as white, sheer curtains wafted in the wind before him. He turned his head and saw the wooden beams above him, the bed off to the side and the bare wooden figures where he and Vara kept their armor when not in use.

"Alaric?" Cyrus called, looking around the Tower of the Guildmaster in stunned disbelief, a sense of warm memory washing over him and replacing the momentary fears, the doubts that had so covered him only a moment earlier.

"I'm afraid not," came a vibrant voice from behind Cyrus. He turned to see a dark elf standing there, hair as black as tar, eyes alight with the same vitality that had been so obvious in the man's voice. He wore a half-smile, something that hinted at mischief to Cyrus. "He couldn't make it today, but it was important that someone came," he held his hands out, "so here I am."

"Who are you?" Cyrus asked, letting the disappointment fade lightly.

"An interesting question," the dark elf said, stepping toward him lightly. "One I suspect you have been asking yourself quite a bit lately."

"Nice dodge," Cyrus said.

The dark elf bowed his head. "Thank you. But I wasn't really dodging, just answering in a roundabout way. My friends—and I extend that courtesy to you because we have a mutual friend or three—some more friend than mutual, and vice versa—but still. My name is Genn."

"Genn?" Cyrus asked, frowning. "Who are you?"

"Oh, that question again," Genn said, shaking his head. "Do you even know? Never mind," he waved a hand. "Oh, all right. Add a 'Terr' at the beginning and a 'den' to the end, and you have me." He waved a hand with a flourish.

"Terrgenden?" Cyrus asked. "The God of Mischief?" His hand fell to Praelior, which was now sheathed in his scabbard. "What are you doing here?"

"I told you," Terrgenden said, and now the amusement was all gone. "Someone had to come … and I drew the short straw."

"Short straw?" Cyrus asked, his sense of calm fading. "What the hell are you talking about?"

Terrgenden's veil of amusement vanished, and he took a deep breath, sighing it out as though he were under great duress. "Because someone had to save your life, since you seemed unwilling to do it yourself ... and so here I am." His eyes glittered, but there was no hint of humor there. "And now we will have a talk."

66.

"What are we going to talk about?" Cyrus asked, noting the hint of chill coming off the wind whipping in from the Plains of Perdamun. "Mischief?"

"Ohh," Terrgenden said, shaking his head, sounding mildly distressed. "Everyone always says that to me. 'Oh, you're the God of Mischief,' 'Oh, you're responsible for the trouble I got into that one time I decided to run paint over my neighbor's donkey and parade him through the square,' 'Oh, it's your fault my brother played a prank on me when we were twelve.'" He made the noise again, a high note in the back of his throat. "It's exhausting, being the scapegoat for so many." He looked Cyrus over. "Probably not half as exhausting as being the scapegoat for yourself, though."

"I'm about to get an Alaric lecture delivered by proxy from the God of Mischief in the middle of my own quarters," Cyrus said to no one in particular. "This is a heady thing."

"I'm not the God of Mischief, in point of fact," Terrgenden said. "You, though—you're in the process of trying to trick the dragons into getting involved in a battle you don't think you can win." He placed a finger on his lip as though contemplating. "Really, which of us is the trickster in this tower?"

"I'm doing what I … have to," Cyrus said, but he lost all feeling for what he was saying halfway through, his words sounding tinny and far away.

"What you have to? Hm." Terrgenden's high voice lowered an octave. "They question I would ask, in my official capacity is … are your actions *just?*"

"Letting the titans continue to rampage across whoever they can crush is about the most unjust thing I can imagine," Cyrus said, finding a little of the fire that had left him.

"That's not what I asked." Terrgenden strolled over to one of the balconies and looked out, apparently admiring the view. "The titans serve the same master you followed once upon a time, Cyrus Davidon." He turned, a slow spin that almost looked like a movement from a dance. "Who do you serve now? The God of War?" He held a hand high, like a scale. "You are too ... soft for him now, aren't you?" He stared at Cyrus, and it felt as though he were burrowing right into Cyrus's soul. "Or do you follow ... the Ghost of this place?" He waved his hand around the Tower of the Guildmaster. "And who does that make you? Child of Bellarum? Or a protector of Arkaria?"

"It makes me the Guildmaster of Sanctuary," Cyrus said roughly, his voice under a little strain.

"What we believe in defines us," Terrgenden said. "What we tell ourselves we are is part of it as well. So ... Sir Davidon ... who are you?"

"I'm a man rapidly losing patience."

"You're a man who needs to look inward more often, then," Terrgenden said. "Or perhaps ..." And with a flourish, he disappeared and reappeared next to the full-length mirror, "... take a look at yourself?"

"Why would I—" Cyrus started, but he looked at the mirror and saw a flash of a warrior in stained armor, blood running fresh down the black metal, the face visible where it peeked from the helm covered in red, staring out at him with soulless eyes that were blank and yet dark, and he heard a rising scream in his mind—

Cyrus blanched and looked away, bringing a hand up to his forehead to block his sight. When he removed it as the cacophony in his head subsided, Terrgenden was standing right in front of him, watching him carefully. "What did you do?" Cyrus asked.

"I saved your life," came the reply.

"You keep saying that," Cyrus said, rubbing at his eyes. "Saved it from what?"

"You were about to charge headlong into the mouth of a fire dragon," Terrgenden said quietly. "You were going to take its undivided attention upon yourself. Now, listen ... anyone inhabiting the responsibility of this place," he swept a hand around to indicate the tower of the Guildmaster once more, "is bound to develop at least some belief in themselves, some little whisper of ego and ambition to change everything, their own personal god complex ..." He shook his head. "You are no god, Cyrus, in spite of whatever you might think. You are no child of a god, no being of incredible power and magic," he swept his hands in front of him in light circles, twirling his fingers in mockery. "In spite of your armor and sword, you are a man. You live like a man—a brave one, but a man—and you can die as easily as any other." He words came with a quiet solemnity. "But your time to die is not yet. You have work still in front of you—a man's work."

"I'm going to challenge that dragon," Cyrus said, staring hard at Terrgenden's surprisingly gentle eyes. "I'm going to do whatever I have to in order to—"

"Oh, yes, yes," Terrgenden said, nodding as he cut him off. "I'm sure you would be very brave, charging right into the thick of the battle, leading from the front ... if you were there when it started."

Cyrus felt a chill roll over him, like a thousand spiders making their way up his back and scalp. "What ... did you say?"

Terrgenden took a slow breath. "You are brave." He nodded, looking a little sad. "Too brave, sometimes, I think. Fearless for the wrong reasons, occasionally, and not fearful enough at the right ones. A man like you could change the world, Cyrus Davidon." He let that breath out. "And you will. But not today. And certainly not if you died instead of—" And with a wave of his hand, Terrgenden brought down the curtain of night around him—

—and—

—and—

The flash of flame leapt somewhere in front of him, orange fire pouring forth from a dragon some hundred meters ahead of Cyrus, lighting the world around him now that the Tower of the Guildmaster and its blue sky had faded away. Cyrus blinked, and realized he was standing, alone, in front of the door in Merceragg, the dragon of fire's quarters and—

The entirety of his army was already engaged in the fight.

"No," Cyrus whispered as he clenched his fist, realizing that Praelior was back in it. He started forward, watching the dragon breathe flame once more, small figures dancing around his head in circles as they swept in and struck—

—without him.

Cyrus charged, dread welling in him, threatening to overflow like water pouring out of Wellsheverr's quarters. He broke into a hard run, his eyes taking in the sight before him—Odellan, Vara, Thad, Scuddar and Longwell on high, swarming around the dragon's head, fighting for his attention—

Merceragg whipped back and forth between his choice of targets, each of them moving slower, not endowed with a weapon of the gods, spell magic flashing below the dragon's dark skin and pale eyes, a thousand blasts of ice and lightning having little effect on the creature but to antagonize him. Cyrus was still some fifty meters away when Merceragg locked eyes on Odellan and—

—and—

A wash of flame bellowed forth from the dragon's mouth and Odellan was gone in a burst of orange mingled with scarlet. Merceragg swept his snout sideways as Vara rushed out of his path faster than the warrior next to her, his scuffed red armor caught for an instant in the glow of another burst as Thad was swallowed in flame—

"NOOOOOOOOO!" Cyrus screamed as he charged ahead, racing over the heads of the spellcasters on pounding legs.

Merceragg heard him, though, and his eyes locked on Cyrus, on the target streaking toward him. Merceragg's nostrils flared to take a breath, and Cyrus zagged sideways, trying to remove himself from the thick knot of spellcasters below, tearing free of them to open ground where only one lone figure stood, away from the rest, his white robes and ruddy face staring up at Cyrus as the warrior tore past, trying to lead the inevitable, fiery cataclysm away from the eyes watching just below—

—the eyes of—

Oh, gods.

—of Andren—

The flame surged in Cyrus's wake as he spun in blind panic, turning on air and nearly twisting himself into a knot. The breath of flame came out of Merceragg's mouth just a few paces behind Cyrus, falling like a blanket of snow dropped from above, almost wafting down on Andren where he stood—

It danced as it landed, a small lake of fire that existed only for a second before it sputtered out, but long enough to turn the figure of

Andren, white robes bright against the stone floor, into a shadow in the fire, then, as it disappeared—

There was nothing left of the healer, not even a trace of ash.

"NOOO!" Cyrus screamed again, and he ran at Merceragg, the world gone red around him. He flailed at the beast, but before he could even reach it, a flash of blood-red light glowed below him, and then came another burst, harsh green. Merceragg jerked, his head wavering atop his neck, recoiling as he staggered under the impact of magics that came from somewhere behind Cyrus.

Merceragg's eyes went dead, and the dragon sank to the ground, splashing lava out of his nest as he fell onto his back, ungainly in death. His belly was scorched, scales torn free, scars of some powerful magic written all over his corpse. Cyrus looked at the wound as he sank to the ground in a slow spiral, letting the stone floor rise up to meet him as the Falcon's Essence spell brought him back to earth.

"Are you all right?" Vara asked, sliding up next to him, breathless, from out of the air. She did not wait for his answer but slammed her armor into his, wrapping her arms around him and clanking her helm against his pauldrons.

Cyrus did not answer, merely stood in the silence as Curatio staggered forward, face utterly grey and spent, looking far, far worse than Cyrus had ever seen the healer. He looked as though he might fade away at any moment, keel over and hurt himself in the process. He fell to the ground on his knees, and it looked dimly to Cyrus as though it might have hurt, tears welling at the corner of the healer's eyes.

"Odellan," Cyrus said quietly, no one speaking. "Thad." He heard a choked noise behind him and turned to see Martaina, her grief welling up and threatening to overwhelm her. "Andren."

The names of the fallen hung in silence in Merceragg's chamber, the only sound to break it the choked sobs of Martaina Proelius, whose loss was thick in the air. They all felt it, but none dared say anything at all.

67.

"What now?" Vaste asked when they had assembled the officers, outside the dark of Merceragg's chambers, the army gathered in silence around them.

"You know what now," Vara said quietly.

"Ah, yes, the Sky dragon," Vaste said, leaning against an interior wall as though he needed its strength to hold him up. "What's his name?"

"Vervahz," Curatio said, voice a thick whisper, gravelly and weak. "He's the last."

"Fine," Vaste said, his own voice lower, heavy with grief. "Let's get this over with."

"Not yet," Cyrus said, almost hollow.

"I just ..." Vaste's whole face sank. "This has been ... just a day. Just a ... I can't even find a descriptor, but whatever odious term you'd like to come up with, I'm fine with. In fact, if we made another, even worse term, to describe a day of this sort, something beyond wretched, horrific, tragic, gods-awful—"

"It's been a Goliath of a day," Longwell said, sounding utterly drained.

"That just about covers it," Vaste said, nodding.

"We can't go yet," Cyrus said, staring straight ahead at the grey sky between the columns. It truly was like a tease, like he'd been yanked away to a place of beauty and wonder, far from this hellish, torchlit nightmare, and then thrust back into it at the worst possible moment, just in time to see Thad and Odellan die, and to draw fire upon Andren himself. The guilt was like spears, magnified from the daggers of Belkan's death and Nyad's and those of the rangers, stabbing into him at all points.

"What happened to you back there?" Vaste asked, focusing on Cyrus. "You just ... disappeared. I didn't get into the room in time to see it, but I caught Odellan and Thad arguing over it, saying it was like you were teleported away."

"I was in the Tower of the Guildmaster," Cyrus said, staring straight ahead.

Silence greeted his proclamation. "Did you ... see Alaric?" Vara asked finally.

"No," Cyrus said, his voice growing hoarse with grief. "No, it was someone else." He glanced at her. "Said Alaric couldn't make it, so he came instead."

"Was it anyone we'd know?" Vaste asked with a surprising level of calm.

"Said his name was Terrgenden," Cyrus said.

"You were pulled from the fight by the God of Mischief?" Vara asked.

Cyrus just stared straight ahead. "So he said."

"To what purpose?"

Cyrus swallowed heavily. "He said he was there ... to save my life." His voice came out unrecognizable.

Silence fell once more. "To hell with these gods of yours," Longwell said at last.

"I was thinking that very thing myself," Cyrus said, and suddenly the howl of a drake in the far distance reached his ears. He came to his feet in an instant, the sound of another screech somewhere, miles away, came to him, followed by another.

"Uh oh," Vaste said.

"It's time," Cyrus said. He listened carefully, but heard nothing. Vara, on the other hand, was standing at rapt attention, listening intently. "Do you hear—?"

Before he even got it out, he heard it as well, the deep thundering of boots on stone. It came from behind them, and the Army of Sanctuary came to their feet in urgency, weapons drawn, frozen out of formation, the grey sky lighting them between the columns of the shrine.

The thundering of feet drew nearer and nearer even as the shrieks of distant dragonkin grew louder. "We won't have long," Cyrus said, casting a wide gaze. Everyone was on their feet, save for Curatio, who had pulled himself to one knee, his face sagging in a way Cyrus had not seen from him before.

"It'll have to be enough," Vara said, her sword drawn as the sound of the approaching footsteps turned the curve in front of them and burst into their sight.

Five titans came at a run, bellowing as they approached the Army of Sanctuary, roaring with a madness and rage that harmonized well with what Cyrus was feeling at the moment. They came sweeping toward the front of the army, utterly unprepared for assault—

And stopped short just before the edge, slowing to stand in a line, eyes dull and facing forward, staring over the army at their feet.

"Hello there," J'anda called from atop the titan at the fore. Cyrus saw Mendicant and Ryin each holding onto the necks of their own mounts, the goblin and the man both looking considerably less comfortable than the enchanter. "I apologize for our tardiness, but as it turns out … titan pets are somewhat hard to control for a run as long as the one we just made, even for me." He twirled his staff slightly as he looked down at them, and then stopped as he met a sea of faces swallowed in grief. His own fell, and he lowered his staff. "Oh, no."

"You're a grim lot considering you've been slaying dragons all the live long day," Ryin called from atop his own titan. "It's almost if someone di—" He froze as the words hung in his throat, and silence once more engulfed the Army of Sanctuary.

68.

The path to the inside of the volcano was wide and obvious, and Cyrus ran along it with Vara and Longwell just behind him, Vaste trailing in tow. He knew from Ehrgraz that he would find no defenders here, and indeed the path to the center of the mountain was empty, a straight rock road that led through the side of the peak. The heat grew more intense the closer they got to the middle, and soon Cyrus was left feeling as though he were in the middle of the battle with Merceragg again, but with a closer look at the inside of the mouth this time—

Like Thad.

Shaking off that thought, he pushed on, his weary legs protesting. They ran in silence, the glow of hot magma ahead lighting their way. The army behind them was already leaving, teleporting out in segments as the final pieces of the plan were being put in place, executed like—

Like Odellan.

Cyrus forced that thought away as he broke through the wide tunnel and into the heart of the volcano. Here the air was searing and heavy, shimmering like the heat of a mirage where he stood a few feet from the edge of the path. He sauntered slowly over to it, half afraid a dragon would come leaping out at him. *I have had enough of dragons for today, for a lifetime—*

Like Andren, probably, his long lifetime cut considerably short.

Cyrus rummaged on his belt for the small leather sack that had hung there for more miles and more days than he could remember now. The journey had all blurred together in his tired mind, days and nights of unrest now punctuated by events so horrific that they almost seemed surreal. He cradled the small bag in his gauntlet, feeling its weight, and after another moment considering it, he tossed it over the edge into the pit below. He leaned over enough to watch it sail down into the pool of bubbling magma a hundred feet beneath them, and felt the others do the same, as though it were some grand sight to see, some final closure for this expedition into the jaws of utter death.

"That feels anticlimactic," Vaste said.

"I could push you in if you desire a more exciting ending," Vara said, but her voice broke at the last.

"I—" Cyrus began but paused as a stir went across the pool of white-hot lava. It rippled like a rock had been thrown into a pond, the surface writhing as the effect spread. Folds of lava bubbled up and came crashing down again, molten rock slung up the sides of the crater.

Cyrus stood on the path and watched the pool of the volcano come alive with motion, a cauldron stirred, sloshing, like a tornado had been unleashed in its depths. It came to a crescendo, bursts of hot lava exploding into the air, and then it died just as suddenly, the red surface turning black, the heat fading dramatically, like someone had poured cold water all around them, or unleashed a blizzard—

Like Nyad.

The rock hissed as it cooled and came to rest, the volcano dying before their eyes. There was no steam, no release, just a sudden change from liquid to stone, solid enough that Cyrus knew if he jumped, he would be smashed upon it—

Like Belkan.

He turned from the edge of the path and started his run back to where he'd left his army. The others fell in behind him; he could hear their boots. Vaste's were creaking, the leather moving. Vara's were quietest of all, the small plate barely clanging with each step against the stone. Longwell's were punctuated with the haft of his lance hitting on each step, and Cyrus wondered if it was merely habit or a deep-seated weariness that made the dragoon do it.

They came back to the wide circle around the shrine's upper floor to the sound of a thousand drakes and wyverns howling in the distance, ever so much closer than when they'd left. Cyrus paused, less than three hundred of his army remaining before them, the last of their number before the retreat was to be sounded. J'anda was gone, of course, with his titans, but the rest of them were there, even Ryin and Mendicant—

Howls of rage came from their right, and Cyrus turned his head with the rest of the army. The last dragon's quarters were just a few hundred meters down the way. Vervahz of the sky was awakened, it seemed, his ire raised as surely as any of the lesser dragonkin that howled in the distance as they approached even now.

"Launch the teleport spells," Cyrus said to Mendicant, and several hundred orbs glittered into existence before them. Cyrus made but a motion and the flashes began, the last members of the army making good their retreat back to Sanctuary.

Cyrus waited and listened, hearing the sounds of battle, of combat, skin against scale. There were grunts and moans, the rush of air as Vervahz turned loose his breath on the titans attacking him in the chamber.

Now it was down to the officers and a few more. Calene Raverle and Scuddar waited next to Mendicant, Larana stared at Cyrus with worried eyes, and Menlos Irontooth stood silently in the middle of them all, his wolves surrounding him.

"Get out," Cyrus warned them without much force. He saw Calene reluctantly take the orb first, then Menlos, his wolves clutched tight under his arms. Larana lingered a moment longer and then left with Scuddar.

Curatio vanished next, the light of the spell not making his face any whiter than it already was, so worn and ragged from his expenditure of magics against Merceragg. Erith took her orb with reluctance, and she too was engulfed in pale light whiter than her robes.

The sounds of titans battling a dragon spilled out of the door ahead and someone slammed into the wood, breaking it free of its hinges. Cyrus saw shapes crashing through, a titan clinging to the back of Vervahz, another with his arms wrapped around the dragon's neck. Two more flanked him, punching at his sides and ripping at his tail as the dragon broke out of his quarters and into the hallway.

"Go," Cyrus said quietly. Vervahz's attention was still on the fight at hand, his head never once veering toward the cluster of Sanctuary officers still standing down the circular hallway. Ryin took his orb and vanished, his druid robes seeming to implode with the magic of the spell swallowing him whole. Mendicant took his next, a small flash following him.

Vara and Vaste stood with Cyrus, as did Samwen Longwell, watching the combat before them. Vervahz lifted the titan hanging on his back and slammed him into the nearest pillar. The titan crashed through stone like he was pushed through a column of dirt, dust billowing out, and fell from the third tier, screaming all the way to the bottom, where they heard a thud.

"Longwell, you're next," Cyrus said as he watched J'anda come creeping out of the shattered door, hurrying along toward them with the alacrity granted by his godly weapon.

"I told you after Termina I wouldn't leave before you again," Longwell said, holding firm as the enchanter scampered toward them.

One of the titans grasped Vervahz in a tight grip around his throat, pressing his fingers into scale and ripping them free. The blue dragon bled pink, the titan's fingers covered in the slick substance. The titan ripped at the wound it had created in a frenzy, tearing at the flesh hidden below the scale.

Vervahz came around with a snap of jaws and tore the titan's throat out, ripping it free with a flash of blood and flesh. The titan's hands pulled from the dragon in an instant, clamping down on his own neck desperately, trying to staunch the flow. The wounded titan hit his knees, already forgotten by the dragon as he moved on to his next prey.

"Why are we all standing around?" J'anda asked as he reached them, tossing a look back to watch the battle.

"Making sure the job is done," Vaste answered for all of them. "Making sure that ..."

"That it wasn't in vain," Vara said.

"If we get caught here, it will be worse than in vain," J'anda said, and he whirled his staff in front of him before the light of his return spell carried him away.

"It would be death," Longwell finished for him. Reluctantly, he reached out for the orb of teleportation, pausing a second away from it. "We should go, all of us."

"Just a minute more," Cyrus said, unable to tear his eyes away even as the hooting, furious sounds of the drakes and wyverns built in the air, coming closer and closer.

Longwell inclined his head slightly and took hold of the teleportation orb, flashing away as one of the titans seized hold of Vervahz's wing and ripped hard upon it. The sound of bones breaking was loud even as far away as they were, but the dragon did not scream in pain. He flailed instead, kicking out with a razored foot, catching the titan in the gut and opening him wide. Cyrus saw blood and intestines, and the smell hit a moment later.

"Gah," Vaste said, the smell overwhelming. He seized his orb without a word, disappearing away with a flash.

"We should go," Vara said, her fingers finding his, their orbs glowing brightly in front of them. "This is not safe." The howls of furious dragonkin put urgency and truth to her words.

"Just ... wait," Cyrus said quietly as he watched the last two titans struggling against their foe. One punched Vervahz in the side of the head, smashing him into a column. Vervahz kicked against his attacker, laying open the titan's leg. The titan gritted its teeth and grabbed the sky dragon around the neck, yanking it down, closer to the edge of the shrine.

Cyrus began walking forward, the orb following him along with Vara. Vervahz was fighting a losing battle, of that Cyrus was certain, and the melee spilled right to the edge of the shrine, the flash of the blue dragon's lone working wing trying to extend, to carry him forth—

And then the last two titans, still clutching and tearing at the dragon even as he tore at them, went cascading over the edge of the walkway, smashing through another column on their way out.

Cyrus ran to the edge and made it in time to see them all land, flailing wildly until they struck the ashy ground. The two titans landed atop the blue dragon and bounced, rolling away from the carcass. And it was a carcass; Cyrus could see the light gone from Vervahz's eyes, the dragon limp across the grey dust. He stared down at them, at his triumph ...

And felt nothing.

"Now?" Vara asked into the pitched shrieks growing closer behind them, the dragonkin coming for blood, for vengeance.

"Now," Cyrus said, and they took their orbs as one, leaving behind the ashen battlefield and whatever remained of the fallen.

69.

Silence hung heavy over the Council Chamber like ash over the raiding party only a few hours earlier. Cyrus sat in his place at the head of the table, wishing he were anywhere else but there. He looked slowly around the table, starting at his left, noting the two empty chairs of Nyad and Thad immediately past Vara, who sat with her head down, staring at the table's edge, ash still stuck in her blond locks.

Vaste and Longwell sat just past the empty seats, the troll still as Cyrus had ever seen him and Longwell looking around, observing all that was going on within the chamber. Odellan's seat sat empty just to the dragoon's left, and Erith sat lonely and pale, between it and Andren's chair, also empty and slightly askew. Mendicant, Ryin and J'anda sat to the left of that empty seat, each in their own sullen silence, none of them looking about save for the druid. Just past them, to Cyrus's immediate right, Curatio's chair also sat empty.

"Where's Curatio?" Cyrus asked, barely above a whisper, as if afraid anything louder would be as unto a breath of fire descending into the chamber from on high.

"He looked exhausted when I saw him, said something about needing to sleep," Vaste said, his voice barely louder than Cyrus's. "He used one of those powerful heretic spells on—I can't even remember which dragon. One of the 'errs. The one that breathed fire." His voice turned even more sour. "The one that killed more of our officers than anything else, ever."

"It was actually Merceragg," Erith said quietly.

"Well, take me for a country whore and throw me into a city brothel," Vaste said hotly. "As though I give a single damn what the name of that dead creature is."

"We'll need to arrange funerals," Ryin said, looking around, face grey. "And the families will need to be informed."

"I'll handle it," Cyrus said, looking down.

"You won't be alone," Vara said, and he did not even think to argue.

"What now?" Erith asked, and her voice broke.

"Could we declare war on the dragons?" Vaste asked. "Because I'd like to declare war on the dragons."

"This was our fault," Cyrus said, drawing the attention of everyone. "My fault. My plan, along with Ehrgraz, anyway." He looked around the table, and it seemed … so empty.

"Then what do we do next?" Longwell asked.

"We mourn," Cyrus said, "and we wait. For Ehrgraz to do his part." He lowered his head. "Gods know we've got plenty to do with just the mourning."

"Hard to believe this all started with a hostile visit to Kortran years ago," Mendicant said, his low voice almost melodic as the goblin lapsed into contemplation.

"I just want to know how it's going to end," Vaste asked, looking very pointedly across the table at Cyrus.

Cyrus did not meet his gaze, some vague hint of fear keeping his eyes from meeting the troll's. "I want to know the answer to that question myself," he said quietly. "But I have a feeling it's going to be a while longer before the answer is clear."

70.

The wait at King Danay's court was interminable, hours of pacing in a grand room designed for the purpose of impressing and intimidating visitors to the Elven Kingdom. There were pillars of greenery and skylights and a wide-open hall so large Cyrus could scarcely see from one side to the other. The tinkling of water echoed from some of the fountains and waterfalls built into the cavernous room. A sweet scent lingered in his nostrils, sharper than rose petals, though by now he felt well sick of it. *This is the price of admission when you don't make your appointment ahead of time,* Cyrus thought.

This is the price I will pay to come to tell a father that his daughter is dead.

He walked in a steady circle around one of the pillars, a garden unto itself built in tiers, blooming just fine in the face of winter beginning to settle in on Arkaria. On the walk through Pharesia, Cyrus had scarcely noticed the light chill in the air. It did not seem like autumn here, not even the earliest version of it.

Here in the waiting chamber before the throne room, however, it was not as cool as out of doors, the skylights keeping the room in the steady warmth of the sun, giving the plants life and courtiers and visitors a pleasant enough place to while away the hours before an audience with Danay. For Cyrus's part, though, he could not imagine this room without linking it inextricably with Nyad, and it caused a pain in his chest and lower, a roiling in his guts he could not escape.

"This palace has stood for thousands of years," Vara said, voice echoing slightly through the chamber, "and I would imagine it has looked much the same for all that time—until now, when you wear holes in this marbled floor from your interminable pacing." She looked equally cross and amused, and he marveled at her ability to carry off that expression.

"I find myself filled with a nervous energy that you apparently do not share," Cyrus said, eyeing Vara, who sat next to a fidgeting Mendicant. The goblin looked more than a little discomfited sitting in the court of Pharesia, though to someone not well versed in goblin behavior, he probably looked quite normal—which was to say, strange. Cyrus could read the nervousness in the hunch of the wizard's shoulders, however, in the grimacing way he bared his teeth and kept his head down. "Well, it looks as though Mendicant might."

"Hm?" Mendicant looked up, head turning rapidly, snapping from Vara to Cyrus in an instant as though he had missed something truly important. "I am sorry, my Lord and Lady Davidon, but I—" He stopped, twitched, and his mouth froze in a line of sharp teeth. "I apologize again."

"I've been called worse," Vara said with a faint smile. "Probably by Lord Davidon, in fact."

Cyrus looked at her, pensive, for a moment, then back to their wizard companion with a hint of sheepishness. "How are you doing, Mendicant?"

"This is frightening duty for me," Mendicant said, looking very earnest as he raised his head and lowered his voice. "Are you not ... worried that the king is going to be particularly vengeful when he finds out that his dau—"

Vara clasped a hand over Mendicant's mouth before the last bit could come out. Even so, Cyrus could see elves some distance away raise their heads, snapping their gazes away quickly as they realized that they had been caught eavesdropping.

"That is for the king's ears," Cyrus said as Vara relinquished her hold on Mendicant's face, but kept it close by in case she had to grab him again. "And since there are so very many ears in this place that seem keen to listen in on every conversation being had in these chambers ..."

"There's quite a bit of profit in doing so," Vara said, matter-of-factly. "In politics, information is power, and having the ability to tell a monarch news of any sort—bad or good—before the person here to deliver it does so ... well, that's a power all its own." She looked around. "Though it would be quite bad for us."

"There's every possibility he already knows," Cyrus said, trying to keep his nerves from showing as he glanced around. "I was left with the distinct impression that there is not much that goes on in Sanctuary that the rest of Arkaria does not hear about."

"It was a small army that came with us," Vara said, her lips a thin line when they came to rest, one that hinted at her own worry. "Perhaps that will insulate us some from word leaking so fast."

"Doubtful," Mendicant said, "everyone in Sanctuary knows. About—" he glanced around, "... her, about Andren, Odellan, Thad ... and about those poor rangers that were ground up by Groz'anarr."

"Word travels fast around our small halls," Cyrus said, pursing his own lips. "Which is why I brought you and the Lady of Nalikh'akur," Cyrus said, looking straight at Vara. "If the king is displeased, hopefully he won't resort to striking out at the shelas'akur."

"That would be a terrible thing," Vara said.

Mendicant frowned. "I'm not well versed in elven culture as I'd like, but as I understand it, the King taking such an action would likely turn the people against him, yes?" He caught a slight nod from Vara, filled with hesitation. "Yes, I suppose that would make it a terrible thing."

Vara's face reddened all the way to her ears. "Mendicant, I was speaking from the perspective of having to strike down palace guards in my own defense being rather an unfortunate occurrence, not from any larger political concerns."

"Oh," Mendicant said, eyes darting as he thought. "Then ... it was somewhat of an understatement, then? For purposes of humor?"

"You didn't catch that?" Cyrus asked, watching the goblin with some dark amusement that he would not have believed he could find in this hour.

"Goblin humor is quite a bit different than your variety," Mendicant said quietly. "It is very much based on the concept of—"

"Lord Cyrus Davidon," a voice boomed behind him, drawing the attention of all three of them to a man in a steward's uniform. Cyrus searched the face, but it was unfamiliar; he was simply a worker of the palace doing his job and not the king himself in disguise, as he had been known to be on previous occasions. "You will follow me."

Cyrus waited for Vara and Mendicant to rise to their feet, and then followed the steward, who was already in motion toward the grand entrance to the throne room. Cyrus did not hurry to keep up, forcing the steward to slow to allow them to catch him, Mendicant's small legs and ungainly walk upon two feet hampering their progress considerably.

When they reached the throne room itself, Cyrus was once more impressed with its sprawling size and the considerable rainbow coloring of the monarch himself, visible at some distance. Once more, the steward began to pull away from them, visibly increasing his pace, and at this, Cyrus realized, they had been had.

"Shit," he muttered, "Mendicant—"

"Do not," King Danay said, loudly enough to be heard over the rustle of movement high above them in the balcony reaches of the room. Bows were drawn and nocked by the hundreds, perhaps even as many as a thousand, crowding around balconies above, arrows pointed down at him in number enough to kill Mendicant at least a hundred times over; Vara might be more lucky and only suffer serious wounds that would lead to her bleeding to death. Surely she would rate a resurrection spell, but probably not until Cyrus was dead and his body well disposed of.

Cyrus stood there, Vara and Mendicant behind him, his hand feeling like it was a mile from the salvation of Praelior on his belt, sure that death was well at hand, and he waited for the command that would spell his certain end.

71.

"Your hospitality sucks," Cyrus pronounced, his fingers eager to dance toward Praelior, but his mind sure that to make even a motion in that direction would spell the end of all of them. "And I'm not just talking about your lack of feast on this occasion."

King Danay sat in his seat at some considerable distance, elevated steps above the floor where Cyrus and his compatriots stood, but his dark countenance was easily visible, and he seemed to be radiating fury. "You come to tell me of the death of my youngest daughter."

"If I'd known you'd be such a prick about it," Cyrus said, eyeing the archers above, "I would have sent a druid to hand a note to your troops before casting a spell for a quick getaway. Apparently personal condolences don't rate very high for you."

"You led my heir into death," Danay said with rising anger.

"Oh, come now," Cyrus said, feeling as caustic as Weck'arerr, "you disinherited her with all the ease of a butcher taking the head off a goat not four years ago, practically an eye blink to your people. You've probably had bowel movements that lasted longer."

"You come into my hall and insult me now?" Danay said, cold fury seeping into his tone, layering over the earlier hot rage.

"I figure I'm not going to make it out of here alive no matter how polite I talk at this point," Cyrus said. "You didn't plan this ambush in the name of theatrics, you mean to kill me." His eyes settled on Danay's, and he found he had more than a little anger to answer that which he saw in the King. "You know there will be consequences for this, and you've decided to do it anyway. Well, I hope you're ready for war, because it's coming your way after this."

Danay laughed. "You think this will end in war?" His eyes

sparkled. "I don't. Your people are already at war, as are mine. We are natural allies, Sanctuary and the kingdom, fearful of the same great enemy. I will return your wizard to your guild, intact and well, and the shelas'akur will, of course, live—"

"Of course," Cyrus said acidly.

"Do you think I'll keep my mouth shut at what you plan to do?" Vara asked, incredulous. "If so, you are even more dim than I ever gave you credit for. If you kill him, you had best kill me as well, for I will lead the bloody war myself and take your throne for my bloody own, leaving your head on a pike atop the gate as an example to the last generation of the elves of what happens to a monarch whose head swells entirely too much for his crown."

Cyrus blanched at her words then closed his eyes. "She doesn't mean it—"

"Of course she does," Danay said icily. "She means every word of it." His voice tilted toward sadness. "Which is a shame, but let us face it ... the shelas'akur is nothing more than a symbol, and if she must die to prevent a war ... so be it."

"You are out of your gods-damned mind," Vara said. "You didn't even care for your daughter that much—"

"You don't know what I cared for," Danay snapped. "You don't *know* anything, you're a child—"

"Here's what I know," a shadowed figure said, barely visible, voice low and harsh, appearing at Danay's throat with an ornate dagger clutched in the blue-skinned hand of a dark elf, pale, barely visible fingers small enough to indicate that beneath the cowl was the face of a woman. "If you kill them, there will be no finding your head." The woman disappeared in an instant, and a scarlet line appeared on Danay's neck before she reappeared at his other side, pulling him roughly against the back of the chair. "And you will be at war with the Sovereignty. Again."

Danay's face broke into a furious grimace. "I did not summon you, Ambassador."

"The Sovereign bade me come," she said, leaning in close to his ear but speaking loudly enough in the human tongue that all could hear her. "And should your men decide to throw a few well-placed arrows my way—" She disappeared again, and now the blade stretched over the top of the throne, perched to stab directly into the top of the king's head, his crown knocked asunder. "You *will* get the point."

"Your Sovereign does not want war with me," Danay said, but there was a hint of uncertainty in the way he said it.

"My Sovereign anticipated you would say exactly that," the woman said, appearing once more at his side, her motions quicker than Cyrus had seen even from Alaric when he turned to mist and disappeared. But there was no mist with her, merely the appearance that one moment she was in one place, and the next, another. *Almost as though she moves with the aid of a godly weapon ... but who the hell ...? That voice is ... Something is muffling it.* "He bade me tell you that as of this morning, we have some ten thousand troops stationed as relief for our allies in the Emerald Fields, anticipating that perhaps you might perhaps think striking down that settlement before committing an act of war on Sanctuary might be a sound defensive move."

She flashed again behind him, appearing at the other side, blade poking into his ornate raiment and tearing it just slightly. He flinched visibly. "We have an agreement with Administrator Tiernan, who is rather fond of Sanctuary and this one," the woman waved faintly at Cyrus, "for some reason. The portal will remain open to us, allowing us to deliver our troops directly onto your shores." There was a hint of malice as she spoke. "How do you reckon a war will go with dark elves and the Army of Sanctuary able to march straight to your capital, furious at the loss of their General? How will it go with your own people once word spreads that you killed the shelas'akur?"

Danay's face was pure fury, suffused anger threatening to boil out. "It will not bring them back."

"It won't bring you back, either," she said, slapping him lightly on the cheek with the flat edge of the blade and making him flinch. "Cyrus, Vara, Mendicant ... be dears and approach the king, will you?" She turned her voice toward the archers in the balcony. "Loose a single arrow and your king will sit headless upon this throne as the dark elves and the largest guild in Arkaria march across your land with the shelas'akur at their head." Her voice echoed, deep and dramatic, and ... damned familiar. "Choose your path—kill your king, kill Cyrus Davidon, kill the shelas'akur ... and watch the heirs in waiting fight over the throne." She dropped her voice conversationally. "How many are there again, below Nyad? Some five hundred, I believe? I hope there's no acrimony between them, no division. Surely they'd line up behind one of their own and not divide into segments, along with your whole kingdom—your legacy." She sounded amused.

Cyrus had taken the woman's instruction and was advancing slowly. The steward who had led them into the throne room moved aside, hurrying to flatten himself against the nearest wall, well out of the way.

Cyrus peered at the cowled figure as he reached the steps to the massive throne. The pale blue hand beckoned him forward, and he rose on the steps, one at a time, drawing fearful breaths of perfume-clouded air, Vara and Mendicant only a step behind him.

He saw the crimson dripping down Danay's front and staining his royal rainbow attire. It was not a small wound that the dark elven ambassador had inflicted, and the first hints of worry were fighting to appear on Danay's face even now. He kept his hands clutched on his throne, but his knuckles were white with the effort.

"Thank you," Cyrus said to the dark elven figure behind the throne. "For ... this."

"I owed you one," she said, nervousness fighting through the distorted sound of her voice. "But I suggest we leave quickly, before some of the archers above grow weary of holding their bows nocked."

"Wise sentiment from the ..." Vara was frowning, "... whoever you are."

"Your daughter died bravely," Cyrus said, staring right into King Danay's face. "She fought to the end to try and bring all the help she could to your kingdom, and her death was tragedy of the highest order ... and exactly the sort we face in battle and war."

"She should not have been with you," Danay said gravely, the fury returned beneath his worry.

"That's an argument you should have had with her," Cyrus said, nodding once at the figure behind the throne. "Not me. Though I didn't hear you complaining when her being with us resulted in Termina being defended by Sanctuary, or the Heia Pass getting our efforts." Cyrus's face went grave. "Our assistance to you ends now. Sanctuary's aid is to the Emerald Fields, and if you ever so much as make a feint at them with an army, you will have me—and Sanctuary—"

"And me," Vara said harshly.

"And the Sovereign of Saekaj and Sovar," the lady in the cloak said.

"—to contend with," Cyrus finished. "We can find more soldiers." He drew himself up to his full height, and the difference between him and the sitting monarch was imposing. "Can you?"

"Get out of here, damn you," Danay said after a moment of silence. "You'll have your peace."

"Your pragmatism is appreciated," Cyrus said. He let his hand drop to Praelior as he signaled to Mendicant. The world slowed immediately, the trickle of blood down the king's neck down to individual beads rolling slowly over pale skin, the almost imperceptible twitch at the corner of his mouth obvious to Cyrus now.

A teleportation orb sprang into existence before Cyrus, the easy transit back to his point of soul binding, but as he started to reach for it, he looked up at the dark elven ambassador. Where before her form had been shaded and dark, as though she were under some cloud, now she was as obvious to his eyes as any of the countless other times he had looked upon her.

"What. The. *Hell?*" Cyrus asked, staring at her in undisguised awe.

He could now see her white hair beneath the cowl as if someone shone a light into the darkness, could see her face, proud and unabashed even though she was hiding under means of darkness that he could not define other than—

He saw the dagger, clearly, and saw the glow from the weapon. It was a faint one but clear to him, now that Praelior was in his hand, one godly weapon shedding light on another.

"I told you that I owe you," Aisling Nightwind said, and then she reached out for the orb in front of her. But she said it with a hint of sadness, and even though her motion was telegraphed to give them plenty of time, Cyrus still had to scramble to take hold of his orb before she grasped hers—but not until he'd seen the flashes behind him from Vara and Mendicant. "Take care, Cyrus," she said and took hold of the spell magic that whisked her away.

Cyrus clutched at the magical orb and let it sweep him along as well, dragging him through space, and back to the Tower of the Guildmaster, unsure if he was more disturbed by the King who had threatened him with death and war … or the former lover and assassin who had just spared him from both.

72.

The funeral for Andren, Odellan, Nyad, Thad and the six rangers was less like a funeral than any Cyrus could ever recall seeing—with the exception of the ones that he had been forced to preside over of late. Without benefit of bodies, there was no need for graves. There was some talk about digging them anyway, but of late the cemetery in the back corner of the Sanctuary wall had grown full, and so a new tradition had begun after the siege two years prior, based on some of the customs of the human Northlands.

The entire guild stood, after a long procession, upon the banks of the River Perda south of Sanctuary. There was silence in the air, the skies were grey as was fitting for the early onset of autumn in the Plains of Perdamun, and Cyrus stood at the fore in his black armor as they set adrift ten small wooden boats upon the river, pushing them out and letting the current catch them, tugging them inexorably toward the mouth of the river at its entry to the Bay of Lost Souls.

The silence was an immovable thing; Cyrus stood basking in it in the absence of the rays of the sun. His officers were a step behind, but he did not look to them for comfort, not even to Vara, who was only a half-pace behind him. *I am the leader. I must bear this burden in silence. I am the example. I cannot appear to be lost, no matter how much so I may feel.*

And so he held his head high, watching the first flaming arrow strike the lead boat, the one prepared for Thad with his original red armor painted up freshly, lying within the wooden beams like a body. The tinder around it caught quickly, and the flames leapt high as the fire arrows landed upon the second boat, then the third in line, until all ten were properly burning, pyres making their way down the river.

The boats drifted aflame, giving light to the grey day but not nearly enough heat to reach them on the banks. Cyrus wanted to feel the fire, to hear its crackle on flesh. *Did they feel it?* he wondered, numb, but not from the cold. *Did it burn and course over them, consume them while they yet lived, breathing in the flame, letting it incinerate them outside and in?* He pictured it blackening flesh, watching Andren disappear under the inferno, imagined it slow rather than so quick it almost defied notice; as if he could have turned his head and never even known that his oldest friend had passed from this world.

Cyrus turned his head slightly to see Martaina standing stonefaced, bow in hand, a lit torch next to her, performing her duty—her last duty—to both husband and lover, her thoughts shrouded behind a black veil that apparently did nothing to impair her aim.

With quiet solemnity, a voice in the audience reached up with a chorus of song in a tongue Cyrus did not quite understand, something that vaguely bordered his knowledge of the human language, but was rooted in some dialect with words that eclipsed his knowing. With a start, he recognized the honey-smooth voice as that of Menlos Irontooth, singing in the manner of his people when they performed this very ceremony.

Other voices took up the song, until Cyrus realized that Vara was adding her own, low and harmonious, and he realized that he had never even known she could sing.

The grey clouds rolled over the afternoon sky as the song broke the silence, repeated twice more, more voices joining in on each chorus as the simplicity of the words washed over the crowd of mourners like a river running over its banks. Cyrus had contemplated a speech, had delivered these sorts of eulogies before, the last only a week or so earlier. Something needed to be said, but he had only a few thoughts on his mind as the chorus closed its song and silence reigned over the river once more, the pyres drifted nearly out of sight by this point.

"We could tell tales all afternoon of these ten brave souls," Cyrus said, his voice strong and clear and ringing. "And I expect we will— later, in the warmth of the fire, ales in hand, toasting them and their sacrifice until the small hours of the morning. We are a company that goes to battle, that goes to war, but that loses few. This a fact we are immensely proud of, but when we do suffer that loss, it is all the more keenly painful for its rarity, in the same way that gold is precious for its scarcity.

"These people were friends, brothers, sisters, lovers, husbands, wives—they were many things to the many of us," Cyrus continued, turning to face the crowd, letting his eyes dance over the officers one by one. Someone was missing, he thought, but he did not stop to consider who; with all the recent loss, he might simply have miscounted. "We knew who they were, their names, their dreams, their ambitions, their secrets," he lowered his voice. "They lived among us, they were us, warriors, rangers, wizard, healer. Members, officers—all of Sanctuary, and true.

"Their loss is a blow," he went on, hearing a sob choked off in the back of the crowd, and his eyes settled on Terian, who stood near the front, solemn, with some of his own procession in attendance behind him. His eyes were downcast, his armor drawing stares from the members of Sanctuary around him. "To lose any of our number is painful; to lose so many so quickly is … almost unthinkable."

Cyrus drew a breath and let it out. "I could spend the whole day telling you all I know of our dear lost, and not even ripple the surface of that particular pond. That leaves off all that I did not know, for many of our dead I would have been have been hard-pressed to name were I to run into them in the halls. I consider that a tragedy, for I know their names now, and have heard many stories about each of them, enough to convince me that we are greatly poorer for their passing. They were our guildmates, and they were exemplars of courage, which is the tie that binds our membership. We take none but the brave," Cyrus went on, "and they were brave, and true, and stood their ground to the last, every one of them." His eyes flitted over Cora, who stood off to one side with Gareth and Mirasa as well as one of their druids flanking her, paying their condolences. *I wonder how they heard?*

"They fought and died for their brethren here," Cyrus said, trying to thread his speech to a close, "as I expect any of you would. For that is the strength of Sanctuary—we are no mean mercenary company that merely goes where the gold compels us; we are called to higher purpose," he felt an ashen sensation within just saying it, as though their attack on the dragons put the lie to the thought, "and they fought for that purpose, giving everything they had to the cause." He straightened. "Speaking only for myself … we all die at some point in our walk through this world, and I can only hope, when my day comes, that it should be to such high purpose as fighting to end such a war as we are in—as it did for these brave souls."

The applause was light, polite, and then grew stronger. But even as it raged while emotions poured out of those before him, there was another thought that was stirred by what he had just said, about all of them dying eventually, and he realized at last which officer was absent from the funeral rites.

Curatio.

The applause faded away, and the crowd began to disperse, some twenty thousand plus mourners and guests, filing silently across the green and rustling plains, back toward the keep of Sanctuary on the northern horizon.

73.

"That was well said." Vara walked alongside him at the rear of the formation, the slow, disorganized march back to Sanctuary holding none of the urgency or discipline of the army at war.

"It was very spontaneous, so I'm surprised it came out at all," Cyrus said, his armor feeling as though it were weighing him down. He nodded sharply ahead as he caught sight of a familiar helm in the procession. "I need to talk to Terian—"

"Well, go, then," Vara said, "I'll catch up."

Cyrus frowned. "I need to talk to Cora, too."

Now it was her turn to frown. "Why? You think she'll have some news of the titan movements?"

He stopped straight away. "I forgot to tell you, didn't I?" He grimaced. "Can you catch her?"

"Perhaps if you were to tell me for what purpose," she said, looking mildly annoyed.

"I'm sorry, I will," Cyrus said, nodding at Cora's receding back in the distance. "Maybe we should stop her first, since I suspect Terian will take an audience with me anytime …" He started forward again, using his aggressively long stride to try and catch the elf, who was already fading into the crowd. "Cora!"

She heard him and turned in a casual manner that reminded him that nothing was amiss in her mind; it wasn't as if she could have known that he had "found her out." *It wasn't as though living next to me in the past was a crime. Though she might have mentioned it.*

Cora held position politely and waited for him to catch up. She must have caught some signal of his mood, however, for she inclined her head with a wary eyebrow cocked as he approached. "Hello,

Cyrus," she said.

"Hello, neighbor," Cyrus said dryly, and watched her eyebrow rise a little further. "I didn't realize until recently how far back our acquaintance stretched."

"And why should you?" Cora asked calmly as Vara caught up to them. "You were, after all, but a child when Belkan came to take you from my house to deliver you to the Society of Arms."

"What. The. Ruddy. Hell," Vara said, more than a little taken aback. She leveled her gaze on Cyrus. "*This* you forgot to mention to me?"

"We had a whole conversation right after I found out, on the bridge, that ended with Curatio dumping water on us, and Ehrgraz showing up to start us into this whole shrine attack," Cyrus said, waving her off. "We've been so busy, I guess I just forgot—"

"Yes, well," Vara said, slightly above a simmer, "when next we're intimate—some fifty years from now, I hasten to add—I might 'forget' to take my ventra'maq, and then you, you spoony warrior, will be left with an offspring at roughly the same time you will have an utterly valid excuse to be forgetting important things."

"By 'spoony,' do you mean 'delicious'?" Cyrus asked. "Because I can agree with—"

"As amusing as it is to watch you 'all grown up' without acting the part," Cora said politely, "perhaps you might save the spat for later." Her eyes honed in on Cyrus, but he could feel Vara's wrath bubbling next to him. *It's not as though she weren't already provided ample cause to be irritable, what with the events in the elven throne room and—uh, who rescued us.* That had not been a particularly enjoyable revelation afterward, when Cyrus had told her who had been beneath the cowl, though it had perhaps improved his pronunciation of elvish curses, hearing them all strung together and repeated so loudly. "You act as though my knowing you as a child has any bearing on my knowing you now," Cora said. "You were obviously not the Guildmaster of Sanctuary when last we made our acquaintance. Despite your childish protestations of fierce warriordom at the time—you would have been of little use in the situation we now find ourselves in."

"It has some bearing," Cyrus said sharply. "You knew my parents."

"Many did," Cora said without expression. "Shall we track them all down and you can have a good row in front of them as well?" She eyed Vara. "I expect this one could stay angry long enough to pull it off."

"Cora, you old sow," Vara said. "This is the sort of thing you might have mentioned."

"I might have," Cora said, almost indifferently, "but I felt to do so might be to try to invoke old loyalties that young Cyrus here does not even have memory of." She smiled faintly. "You did not even recall me, after all."

"I was six," Cyrus said. "And probably somewhat traumatized given all that I'd been through with losing my father and mother so close together—"

"Your mother and father did not die that close together," Cora said with a shrug. "Your mother was around for some time after Rusyl's death. Surely you remember her stories, her tales ... she was quite the teller of them," she said with a faint smile. "She had a way with words, a talent I see might have bred true in you."

"I remember stories," Cyrus said, looking a little furiously at her, "but mostly of the trolls and how horrible they were."

"She was a bit irate with them," Cora said with a stunning amount of subtlety. "You might see some cause for why."

"I damned well know why she hated the trolls," Cyrus said, voice booming loud enough that some in the ranks of the funeral procession turned back to look, dark figures on near-colorless plains. Vaste, in particular, frowned at Cyrus, his head well above the crowd. "You say you didn't want to mention this old acquaintance because you were asking for a favor, fine. Why not mention it after you knew we were going to help you?"

"We haven't had that many conversations since then," Cora said, "and it's not the sort of thing one merely brings up—'Oh, by the by, did you know that you used to come and play at my house when you were a child?' You were a lot shorter then, and somewhat homely. I was worried for you, but fortunately it seems you've done all right in spite of it," she said, nodding at Vara.

"Hey!" Cyrus said.

"There is nothing to say," Cora said, spreading her arms wide. "Do you wish to reminisce about things you cannot even recall? By all means, come to Amti some time when this is over and I will regale you with all the tales I have." Her face grew still and somehow long. "But for now … the titans swirl about the Gradsden Savanna in great number, edging into the Jungle of Vidara and chopping more of it down every single day to feed their war machine." She paused and chewed her bottom lip. "Forgive me for not being interested in discussing the days of old when the days of now so consume my thoughts with worry."

Cyrus took a breath and shared a look with Vara, whose rage had plainly mellowed. "Fine," Cyrus said, still viewing her with some suspicion. "I'm going to take you up on that."

Cora kept her face almost impassive—almost, but not quite. The faintest of smiles played on her lips even though it was obvious in its fakery. "I look forward to it," she said, but that subtle flicker in her expression put the lie to it before she bowed to Cyrus and then walked away.

74.

"Terian," Cyrus said, greeting the Sovereign of Saekaj Sovar at the gate where the dark elf waited, his own entourage—the healer, Dahveed, the druid, Bowe and that enormous warrior, Grinnd—standing off from him about twenty paces. The warrior and healer smiled politely at passersby, but the druid sat with legs crossed, hands up, meditating, a cushion of three feet of air between his backside and the ground.

"Cyrus," Terian said grimly. "Vara."

"Thank you for coming," Cyrus said. "Your presence in this hour is … much appreciated." He looked around, but other than Terian's three servants, all the others from the funeral had already passed through the Sanctuary gates.

"Well, I did know all the officers that died," Terian said. "So I appreciate you allowing me to come and pay my respects."

"I think I speak for both of us," Vara said, "albeit rather surprisedly … but you are welcome at any time."

"Perhaps not in the middle of the night," Cyrus corrected, "unless it's an emergency."

"Davidon, you aren't getting me out of my comfortable bed in the middle of the night *unless* it's an emergency," Terian said. "Besides, I have messengers for the minor stuff now, like, 'Vaste needs a swat upside the head, it's been too long.'"

"A persistent problem," Cyrus agreed.

"Have you heard from Ehrgraz yet?" Terian asked, a little tentatively given his position as leader of a nation.

"No," Cyrus said, frowning. "I assumed that was a good thing, though, given …" He let his voice drift off. "Do you know something

I don't?"

"Not really," Terian said, but there was hesitation in his voice. "I introduced Bowe over there to my sources in the Ashen Wastelands." He nodded at the druid, hovering placidly. "He's been trying to check in daily, but ... nothing."

"That could be good, right?" Cyrus asked, looking from Vara to Terian. "The dragons are cloistered up, debating the course of revenge?"

"Maybe," Terian said, more than a little skeptically. "I would have thought Ehrgraz would have come to you by now, though, or at least sent some word. He has his spies and sources, after all ..." Terian lowered his head. "Silence ... not generally good from one dragon. When you're getting it from all of them, and all their lesser kin ..." He blew air out of pale blue lips. "It's worrying, let's put it that way."

"Well, he wouldn't be the first ally to abandon us of late," Cyrus said a little acidly.

Terian looked pained. "I heard about Danay. I didn't think he'd do that, honestly, but ..."

"But it was a possibility in your mind?" Vara asked.

"Everything is a possibility in my mind, lately," Terian said. "But every conversation I had with Nyad or others about the King suggested that with the exception of my own, he was possibly the least warm and loving father of all."

"True," Cyrus said. "This feels like something else other than fatherly regard. Pride, perhaps. Whatever it might be, it loses us an ally when we should all be steadfast in our opposition to the titans." He looked up at Terian. "Still, the fact that you stand with us ... and sent ... uh ... your ambassador to help us ..." He raised an eyebrow, trying to stay away from condemnation. "Well, I appreciate it, even if I didn't exactly expect the form that help took."

Terian turned quite serious. "She helped me with the Sovereignty in invaluable ways. And when she did what she did to you, she was in a difficult spot—"

"She was a traitorous whore," Vara pronounced with sheerest loathing, "and the only positions she was in were on her back, and astride—"

"Let's not," Cyrus said, grimacing, "get into exhaustive detail." He paused. "My regards to her nonetheless." He tried to ignore the scandalized look in Vara's eyes. "She saved our lives."

"She owed you considerably more than that for the gift of the scar that graces your lower back and that still seems to ache in moments of exertion—"

"There's an argument and I'm not part of it," Terian mused idly, "I feel like I've done something wrong."

"I have another question for you," Cyrus said, changing the subject. "Uhm … about your armor, err … Alaric. Has he ever …" Cyrus took a deep breath, "… appeared to you, in, say … the Tower of the Guildmaster?"

Terian's eye bucked upward, then settled as he went from surprise to amused resignation in the space of a few heartbeats. "He appeared to you, too, huh?" He nodded, now resolute. "That makes sense. It'd be the two of us, I guess."

"Oh, you're both so very special," Vara said acidly.

"Well, I think we just need more help than you," Terian said.

"You're about to need help of the sort only a healer can render—"

"What did he say to you?" Cyrus asked.

Terian blushed a deeper navy. "He … encouraged me … taught me to be a paladin, actually, in those moments." He reached back, slowly, and pulled the black axe from behind him, then muttered something under his breath as it flamed to life, drawing a gasp from Vara. "He taught me this."

"That bastard," Vara said, "pretty soon he'll be teaching that to everyone."

"You're still special," Terian said with a grin.

"Healer, you're going to be needed over here."

"Peace," Terian said, extinguishing the flame. He paused then nodded to Cyrus. "What did he tell you?"

"He reminded me I wasn't alone in the fight with Yartraak," Cyrus said simply, giving Vara a look that immediately caused her own to soften. "And more recently, someone else summoned me to the Tower while invoking his name—Terrgenden, the—"

"God of Justice," Terian breathed, nodding. "He's quite the fellow, isn't he?"

"And now *you* sup with gods?" Vara asked, under her breath. "This land has gone truly mad."

"I met him and Vidara both, actually," Terian said, drawing an even more ireful look from Vara. "She seemed nice, your goddess. They named you after her?"

Vara's eye twitched. "Yes."

"She seemed … calmer," Terian said. Vara's reply was lost under her breath.

"You think he's still alive, then?" Cyrus asked.

Terian seemed taken aback at that. "Actually, I thought I was having a delusion, but now that you're telling me you saw him in the exact same setting—and I assume he sort of … pulled you out of the middle of a battle going unfavorably?" Cyrus nodded. "Then yes, I think …" The white knight nodded, "… it stands to reason he's still alive, somewhere, somehow, though how he's doing this is a bit mystifying."

"Any idea what we should do about it?" Cyrus asked, the wind whipping around him.

"Have you thought about searching your quarters thoroughly?" Terian asked with a grin. "Maybe look under the bed?"

"I assure you, no one could have survived under there the last few months," Cyrus said, earning him a gauntleted slap to the upper arm from Vara that rang out under the grey afternoon sky.

"If he's appeared to us but is not showing up," Terian said with a shrug, "then I daresay he doesn't want to be found. And while trying to hunt a ghost through the countryside of Arkaria sounds like so much fun—stopping at every house, 'Hey, have you seen a man who can fade into insubstantial mist?' slamming of doors in your face, repeat endlessly—" He shrugged once more. "He's the Ghost. What he does is at least as mysterious as how he does it, and if he doesn't want to be found …"

"Then we're on our own, I suppose," Cyrus said.

"I think that might be how he wanted it," Terian said slowly, and when both Cyrus and Vara were looking at him, he went a little further. "Think about it … he was the Guildmaster of Sanctuary. While he was here, I might have always had somewhere to run back to, and while you were the General, you had essentially topped out on how far you could go in this guild." He gestured to the central tower somewhere hidden behind the wall at his back. "But now … well, look at us. You're the Lord of Perdamun, I'm the Sovereign, she's the Guildmaster's woman—" His grin broke loose and he received a slap of his own from Vara, hard across his vambraces, the metal clanking as he broke into laughter. "Kidding! Only kidding!" His smile disappeared. "We were in his shadow. But now …"

Cyrus stared at the dark elf, taking his meaning. He exchanged an uneasy look with Vara, all thought of reprisal for Terian's comment clearly struck from her mind by one that was causing worry lines to crease her brow. "So we really are on our own," Cyrus said, and this time no one answered, for none of them had one that gave them even the slightest feeling of reassurance.

75.

The knock at Cyrus's door sounded as he was almost ready to extinguish the torches for the night and call it an evening. The white silken sheers that stood in front of the four balconies in the Tower of the Guildmaster were wafting lightly in the wind. Vara was still absent, gone down to the foyer some hours earlier to "put in an appearance," as she had said it, kissing him before she had left. It had been necessary, he figured, for one of them to go, but he did not feel like putting on the brave face, not this evening, though at the sound of the knock he marshaled his reserves for that very purpose.

"Come in," he called, his armor still on, rising from the chair in the corner of the room as the door squeaked open down the thin slit of the stairway passage.

He waited where he stood, knowing full well that Vara would not have knocked unless she brought someone with her, and when he saw the green cloak and cowl, he relaxed a little. "Martaina," he said.

"Guildmaster," she said, oddly formal, looking around. Her eyes fixed on a white sheer as the wind caught it, and Cyrus struggled to remember if she had been here before.

"What can I do for you?" Cyrus asked, easing toward her, his armor making soft noises, metal boots scraping against the stone floor.

Her passage toward him was slower, with yet more reserve, hands threaded behind her back, but her eyes were clear as they took in the details of the tower around them. Her bow was absent and so were the blades she kept on her belt. It was a curious thing, seeing her like this, and he realized at last her bun of hair was freshly done, though poorly. "There's nothing you can do for me," she said, finally looking directly at him. "I've come to tell you … I'm leaving."

Cyrus felt as though a physical blow had struck him, as though he might teeter back and fall into the seat he'd just left. "Leaving? Now?"

"It seemed the time," Martaina said, voice a little hoarse.

"There are others that might be more opportune," Cyrus said, "such as when we have not just had funeral rites for—"

"I know full well how many we just said our farewells to," Martaina said with more than a little edge. "I trained those rangers myself, two of them from farmers with no skill, one from a simple shop clerk in a small town, and the other three from little experience." She did not blink. "And of course I knew all the others, though two better than most." She bowed her head. "And one of them I had known almost all his life."

Cyrus blinked, looking up. "You knew Thad since …?"

"Since when he was a child," she said succinctly, "and I was most definitely not."

Cyrus let the quiet hang between them as he digested that. "Where … would you go?"

"Amti," she said simply. "Gareth is there for a reason. Amti is the place in Arkaria most like where we were raised." She drew her arms up across her chest, cradling her own elbows. "I see in that jungle the seeds of olden days, the days of my childhood long gone. I see people in need of hunters—"

"We need you here," Cyrus said.

"I have nothing more to give to Sanctuary," Martaina said simply, "and if I stay, I will be hollowed out and left as empty as I heard Terian once accuse you of being." She met his gaze with something akin to guilt. "I will be on hand to help as I can between now and the end of this present crisis with the titans, because it benefits my new home, but after that …" Her voice faded, and she made her retreat, pausing at the top of the steps, "seek me no more, for you will not find me willing to return to this place."

Cyrus tried to find some words to say, some small comfort, even something so little as *I know how you feel*, but he found it rang false in his mind. He faltered, and she lingered only a moment longer, then retreated as silently as ever, shutting the door so expertly he was not even sure she was gone until he walked up to the edge of the dark of the stairs and checked for himself.

76.

The Council Chambers were once more marked with quiet on the following morning, an air of mourning still hanging over them. Cyrus wondered if it would ever lift again, but seeing only a few days separated them from the event itself, he did not dare to call into question the finite nature of grief, instead tending toward more prosaic matters—even the ones that were not at all pleasant to contemplate.

"Martaina, too?" Erith's shocked whisper penetrated the silence. Dark clouds were gathered outside the windows behind Cyrus, and the torches and hearth burned with quiet warmth that he found himself deeply grateful for. "Gods, we're losing the old guard quickly now."

"Yes," Vara said, "with the exception of Curatio, I am the longest-serving member of the Council now." She shook her head. "Next in line stand Cyrus, Vaste and J'anda."

"I'm olllllllllld!" Vaste cried, leaning his head back. "Why, I'm practically the Elder at this point."

"You've been an officer for five years," J'anda said, a little nonplussed.

"The same could be said of our esteemed Guildmaster," Vaste said, pointing at Cyrus, "and just look how it's aged him!"

Cyrus suddenly longed for a mirror. "I ... uh ..." He looked at Vara and lowered his voice to a whisper. "Am I really that aged?"

"Like a good cheese, dear," she said, "better with time and all that."

"Or possibly just rank like one," Ryin muttered with a wry smile that was the first bit of good humor that Cyrus could recall in the chamber in days.

The laughter echoed over the empty seats between them. "Shall we discuss the business at hand?" Longwell asked once it had faded.

"How are the Emerald Fields doing?" Cyrus asked.

"The recovery proceeds," Longwell said, now a little stiffer. "We're almost two months on from the attack now, and with our troops matched by Terian's, I think our survivors are sleeping rather soundly at the moment. The crop is in, and it was bountiful, so I believe the mourning period after the attack is … more or less over for those not directly affected, of course." He lowered his head. "The threat, is, however, still present, somewhere beyond those mountains to the south."

"I should visit soon," Cyrus said, feeling a bit stiff about it. "I owe Administrator Tiernan my thanks for giving Terian leave to make the move that saved our lives." He nodded to Mendicant and Vara. "And I should inspect the troops, seeing how anyone stationed down there is in the most immediate harm from both elf and titan."

"The elves aren't going to do a damned thing," Vaste said.

Cyrus raised an eyebrow. "I was very certain of that as well, until recently, but then a thousand arrows pointed at my head reduced that quaint notion to vapor."

"Yes, but that was before Terian humiliated Danay in his own throne room," Vaste said. "Now I have to believe that the dark elves have attained their place firmly at the top of his hierarchy of anger."

"He did somewhat give his word that he was going to let us slip on this," Vara said, showing a little anger of her own, "though I would not suspect he will be forgiving or forgetting any of this anytime soon."

"As well he shouldn't," Cyrus said, leaning back in his chair, all his energy for matters at hand nearly gone. "For I certainly won't be doing either anytime soon, and I expect if an opportunity presents itself for him to strike back at us without causing himself undue inconvenience—or an invasion of dark elves—he'll do it in a second."

"But for the moment," Vaste said, "we have peace! Lovely, lovely peace! Except for the titans. And possibly the dragons." he ticked them off on his fingers. "And are the humans still mad at us? I can never tell, it changes so quickly …"

"At least the trolls like us now," Cyrus said with a smirk.

"Some of them, perhaps," Vaste said, giving him a sidelong look. "Some of us are still not so keen on you, Lord of Perdamun."

"What do we do next?" J'anda asked, tapping his staff against the table. "It seems ill-advised to simply wait and see if the dragons take some form of action."

"Short of a full-scale invasion of the south over the mountains," Cyrus said, shaking his head, "I'm not sure there's much else we can do at the moment." He glanced at Curatio's empty chair. "And while that's certainly an option, I'd rather wait and see if the solution we paid so heavy a price to effect has any … well, effect." That settled the room into a quiet, and Cyrus nodded at the empty seat to his right. "Has anyone seen Curatio since the shrine?"

"Since the fiery, icy, rock-flinging slaughter, you mean?" Vaste asked, letting the sarcasm drip. "Why, no, no I haven't. I can't imagine what he'd be doing other than perhaps mourning and recovering some of that eternal life that he spent to save all of the rest of us."

"I feel like I should check on him," Cyrus said, waving a hand to silence the troll. "Meeting adjourned, provided there's nothing else—"

"I was thinking of having a memorial marker carved for the recent dead," Erith said. "Just something we could place in the corner outside the cemetery."

Cyrus paused, hands flat on the table, prepared to scoop his helm off the wooden surface to leave. "That sounds … like a wonderful idea," he said, guilt suddenly ripping through him unexpectedly. It started a churning in his stomach, a weak sense of inadequacy, like he was far, far too small for the chair he was seated in, a child in the middle of it, really.

Cyrus forced himself to rise quickly, thumping the table with fumbling hands as he gathered his helm to him. "All right, that's it for today, then." He smiled weakly and made for the door, reaching it before anyone else did. He heard the footsteps behind him and did not close it, instead hurrying on and up the steps to the level of the officer quarters.

He had made it nearly down the hall to Curatio's quarters when Vara came out of the staircase behind him. "What the hell are you doing?" she asked, hissing into the empty hallway.

Cyrus turned and held a finger to his lips. "I'm checking on Curatio," he lied, just a little. He was checking on the healer, though that was hardly all.

"What happened back there?" she asked, lowering her voice as she approached.

Vaste emerged from the stairwell behind her. "Don't mind me," he said, steering around Vara, "I'm just going to go back to my quarters. Feel free to have a loud argument about your feelings just outside my door, I won't judge. Much."

Vara let out a long breath. "Why must you vex me so?"

"Hey, you're in my hallway," Vaste said.

"My quarters are right over there," Vara said, pointing at her door.

"No, yours are one floor up," Vaste said, pointing at the ceiling. "I haven't seen you down here for anything other than the purposes of getting some of your festive shoes in months."

Cyrus frowned. "Festive ... shoes?"

"Oh, is this where the argument is being held?" J'anda asked, thumping along with his staff in hand as he emerged from the stairwell. "Try to keep it down; I need a nap."

"I'm just here to check on Curatio," Cyrus said, more than a little annoyed.

"Well, after that, do try to make it upstairs before the fight begins, eh?" J'anda asked, yawning as he passed by a torch, causing the flame to flutter.

"There's not going to be a fight," Cyrus said.

"Oh, I beg to differ," Vaste said, easing past him. "And it'll probably be loud and filled with screaming—"

"I say we turn our combined irritation on this lump," Vara said, locking eyes with Cyrus and tilting her head toward Vaste.

"I have to check on Curatio," Cyrus said, the irritation bleeding out of his voice as he walked the last steps to the healer's door. He knocked his knuckles solidly against the wood, holding back just a little on the first rap. He waited, and so did the others, listening, and when he heard no movement, he raised his hand to knock again.

"Put some effort into it this time, will you?" Vaste asked, moving over. "Like this—"

He and Cyrus slammed the door at once, Cyrus's hand open and flat, Vaste's enormous knuckles bigger than a small melon. Their combined strength pushed hard enough against the door that it opened, squeaking as it did so, to reveal—

"Goddess," Vara breathed as she looked inside.

Absolutely nothing.

There was a chair, and a desk, and a bed, and a hearth with no sign of a recent fire. The torches snapped to life as Cyrus crossed the threshold, but there was nary a sign of clothing, nor books, for the shelves and armoire were utterly bare. There was not even a hint that the quarters were lived in, not for days, and as the four of them quietly searched for some sign of life, and the silence stretched into the minutes until they were done, Cyrus's heart sank lower and lower, until the inescapable conclusion was reached by all, but given voice by J'anda.

"He's gone," the enchanter said, and the mournful tone in the empty quarters settled upon them as surely as the complete lack of life had settled on this place, where the oldest among them had once lived.

77.

In the wake of Curatio's departure, the days settled in a hard pattern of council meetings and silence, the slow pull of time dragging them unerringly forward. Cyrus felt each day's passage most acutely. The long days passed into months, and autumn turned to winter, and the year they were in departed to be replaced by another, and then spring settled on the Plains of Perdamun. The time he spent with Vara was the easiest, but she busied herself with her duties, taking up some of the considerable responsibilities left by the loss of so many officers.

Cyrus himself found, if anything, less responsibility on his shoulders. Sanctuary was at alert, but not actively at war. The army was on guard but not in the midst of any expeditions which required planning nor deployments other than to the Emerald Fields and the occasional march through the Plains of Perdamun as a show of force for the locals; no threats presented themselves, not even bandits, and thus Cyrus left the business of marching with the armies to Longwell, his newly appointed General.

He had a made a few such appointments with the approval of the Council—Calene Raverle had taken over as informal leader of the rangers, much to her surprise. She had shown some reservations, her tentativeness plain and fears of the sort of job she might do as obvious as the blond hair on Vara's head. Since taking over, though, Calene had done fine work, carrying on Martaina's training program with an enthusiastic eye toward aim improvement among the archers.

Scuddar In'shara had reluctantly taken up the post of Castellan and had seen to the defense of Sanctuary itself with an uncompromising eye toward the security of the place. He was quiet as ever, but his orders were crisp and clear when given, and there was no mistaking his ever-present watch on the walls and the foyer, when the portal was open. He stood up front of any guard group he headed, his robes billowing about him, his scimitar always at the ready.

The other appointment taken up by one of the council had been met with nearly as much enthusiasm as the other three; Vaste had been forced into the position of the keeper of the Halls of Healing, something he bitterly complained about on every occasion Cyrus encountered him.

"Is there something about me that would indicate that I might enjoy sitting inside every single day, waiting for idiots who have sprained their ankles whilst walking the grounds, so incompetent that they cannot even manage their footing on flat plains, to come in so that I might heal them?" His belligerence might have met with a more sympathetic audience in that Council meeting had he not stood up and tripped over his chair while exiting the room not five minutes later. There were many guffaws as Erith healed him back into consciousness, but Cyrus could not help but feel that the troll had missed the lesson entirely.

And so Cyrus's days were spent in the Tower of the Guildmaster or in the Council Chambers, largely alone, reading when he could find it in himself to concentrate and brooding quietly when he could not. Vara was out on some detail, he recalled, taking up the tasks that Curatio had handled as Elder. He had it in his mind to appoint her to the post, and felt the Council would approve as soon as a little more time had elapsed. For his part, Cyrus did not believe that Curatio would return; the healer's disagreement with the attack on the shrine stuck in Cyrus's mind like a chicken bone in the throat. If the healer's quarters only had been cleaned out of all possessions, he might have believed that a return could be in order. However, Curatio's office in the Halls of Healing, with its thick volumes of journals that the elf had amassed over his long lifetime of experience, had also been emptied. To Cyrus's mind an endeavor of the scale required to move those books suggested that Curatio would not be returning soon, if ever.

And so Cyrus sat in the Council Chambers on this day, some six months removed from the Elder's departure, this one like so many other unremarkable ones that had passed in that interval, in his chair, helm on the table at his side, taking his breaths slowly and watching the light slowly fade from the day as he awaited Vara's eventual return

... Or dinner, perhaps. Whichever comes first.

The smoky aroma of the hearth burning to keep the light spring touch of the plains at bay seeped into his very pores. After a long day spent in the Council Chambers, Cyrus would often find the smell of that faint smoke on his skin. He had never noticed until Vara had pointed it out to him after one of their trysts—the only thing he could seem to find energy for at present. Since then he had scarcely been able to avoid noting it on all occasions, though it did not remind him of home as much as it might once have.

Cyrus took a breath, the taste of his luncheon from hours earlier still on the back of his tongue, the sourdough bread hot from the ovens coupled with sliced beef and fresh vegetables. His eyes traced their way over the deserted chamber until he heard footsteps outside, straightening up just slightly in anticipation, hoping they would come his way rather than fade up the stairs to the officer quarters.

He was not disappointed when the door slid open a moment later and Mendicant scampered in, robes trailing against the stone floor with a quiet swish. The goblin shut the door behind him and paused as he caught a glimpse of Cyrus in darkness and shadowed by the light beyond the balcony windows. Mendicant gasped slightly, causing Cyrus to stare at him in curiosity until the wizard let out a sigh of relief. "Oh. Sorry. It's just you."

"You were expecting someone else?" Cyrus asked. "Sitting in the Guildmaster's chair, wearing my armor?"

"I didn't know it was your armor without the helm," Mendicant said, taking a couple steps forward, claws dragging the floor. "You looked like, uh ... well ..."

"You thought I was Alaric?" Cyrus asked with a faint smile.

"For just a second," Mendicant said hastily. "No insult intended—"

"On the contrary," Cyrus said, "I take it as a compliment. What brings you into these deathly quiet chambers in the absence of a meeting, Mendicant? Looking to commune with ... ghosts?" A trace of sadness leaked out as Cyrus spoke.

"No," Mendicant said, shaking his head, "I was bound for the archives." He pointed with a thin, clawed finger to the door on Cyrus's right, tucked away next to the hearth.

Cyrus frowned at the door; he had seldom been inside, and indeed, often forgot about the room entirely. "Huh. What are you looking for in there?"

"I go in there from time to time to read old passages about the formation of the guild," Mendicant said. "To seek the wisdom of the past in reading about the trials they went through in those days."

"There were less than two hundred people in Sanctuary when I joined," Cyrus said, looking at the goblin with a sense of amusement, "and now we have more than twenty thousand, even with the recent losses. I'm not sure what wisdom you'd find there about running a guild of this size."

"Oh, there is much to be found in there," Mendicant said, his voice filled with quiet awe. "The notes that were kept on the Council meetings of old were extensive, and I find it interesting to go back and read about the great debates of the day. The names of the founders stick with me, and it's almost as though I can hear their voices in these walls as I read. Cora, Pradhar, Erkhardt—" Cyrus felt a strange tingle at this name, a prickling at the back of his neck that he did not entirely know the origin of, "Alaric and Raifa. They founded something that exists to this day, and stronger than when each of them left it." Mendicant rubbed his palms together. "They were the origin of a tradition that has stepped forth to protect Arkaria from so many threats over the years, threats that no one else would have, or could have dealt with."

Cyrus opened his mouth to argue, to balance the scales with their failures in Luukessia and elsewhere, but shut his mouth just as quickly. *Why debate? It's pointless. Let him have his illusions, let him believe that we are some great good instead of a force that occasionally and unwittingly causes harm in the process of doing good.* "It's good to have respect for the traditions, I guess," he said instead.

"These were men and women of integrity," Mendicant said, possibly not even hearing Cyrus at this point, so deep was he in his lionization of the past, "with singular vision. To even meet Lady Cora was such an honor as I cannot describe."

Cyrus felt a twinge in his eyelid. "Yes, she's quite something, that one. And I can see why she and Alaric got on so famously as to start a guild together."

"I sense sometimes there are things missing from the record," Mendicant went on, "as though there is a gap in the meetings—"

Cyrus frowned. "What are you talking about?"

"There are references to people that are scrawled over in the journals," Mendicant said, making a popping noise in the back of his throat. "Covered with smudges of ink too dense to read, but that fail to bleed through onto the back of the pages."

"Sounds like magic," Cyrus said with an ironic smirk.

"Perhaps," Mendicant said, though he sounded unsure. "Magic is certainly an element I felt I understood well before I arrived here. But since seeing Lord Soulmender's efforts—"

"Who?" Cyrus asked.

"Oh, uh," Mendicant said, looking greatly abashed, "Lord Soulmender. You know ..."

Cyrus blinked, searching his memory for that name, which did sound vaguely familiar. "I ... uh ..."

"Curatio," Mendicant whispered under his breath.

"Right," Cyrus said, squeezing his eyes tight. "I sometimes forget that he had adopted a surname, he uses it so little."

"Since seeing his magic at work, so expansive," the goblin said hungrily, "so different from what even we wizards, the most powerful offensive spellcasters, can achieve ... it has redefined everything for me. I am afraid I must confess to some feelings of guilt in the wake of his departure ..."

"Lot of that going around," Cyrus said. "But why do you feel guilty?"

"I hounded him," Mendicant said, head bowed. "I asked him many, many questions about the nature of magic, most of which he declined to say anything about save for, 'I cannot answer that,' but a few which expanded my knowledge in other directions. For every answer he gave or did not give, I felt ten more questions spring up, and thus ..." He paused, and his voice fell, "... I feel I may have led to his departure."

"Pfft," Cyrus said so dismissively that Mendicant's head snapped up in surprise. "You were no more guilty of driving off Curatio with questions than you are of teaching me a fire spell simply because you mouthed the words in front of me." Mendicant blanched and Cyrus waved a hand to absolve him. "There were other things going on with Curatio, things in his mind and arguments he had with me that weighed on him, I think. Do you recall last year when he resigned as acting Guildmaster, that fit of temper he had in Council?"

"I ... was not an officer then," Mendicant said.

"Right. I forget these things," Cyrus said. "He had a full-on blaze of emotion come burning out of him like a gout of flame off one of you wizards. And he's looked wearier and wearier over the last few months." Cyrus shook his head. "You ask me, he hit his limit, either with the matters of we child races, or simply with my failure to listen to his good advice." Cyrus felt the burn of shame on his cheeks. "Either way, the fault is not yours, I don't think. There are far too many other more likely culprits."

"You are kind to say so," Mendicant said, bowing. There was a pause before next he spoke. "What are you doing here in the dark, if I might ask, Lord Davidon?"

Cyrus looked around the room, the torches not yet lit, only the hearth's faint glow for light. "I think I'm brooding."

"... You *think* you are? Do you not know?"

"I'm afraid to call it such," Cyrus said. "I don't know why; perhaps it's my upbringing in the Society, where they eschewed the idea of pensive reflection entirely in favor of seeking out and killing all that vexes you in the name of Bellarum. Alaric was good at brooding, though, sitting quietly in a dark room and mentally attacking even the impossible problems. Yes, I think I'm brooding," he finished.

"If Lord Garaunt embraced this as a strategy of life," Mendicant said, rather delicately, "then why do you hesitate to embrace it for yourself?"

"Because I'm not Alaric," Cyrus said, and with the words came a weight off of him, a most curious one at that. "I'm not as good as him," he went on, finding each additional statement carried its own relief, "I'm not as virtuous, or honorable—which is why I'm not a paladin, I suppose, leaving aside the lack of magic—I don't lead nearly as well or wisely, and I contemplate darker solutions to these wars and enemies than Alaric ever would have considered." He stared at the door behind Mendicant as the hearth crackled. "I'm somewhere between where I started and where Alaric would have me, I suspect; too dark to be truly virtuous, too held down by virtue to be a great warrior—or warlord at this point, I suppose is what the doctrine of war would call a man of my position. Too dirty to be called clean, too clean to be properly dirty. It's a vexing thing, being a man in the middle. Even Terian is now more assured of his place than I am."

Mendicant's face was a confused frown, lips all askew. "It is a bad thing to be open to good change?"

Cyrus laughed. "I don't ... I don't know, actually. I suppose I'm torn because I look at the problems facing Sanctuary and ... even if I were as noble and virtuous as Alaric, I don't see an answer to our current dilemmas down his path, at least not one that wouldn't result in so many dead as to defy the counting."

"And what do you see down the other path?" Mendicant asked. "Down the path of the warlord?"

"Death," Cyrus said grimly. "Abundant death and war ... but I also see, perhaps, an end somewhere down there."

"It would be ... easy, I think," Mendicant said, "to tell you that an end down that road is a mirage, for perhaps it is not."

"It's not," Cyrus said darkly. "Wiping out your enemies to the last man is a fairly definitive end, at least to that conflict."

"Those are deeds that would blacken the soul, though, are they not?" Mendicant asked.

"They are," Cyrus said. "Deeds worthy of a warlord, and not a paladin." *Which I am not in any case.*

"I am but a simple goblin," Mendicant said, and Cyrus detected no falseness in the modesty he presented, "and I come from a place of ... well, you knew Enterra. Low brutality and repressive means ... the Imperium was all darkness, and not just from being underground. When I grew up there, I saw those examples presented—the guards with their unending violence, unwilling to take so much as an ounce of disrespect without answering it with furious reprisal. It gave me an example, which was what they wanted, but of exactly what I did not want to be." His eyes flicked up. "It seems to me, Lord Davidon, there is no shame in leaving behind your raising to embrace what you want to be rather than who you were taught to be."

"There's no victory there," Cyrus said quietly. "Not down that road." *His road.*

"Is the other victory—the one down the path of the warlord, the one wherein you slaughter every titan to the last woman and child ... is this a victory you want?" Mendicant asked. "Because if so ... then I would say your answer is already evident, and your path ... is most assuredly set." He shuddered, his green, scaly skin catching the orange reflection from the hearth. "But I do not think it is a path that even your army would follow willingly ... or that you would, if I may say."

"I certainly had the seeds planted in me," Cyrus said, thinking of moments in the Society when he was told to kill, forced to harm, cheered to it, without guilt or remorse.

"Perhaps, when you were a child," Mendicant said, and now he was easing toward the door to the archive. "But now are you are a man, and have the ability to choose what grows within you—what seeds to plant, as it were." He bowed his head in respect. "Good evening, Lord Davidon." And he went to open the door.

"I think some of that wisdom of the founders might be rubbing off on you, Mendicant," Cyrus called after him.

"I can think of no better reason to immerse myself in these texts, then," Mendicant said and shut the door to do exactly that, leaving Cyrus with slightly lighter thoughts than he'd had when the goblin came in.

78.

Vara found Cyrus in the Tower of the Guildmaster later that night. There was a look of exhaustion upon her face as she came in, already unfastening her armor before the door was closed. She made a face as she slipped out of her boots, and they clanked as they fell over on the stairs, and she did not bother to pick them up.

"Long day?" Cyrus asked.

"As long as any other, I suppose, though it felt longer," she said, dropping her breastplate and backplate on the ground. He eyed her tight-clinging shirt, damp with sweat. "I just marched to Prehorta and back without benefit of a horse."

Cyrus frowned. "I didn't know you were going on a march. I would have accompanied you."

"I was not intending to," she said, slipping out of her greaves, the chainmail she wore beneath her armor already hanging around her waist, ready to fall to the ground. "But I got a bit caught up in talking with members of a patrol heading out on a routine trip to outlying villages from the next portal north. Soon enough, I found myself marching with them."

"You? Conversing like a normal person?" Cyrus asked. "Did you cast offensive spells at any of them?"

"No, nor even any offensive words," she said, her voice light despite her obvious fatigue. "I did, however, listen to them—their worries, their complaints, their hopes for the future."

Cyrus just stared at her. "I'm waiting for the other boot to drop." He looked past her. "Not yours, not literally, as both of those have clearly toppled over, but figuratively ..."

"I'm doing my best," she said earnestly, the chainmail clattering as it fell around her ankles and she stepped out of it, making her way to the room in the corner where the toiletry was kept, and turning the faucet to unleash a spattering flow of water just out of Cyrus's sight.

"I know you are," Cyrus said, still a little amazed. "Did you learn anything of note?"

"Most of our guildmates are concerned about the lack of expeditions and how it will affect their purses in the long run," Vara called from just inside the door as her soiled shirt flew out and landed on the floor outside. Her pants followed with her next statement. "But the Luukessians, of course, are concerned about the security of Emerald Fields, and most of the Arkarians are tied enough to our brethren from across the sea to be worried as well. All want a solution to this southern conflict, though, be they goblin, elf, human or dark elf."

"Of course," Cyrus muttered as he heard her step under the running water. She let out a sharp intake of breath at the temperature, and he could hear the subtle change in sound as it began to land on her skin rather than on the stone floor.

He waited quietly for her in his chair, probing at the padding atop the arms, wondering if Alaric had been the one to buy this particular furnishing or if it was too stylish to have been his decision. Vara came out of the door a few minutes later, her hair wrung out and snaking over her shoulder, faint hints of moisture still hanging about her fair skin where the towel had missed its mark. "I was left with quite a bit of time to think on this journey, of course," she said, stark naked.

"And what did you think about?" Cyrus asked, not wanting to move his eyes.

"Us," she said, walking across the floor somewhat daintily for her. She circumnavigated around the bed and knelt before him, which surprised him more than a little as she placed her elbows on his knees and stared up at him from between his legs. "The future."

He blinked. "And what did you think about, *vis-à-vis* this future of ours?"

She steadied her gaze, and took a breath. "I think we should marry."

Cyrus could not help but blink again. Then once more. And yet again. "This is an odd thing."

"That I have just proposed marriage?" she asked, cocking her own eyebrow at him.

"Well, you've certainly chosen an interesting way to go about it," he said, glancing once, surreptitiously, down at her nakedness. "Effective, too, I would think—"

"Don't be an arse," she teased.

"I'm sorry," Cyrus said, drumming fingers nervously along the arm of the chair where the wood met padding, "the timing feels strange. I know it's been over half a year, but it feels like just yesterday we had rather a lot of funerals."

"That's actually what got me thinking about it," she said, lowering her gaze to somewhere in the vicinity of his breastplate. "We have no family but ourselves, really—"

Cyrus felt the frown crease his forehead again. "You have a sister."

Vara blew out an exasperated breath. "Right. Yes. Well, of course we could invite her as well, but my point, if I might make it, is that you and I, on a day to day basis, are somewhat alone outside of the members of this guild as our family."

"True," Cyrus said. He had been feeling that exact sensation most acutely since the death of Andren, something he felt keenly in moments of quiet like he'd had on this night. *On every day since it happened, really.*

"I feel like we have circled each other for long enough," Vara said, and he could tell she had very specific points in mind that she had perhaps practiced rehearsing for this very moment. "For years. Enough to know each other well—as well as can be expected, especially over these last months, when we found that truly, we are quite compatible—"

"I love you, too."

She gave him a faux dangerous look at the interruption. "Do you want to marry me or not?"

"Since you asked so nicely," Cyrus said with a smirk that dared the danger even further. He took a breath and let it out. "Of course I want to marry you." She relaxed slightly in clear relief and slid a little further up. "You didn't think I was going to say no, did you?"

"Well, you could have been a little less dramatic about it," she said accusingly as she sat on his leg and wrapped her arms around his neck.

"Said the woman who crouched naked between my legs and

proposed marriage. Not very subtle, dear—"

A thundering knock came at the door, and both of them stiffened in surprise. Vara slid from his grasp easily and he watched her go, sliding into the bed and covering herself before he allowed himself to shout, "Enter!"

The door opened and shut quickly, and the sound of leather boots on the steps was short as the messenger climbed the stairs and presented herself in mere seconds.

"Cora?" Cyrus asked, standing, small droplets of water that Vara had left behind on his armor showering off at his quick motion. "What are you doin—"

"There is no time," Cora said, breathless from the climb, holding her side. She looked directly at Cyrus, and the urgency in her voice told him what had happened even before she finished speaking. "The titans. They're coming.

"Now."

79.

The alarm was sounding, ringing through the towers and halls as Cyrus descended with Cora at his side, his call taken up by already vigilant listeners at every level who had perhaps seen Cora tear by on her way to get him. Vara was surely not far behind, but he had left her to dress in order to get the jump on this crisis. He silenced Cora as she began to explain, allowing her to tell him nothing until the officers were assembled. They surged into the Council Chambers and waited, the doors open, and Cyrus called out to each officer as they passed on the stairwell, the room slowly filling up as they came in.

"Sit there," Cyrus told Cora, pointing her to Andren's seat without thought. He cringed as she took it, irritated at himself for his thoughtless direction.

"Where are the titans now?" Vara asked as she breezed in with Erith and Vaste, the last of the officers that they had been waiting for. Her wet hair was laid over her shoulder, water still dripping down her breastplate. The torches flickered at her speedy entry, striding to her place at Cyrus's left, none of the coyness she had exhibited to him only five minutes earlier present anywhere in her bearing. She was paladin now and officer, not lover or would-be wife, and he smiled faintly at the beautiful contradiction he saw there.

"They are approaching Amti in force," Cora said, her usual calm clearly disrupted. "One of our small groups of hunters went missing on a ranging. They have been gone for days."

"The titans got them, then," Vaste said.

"They have been coming deeper into the jungle all the time," Cora said, "since their failure at the pass."

"So nothing from the dragons, then?" Erith asked, utterly

crestfallen.

"No," Cora said, shaking her head. "The titans are still fully attending to their northern interests, presumably building up their supply lines for a northern push ... and I would imagine having Amti at their backs, able to strike at their stores, is something of a slight inconvenience."

"Not slight enough to ignore, though," Longwell said, doing a little head-shaking of his own. "This is about to be it for you lot. Best get to evacuating."

"We will not leave," Cora said stiffly.

"If you stay, you die," Longwell said simply, shrugging his shoulders. "Trust me, I know it's hard. I've had these very discussions with Administrator Tiernan in the Emerald Fields; if you value the lives of your people, you'll move out of the way of the damned near unquenchable enemy, because their thirst for violence is like nothing I've ever seen, even from implacable death."

"We will not abandon our homes," Cora said.

"It was nice knowing you, then," Longwell said sarcastically, adding a short salute.

"Can we defend them?" Cyrus asked, just throwing the question out.

"No," Longwell said before he finished.

"Maybe," Mendicant said.

Every face in the chambers turned to the goblin. "How?" Longwell asked. "We can't get a force onto the savanna; even J'anda's little gambit to bring titans into the dragon shrine nearly got wiped out by—"

"We can teleport directly to Amti," Mendicant said nervously, his eyes dancing around the table's top. "They have druids that can bring a couple spellcasters in at a time with return spells by putting ourselves in closest physical proximity to them—"

"Uncomfortably close, some of us might say," Vaste said with a cocked eyebrow.

Mendicant continued. "We set up a simple chain, bringing in a few spellcasters at a time to Amti, letting them anchor their souls, and then having them cast their teleport spell to bring them back to the great seal in the foyer. They take a couple more spellcasters, until all our spellcasters are bound in Amti—"

"That's insane," Ryin said, leaning forward, eyes wide. "If Amti falls, the quickest route out is a wizard teleport spell spread over a wide area, and the widest radius teleport spell is the one that returns you to your point of binding. If you execute this particular plan, all our spellcasters will be bound in a place being torn apart by the titans. They'll be trapped; unable to escape, save for the druids and wizards who can cast their own teleportation elsewhere."

"It's not without risks, certainly," Mendicant said with a shrug, "but the question was 'Can we defend them'? The answer is 'yes.'"

Cyrus cast Vara a look and was met with a somewhat stricken one in return. "He is right," she said. "On all counts. This is perhaps the most dangerous strategy we have ever embraced. There will be no effective retreat from this."

"And defending a people that are mad and choosing to stay there," Longwell said.

"We've fought gods," Vaste said dismissively. "Did we have a possibility of escape when we fought Mortus, trapped in his realm? Or Yartraak, when we were stuck in Saekaj?"

"These are long odds," Longwell said cautiously. "I'm not above nasty battle, but if we're already counting dear our losses, this idea will cost us more. Sure and certain."

"Can we even defend them when we get there?" Cyrus mused. "The whole of the army of the titans in the Gradsden Savanna, probably pouring toward Amti even now?" A faint desperation clawed at his thoughts.

"It would be the sort of battle an adherent of Bellarum would charge into with sword held high, I would think," J'anda said, his eyes sparkling faintly.

"It is the sort of battle that a paladin would go into believing that even the hopeless causes should be fought for," Mendicant said, looking at Vara. "Am I wrong?"

"You are not wrong," Vara said, giving the goblin a nod. "Not at all."

And so it comes down to this, Cyrus thought, his mind aswirl. *Two choices before me, to stay and let them die, or to fight and lead us to almost certain death ...*

The bloodthirsty warrior would fight for the sake of it, and the paladin would fight to protect the people. Two paths, and both lead the same direction.

Who am I? The question whispered through his mind unbidden. Either way, the answer was the same.

"This is to be utterly voluntary," Cyrus said, and he could feel the blood draining out of his face. "Pass the word that no one need come unless they are prepared to die in the south, with no hope of revival." He looked at Mendicant. "Even with your plan, how long will it take to get our army down there in its entirety?"

"Days," Mendicant said. "Accounting for magical regeneration, the sheer number of spells we'd have to cast, and—and you'd have nearly no magical support during the period we're bringing people in, which would leave the army—"

"Vulnerable," Cyrus whispered.

"Fighting titans without healers or aid of magic?" Vara asked, her own eyes wide. "That's putting it a bit mildly."

"No one but volunteers," Cyrus said, shaking his head. "If I find out any person coming on this has been coerced in any way—"

"You'll what?" Vaste asked. "Kill the responsible parties? Assuming the titans don't do the job for you—or on you—"

"I'm going," Cyrus said, and he stood.

And every other officer in the room stood a second later.

"So that's how it's to be, then?" Cyrus asked, looking at each of them in awe, from J'anda, who nodded, his staff standing taller than he in his grasp, to Ryin, who held a look of flickering hesitation that turned into resolve before Cyrus's eyes, to Mendicant, holding himself high as he could, and Erith, whose shoulders were hunched in calm resolution. Longwell stood nearly at attention, his own lance threatening to put a gouge in the ceiling, and Vaste snatched his staff up and passed it between hands nervously.

"That's how it is, oh fearless guildmaster," Vaste said.

Cyrus turned his eyes to Vara, who stood at his side—and he at hers. "We await your command," she said with a nod.

"If this be our end," Cyrus said, "then let's make it one so grand and glorious that the titans whisper our names in fear for twenty generations." He favored them with one last look and his gaze settled on Cora, who stood now at last, in the middle of it all, the calm, watching eye as the storm passed around her. He saw something there, some approval perhaps, but it was buried under layers and years and came out in the form of the faintest nod. "Let's go to war."

80.

Cyrus's speech to the assembled guild was blessedly short, at least in his eyes, and well received, to no one's surprise but his. His preparation after that lasted only seconds and extended to telling Mendicant to travel to Emerald Fields and Saekaj to carry word of their actions to both their allies. With that, he clutched tightly to J'anda, freshly returned from binding in Amti with the aid of one of their druids, and he and Vara were carried back to the jungle with the enchanter sandwiched between them.

"She smells lovely," J'anda said, nodding his head over his shoulder at Vara as they separated in room entirely composed of wood. "You, though ... you smell like fire."

"I expect that's an omen of some sort," Cyrus said, looking around swiftly as more bursts of light came into being around them, the officers of Sanctuary arriving a few at a time either under their own power or clutching to spellcasters.

"It's not that I dislike you," Longwell was telling Ryin as the dragoon pulled himself awkwardly back from holding tight to the druid on one side while Calene Raverle let go of Ryin's back, "it's just a bit uncomfortable being as I don't feel like we're that ... uh ... close."

"Officers," Cyrus said, snapping them all to. The door opened on the far end of the room and Martaina entered, her bow in hand, her hair looking longer than he remembered and her eyes as dark as he'd ever seen them. The lack of sleep was apparent, and her cloak hung tight behind her as she entered. "Lady Ranger," he said.

She gave him a look of pure annoyance. "Don't be a jackass," she said. "You've known me for years, don't act all formal now, it's not the moment for it." She addressed them all quickly, her haggard appearance trickling down into her manner. "They're on the horizon, and they're making a very direct line for Amti. There's rather a lot of them—"

"How many?" Longwell asked.

"Thousands," Martaina said tightly. "Tens of, perhaps. Enough that our little traps and preparations won't but barely slow them."

"You set up traps?" Cyrus asked.

She favored him with a tired look. "I didn't have that many rangers to train here, so I looked down other avenues to cement my worth. There are small spike pits throughout the jungle, and some log traps made of vine and rope. Not enough to cause significant damage to these numbers; they were meant as a discouragement for casual wanderers."

"You know what I find is a discouragement to casual wanderers in whatever area I choose to be in?" Vaste asked.

"Casual nudity from a bellicose and frighteningly ugly troll?" Vara suggested.

"I'm going to show you my arse later," Vaste said. "Just for that. And you will look upon it and go, 'My, what a firm and supple arse. Perhaps I should have been nicer to Vaste for all these years, seeing as it's such a damned fine apple of an—'"

Cyrus rolled his eyes and kicked the troll lightly in the rump, knocking him off balance. "Enough of that. We've got a sizable battle laid out before us."

Vaste recovered, straightening his robes. "Of all the regrets you're going to take to your grave, not seeing this magnificent troll arse is going to work its way right to the top, I assure you."

"Oh, Vaste," Cyrus said, squeezing past him, "you've shown me your ass more times than I can count." He gestured to Martaina. "Show me what you've got."

He followed her wordlessly up the spiral inside of the tree. The walk seemed infinitely long and was made all the worse by the silence both in front of him from Martaina and behind him from the few officers and others following behind him. Every step on the grain of the wood sounded hollow, like he was being led to his doom, and it was curious, he thought, that he felt no dread at the prospect.

They came out atop the trees, hidden among branches and boughs that were tied off and arranged in such a way to allow this place to be used as a watch post over the canopy of the jungle. Cyrus followed Martaina's careful steps out onto the branches, and looked where she pointed, in the far distance, and saw immediately.

Trees shook as though mighty things were rattling them at their base. It did not worry Cyrus until he remembered the scale of the trees in this jungle. The line of their disturbance was massive, stretching for miles, and it centered entirely on one direction—the one that led to Amti.

"Here it comes," Cyrus said, Vara and Longwell easing up behind him. "How long?"

"Half an hour," Martaina said, "at most. But worse than that," she said with considerable sourness, "we have to fight at ground level."

"That's mad," Longwell said, shaking his head. "We need Falcon's Essence."

"Too few druids," Cyrus said.

"And not to mention that," Martaina said, "even if you do use it, if they cast a cessation spell on our defenders while we're attacking—"

"Splat. Battle over." Cyrus exchanged a look with Vara. "How many people will we have here in half an hour?"

Her lips went pale, pressed together hard as she allowed a moment to contemplate his answer. "Less than a thousand."

He looked to the sky and saw the sun beginning to set, then surveyed the jungle before him, with its myriad paths and utter lack of bridges or passes to make defense even marginally easier against the gargantuan titans. "This is either going to be a long night," Cyrus said, staring into the growing purple dusk, "or a very, very short one."

81.

The view from the ground was no more encouraging, certainly not with only a few hundred melee fighters spread out around the trunks of the large trees that comprised Amti. Cyrus stood between the tangled roots, wondering if the footing was even a quarter as inhospitable to the titans as it was for his army, and deciding that no, this was exponentially worse for the shorter party.

Gareth slid down the nearest tree trunk, his cloak acting as a sort of sled as he perfectly balanced the angle of the roots as it furled around. He sprang off and landed next to Cyrus, recovering his footing flawlessly as he came to stand next to the warrior.

"Five minutes or less," the ranger said, pulling his bow off his shoulder casually. "Your glorious battle is coming."

Cyrus eyed him. "I'm not convinced it's going to be all that glorious." The smell of greenery was in the air around them, and the jungle felt close and heavy, not quite steamy but only a few degrees off.

Gareth smiled. "Isn't your guild founded on these sorts of defenses? All give, no quit, fight to the last?"

"It's easy to say that, I suppose," Cyrus said, "and I've certainly professed it a time or two myself." He lowered his voice. "I don't even mind for my own sake, but ... leading these good people into death?" He shook his head. "Not much glory in that."

Gareth's face fell. "I convinced them to get as many children and non-combatants out as I could, but ... it's a low number."

"Every little bit helps," Cyrus said, pulling Praelior out of its scabbard and kicking at the edge of an exposed root that was almost as tall as he himself was.

"Your help is more than a 'little bit,'" Gareth said with a faint, fleeting smile. "It gives us a chance."

Cyrus chewed that one over as thoroughly as the dried meat he'd supped on a few minutes earlier. "I don't believe it does, not against these numbers." He nodded to the distance, where the sound of crashing through the underbrush could now be heard easily. "Unless they run right past, these odds are so long that even the most foolish gambler in Reikonos would fail to take them."

I believe in you, whispered a familiar voice, faintly, somewhere in the distance.

"What?" Cyrus jolted upright.

"I didn't say anything," Gareth said. "Couldn't think of anything *to* say to that."

They fell into silence, and once more Cyrus surveyed his impromptu army. Erith lurked by a tree trunk, hiding one of the hollows, barely peeking out. She was the only healer on the field of battle, and so far as he knew, the only one who had not bound herself here in Amti. She watched tentatively as the crescendo of noise approaching out of the west grew ever louder, and the battle lines of the Sanctuary army grew ever more restless. Weapons were clutched in hand, bows were nocked with arrows, and Vara drifted to Cyrus's side at the last, as he guessed they were no more than a minute from the first of the titans breaking through into sight.

"Are you sure about this?" she asked at a whisper.

He looked at her in surprise. "You're not?"

She smiled, both impish and sad in one. "It does rather put a halt to that marriage proposal, doesn't it?"

"I could marry you right here," he said with a smile of his own, "with battle as the backdrop. It'd be very 'Warlord of Bellarum,' really, almost a holy rite—"

"Yet somehow not exactly what I dreamed of in my youth on those exceedingly rare occasions when I contemplated my wedding day." Her expression softened as the crash of the underbrush grew to a pitch. "How did you imagine it?"

"I didn't back then," Cyrus said, staring into the dark of the canopy, no light coming in from above, his eyes only able to see via spellcraft. *Another thing I'll lose if they cast a cessation spell.* "I never once imagined it—which is probably why I jumped on the possibility so quickly with Imina." He smiled wanly. "The thought of relying on others ... it wasn't part of who I was back then, so the thought of sharing my life with someone ... well ..." He lowered his gaze. "It was a little too farfetched for me to believe." He took her hand. "But now? I can't imagine my life without you."

"That's so precious," Erith called from her place between the roots. "Kiss her already!"

Cyrus did, but it only lasted a second, perhaps a little less, before the warm, tenderness of her lips was pulled away as the first of the titans broke through the jungle into sight less than a hundred meters away.

82.

There was no exchange of wit when the titans came, no fiery repartee, words thrown and challenges made. The beasts from Kortran carried a branch at their fore with an elf tied upon it, both legs and an arm pinched off, almost limp within its bindings, but his remaining hand pointed out, croaking, "There … there …" directly at the trees of Amti.

The titans charged without hesitation, without pause, without mercy. Cyrus met them, as he always did, on the fore of the battle line, Praelior finding a knee above the metal boots of his first attacker. His attacker faltered at the strike, failing in his counterattack, an unarmed slap of the hand. The titan tumbled down and was stabbed through the face by Longwell.

A blast of force from Vara spit into the face of the next titan coming at Cyrus, slamming him back into a tree and splitting his skull with a mighty crack. He slid down the bark, dropping his prize of the elven hunter on the stake, and the poor man went face down in a root.

The ground was thick with roots, and it made for an uneven charge for the forces of Sanctuary, vaulting the living wood obstacles before them even as the titans walked easily over them. Cyrus found himself battling for breath as he took down his next foe, the titan hordes coming as exactly that—a horde, not lines of an army, led into the fight by a tortured man on a stake, with much cheering, like a hunt with near-wild dogs and men that Cyrus had once had the misfortune to witness.

Even now, the titan jeers filled the air in that peculiar language of theirs, full of glee and rage all at once. The smell of them was in the jungle air now as well, musty and deep, the first few dead adding their own particular scent to the early night air.

Cyrus severed a hand that reached for him, fighting furiously against all threats. Calene lanced an arrow into the face of that titan, sending him flinching back. Menlos Irontooth followed it with his wolves, attacking the exposed ankles of this particular titan.

The line of battle was already chaos, though not somehow as bad as it had been in the Heia Pass. The titans fell at a faster pace here, even without spellcaster magic at Sanctuary's easy disposal. Cyrus watched three titans turn on their brethren, and knew as a fourth and fifth joined the fray on the Sanctuary side, that J'anda Aimant had entered the battle.

Still, the titans were relentless, flooding into the battlefield as they had into the arena in Kortran, enthusiastic if not skilled, trying with everything in them to overmatch their tiny prey and constantly outmaneuvered by them nonetheless.

"Sure you don't want to do that wedding now?" Cyrus shouted as he launched himself up and landed on the back of a stooped-over titan's neck. He plunged Praelior into the sweet spot between vertebrae, and exited with a leap before the titan toppled over.

"I hope you're not asking one of these dead beasts to marry you," Vara called back from some fifty feet away. "Because I would expect that from the Guildmaster of Goliath, but we hold you to a somewhat higher standard in Sanctuary."

"Is that so? Then should I take aim for royalty of some sort, then? Perhaps hold out for a dwarven princess or some elven royal—?"

"It'll be a frosty day in the Realm of Fire before you get any offers from elven royals, I'd wager, other than a few opportunists who have more issues with their father than even you do," Vara said, leaping from the shoulders of one titan that she had just struck down to the next. "But I might know a certain elf of some importance that could be interested."

"Is that so?" Cyrus asked, splitting a leg from a titan to the howls of his victim.

"Don't be coy," Vara said, smirking as she vaulted down, "or you might lose your 'last hope.'"

"Never, shelas'akur," Cyrus said, not entirely able to cover the anxious feeling that followed his braggadocio, and instead planting his blade in a leaning titan's skull. "Never leave me."

The titan numbers were increasing, but Cyrus saw little sign of his own troops growing in number. A trickle of Sanctuary fighters were coming out of the trees of Amti, a few at a time, and then they stopped altogether for some several long moments, during which J'anda, still unseen, seized a never-ending procession of titans and reversed them upon their own, single-handedly holding off any assault from their left.

"This lack of reinforcements is concerning," Cyrus muttered as he was kicked by a passing titan. He clipped a tree and caught himself on one knee, the wind knocked out of him.

"Perhaps your people thought the better of throwing themselves into this fruitless endeavor," Gareth said, running past in a flash, yanking Cyrus back to his feet as he went.

"We're not that smart," Cyrus replied, straightening up with some effort.

"You're also not alone!" came the call from above. The armor of Alaric Garaunt came raining down into battle from on high, the axe of its new wearer brandished above. Terian's blow found the back of a titan's neck and separated it cleanly as the white knight swept down to Cyrus's level on the wings of a Falcon's Essence spell.

"Glad to see you," Cyrus said with a grin as Terian sped down to him. "Might not want to rely on that for loft when the cessation spells come to call, though."

"True enough," Terian said, and with a wave of his hand his boots slapped back to the earth. "Sorry for the tardiness. It took a few minutes for your spellcasters to coordinate and bring mine in, but ..." He grinned. "Now we're here, and more of us are coming all the time."

"Then maybe we've got a little more of a chance," Cyrus said, with a grin of his own, as the next wave of titans burst through the trees in front of them.

"I wouldn't call it even just yet," Terian said, and now he was back to grim. "You got a plan for ending this?"

"I was thinking we'd just fight to the death."

"Oh, hell." Terian puckered his lips. "I should have known." But he swung his axe, delivering death to the next titan, and the one after that, his army falling in behind him, a trickle of spellcasters joining them now in the battle at the trunk of the trees.

The titans came thicker now, and more armored, sweeping in under branches as warriors and rangers of Sanctuary and the Sovereignty fought side by side. They gave against the onslaught, surrendering ground and pressing back, and Cyrus was reminded of the days of Luukessia once more, of the ceaseless drive of the scourge to knock them back.

And that didn't end so well for us, Cyrus thought, *with just as implacable a foe, but weaker, and more easily channeled along controllable lines.* He watched Vara blast a titan with her force spell so hard that its neck was snapped back and was broken. *Still, though ... we aren't failing ... perhaps we could—*

"YAAAAAAAAAAH!" the low, rumbling shout came from somewhere above, and the entire battle seemed to pause as everyone looked skyward. A black blur, a dark shadow in the night came falling down like a stone, crashing into the back of a titan's neck and hammering him into the ground with fury. Rocky hands rose up and pummeled the already downed titan, shattering skull and drawing blood.

"I AM LORD FORTIN THE RAPACIOUS OF ROCKRIDGE!" the rock giant shouted, voice crackling in fury over the suddenly quiet jungle. "DEFENDER OF THE EMERALD FIELDS AND GRAND KNIGHT OF SANCTUARY!"

"I don't remembering anyone bestowing him that particular title," Vara said into the silence.

"I'll do it later," Cyrus said, transfixed as everyone else by the rock giant's entry to the fight. "I like it."

"IF YOU SEEK BATTLE, GLORY AND DEATH, SEEK ME, COWARDLY TITANS!"

With that, the fray resumed, but in a suddenly unbalanced shift. Titans that had been advancing toward Cyrus and the others, even some who had been in the throes of combat, broke loose and turned toward Fortin, coming at him in a knot, fighting amongst each other for their opportunity at the rock giant's challenge. Cyrus watched a few breaking into fights with each other, jabbing out eyes, crushing throats, throttling their fellows, and he was hard pressed to say whether J'anda had even had any sway on this particular outbreak of feuding among the titans.

Cyrus fought to the side as well, the rock giant still in the midst of a thrashing ocean of titans. Body parts were being flung, knees were being crushed, and the anguished screams of titans were enough to suggest to Cyrus that the rock giant was in the thick of it, but he hurried along nonetheless, plunging his sword into the backs of exposed knee joints and slitting throats among the fallen in a race to move with the line into place to defend Fortin—

The sound of feet crashing into the clearing, louder than any others, made him turn his head to the side. He looked once, then did a double take and turned again to be sure he had seen what he thought he had.

It was exactly what he had feared.

A titan stood at the edge of the fight in full plate armor, covered from head to toe in the manner of Arkarian warriors. As Cyrus watched, awestruck in contemplation of trying to fight through even folded steel smithed at such a scale, the armored titan spoke in the familiar voice of Talikartin, but with an even rougher edge, the bucket-shaped helm's dark eye slits focused right on him.

"Cyrus Davidon," Talikartin said, "you let a creature of the earth do your fighting, issue your challenges for you? How cowardly you have become, to hide in the shadow of such things rather than fight your own battles—and scarcely worth the battle I came all this way just to have … with you."

83.

"You came all this way for me?" Cyrus asked, staring across the darkened forest at the armored titan, whose head was held high, eye slits shadowed. "Well, then what are you shuffling toward that rock giant for?" He waved. "Come on over here, Tali, and let's finish this properly."

Talikartin's nose flared in fury, snorts echoing in the dark under the canopy and the night sky. "Do you think me a fool? How many times have you run from me now?"

"Only every time your army tries to rush in and crush us," Cyrus said, swallowing his nerves. "If you came here for me ... fight me."

The battle around Fortin had ceased, and every eye in the forest was on the challenge being offered to Cyrus. "You negotiate like a merchant," Talikartin scoffed. "Too long in that human capital and its profane markets has soured you, turned you into something weak and incapable of staring into the true face of combat, meeting it with your eyes and striking out at it."

"Yeah, well, I didn't get to choose where I grew up," Cyrus said, stalling for time. He saw Vara edging around behind him, circling up a tree. "Neither did you, big boy, though I suspect if you'd grown up in Reikonos like me, you might have also had some civilizing influences on you, unlike the sort you run into out here in the savage wilds." He waved a hand around. "Like for example, you might have learned— very merchant-like—that you don't necessarily throw your best warrior stupidly into a contest with a creature four times their size without some guarantee of gain."

"You truly are haggling," Talikartin said in disgust.

"I don't hear you making a counter-offer," Cyrus said, narrowing his own eyes, "so listen to this: I beat you, your people get the hell out of this jungle and don't come back."

Talikartin bellowed out in laughter that seemed to shake the trees around him, laughter that was quickly echoed by the titans standing around listening to the discussion play out. "You wish to barter for the lives of these elves?"

"They've never been a threat to you," Cyrus said, clenching Praelior tightly. "They've kept to their lands and—"

"You think we would countenance invaders?" Talikartin asked, still tall, still implacable, still refusing to bend to so much as look down at Cyrus through those eye-slits of his helm. "Tolerate this weak elven scum to sit in our lands unchallenged? How far you have fallen from the height of a warrior, how low you are in my estimation, how feeble in the beliefs that I was so sure bred true in you."

"You don't know me," Cyrus said darkly.

"Indeed not," Talikartin said. "You wish to bargain? Very well, I offer you this: Fight me, now, alone, without your healers or other spellcasters as aid, to the death, or I will slaughter without mercy or weakness every one of your guildmates I can lay hands on, tearing them to ribbon and mashing their little heads to paste beyond any hope of healing magic to repair them."

"Here endeth the vendetta," Cyrus whispered, looking up at the titan. "All right. Fine. I—"

"Don't!" Vara slid into place next to him. "That thing is armored from heel to crown."

"So am I," Cyrus said, nodding at Talikartin.

"It doesn't matter," Vara said with a frown, "even Praelior is going to take time cutting through that—assuming it's even possible."

Cyrus eased in her closer to her. "We always knew it was going to come down to this—coming here, I mean. This was always a fight to the death."

"Yes," she said archly, "but I was supposed to die first."

He frowned. "All these years, you told me that you were afraid you'd die last—"

"Well, yes, and that was why I didn't want to be with you—"

"But now you are—"

"And you don't even have the good grace not to go feeding into my greatest fears about our relationship, you inconsiderate arse—"

"ENOUGH!" Talikartin bellowed. "Enough bickering!"

"I haven't had enough yet." Cyrus leaned in and gave Vara a kiss, short, but filled with meaning. He saw the regret in her eyes, the fear, and he tried to smile. "Don't get involved in this one," he said.

"I will try not to," she said, looking as troubled as he'd ever seen her.

"Talikartin the Guardian," Cyrus said, turning back to look at the titan, "I accept your challenge."

"Good," Talikartin whispered, and finally, at last, he looked at Cyrus. His helm moved just enough to give Cyrus a full view of the eye-slits beneath, like windows into the soul of the titan he was about to do battle with.

And it was enough to drive the cold of winter into Cyrus's very soul.

As he stood there, staring at his considerably larger opponent, it was not the armor, nor the disparity in height, nor even the challenge of strength that caused Cyrus to hesitate, to feel that ephemeral sense of fear that he thought he had long ago banished from his life, at least for himself. None of that weighed in his considerations at all, in fact.

It was the glowing red eyes that sent the twist into his stomach and the hint of weakness into his knees, for Cyrus knew at once that they were eyes he had seen in a thousand dreams over his many years, eyes that had looked into his very soul and handed him a mission to collect the pieces to put together the very sword he held in his hands.

The eyes of the God of War himself—Bellarum.

84.

"My Lord Bellarum," Cyrus said, mouth suddenly dry. "You're ... here. You ..." A thought tumbled loose. "*You* taught the titans magic?"

Talikartin the Guardian smiled a viler smile than Cyrus had seen from him before, visible underneath the helm's gap. "I gave them no spells of teleportation to go to the north, nor healing magics to give them silly regard for fixing weakness; no, I gave them the power to strike out, to build my kingdom in the south and to go north by the pass if they could."

Cyrus blinked, feeling like the jungle was closing in around him, the air reaching out to strangle him in his armor as he stared, helplessly, at the red eyes that had followed him through a thousand dreams, and had reached out to him in one vision in particular that had changed the course of his life. He held Praelior weakly in his fingers, afraid to clench his hand around it for fear it might strike out at him with the anger of the one who had as good as put it in that hand. "Why?" he asked, voice cracking.

The red eyes narrowed, and the voice of Talikartin changed into a deeper timbre, that strange tone taking over. "I wanted to give you room to grow, to build a kingdom for me in the north while the titans did the same here." He made a scoffing noise. "You were handed those plains and what have you done with them? Nothing." He sneered. "You've grown weak, Cyrus. And weakness must be purged."

"I'm not ..." Cyrus felt staggered, as though the titan had already punched him squarely in the jaw. "I'm the strongest warrior in Arkaria."

"On the contrary," Talikartin said, thumping his chestplate.

"You've taken him over?" Cyrus stared at the God of War in the titan's form. "He's your ... avatar?" A nod followed, and the sense that battle could resume at any moment hung about them. "Why? Why bring an avatar to Arkaria?"

Bellarum laughed. "You of all people should know why, Cyrus. Did I not work that sword into your hand and place Mortus into your path, knowing that he wanted nothing more than to kill the woman you fawned over?" A discordant guffaw sounded like a blade jabbed into Cyrus's ears. "Did I not set Yartraak in motion on his grand plan to destroy the lands that you loved?" He glared down at Cyrus with amusement. "Oh, yes. My hand has been guiding the events of your life to my purpose—that to which you swore your loyalty!" The voice of the God of War caused a pain soul-deep in Cyrus. "I have done more for you than you even know, and you have turned away from my path. You were my loyal servant. I saw potential in you, strength in you. I groomed you for greatness ... and you embraced mediocrity." He pointed into the stunned crowd of fighters that encircled them, singling out Terian. "You might as well be wearing *that* armor."

"Hey!" Terian said. "It's ... well, it's comfortable. A little loose around the—"

"SILENCE!" Bellarum shouted into the night, and the command was obeyed by sheer force of the volume it carried. "Now," the God of War said from his earthly form, "Cyrus ... the time has come for me to beat the weakness out of you." He smiled. "I know your armor protects you against most attacks, so this may take some time, but we will get all the pesky disease of compassion ... of the heart ... that your former Guildmaster seeded in you, I will have you strong ... or I will have you dead." The eyes burned. "And at this point, I have lost all care which it will be."

85.

The first punch was fast, faster than Cyrus remembered either Yartraak or Mortus being. It came with a speed that Cyrus recalled of wagons racing through the streets of Reikonos when he was a child, the wheels threatening to roll unceasingly over any child or man that got in the way. So too was this punch, a metal-encased hand as big as Cyrus's entire chest, thrown at his midsection and dodged only just in time.

Cyrus landed face first in a patch of grass. The scent of greenery invading his sinuses forcefully, the tickle of the blades ironic at a moment when he feared death itself was coming for him in the form of his angry god. He rolled as hard as he could to the side, already knowing that a killing attack would follow. It did, only a moment later, a fist slamming into the ground with merciless force where he had lain only seconds earlier, shaking the earth and rattling him in his armor, down to his very teeth.

"You are running from your fate like a coward!" Bellarum's voice echoed angrily in the night. "Stand and take your punishment like a man of war!"

Cyrus rolled once more, narrowly avoiding another hit, his head swimming. *Is this really happening?*

Is Bellarum really attacking ... me?

The world shook at the landing of another punch, and Cyrus rattled once more.

Yes.

This is happening.

Cyrus lurched to his feet as Bellarum's titan shell took a step back and surveyed him with unmistakable anger. The eyes showed a seething rage, furious at being thwarted even slightly in front of an audience. Bellarum balled Talikartin's fists and shifted on his mighty feet, and Cyrus knew he would be much more sure before the next attack came.

"If it is as you said," Cyrus looked up at the red eyes, "and you placed Mortus and Yartraak against me to get them killed ... why are you so damned displeased with me now? I have an army. I have done what you want—"

"You have failed!" Bellarum swung a shorter punch this time as he stepped forward, and there was no avoiding it. Cyrus clung tight to Praelior and pointed it outward in exactly the manner that had once cost Mortus a few fingers.

The blow struck and Cyrus felt it, the force running through his armor and sending him flying into a tree. When he hit, the breath was knocked from him for a moment and he fell to his knees on the roots, some ten feet above the jungle floor. He put down a hand to steady himself as he pushed up and found his opponent once more, standing, resolute, looking him in the eye, almost level with him.

Blood ran down the titan's hand, but a faint glow faded as Cyrus watched it, the healing spell subtle where Bellarum held his hand out of sight, but the glow unmistakable in the forest dark. "You hypocrite," Cyrus said, and the jungle around him came to life.

Vara was the first to spring, lunging in a leap at Bellarum, but she was knocked from the air by a titan who roared in disapproval. Terian came forth next, shouting his anger in the night, axe held high, but he was blocked by six titans suddenly in his path. Other titans sprang forward to defend the circle around Cyrus and Bellarum, and others fought them—J'anda's pets, trying to force their way through the line, a wrestling match at the edge of the battle as the fight carried on around them, unable to penetrate through to where the God of War stalked his prey.

"Your people were loyal and true," Bellarum said, "and they would have followed you in doing my will."

"No," Cyrus said, steadying himself as he watched the chaos unfolding around him. "Not all of them."

"Those who will not serve," Bellarum said, eyes flashing, "will die."

"I will not just die—"

The strike hit Cyrus unawares, from a titan that had crept up behind him. It was hardly a punch like the world ending sort that Bellarum was throwing about, but it knocked him firmly off the root on which he'd been standing, sending him headfirst to the floor of the jungle. A smaller root caught him in the lips, and he tasted blood, pouring down his chin. He started to get to his feet, Praelior clutched in front of him, but—

Bellarum's titan foot descended onto his fingers, bending the joints of his armor back just far enough to cause Cyrus immense pain. The titan's ground down upon his fingers with all their weight, and then skidded hard against the ground—

Yanking Praelior out of his grasp.

The Champion's Sword slid across the jungle floor and came to rest in the shadow of a root some ten feet away. Without the aid of its power, it might as well have been a mile away, for now he stared into the red eyes of a furious, smiling, satisfied god and knew that he was powerless.

86.

"You were supposed to be an instrument of war," Bellarum said, "but without your weapon *you are nothing*." He leaned down closer to Cyrus and grabbed him around the chest so quickly that Cyrus could not respond, pulled him aloft, and shook him. "Without me ... you are nothing."

Cyrus felt the squeeze of the God of War held at bay by his armor, but the tension, the power of the grip was evident. "Alaric!" Cyrus called out impulsively.

Bellarum's eyes glowed harder crimson in fury, but his voice sounded almost amused. "He can't help you now." The God of War chortled. "Do you know what I did—what I have done to him?" The red eyes drew closer as Cyrus was raised up to Talikartin's horrendously glowing eyes. "I sent this shell north into the Plains of Perdamun all those years ago to kill Raifa Herde out of sheerest spite for her husband. Talikartin, unlike you, is a loyal servant, and he did my bidding well." Bellarum's mouth twisted in rage and glee. "He remains uncorrupted by the pox that is Alaric Garaunt. *Unlike you.*" His nostrils flared. "Yes, I see it now. The weakness cannot be burned out of you by any cleansing fire. It is soul-deep, this filth."

He paused, and his voice grew deep as Cyrus blanched away from the pressure through his armor. In some of the cracks, the chainmail picked up the pressure and pushed inward on Cyrus, in the soft spots around his stomach and waist. He could almost taste the metal in his mouth ... or was that simply the blood?

"Now," Bellarum said, resolved, "die like as much of a warrior as you can ... by looking me in the eyes as I kill you."

A tingle ran over Cyrus's scalp and down his entire body, and he brought his head around to look the possessed titan in the eyes.

I meet you.

As Bellarum brought back his other fist to finish the task at hand, there was no mistaking the lethality of the maneuver. He would pummel Cyrus so that his own armor would cut him cleanly in two. Perhaps after that he would rip off the head, tear off limbs, shred him into a paste while the Army of Sanctuary watched, unable to reach him—

Cyrus swept his gaze in the cool second before his death and saw the fight continuing, futile, the titans having taken advantage of the moments of truce to pour reinforcements into the trees around Amti—while no such numbers could possibly come on Sanctuary's side.

The world seemed to slow as the fist of a god came crashing toward Cyrus, reaching its high arc, the height of its force and beginning its descent to crush him. The air around him was still, the call of battle was like the silence of death, closing in, unerringly.

And a voice spoke into that silence.

Arnngraav, urnkaaav.

The words came in a voice he trusted implicitly, a voice deep and resonant that seemed to pluck at the very heartstrings deep within him. Cyrus blinked as the fist of Bellarum came toward him, and he put up a hand to ward off, instinctively, even knowing deep within it would do no good.

Arnngraav, urnkaaav! the voice came again, saying words that Cyrus did not know, but had heard—somewhere, once, perhaps?

ARNNGRAAV, URNKAAAV! the voice of Alaric Garaunt bellowed in his ear, snapping him out of the stunned, fearful wait for death that had consumed him and spurring him into simple, mad action.

"Arnngraav, urnkaaav!" Cyrus shouted into the night, and the hand of Bellarum wavered just a second in its fall.

Long enough for a billowing blast of flame to spray forth from Cyrus's hand and consume the head of the Avatar of the God of War.

The shrieks of a burning god spilled into the jungle night. The frightful grip around Cyrus faltered, and he fell some fifteen feet to the jungle floor, hitting soft soil and a patch of small ferns. He landed with a thump and looked up in surprise.

Bellarum clutched at Talikartin's face, fire still burning the flesh as though it had been brought to life behind the titan's very eyes. He fell to his knees and scratched at his eye sockets as he tried to beat out the fire that had struck him and caught eyebrows aflame.

Cyrus did not wait, did not watch; he scrambled forward on uncertain legs, lurching toward the glowing blue sword some ten feet away. He moved unsteadily, swaying from side to side, fatigued in a way he could not recall ever feeling, as though something had been drained from within him, some energy that he had never before noticed, until it was gone.

Cyrus's pained fingers closed in on the hilt of Praelior, and the world slowed around him. He scooped it up with the aid of its dexterity, and turned on the God of War, still kneeling and striking at his own face, the flames gone but the pain still clearly there.

Cyrus did not hesitate, but simply followed the training of the Society of Arms. He leapt like the paladin he now loved more than any other, using the strength provided by his sword to fly over the back of the God of War's mortal form. He swept down with Praelior as he did so, burying his blade into the back of Talikartin the Guardian's thick neck. It took a good, hard twist to land it right, and then Cyrus let his own weight carry him down—

And he cut off the head of the Avatar of the God of War.

A silence fell over the Jungle of Vidara, whispering through the trees quieter than the rasp of crickets. It was broken by the first scream, then another, then another, the roar of titans not enraged, but terrified.

Terrified, for they had seen their own god die before them.

Cyrus listened to the shrieks, the wails, the plaintive moans, the first footfalls as titan after titan broke from the battle and ran, their opponents forgotten, their helms knocked aside and cast away, massive gauntlets shrugged out of and dropped in the underbrush like so much refuse.

"I think we just …" Terian staggered up to Cyrus, navy blood running down his jawline, splattered on his breastplate. "Did we just …?"

"We won, yes," Vara said, sword in hand, moving into view on steadier legs than Terian exhibited. She looked sideways at Cyrus, with more than a little suspicion. "Or you did, at least."

Cyrus lifted his hand, transferring Praelior to the other, and held his gauntlet up, staring at it. "Did you see ...?"

"You shoot a big damned fire spell out of your hand into the face of the God of War?" Terian asked, sounding more than a little wary. "It would have been to hard to miss in this light."

Cyrus studied the lines of his gauntlet, staring at the traces of the folds. "How ... how did I?" He looked up, feeling the cool trickle of something like fingers rubbing across his scalp. "What am I?"

"I don't know," Vara said, swallowing hard. Cyrus looked around them and saw every face on them—on him. "But I do know what they will call you, when the Leagues hear about this.

"Heretic."

87.

Falcon's Essence carried Cyrus along, Terian racing beside him as they ran through the Jungle of Vidara, the first hints of blue appearing in the gaps of the canopy above. The run was oddly uninvigorating despite the crisp morning air. The taste of blood and bitterness was still thick on his tongue, and Vara's speaking of the word echoed in his ears.

Heretic.

She was behind them a little ways, the power of Noctus and Praelior speeding them forward. J'anda and Fortin had gotten even farther ahead, the rock giant's mighty strides carrying him away from Amti even before Cyrus and Terian had made a start of their run. J'anda had followed, five titans still in his sway, riding atop the tallest of them.

"Do you want to talk about it?" Terian asked as they circled around a particularly large tree trunk.

"Not really," Cyrus said, his head still awhirl. "I just want to make sure the titans don't rally and come back for more." The word bounced around in his mind like thrown mud, sticking to everything.

Heretic.

"Where'd you learn it?" Terian asked. "The fire spell?"

"I heard it from someone," Cyrus said, thinking of Mendicant but not daring to say his name aloud, "while they were trying to save my life."

"Good instinct," Terian said with a sharp nod, "keeping it to yourself. Whoever slipped up, well, they're going to get the full fire of the Leagues on their tail as well."

Cyrus frowned, and it felt like mud stuck in the creases of his face, freezing it into place. "It's going to be bad, isn't it?"

Terian cocked his head. "You have trouble coming your way, my friend. I hope you'll call for my help if you find yourself needing it."

Cyrus felt a grim, ashen smile take root on his face. "It's very strange to hear the Sovereign of Saekaj Sovar say that."

"It's just a title, Cyrus," Terian said, looking at him as earnestly as the knight had ever appeared to Cyrus's eyes. "It's not who I am—or at least not all of it."

"Lord Davidon!" Fortin's voice rumbled as the first breaks in the jungle appeared ahead, deep blue sky of early morning shining through beyond. Cyrus slowed as he caught up to the rock giant, who crouched behind a tree, J'anda atop a titan behind another. "You will want to see this!"

Cyrus ran the last hundred meters or so to where the two of them crouched at the edge of the jungle, but it did not take him that long to realize what the rock giant was referring to.

Cyrus slowed his pace and felt Terian do the same behind him. Vara huffed as she caught up then stopped. He did not turn, but he felt certain that Vara's mouth was as agape as his surely was.

The Gradsden Savanna burned.

The fire started only a few hundred meters past the end of the jungle, scorched ground already giving way, the grass fire having nearly burned itself out already, black soil and ashen remains all that was left—that and scorched bones, too massive to be those of anything but titans.

"Gods," Cyrus murmured.

"Probably don't want to be invoking them right now," Vara corrected gently.

"Shits," Terian said, staring out at the spectacle of destruction before them.

"Probably shouldn't invoke that, either, for fear of—"

"Too late," Terian said, stepping forward.

"Poor Alaric," she said. "I hope he doesn't ever plan to get that armor back."

There was little smoke, but the damage was plain from what had been done. Fast-burning fire had consumed the retreating titan army, and it was obvious and visible that the fire had not stopped with just that army. Black clouds were strung over the flat savanna in patches that Cyrus suspected corresponded to every single titan supply camp.

"What do you think did this—" Terian started to ask, but the question was answered before he even finished.

A deafening screech of anger was followed by a sweeping shadow flying overhead, and five more after it. The wings whispered with each flutter as they caught the dawn's light behind them. The dragons flew overhead, bellowing their anger out upon a savanna devoid of life—as they had made it.

"Look," Vara said, and she pointed to the mountains in the distance, far, far to the south, around the valley where Kortran was nestled.

Black smoke hung thick here, still alight with red flame on the dark edge of the horizon, and Cyrus knew that below the edge of the valley was a pyre that would stay lit all the day.

"I believe that is the end of the titans," Cyrus said, that ashy taste still in his mouth. They stood there for quite some time, in the dark of the jungle, watching the shadowed dragons fly overhead, occasionally swooping down to inflict their wrath on some poor unfortunate out of sight—the fulfillment of a promise that had come at the highest cost.

88.

The journey back to Amti had been strangely swift, barely noticeable to Cyrus after long hours spent watching the dragons do their horrible work over the savanna. The jungle had been cleared in Cyrus's absence, no titan stragglers found, and by the time that all that had been declared to be sure, the dark elven army and Terian gathered and left in shortest order with only the kindest of regards on their way out.

The Sanctuary army began to clear, albeit slower, and Cyrus found himself in Tierreed with the four members of Amti's council as well as Martaina as he waited for the druids and wizards to do their slow work of teleporting everyone home.

"Are you sure you want to stay?" he asked Martaina, who stood off from Gareth just a little, the distance between them telling Cyrus quite a bit.

She thought about it before answering. "I don't want to go back to Sanctuary, no. Too many ... unfortunate memories."

Cyrus could not help but think of Andren, and the thought was like a physical pain punching into his chest under his armor. "I understand. If you ever change your mind ..."

"I know where to find you," she said with a ghostly smile that told him that she would not be changing her mind.

"And you—" Cyrus said, turning to look at Cora, who stared back at him with an effervescent smile of her own.

Cora held up a finger to stay him. "I will say my piece first, and then you may remonstrate with me for my furtiveness however you desire." She led Gareth, Fredaula and Mirasa in a long bow, during which Martaina rolled her eyes. "Thank you, Cyrus, Vara, and Sanctuary," Cora said when she came up, smiling, "for by your efforts, you have saved Amti."

"You're welcome," Cyrus said, but could not help but add, "it's what good neighbors do." Vara smacked him on the shoulder.

Cora's eyes faltered. "I was not a good neighbor, though, was I? For if I had been, I would have kept you longer than the time I did." She looked him up and down, at his armor. "I might have kept you from … that place."

Cyrus frowned at her. "The Society?"

"The Society, aye," Cora said, sounding a little disgusted. "It was not where your mother and father wanted to you to go."

Cyrus straightened a little. "What? Why not?"

"Because warriors go off to war for years at a time, of course," Cora said, as though it were evident. "Most of them have no magical support, no hope of resurrection in death, and then … there was the training." She looked away. "But you know about that."

"I know about that," Cyrus said, and smiled wanly. "I made it through, though." He paused as a thought occurred to him. "What did they want me to do? What did they want me to be?"

Cora started to say something then stopped, breaking into another wan smile as she reached out to brush a hand lightly against his cheek—like a mother might have. "They wanted for you what any parent wants for their child—for you to be safe, and happy, and assured of your place in their affections." Her eyes twinkled with a hint of sadness. "But beyond that, all they desired for you … was for you to be yourself."

89.

When they appeared back in the Sanctuary foyer, Cyrus finally dared look at Mendicant, who had cast the spell to bring them home, but when he did, he found the goblin looking coolly back at him, without a trace of fear. They stood in the middle of a quiet army, the whispers of those who had gone along rippling through the ranks of those who had not been there to witness their guildmaster commit his heresy in the jungle.

"Well," Vaste said bracingly, a little too relaxed and a little too loud for Cyrus to properly believe him, "we should probably have an absolutely standard and rudimentary Council meeting in which we will discuss nothing but the very ordinary events of this particular action."

"That will have to wait," Scuddar In'shara said, sweeping in from the open doors of the foyer. Blue skies shone outside, the sun already up in the sky. A soft breeze wafted into the room. "You have a visitor at the wall."

"Ehrgraz?" Cyrus asked and received a nod in return. He started for the door, but Vaste landed a hand on his arm.

"We are going to have that very ordinary Council meeting afterward though, yes?" Vaste asked.

"I'm sure you'll hound me until we do," Cyrus said, and the troll's grip relinquished him.

"Ehrgraz has picked an odd time to break his silence," Vara said, stepping into line beside him as they walked toward the wall.

"I expect we'll get an explanation for that," Cyrus said tightly, his boots mashing into the soft lawn with every step. The day around him seemed like it was excessively bright, and then he realized there were no clouds in the sky. "Though whether it's to our satisfaction is

414

anyone's guess."

"About the other thing—" she said quickly.

"Later," Cyrus said, and paused as she stopped. He looked her in the eyes and saw the same worry and fear there that he felt sure were in his own. "Truly. After the Council meeting, we can—" He smiled faintly. "Why don't we go to Reikonos and have a walk?"

Her eyes flickered. "Like you used to do with … Andren?"

"Exactly," Cyrus said, barely a whisper.

"Very well," she said, nodding once, in discomfort, before they made their way up the nearest tower to the top of the wall, the clank of their boots against the stone pathways resounding in Cyrus's ears.

"If you're here to give condolences, you're months late," Cyrus said as he strode out onto the wall where Ehrgraz's head waited, glaring at him with one eye cocked.

"I will only say this once," Ehrgraz said dangerously, "so listen carefully—I am sorry for your losses." He sounded slightly contrite when he said it, though his tone still indicated deep contempt or irritation; which, Cyrus could not rightly say.

"Your regrets are appreciated," Cyrus said, watching him with both eyes. "I saw your handiwork in the savanna this morning."

"I heard you were watching," Ehrgraz said, looking at him in a way that Cyrus found suddenly uncomfortable.

"Did you?" Cyrus asked. "What else did you hear?"

"Everything," Ehrgraz said, leaving Cyrus in little doubt that he spoke the truth. "Your days are soon to become more difficult."

"Well, at least I don't have to worry about an army of titans coming out of the south," Cyrus said, a little sourly, "though now it's something of an open question if I ever really did, once the pass was shut."

"Do you think Bellarum would have been content to let you sit idly here in the north without challenge? That he would not have given the titans the keys to every kingdom here in the north eventually?" Ehrgraz asked, yellow eyes on him in near disbelief once more. "Your failure to follow his path is what spurred him to foolish action with the titans. He hoped to move you cleanly back to his side." The dragon puffed black smoke. "Apparently he underestimated the other ties that bind you." Ehrgraz looked pointedly at Vara.

"Me?" she asked, hand falling to her chest.

"You know an awful lot about the affairs of gods," Cyrus said, watching the dragon with suspicion.

"Hmpf!" Ehrgraz scoffed. "I bid you farewell now, Cyrus Davidon, for our paths are now diverging." He flapped his wings once. "Pray to whatever gods you still hold dear that they do not cross again in an unfavorable way, for I think you have seen what end that holds for those who challenge us."

"Same to you, Ehrgraz," Cyrus said, drawing another sharp look from the dragon, which he returned in kind. "I don't suppose I need to remind you that I've killed more dragons than I have gods—and I don't really care which is on the end of my blade, if they cross *me*."

Ehrgraz stared back at him, unrelenting. "I think we understand each other perfectly." And he flapped his wings and shot off into the sky impossibly fast, disappearing out of sight into the distance in mere moments. The mood that his threat left Cyrus in, however, was not nearly so quick to depart.

90.

"The way I see it," Vaste said in the Council Chamber, the warmth of the hearth keeping some of the day's chill at bay, "we're as blind as the Dragonlord just before Cyrus rode him right into the ground. And furthermore," the troll said, looking pointedly at Cyrus at the head of the table, "probably just as stuck with our esteemed Guildmaster riding us into oblivion."

"I'm not trying to ... ride you," Cyrus said, faltering partway through.

"Except her," Erith said with a nod at Vara.

"Actually, I prefer to do the riding," Vara said a little stiffly.

"Oh, how I hate you two," Vaste said, lowering his head and cradling it in his hands. "I miss the fighting. Where is the fighting?"

"Does anyone else have that ... that sinking feeling of stepping off a high stair when your Falcon's Essence has just worn off?" J'anda asked, his voice filling the chamber.

"That more or less sums up how I feel as well," Ryin said, mouth buried behind his hand. He glanced around. "I mean ... we'll all be heretics together if this stands, won't we?"

"I think technically if you're merely aiding or supporting a heretic you're called a—" Mendicant started.

"The effect is the same, yes?" Ryin asked the goblin, looking down at him.

"A veritable death sentence, yes," Vaste said.

"Can we just discuss how Cyrus used a fire spell?" Longwell asked, looking at Cyrus. "I mean ... does that mean any of us could?"

"Try it," Cyrus said with a shrug. "The words are—"

"NOOO!" Ryin shouted, face red.

"Arnngraav, urnkaaav," Cyrus said, looking sideways at the druid, who slumped with his hands on his forehead in much the same way Vaste just had.

Longwell pointed his hand at a blank stretch of wall. "Arnngraav, urnkaaav!" They waited quietly for a second, then two, and the dragoon shrugged. "I guess I'm just not magical enough." He pursed his lips. "Damn."

"He didn't cast it just now either, when he said it to you," Vaste noted, looking at Cyrus with suspicion.

Cyrus shrugged languidly. "Wasn't trying to, but …" He stood and unlocked the balcony door, then stuck his hand out. "Arnngraav, urnkaaav!"

Flame bellowed out over the balcony and Cyrus felt a curious tugging sensation within him, like breath being sucked from lungs he didn't know he had. The fire was small compared to the spells of the wizards he had known, or even the druids, and faded quickly.

"Oh, will you just stop committing heresy?" Ryin asked, now hiding his eyes.

"Wow," Erith said and pointed her hand at the hearth before whispering something under her breath. A gout of flame leapt out of her hand, larger than the one that Cyrus had just loosed, burning into the hearth and upward, setting fire to the painting hanging above the frame. "Oh, damn."

"Yes," Ryin said, watching in consternation as the picture and frame were consumed by yellow fire, smoking into the air above the stone hearth's mantle. "Burning our art is certainly cause for concern at a moment *when we're all sitting around committing and aiding heresy!*"

"Well, now I have to try," Vaste said and led the way out to the balcony. Vara and J'anda followed behind her, each of them belting out a flame spell in turn, Vaste's mild and long, like a tongue, Vara's short of duration and fury, her hesitation causing her to pull back some of the power Cyrus suspected she could have applied.

J'anda's, on the other hand, blew out like the breath of a dragon, making Cyrus and the others flinch away from the heat and intensity. When Cyrus opened his hand again, he found the enchanter clutching his staff tightly, a look of satisfaction on his face. "Hmmm," the dark elf said, clearly contemplating possibilities.

"I guess this explains why that heretic we ran into in the Bandit

Lands was so hunted by the Leagues," Vaste mused aloud as they came in from the balcony, the smell of fire and smoke following behind them.

"Yes, it's amazing how heretics get hunted for being heretics," Ryin said, his face on the table.

"Do you realize what this means?" Vaste asked.

"For some of us," Longwell said, a bit sourly, "not a damned thing."

"It means the Leagues have been controlling magic," Mendicant said, looking more than a little hungry. "That like Lord Soulmender said—"

"Who?" J'anda asked with a frown.

"Wasn't that Curatio's surname?" Vaste asked. "I think I heard him say it once."

"—there are practices forbidden and controlled," Mendicant went on, ignoring the interruptions. "That they've been—"

"Holding out on us," Vara said quietly.

"The Leagues are not 'holding out on us,'" Ryin said with more than a little outrage. "They put guidelines in place for our own safety, and to keep dangerous magics out of the hands of nutters like—like—like the bloody Sorceress Quinneria!" He looked at Vaste.

Vaste blinked in surprise. "Uh ... yes. I suppose that's true. You don't want dangerous magics falling into the hands of people who want to wipe out all the trolls, after all." He rubbed at his chin. "But, uhm ..." He scratched at his chin, "... I'm not sure that saving my not-so-noble people was the purpose behind the League control." He flicked his gaze to Cyrus. "Because ... as we learned just a few short years ago, the Leagues are probably under the same guidance as the major powers, which means their patrons—"

"Are the gods," Cyrus finished for him.

Vaste nodded once. "Exactly. And I'm guessing ... now that we've killed two of their number plus one of their avatars—"

"The Leagues are going to come after us," Vara said quietly.

"Entire nations are going to come after us," Ryin said miserably.

"And we'll stand against them all," Cyrus said, that uncertain feeling that had wracked him for months dissolving in one moment of absolute belief. He looked his officers in the eyes one by one, and saw a mixture of disbelief waiting there. "Just like we always have, against all challengers.

"Whatever comes our way ... we will fight," he said. "Because that's what we do. It's who we are." Cyrus straightened, and he felt the others stand a little taller with him. "We've fought for others, for what was right, for the defenseless, and for Arkaria. All noble causes." His breath caught in his throat, but he felt sure that this was it, the words that needed to be said, the cause that needed to be embraced.

They're coming.

"Now," Cyrus said, "we're just going to have to fight for ourselves."

91.

Cyrus and Vara strolled hand in hand along the darkening streets of Reikonos, Cyrus trying to take in every line, every trace of the city for fear he would not see it again soon, if ever. Even the stink of so many people and their waste in this close proximity seemed less foul, now that he feared his days of being able to visit freely were drawing to a close.

"This whole sequence of events and what is to come," Vara said, musing quietly, "brings to mind what happened four years ago, when Goliath blamed us for the goblin attacks on the plains convoys and got us barred by all the major powers."

"Except we have no one to blame this time but ourselves," Cyrus said. "Or at least myself."

"I don't think anyone can blame you for something done in such extremes," she said, her boots finding the soft, dust-covered streets of this part of town. They had strolled toward the remnants of Cyrus's old house and talked the whole way—of the battle near Amti and its consequences, and all that had come after, though in hushed tones, for fear of being overheard.

"When things get bad," Cyrus said, feeling a little like a man with his head on the block, axe poised above it ready to fall, "they'll find a way to blame me."

"You are still the Guildmaster," she said, stopping him. They stood in the street, and she raised his hands in hers to clutch them against her breastplate. "You are still the foremost warrior in Arkaria." She smiled faintly. "And you will be my husband, do not forget."

"We should set a date," Cyrus said with a faint smile of his own. "Before we get all caught up in what's coming."

"Yes, a couple months will do it, I should say," she agreed, going back to strolling along with him, her hand in his. "We'll need to do it on the Sanctuary grounds, of course, by then—"

"Do you think everyone already knows?" Cyrus asked, looking around in the deepening evening, the buildings on either side of them looking shadowy, as though they could hide any number of assailants in their windows and alleys.

"I think the governments know and the gods know," Vara said. "But as for what follows that—the people … no, I don't think so. Not yet. The rumors have yet to spread."

"But when they do," Cyrus said, "they're going to be wildfire."

They slowed as they came up to the empty lot, Vara following Cyrus's lead as he halted outside the remains of the stone fence separating the disused lot from the street.

"Was this it?" Vara asked, looking at it curiously.

"Apparently so," Cyrus said, letting out a sigh. The foundation still stood just as he'd last seen it, stones buried in the dirt and covered over by the dust of the city and the wind, weeds threading through the cracks.

"Why is it still empty?" Vara asked, nose wrinkling as though she smelled something unpleasant.

"Maybe I own it now," Cyrus mused, then hastily added, "though I won't be going to the Citadel to try and claim it anytime soon, I suppose."

"Oh, it's you again," came a voice from the next house over, and Cyrus turned his gaze to find the older woman he'd spoken with last time, her pipe glowing in hand in the early evening light. She turned to a woman standing next to her, one he could not quite see in the shadow, and pointed at him with the stem. "That's him, Joenne—you remember? I told you about him."

Cyrus let go of Vara's hand and paced along the edge of the stone fence, gauntleted fingers dragging along the half-dismantled wall as he peered into the shadows created by the overhang at the woman's house. "My name is—"

"Gods, you look like him," Joenne said with a gasp, stepping out of the shadows to reveal a look of disgust on her aged face. "Just like Rusyl, with that armor. Knew it was you when I heard tell of Cyrus Davidon the damned mighty." She spat at his feet as he approached, her spittle missing him as she circled to keep the distance between them. *"Heretic,"* she hissed in a voice that sounded like a snake in the Reikonos eve.

"You were saying about wildfire?" Vara eased up next to him.

"Spreads fast, doesn't it?" Cyrus asked, shaking his head. He looked at Joenne's companion, the woman he'd spoken to when last he'd been here. "I guess we're not welcome here."

Joenne spoke loudly, again. "And why would you be, child of the heretic?"

Cyrus blinked as though he'd been slapped but kept his mouth shut until he'd processed what she said. "'Child of the heretic'? You're talking about my father? He was a damned hero—"

"I'm not talking about your bloody father," Joenne said, spitting at him once again. She pointed at the house. "Your father died a hero, yeah, we all know that." She took a breath of pure anger, hot as the ash flaking out of her companion's pipe "I'm talking about the woman that raised you, the one that used to live there," she pointed at the empty lot, the shattered foundations, as Cyrus felt just about as broken as the remainder of the house, leveled to the ground, "I'm talking about the bloody Sorceress Quinneria, I am.

"Your mother."

92.

Alaric

The God of War burst into the room in the midst of a torture session so brutal that Alaric Garaunt had nearly lost his voice from screaming. But Alaric was not too far gone to realize that the sound of the door slamming so hard was a clue as to how this conversation would unfold. The torturer—a singularly humorless fellow named Boreagann—straightened at the sound as the footsteps came racing over to him, fury clapping against the floor with each booted step. Alaric steeled himself for what was surely about to follow.

"Hello, Mathurin," Alaric said, fighting to put on a smile, his voice so strained and hoarse that it came out lower than a whisper. He watched the name sail home like a lance straight to the heart, though, the God of War's eyes burning brighter scarlet as it hit. He hated being called Mathurin, after all, preferring Bellarum.

Mathurin did not slow as he approached, throwing a punch that slammed into Alaric's jaw, crushing the back of his skull into the hard steel table that he was pinned against. The flash of light was as sudden as if someone had cast a spell in his eyes, but Alaric blinked them away after only a minute, as the God of War cast a healing spell upon him that stitched up all the wounds that had been inflicted on him.

Alaric took a short look at Mathurin's face, planning to get another stab in before the God of War spoke. "I heard you had a bit of a rough time in the jungle recently," Alaric said, taking a soothing breath as Mathurin's face tightened even further; it seemed possible the man's cheeks might just explode in his helm. "Perhaps you should avoid travel for a while."

"You heard?" Mathurin asked, clearly trying to restrain his rage and losing.

"You are hardly my only visitor," Alaric said with a satisfied smile. Mathurin stared at him tightly for a moment. "Right you are, Alaric. Right you are." He nodded, and began to pace. "So you heard about my setback?"

"I heard you lost our little wager," Alaric said, and the God of War stopped pacing. "I assume you'd thought I'd forgotten our conversation about how you would win the soul of Cyrus Davidon? I haven't. Torture does terrible things to the mind, it's true, but it hasn't allowed me to forget how wrong I told you that you'd be."

Mathurin looked up, coldly at first, and then a malicious grin spread across his face. "You've been here for years now, Alaric, for years, and—even with this, every day—you're still defiant." He eased over to Alaric and placed a cold, gauntlet-encased hand on the old knight's shoulder. "My friend, you are truly a wonder, in every way. But on this—this business of Cyrus Davidon ..." Mathurin put on a face of absolute false sympathy, "... you realize he's as good as dead now, don't you?"

"I realize that he's slapped your hand bloody," Alaric said without feeling. "That he's made you look the ass, getting caught moving on the southern lands so openly. Why, you even admitted in plain hearing of countless people that you were the one who orchestrated the deaths of Mortus and Yartraak."

"That was always bound to come out," Mathurin said, shaking a hand as if it were nothing. "I mean, I invited Mortus to my realm and started a quarrel with him once I knew you and your guild were safely ensconced in the Realm of Death. As for Yartraak ..." Here he showed rampant glee of the sort that made Alaric's stomach twist. "Well, I must confess, here, where you no one but you can hear me ... I was the one who told the God of Darkness he should kidnap Vidara to solve his problems of supply for his army."

"I just warned you I have other visitors," Alaric said stiffly, "and you tell me this anyway. Because—"

"Because it doesn't matter what you say," Mathurin said good naturedly. "You could tell them I'm planning to kill them all—which I am, by the way, all who will not serve *will* die—and it doesn't matter." He threw up his hands. "I have planned this for longer than anyone imagines. There are no defenses against the hells I have unleashed on my brethren, and they have no choice but to listen to me at this point. What are they going to do, after all? Band together against me?" He made a quivering motion, his face torn with false fear, then broke into a smile. "They tried that once, and look how it turned out for them." He leaned in close to Alaric's ear, as though he did not wish to be heard by anyone else. "They're afraid. That's the problem with being prey, with being weak, with having to cluster around—none of them have stood on their own in forever." He pulled back, a glint in his eye. "But I have. And I've learned to adapt. To move in the shadows, to manipulate, to do whatever I have to do to win wars.

"And I am about to win this war, Alaric," Mathurin said with eyes aglow, "though now I'll be doing it without your faithful dog Cyrus as my servant."

"You may find yourself somewhat surprised if you continue to underestimate Cyrus and Sanctuary," Alaric said.

"He killed an avatar, Alaric," Mathurin said with another wave of his hand. "Anyone can kill an avatar, even mine, apparently. It'll take more than the sword of our old friend the Drettanden for a mere human to bring me low."

"You know he's not a 'mere' anything," Alaric said quietly, cursing himself for allowing the slip, for drawing the attention to it.

Mathurin—no, he wasn't that anymore, not really, now he truly was Bellarum, the God of War—he smiled. "It's been so amusing to watch these—these little people," he gestured vaguely into the ether, "doing their little frightened runs, spinning in circles while the two of us turned them about." He broke into a wider grin. "They made their move, you and I made ours—independently, but toward the same end. Saving Cyrus Davidon.

"Of course the real treat for me now," Bellarum said with a hearty sniff of the air, "is to watch Cyrus himself, because while we all—all of us—manipulated him, he stumbled blindly in the dark, always thinking he was following in the footsteps of his father. But he never once realized that all their desperate action was just an attempt to keep him from following in the footsteps of his mother." Bellarum leaned in again. "They're all going to come after him now. There will be no mercy, not from any of them."

"And if he defeats them all?" Alaric asked, his voice rasping from the torture.

"Then he'll be doing me the grandest of favors," Bellarum said, as he started to walk out. Boreagann stepped up and grabbed one of the countless sharp implements on the tray, as though he'd been waiting for this very moment. "It's not every day you find a way to pit all of your enemies against each other, after all," Bellarum said, pausing at the door. "And no matter what ... when he's done with them, or they're done with him ... all that's left will be simply mopped up by me." He brushed his hands together, the metal squealing as he rubbed them against one another. "War will always win, Alaric ... *I* will always win. You ought to know that by now."

The cutting began once again in earnest, but this time it seemed to hurt all the more, for the truth that Bellarum had spoken carried its own sort of pain ... and it was a kind that was far, far worse than any blade.

NOW

Epilogue

"I'm starting to worry about you," Vaste said, almost to the foyer doors. "I'd say you're not really acting like yourself, but the truth is ..." His voice trailed off as Cyrus lost focus on what the troll was saying.

Cyrus looked up at the grand structure of Sanctuary, so much the worse for the wear now. He paused as he followed Vaste back toward the keep, his eyes stumbling over every line of the exterior, the damage from the last fight as obvious to him on the lines of the old structure as a blemish would have been on—

Her.

"You're not death," Vaste said, jarring Cyrus as he realized suddenly that the troll was now standing just behind him. "I met that fellow, remember? You lack the teeth to be him. Also, a few limbs."

"It's a metaphor," Cyrus said quietly.

"Come on," Vaste said, motioning him forward. "Come upstairs, read some more of her diary. It'll make you feel better."

"I don't want to," Cyrus said with a shrug, letting his hands fall to his belt and resting them there. "I don't care to read any more."

"Because your aging eyes are tired?"

"Because there was a lot hidden from me over the years," Cyrus said, feeling the resentment bubble up.

"Alaric had a tendency to do that, yes," Vaste said, his enormous boots squeaking as he walked on the damp ground, bare of any grass.

"I meant Vara," Cyrus snapped. After a pause, he said, "Though obviously not only her."

"She loved you," Vaste said.

"Yes," Cyrus said sharply, "apparently longer than I thought she

WARLORD

did." He bowed his head. "She didn't tell me how she felt before, when we could have had even more time—"

Vaste brought his hands up and slapped his own cheeks, forcing his mouth open in feigned shock. "No! No, impossible! This must be the first time a woman has ever hidden her feelings from her lover!"

"Don't be a dick," Cyrus said, turning away from him and freezing as his gaze fell upon something unexpected on the dead ground.

"What?" Vaste eased up behind him. "What is it? Not like you to bow out in the middle of a good fight." He peered over Cyrus's shoulder. "I don't see—oh. Well. That's ... rather pedestrian, actually."

Cyrus felt a sharp sense of dark amusement at the sight, however. On the barren ground stood a lone patch of weeds springing from the dark earth, the first hint of life returning to this dead place.

"Propitious, though, I suppose," Vaste went on. "Symbolism and all that."

Cyrus turned his head to look at the troll, whose jutting lower lip gave his normally placid expression a look of concentration. "What?"

"You know," Vaste said, nudging him gently, the troll's robe against Cyrus's pauldron. "What with you returning here as new life is springing up." The healer arched his eyebrows. "Though I will say, it seems strange that you came back to live here in these grand and empty halls—"

Cyrus broke into a laugh out of pure morbidity, drawing a sharp look from Vaste.

He doesn't know.

I haven't told him.

Cyrus felt the short, sharp laughter subside, and glanced at the small weed, stretching out of the dead earth, eyes caressing its blades of green. "I didn't come back here to live, Vaste."

"You didn't?" The troll's voice was earnest, curious, and there was a hint of the dread in there that told Cyrus everything about what Vaste suspected about his own intentions.

No point in hiding it anymore, Cyrus thought, and he suddenly felt warm under the sense of coldness that had permeated his world of late, that had settled over him like the least comfortable blanket he could imagine. "No," he said, and there was relief in admitting the truth at last, like that old ragged blanket could finally be flung off—

and its weight was significant, for both of them. "I didn't come back to live here, not at all.

"I came back here to die."

Cyrus Davidon will return in

HERETIC

The Sanctuary Series, Volume Seven

Coming March 17, 2016!

AND

The Sanctuary Series Will Conclude in

LEGEND

The Sanctuary Series, Volume Eight

Coming June 16, 2016!

Author's Note

If you want to know immediately when future books become available, take sixty seconds and sign up for my NEW RELEASE EMAIL ALERTS by visiting my website at www.robertjcrane.com. I don't sell your information and I only send out emails when I have a new book out. The reason you should sign up for this is because I don't always set release dates, and even if you're following me on Facebook (robertJcrane (Author)) or Twitter (@robertJcrane), it's easy to miss my book announcements because...well, because social media is an imprecise thing.

Come join the discussion on my website: http://www.robertjcrane.com !

Cheers,
Robert J. Crane

Acknowledgments

Editorial/Literary Janitorial duties performed by Sarah Barbour and Jeffrey Bryan. Final proofing was handle by Jo Evans. Any errors you see in the text, however, are the result of me rejecting changes.

The cover was masterfully designed by Karri Klawiter.

The map of Southern Arkaria was once again skillfully drawn by Robert Altbauer.

Alexa Medhus, David Leach and Nicolette Solomita pulled first reader duties on this one, so many thanks to them for reading my mess of a manuscript.

As always, thanks to my parents, my kids and my wife, for helping me keep things together.

Other Works by Robert J. Crane

The Sanctuary Series
Epic Fantasy

Defender: The Sanctuary Series, Volume One
Avenger: The Sanctuary Series, Volume Two
Champion: The Sanctuary Series, Volume Three
Crusader: The Sanctuary Series, Volume Four
Sanctuary Tales, Volume One - A Short Story Collection
Thy Father's Shadow: The Sanctuary Series, Volume 4.5
Master: The Sanctuary Series, Volume Five
Fated in Darkness: The Sanctuary Series, Volume 5.5
Warlord: The Sanctuary Series, Volume Six
Heretic: The Sanctuary Series, Volume Seven* (Coming March 17, 2016!)
Legend: The Sanctuary Series, Volume Eight* (Coming June 16, 2016!)

The Girl in the Box
and
Out of the Box
Contemporary Urban Fantasy

Alone: The Girl in the Box, Book 1
Untouched: The Girl in the Box, Book 2
Soulless: The Girl in the Box, Book 3
Family: The Girl in the Box, Book 4
Omega: The Girl in the Box, Book 5
Broken: The Girl in the Box, Book 6
Enemies: The Girl in the Box, Book 7
Legacy: The Girl in the Box, Book 8
Destiny: The Girl in the Box, Book 9
Power: The Girl in the Box, Book 10

Limitless: Out of the Box, Book 1
In the Wind: Out of the Box, Book 2
Ruthless: Out of the Box, Book 3
Grounded: Out of the Box, Book 4
Tormented: Out of the Box, Book 5
Vengeful: Out of the Box, Book 6
Sea Change: Out of the Box, Book 7* (Coming February 17, 2016!)
Painkiller: Out of the Box, Book 8* (Coming April 14, 2016!)
Masks: Out of the Box, Book 9* (Coming June 9, 2016!)

Southern Watch
Contemporary Urban Fantasy

Called: Southern Watch, Book 1
Depths: Southern Watch, Book 2
Corrupted: Southern Watch, Book 3
Unearthed: Southern Watch, Book 4
Legion: Southern Watch, Book 5* (Coming in 2016!)

*Forthcoming

Made in the USA
Las Vegas, NV
05 October 2023

78577682R10243